ALL THE DEAD MEN LIE

Copyright © 2024 Barry N Rainsford

Published by Sleeping Dogs

Paperback ISBN: 978-1-0686335-0-8
eBook ISBN: 978-1-0686335-1-5

Cover design by Spiffing Publishing Ltd

All rights reserved

No part of this book may be reproduced in any form or by any electronic or mechanical means including information storage and retrieval systems, without permission in writing from the author. The only exception is by a reviewer, who may quote short excerpts in a review.

This book is a work of fiction. Names, characters, places, and incidents either are products of the author's imagination or are used fictitiously. Any resemblance to actual persons, living or dead, events, or locales is entirely coincidental.

ALL THE DEAD MEN LIE

BARRY N RAINSFORD

To the miners and their communities: those past, those current, and those whom Thatcher ensured never would be.

Set in the midst of the 1984 Miners' Strike, some of the attitudes and language in this work of narrative fiction are representative of the era and may cause offence to modern sensibilities. The miners fought for their livelihoods and for the future of their communities. The police were too often caught between a sense of duty and Thatcher's ambition. Such tensions fashioned the visceral differences and deep seated bitterness that has continued to shape communities and lives long after the dispute ended. It is the dispute that fractured UK society forever.

Moncygrub, as he sips his claret,
Looks with complacent eye,
Down at his watch-chain, eighteen carat -
There, in his club, hard by:
Recks not that every link is stamped with the
Names of the men whose limbs are cramped,
Too long lying in grave-mould, cramped with Death,
Where all the dead men lie.

Barcroft Boake: 1897

Prologue:
October 1984

Clenched tight, hands gripping his thighs just above the knees, he strained to catch his breath. After a moment of gasping for air, he raised his head from staring at the ground, inching his hands up to his hips.

Christ what a day. And it was only what…? He checked his watch; *six fifty-five. How long had he been at this? Since four.*

He looked down at his feet. His boots were covered with mud from the overnight rain. His trouser legs were soaked. There was mud down the front of his dark blue tunic. '*Bollocks!*'

He straightened, looking up, scanning the landscape to the horizon.

The thin early morning light was grey-blue laced with smeared lines of red. Finally, with the sun's rise his surroundings resolved into understanding: fields, hedges, the humps of the slagheaps. The winding gear of the colliery stood beyond, barely visible.

Where were the others? Where the hell was he?

He turned and looked around.

No-one.

The plastic visor on his helmet was scratched and scuffed, obscuring his vision. He flicked it up.

The baton charge had been intense, not like the training. They still had a lot to learn about the short shield, about working as a tight unit. What could they expect, drafting them in from what… *six different forces?*

He'd lost track of the others in the first field, him going for the big bastard in the red-check shirt chucking the bricks whilst the rest of his squad had set about containing a group of miners waving placards and chanting. At least two other officers from his snatch squad had gone with him, but then he'd tripped in the ruts of the second field and lain watching as they'd raced off after the man. By the time he'd got to his feet they'd cleared the horizon, and now, after five minutes of fruitless chasing around, he had to admit to losing both them and his sense of direction.

He turned his head, catching on the drifting breeze the distant sound of shouting; the clatter of what he assumed to be the last of the bottles and rocks against tarmac and plastic shields. From the direction of it, it seemed the confrontation had moved on from the field by the colliery entrance towards the main A5 that skirted the pit. He picked up his shield and baton from where he'd laid them on the grass and started towards the sound.

At least there was the overtime and special duty pay to compensate for the long hours, the twelve-hour shifts, the aggro. At least he wasn't in Yorkshire. The squads who'd been despatched there were having it tough. The news each night was full of the running battles there. Bricks and bottle throwing was a permanent backdrop to the picketing at most pits, had been for months, but everyone knew it was worse there. Bitter.

Like Ireland.

His younger brother was serving in Belfast. He'd told him of the hatred the troops faced over there, the resentment on the faces of the civilians whenever his patrol was sent out. *What did he expect? Policing civil disorder in Belfast or Tamworth wasn't going to be done with a nice quiet chat. You went in and you sorted it out. Shields' banging.* They'd seen that on the news. Learned the lessons.

Orgreave. Put the fear of god in the bastards. Let them know you were coming. Let them know you meant business.

He stopped and looked to his left. PC Rogers and Reid ambled towards him, laughing, visors raised, shoving a large man in a red shirt - the one he'd been after. The man's hands were behind his back.

'What the fuck happened to you?' Reid shouted.

Clarke indicated the mud down the front of his tunic and trousers. 'Fell.'

The two constables laughed.

'You tosser!' Reid offered, ever sympathetic.

'What about you two?'

Rogers nodded at the man in the red-check shirt, shoving him hard in the back. 'This one. Caught him over the other field.'

'Bastards!' the man spat.

'Here,' Reid said, prodding him with his baton, 'less of the bloody language.'

'Fascist fuckers!'

Reid laughed. 'He's a regular Karl Marx this one.'

Rogers shook his head. 'Who gives a toss? Let's get back.'

The bulky figure of the protestor was nudged forward onto the dirt track bisecting the field. Clarke turned and followed his fellow officers.

Crossing the fields, the growing light revealed the remains of the earlier pitched battle between police and pickets; bricks, stones, torn clothing, a police helmet or two, along with broken placards and the wooden staves that had held them. The police line had once more succeeded in pushing the pickets back from the entrance, the coaches carrying the working miners racing through with the morning shift. They'd pushed them into the fields; pushed them into the hedgerows, pushed them until they'd broken into smaller groups. Pushed the main body back towards the access road where they would be dispersing to regroup for the later shifts.

Ahead of him, Clarke saw that Reid had stopped and was looking back at the hedgerow of the field they'd entered. Following Reid's gaze, Clarke noticed the hedgerow had a dip in front of it forming a shallow trench. In it, about thirty yards from the gap where the path cut through, he could see what looked like a figure lying there. 'Alright!' Reid shouted. 'Come-on. It's finished. Get yourself out and get off home!'

There was no response.

'Come-on,' Clarke called out, encouragingly. 'I'm not about to clobber you, and I'm not interested in arresting you.'

There was no movement.

Closing, Clarke saw that it was a man dressed in denim jeans and a donkey jacket. The jacket had a bright orange plastic yoke across the back. Letters were picked out on it in faded stencilling like those worn by many of those he'd seen on the picket lines over the past few weeks. *NCB*. A miners' jacket.

It took for Clarke to stand almost directly above the recumbent figure before he realised that the man's head was covered in blood, as was the grass around it. Across the back and centre of the skull was what appeared to be a large gash where something round and heavy, something like a baseball bat or a baton, had made terrible impact.

'Shit!' He knelt down, turning the figure over onto its side. *Recovery position*. He frantically re-called his first aid training, tearing at the buttons around the shirt collar and thrusting a hand against the side of the prone man's neck.

There was no pulse.

He put his head close to the man's mouth, listening for sounds of breathing.

There was none.

Reid and Rogers with their prisoner came up behind and stood looking down. Clarke looked up at them and shook his head.

'Fucking bastards!' the prisoner screamed. 'Fucking bastards! You've killed him!'

One
Day One

It was cold. Bitterly cold.

Shivering, DC Peter White turned the collar of his overcoat up, tugging the wing tips together as a rudimentary seal against the icy wind gusting across the field.

Shoulders hunched, tired, cold and hungry, he stomped his feet on the clumps of coarse grass, a process splattering his own trousers and those of the three other detectives standing close-by with flecks of clinging red Staffordshire clay.

'Sorry,' he half-muttered.

Detective Inspector Richard Mallen looked down. 'Shit!' he cursed, gazing from the flecks of mud to White and back again. 'For Christ's sake, Peter!' he howled.

'Sorry,' White offered once more.

Mallen bent, attempting to brush the specks away. All he succeeded in doing was creating larger, more conspicuous smudges. 'Isn't it bad enough having to wade through all this shit without you kicking it everywhere?' he demanded.

White nodded acceptance of the point. 'Sorry, guv.'

'Bloody rookies!' Mallen spat, turning back to the loose circle of officers. 'How much longer are we going to be left standing here, anyway?' he asked, his level of irritation fuelled.

DCI Peter Kalus, hands thrust deep in overcoat pockets, stirred from a distant reverie. 'God knows. Until pathologist gets finished. He's been down there a while.'

'What takes them so long, anyway?' Mallen complained, shoving his own hands firmly into the pockets of his three-quarter-length coat. Straight-jacketed, he nodded in the direction of the bottom of the field. 'The say the bloke's head's been stove in. Pretty obvious he's dead. Unless, of course, *Doctor D's* got powers we don't know about to raise him up again.'

Kalus shrugged. There was little else he could add. Doctor Eric Doyle was not a man intimidated by the pressures of an investigation. The on-call pathologist followed his own methods, his own routines, his own finely detailed procedures.

'Any idea who he is?' Mallen asked.

Kalus shook his head. 'Some miner. Not certain. Apparently he was wearing a colliery coat. The uniforms who found the body had a picket they'd arrested with them. He says the bloke's a miner.'

'Well doesn't he know who he is?'

Another shake of the head. 'Just says he's seen him on the picket line over the past few weeks. Means nothing. The bloke they arrested is from Nottingham. The dead man could be local or from anywhere between here and Scotland or Kent. For all we know, he may not even be a miner. Some of the pickets are known militants and agitators.'

'Bloody Marxists.' Mallen kicked at a tuft of coarse grass, watching a chunk of it skitter away. 'Had run-ins with that lot in Handsworth in eighty-one. Stirring things up!' He scowled at the recollection of uniformed officers armed with little more than truncheons and scavenged dustbin lids taking on violent rioters. Stuff like that was why the current riot squads had full-length plastic shields or short snatch shields and batons. Lessons learned.

Handsworth.

Kalus pushed his hands deeper into his pockets, fingers seeking sanctuary from the biting cold. Fumbling amidst the loose change, he found a folded slip of paper. His wife's reminder, written for him as he'd left that morning; the reminder to call in on his father, to drop off the package sitting in his car. He squeezed it tight, clenching it till its crumpled edges dug into his hand.

His father.

He shook his head, clearing his thoughts, pushing back to here. To now.

Focus.

He turned, shielding his face from yet another gust of icy wind, and found himself gazing across the open ground towards the main colliery. Scattered across it, groups of police and emergency services stood gathered in tight knots. A little further on looser groupings of uniformed PCs had formed, their breath steaming in the cold air. Beyond them he could make out others. Those bunches of officers, some still in riot gear, waiting close to the vehicles that had brought them. By his estimate there was well over three hundred officers within the boundary of Tamworth's Birch Coppice Colliery. Three hundred men waiting for command.

His command.

But none of them looked his way. Not a head turned towards him. No eyes met his own. He knew what they were thinking: *Why are you back so soon? Why are you in charge? Handsworth. What really happened? What makes you so special?*

Nothing.

People were dead because of him. He couldn't change that.

He looked down. Surreptitiously holding his hands out in front of him, he clenched them like a footballer in the wall of a free kick. They trembled.

Not here. Not now.

He clenched them tighter. Dug nails into palms. *Focus.*

When had he last felt okay? When had he last felt *normal?*

He knew the answer.

Handsworth.

Reuben.

'Guv?' Mallen's voice cut in.

Kalus turned, aware something had been said. 'What?'

'I said, some bloody crime scene.'

'Sorry?'

'This lot.' Mallen nodded his head in the direction of the groups of police gathered where Kalus had been staring. 'How many people do you think have trampled over these fields in the past few hours?'

Kalus shook his head. 'Hundreds.'

Mallen let out a short plosive snort of derision. 'How do we go about identifying who was where or what they saw amongst this lot? Chaos. Three hundred or more officers, as well as what...? More than four hundred miners and pickets? All of them likely within a hundred yards of a killing - a man beaten to death - and not one of them saw a bloody thing!'

'Do we know he was? Beaten to death, I mean?' White asked, looking up from further study of his muddy shoes.

'A very good point, lad,' the unmistakable voice of Eric Doyle boomed. Each of the detectives heads turned towards the pathologist's heavy footed approach.

It was said that *Doctor D* had been going deaf for years. That his alarming decibel level in conversation was the result of that fact. Others argued that the volume was rather a sign of the pathologist's certainty of the undisputable truth of every utterance he made. The man was right. Always. He brooked no dispute, allowed no dissent. It made him a godsend in the courtroom where juries and defence counsel alike found him intimidating in his self-belief. Eric Doyle's evidence was delivered as Holy Writ. Words from the Mount. Fact.

'No point in idle speculation,' Doyle continued, drawing near. 'Wasting all that time running around chasing clues if you don't start from the right place. *Question: How did he die? Was he beaten to death?* Good questions, lad. Make a detective of you yet.'

'And?' Kalus asked.

Doyle turned to take in his questioner. 'Ah, DCI Kalus. Good to see you back. Blunt force trauma.'

'In English?' Mallen asked.

Doyle smiled. It had no connection to any known form of humour. 'Ah, DI Mallen! Sorry, didn't realise you were here. The *A-B-C* version then. Battered to death. Several blows with a large heavy object.'

'How large?' Mallen prompted, ignoring Doyle's patronising

manner.

Doyle looked around. He pointed at one of the riot police standing a few yards off, shield and baton hanging loosely in the officer's hands. 'Like one of those.' He nodded in confirmation of his own insight. 'Yes. One of those. Do the job just right.'

There was silence. Words sinking in. Implications taking shape.

'Time of death?' Kalus asked.

'Oh, won't be certain until I get him back to the lab.'

'Roughly?' Mallen asked, almost immediately wishing he hadn't.

Doyle span round, this time fixing the acting DI with his best courtroom glower. 'Roughly? *Roughly?* What do you think I am lad? Some sort of mystic? A *Maharishi Yogi* or something? You want roughly then you go and consult with the gypsies. I don't do roughly!' He turned on his heels, calling in the direction of an assistant labouring up the slope laden with medical bags. 'Come on Hardy! Get a move on man!'

With that, the rotund figure of Eric Doyle wheeled away towards the colliery pithead and the waiting cars.

'You finished down there, Doc?' Mallen called after him in a vain attempt to regain some semblance of status.

By way of reply, the departing Doyle waved an arm around in the air. 'All yours!' he boomed over his shoulder as he strode up the incline.

Thomas Hardy, Doyle's loyal medical technician of some ten years, trudged up the grassy slope toting the tools of his master's gruesome trade. As he passed the group, Kalus put out a hand. Hardy stopped and looked about him. 'Three hours,' he whispered out of the corner of his mouth. 'Maybe four. Not more than five,' he clarified before scuttling off in pursuit of the great man.

'Who the fuck?' Mallen began, before letting his question fade. Understanding passed like a Mexican Wave around the group of detectives. Mallen remained far from mollified. 'Wanker!'

That was the good doctor, Kalus thought. The man had at one time or another reduced every detective on the squad to wild meaningless statements of raging incomprehension. And acting Detective Inspector Richard Mallen was easy prey.

At thirty-seven, Mallen ought to have been in the prime of his life, but anyone knowing him thought that any prime must have already been - certainly before his fondness for Marston's Pedigree and late night take-aways. A Birmingham boy, he had grown up in Aston, little more than a slight breeze from the twin towers of the *HP* sauce factory and the *Ansell's* brewery. They had become the twin pillars defining his tastes if not his life.

Where Kalus was slight of build, Mallen was full, rotund. He was a barrel, with a stomach sliding easily over the thin plastic belt of his trousers, the lip of fat circling his waist like the rings around Neptune. His brown hair was greased, combed back off his forehead. It was a style requiring regular smoothing into place, a mannerism that had become almost a tic.

If Kalus' career had till recently been one of perpetual ladders, Mallen had always rolled snakes. The acting DI had been *acting* for some time. He had a hair-trigger temper, and what his superior's believed to be *'a deep brooding suspicion of change'*. It had made him difficult to promote in a force that was in permanent transition, scrabbling for the future. Privately, those on the promotion boards who'd interviewed him put it down to more than that. It was his face. He wore a look of almost perpetual disdain, an enduring sneer. A permanent slight curl of his top lip was the memento of a football game that had turned into a war, one leaving him with a severed facial nerve and the legacy of a lip rolling permanently upwards. In a teenage boy it looked cool - Marlon Brando *The Wild Ones* cool. In a man approaching middle age it gave an air of discontent, a seemingly continual dissatisfaction of all he met.

Like the look he wore now watching the receding pathologist.

DS Roberts nudged the young DC White. *'Ghoul Squad.'*

Alerted by the passing Hardy, two mortuary attendants were

making their way down from the black panelled van that for the past forty-five minutes had sat in the road nearest to the field.

Roberts turned to Kalus, who had also seen the two men.

Kalus nodded. The pathologist's indication that this was no accident was the signal unleashing them from inactivity. He turned to Mallen. 'Rich, we'd better get ourselves down there. Mick, you and White set up a base in the offices. Talk to the pit manager, see if you can get us some space and some phones.'

'Okay, Guv,' Roberts responded.

The group split. If nothing else it was movement, and that in itself was a welcome relief from waiting in the numbing cold.

* * *

From the lip of the shallow ditch they were better able to take in the scene.

Already the SOCOs had marked out an area of some twenty five yards around the locus that was the corpse. They'd stretched yellow tape outlining what was now to be declared the crime scene, fixing it at regular intervals to metal spikes they'd sunk into the ground. At the edge of the marked area stood the two mortuary attendants, a black body bag crumpled on the floor between them. Watching them as they awaited their turn at the corpse, Kalus was reminded why they had the epithet '*Ghouls*'.

Mallen ducked under the tape, holding a section of it up for Kalus who followed. The two walked towards the hub of activity that was the tight grouping of SOCOs kneeling around the corpse. 'Morning, Donny,' Mallen offered as they approached.

One of the three SOCOs turned, his face registering recognition of the man calling his name. 'Oh, morning sir. Didn't see you there.' Donald *Donny* Osborne grinned a broad, toothy smile. For someone with such a lurid job, the lead SOCO retained the same youthful face and disposition that he probably had in his school photo when he was fourteen - the same buckled teeth crowding out his mouth, the flop of hair bouncing around his brow whenever he spoke.

'Good to see you back, sir,' Osborne offered once he saw that it was Kalus who shadowed Mallen's path across the taped-off site.

Kalus nodded, moving quickly forward avoiding any further unwanted enquiries as to his well-being. He waved a hand, a gesture taking in the corpse lying in front of the stooping Osborne. 'What's the score?'

Osborne stood upright, moving out from the trench to stand on a level with the detectives. 'Doc's finished. Usual stuff... *full report to follow... unwilling to speculate on timing.*'

'We met him on the way down. His usual charming self,' Mallen stated.

'Found anything useful?' Kalus asked.

'Not much, waiting for the rest of the team to get down here so that we can start to get more of a shift on. Just about to roll him over.'

'Carry on. Don't let us stop you. Just want to get a feel for the place.'

Osborne returned to the body and began a discussion with his fellow SOCOs of how best to turn and re-position the corpse.

Kalus surveyed the landscape. 'Good spot,' he said to Mallen. 'Lots of cover, what with the hedges and the trench and the lie of the horizon. Relatively secluded.'

Mallen murmured agreement.

'Okay,' Osborne called, indicating they'd manoeuvred the body to one side offering access to the front pockets of the jeans.

Osborne held up a pair of latex gloves, which Mallen slipped on. Kalus followed suit, though by the time he'd struggled into them Mallen had already been through the victim's pockets and placed the contents into a clear plastic evidence bag supplied by the SOCO. Mallen held the bag up. As it slowly span around, he and Kalus stood examining it, children at the fair with their newly acquired goldfish.

'Keys. House keys.' Mallen stated. 'Loose change... about thirty-five pee.'

Kalus took out a biro, using it as a prop to stop the bag from spinning. He nodded his agreement. 'Lighter. Fags. Matchbook from a pub.'

'What about the jacket pockets?'

'Over there,' Osborne said, indicating a tarpaulin spread like the flysheet of a tent some ten paces away. 'The usual. A handkerchief, a penknife… you know, one of those Swiss Army things. There was a paperback book as well. It's a thin one, one of those Penguins.' He smiled, teasing in the manner of a father at Christmas holding the best present back for last. 'Oh, and a wallet.'

The two detectives went to the sheet, Mallen picking up the wallet. It was black; a geometric pattern of sorts crimped into the edges. It was nothing special, the sort of cheap wallet bought in any local market or stall. The sort that had a printed card in a cellophane window as a placeholder for your own details. Inside were two pound notes, a handful of printed till receipts, a couple of vouchers for money off at supermarkets, a driving licence, a Staffordshire library card, and a membership card for the local branch of the NUM. All identified the victim as Stephen Jackson. All identified him as a miner at the colliery where the body had been found.

'So, Stephen Jackson.' Mallen stated, savouring a name he knew would be repeated many times during the course of the coming investigation. He passed the wallet to Kalus.

Kalus thumbed through its slots. Vultures, picking over the bones of the dead. He envied Mallen's apparent indifference to the work.

'Not much,' Mallen offered. 'But better than what we had a few minutes ago. He lived local, worked local. He's a miner. A reader. Shops at the Co-op and he likes a bargain.'

'And someone disliked him enough to smash in the back of his skull.' Kalus offered, flicking the wallet shut and placing it back onto the ground sheet. *Stephen Jackson R.I.P.* 'Or disliked what he was doing. What he stood for. What he represented.'

'You mean the strike?'

Kalus shrugged. 'The strike. The picketing. The violence.

The destruction of a way of life.'

'You mean a copper?'

'At the moment that seems the most obvious. The location, the circumstances, the murder weapon.' He nodded his head in the direction of the officers gathered in the lane beyond the field, 'The number of possible perpetrators.'

'Shit!'

'Shit it is.' Kalus echoed. The investigation of fellow officers was not something relished by any policeman. Policing the police. Watching the watchers. He and Mallen knew that although Complaints would be involved in any enquiry into the morning's events, the investigation of a murder was beyond their remit. It would devolve to CID. To Kalus.

'Makes us popular,' Mallen observed.

'Yeah,' Kalus snorted. 'Shouldn't expect too many cards this Christmas.'

The two stood in silent contemplation of the situation. They were experienced officers - nineteen murder investigations in the past five years between them. But this, this was different. It would involve delving into the lives of fellow officers, probing and pushing into every part of the actions of every one of them over the past twelve hours, and in some cases far beyond even that.

They returned to where Osborne and his fellow SOCOs were stooped exploring the grass from where the corpse had been moved. Osborne himself was crouched low, examining the pool of dried blood. Next to him, another SOCO appeared to be taking temperature readings from the area. 'Checking for moisture,' Osborne explained. 'Might give us some indication as to how long he's been lying here.' He looked up at a sky that remained as grey and brooding as it had at daybreak. 'There was heavy condensation this morning. Been a lot of rain over the past few days.'

Kalus stared at the blood. *Dark. Black.*

Mallen nodded. 'Anything else?'

Osborne considered the question, skimming a cotton bud through the red goo where the dead man's head had lain.

'He was killed here. No doubt about that. Amount of blood... pattern of the bleed. The drops of it on the surrounding grass. Hit from behind with something heavy, something meaty and round. Dropped like a stone. Spatters indicate that there were more blows after he was down.' He looked at the crushed skull of the corpse, 'Three or four good hits I'd say. After the initial blow, and the follow-up one when he was on the ground, the others would have been surplus.' He rose from his crouched position. *Doctor D* will have the details for you, but I'll be surprised if that's not what he says.'

'Thanks Donny. That's a big help. Gives us somewhere to start,' Mallen said. He turned back to Kalus. 'So, a name and an address, and some idea of how and where he was killed. Not bad for the first hour of an enquiry. Had worse.'

Kalus tore his gaze from the blood, the patch of chocolate black grass. 'Absolutely,' he murmured. He thought of the case last year, a female whose headless, limbless corpse had been found in a suitcase in an Aston back alley. No legs. No hands - so no fingerprints. No head - so no dental records or hair colouring, apart from the pubic kind. *Doctor D* had worked overtime on that one. He'd eventually found part of a tattoo that had been burnt partially away with sodium chlorate. A fragment. He and Mallen had put in a lot of leg work for well over a week before a tattooist recognised the partial. They'd got a name and an address, finding there a very surprised partner who'd almost immediately confessed once the SOCOs had started to dismantle the plumbing of the bathtub where he'd butchered her.

'Yeah, well if we get stuck there's always *Crimewatch*,' Mallen offered.

They walked from the scene. Kalus, pulling himself back from contemplation of the dark. 'Fancy seeing yourself in the reconstruction then?' he asked.

Mallen smiled. 'Might be a whole new career. You know, *Opportunity Knocks* and all that stuff!'

'More like a case of *New Faces* in your case. Maybe Derek Hobson might find you one!'

'Bollocks!'

'What's that, your catch phrase? Can't see it catching on with old Mary Whitehouse and her lot.'

Mallen laughed.

None of the officers they passed, or any of the others in attendance at the crime scene, found anything unusual or inappropriate in the sound of their laughter. Each of them were aware of the proprieties that surrounded death, particularly a death that was sudden and violent. They were more than aware of the sensitivities. But here they were among their own. Professionals, men and women accustomed to the horrors of their chosen trade, men and women aware of the need to find some accommodation with their nightmares. Laughing in the face of death might be a romanticised interpretation, but it had resonance with these people.

The two officers walked back the way they had come, moving steadily up the slope in the direction of the access road. As they neared the thoroughfare both were aware of the looks on the faces of the officers grouped close to the coaches that had brought them here earlier that morning. The majority of them had been stood down for some time. They scraped their feet aimlessly as the small talk washed around them. *Overtime...What the fuck was going on?...When were they getting back?...How many more days were they being barracked here?...Bloody Villa, losing again...This fucking weather.*

Some sat on the grass verges, their helmets, shields, and batons lying next to them or by their feet. Others had lain their gear next to the coaches or propped them against their shins as they stood chatting and smoking.

Kalus and Mallen exchanged a look.

'Batons,' Mallen said flatly.

'I know,' Kalus replied. 'Better get someone on it.'

Mallen nodded. 'It just gets better and fucking better.'

Two

They walked along the access road towards the buildings clustered around the winding gear of Birch Coppice Colliery. They walked between lines of police. Some nodded. Most turned away before they had to make that choice.

Kalus glanced to the side, seeing that Mallen walked with his head down.

Embarrassed? What had been said to him? What was he thinking?

Before today they had worked five cases together *Little and Large. Fred and Barney. The Odd Couple.* Kalus: dark hair permanently ruffled, 5 o'clock shadow deepening a high jaw line. Mallen: soft, flabby, a face round where it ought to have been defined. *Before and After*, some had joked. That was then.

Before Handsworth.
Before the doubt.
Before Reuben.
Before the joking stopped.

His appointment as SIO this morning had taken everyone by surprise, none more than himself. Mallen was entitled to ask why. To wonder why Kalus, not him. There were questions to be asked. Lines to be re-drawn between them marking boundaries and borders, the lines connecting them. At some point soon, he would need to address it. First, however, he needed to make sense of it for himself.

The administration block was a two-storey building set to the right at the point where the short driveway widened into a parking area. The block was clearly a more recent addition to the site than those around it, a fact highlighted by the relative cleanliness of its brickwork and by it having larger windows than those blocks lying closer to the pit-head itself. Further along the access road turned, disappearing between Victorian red-brick buildings blackened by years of standing in the lee of the pit. Beyond these would be the bathhouse and the pit head gear that gave access to the colliery workings themselves.

They exchanged nods with the constable on duty at the door before a colliery secretary, a matronly figure in a woollen two piece, led them down a corridor and into the office of the pit manager.

At his secretary's introduction, Gordon Craig rose from behind his desk and extended a firm handshake. Despite the cold he was in shirtsleeves and Kalus found himself noting the dark blue scars lining both of the man's arms. Craig was a man who knew what it was to work the seams he now managed.

'Inspectors,' he said by way of acknowledgement. He indicated the uniformed figure sitting opposite his desk who turned at their entrance. 'Do I assume that you and Chief Inspector Bailey know each other?' Craig asked.

Bailey remained seated. He nodded to the two detectives, a gesture revealing a dome of pink flesh surrounded by a circle of lank brown hair.

'Vaguely,' was all that either man could muster.

'By reputation only,' Bailey offered, his eyes locked on Kalus.

Kalus and Mallen took the chairs indicated to the left of Bailey. 'The Chief Inspector's the local station commander from Tamworth,' Craig stated.

'Johnny on the spot,' Bailey bubbled. 'I was just bringing Mr Craig up to speed with this morning's operation.'

'Dreadful business,' Craig offered, a broad streak of Scot's brogue lining the tiredness straining within his voice. Even sitting it was clear that Craig was a powerful man, an imposing figure topped by a shock of steel-grey hair swept back from a face that the word '*chiselled*' had been coined to describe.

Bailey settled back, nodding agreement of Craig's assessment. 'We've been meeting on and off ever since this whole strike thing began… Months. But it was May when it really kicked off. Up to that point we'd been involved in a mainly advisory capacity. Like a lot of forces, a number of our officers were called into Nottinghamshire during late March. In the circumstances, we thought it advisable we should see about being ready, you know, get on top of things locally here in Tamworth, just in case. For the most part, Birch Coppice has continued its work. A number of the miners here are opposed to the strike, at least sufficient for some operations to continue. With our support their coaches run the pickets every morning. Lately, it's gotten a little more… intense.'

From early on in the strike known left-wing political agitators had been identified as joining the picket lines. Eight thousand police from all around the country had been sent to Nottinghamshire to quell the mounting aggression and violence. The worst had been May. Orgreave.

The so-called *Battle of Orgreave* had seen widespread accusations of police aggression, the claim that there was little in the way of control by senior officers. There were allegations of trained anti-riot police being let off the leash, officers encouraged to take retribution against pickets. The confrontations had escalated, becoming something much more than the policing of a dispute. *POLICE STATE* the pickets' banners now proclaimed. Some thought they weren't far wrong.

A thin line, Kalus thought. A line too easily crossed.

'As you know Orgreave was the real start of the violence,' Bailey continued. 'And we've had the spill over here. The Labour Party conference last week seems to have stirred it all up. Their conference vote, giving the strike their overwhelming support… well, it's given fresh impetus to the picketing. It's been pitched battles every morning for the past week.'

'We've been co-ordinating operations,' Craig put in. 'Coach arrivals and departures. Getting the coal out.' He stroked a calloused hand through his hair. He shook his head, shock and disbelief evident in every part of the gesture. 'But nothing like this. Nothing. I can't believe it. Why now? Why here?'

'Grim. Very grim.' Bailey agreed. He turned to Kalus. 'So, how's it looking? What have you found?'

'Certainly no accident. Blunt object. A man battered to death,' Kalus replied.

'Oh Christ!' Craig despaired, elbows on desk, head cradled in his hands.

'Anything?' Bailey asked. 'Anything at all?'

Kalus shrugged. 'An awful lot of suspects. Unfortunately, at present we've no witnesses and very little to go on.'

Bailey nodded.

'We're setting up a base here at the colliery,' Mallen stated. He turned to Craig. 'Some of your staff will be needed to assist in getting it up and running. We've got some of our own people sorting that out at the moment, but they could really be put to better use elsewhere.'

Craig looked up, nodding his head. 'Anything you need. Anything. I'll give you my best people.'

'Once we're operational we'll need personnel records. The victim first then, as soon as possible, those of the rest of your workforce.'

'They're suspects?' Craig asked.

'It's early days, but we know that he was a miner,' Kalus answered. 'Name of Stephen Jackson. He appears to be local, at least lived locally in Tamworth. From his union card we believe he worked here at your pit.'

'Jackson? Stephen Jackson?' Craig pondered.

'We believe so. Did you know him? Do you know if there are relatives – a wife, kids?'

'It's a large operation Inspector. We've hundreds of employees. I'll need to look at his personnel file. I don't recall too much about the man. Been here a few months, less than a year or so I think.'

Mallen scribbled in his notebook. 'Anything else you can think of?'

Craig shrugged, 'The fact that I don't know him that well suggests that he kept himself to himself. No trouble.'

'Apart from joining the strike. Active on the picket line, too,' Mallen put in.

Craig sat back in acceptance of the point. 'Yes, well... Industrial action... It's the *English Disease* isn't it, or so I believe our fellow Europeans call it. Most of my miners are out there.' He grimaced, 'Some less willingly than others.'

'Coercion,' Bailey observed.

Craig smiled ruefully. 'My background is mining, Chief Inspector. Been a miner all my working life, like my father before me. I know about pit communities. Hard to work in a pit if your fellow miners take against you.' He turned to Kalus. 'Scab and blackleg are more than name-calling around here, of that I can assure you.'

Kalus nodded. 'I suppose so. Motive for murder, though?'

The question was left in the air as each man considered it.

'SOCOs are down at the scene. We'll need to keep it roped off for now,' Mallen stated, breaking the moment.

The Chief Inspector shook his head. 'Easier said than done. There's a dispute going on. There are miners and pickets all over the site. We try to keep it secure, but frankly it's a nightmare. What with the violence on the picket line, I'm not even certain I've got the manpower to detail officers to specifically patrol a crime scene. We've been calling in officers from neighbouring forces as it is.'

'That's the other thing,' Kalus said. 'We'll need a record of all officers who were on duty this morning. We'll need to interview them.'

Bailey laughed. 'Are you serious? You do realise how many men you're talking about? How long it will take to carry out? Some of these men aren't even from my force. We'd need to get records sent over from Kent, Surrey, Lancashire - all over.' He shook his head in disbelief at the absurdity of the request. 'On top of that, I can't spare men from duty for hours at a time while they're waiting to be questioned. We need every man we can get our hands on. I don't know if you're fully aware of the situation here. What it is that we're dealing with. We're stretched beyond breaking as it is.'

'I'm aware of the logistics of it all. I'm also aware that

there's a lot of down time, officers sitting around.'

'Given what they face, they need those breaks.'

'No argument with that,' Kalus conceded. 'But we need to speak with them. We'll keep the time we need them for to a minimum, but there's no way around it. We need to plot where they were, account for every movement. What they might have seen.'

Bailey sighed. Murder enquiry trumped picketing. He rotated his cap in his hands, a man contemplating terms. 'Very well. I'll have my admin sergeants' draw up a list of officers who were on duty. It may take a while.' He made on last effort to re-establish his status. 'The priorities, however, are feeding and tending to those that are injured. Sorting out damaged equipment.'

'That's something else. We'll need their batons, probably their shields too.'

'What?' Bailey's incredulity was obvious.

'Someone's bludgeoned a man to death. The batons are evidence. Those men are suspects in a murder enquiry.'

'All three hundred of them?'

Kalus nodded. 'At present, yes.'

***

They stood in the canteen. A cold, dark oblong of a space; polished parquet floor, insipid green walls, large green curtains hanging limp from frayed nylon cord. It could have been a school hall, a hospital, a prison – it spoke institution. By the time Kalus and Mallen arrived, the team had already begun the process of turning it into something better suited to the needs of a major investigation.

Formica topped tables had been grouped, re-arranged to accommodate the mass of material that a murder enquiry inevitably accrued. There would be paper, lots and lots of paper - personnel records, box files, maps, photos, records of interviews. There would be the need for quiet spaces to conduct interviews and to discuss pertinent lines of questioning and enquiry. There would be typewriters to ensure that all of the relevant details were logged. There would be phones, as many as they could get, and the need to make notes on the calls and the wealth of information that the calls would bring – the truth-tellers, the hoaxers, the concerned citizens, the serial confessors, the nosey neighbours. This space would be their home, the base from which they would foray out. Later, once the principal details were exhausted, they would move to a local station, the space returned to what it once was.

The hall was large, sufficient for over a hundred people to be seated and fed. Kalus knew it was used by managers and office workers, the logistics of ferrying miners out of the shafts at break times was economically wasteful. Travelling time from the coal face to the pit head lifts would take more than ten minutes, and the lifts themselves would only be capable of carrying ten or so miners at a time.

The miners, as they always had, ate, pissed, and excreted where they stood, hands thick with coal dust. They worked the seam; they breathed the coal dust, they drank it and ate it. And at night, at night they coughed the coal dust, wheezing it back up through lungs blackened with its sooty deposits.

Kalus knew it well. His own father had been a miner.

'Getting there, Guv.'

'What?' Kalus turned towards the voice, seeing Roberts, standing next to him, jacket off, a glean of sweat on his forehead.

'I said we're getting there.' Roberts repeated, dragging a forearm across his brow, mopping the sweat. 'Slow going, mind you,' he continued.

Kalus nodded. 'Good job.'

Roberts was by nature an organiser, a fetcher and carrier, a details man. Someone depended on to get the little things right, the things that made the procedure work. Some sought advancement by glory, the great cavalry charge of inspiration. Roberts got there by inches. Kalus knew that when you added it all up, it counted for just as much in terms of getting the job done.

'Looking good,' Mallen remarked, glancing around the room as he made his way over. He had just finished discussing the known details of the victim with White who would be charting the progress of the investigation by opening the Murder Book. The Book was the log of times, dates, places, and enquiries that would be the official record of their work. Part journal, part diary, it currently consisted of the names of the principal detectives assigned to the case along with the bare bones of information they'd gathered regarding the victim and his death. Within twenty four hours it would include official confirmation of the time of that death along with early forensic details of the manner of death. There would be photos of the victim and the crime scene and the contact details of relatives as well as the write-ups of the initial interviews they would make later today. By the close of the investigation. Whatever its outcome, it would run to hundreds if not thousands of pages. The diary of steps taken and the leads chased down. The intuitive leaps and lucky breaks that would form the evidential base of whatever case they could make.

Process. Procedure. The way that crimes were solved. Method, not men as their training manual had it. Though a good detective was often required to see the connections, to find the path that the breadcrumbs marked out to be followed.

Kalus looked around the room.

Why not admit it? Say what they all suspected.

He was broken. Lost.

Certainty was gone - that part that some might have once called his touch. His instinct. Whatever it was, whatever name it went by, it was now as lost as if it had never been. Handsworth. Reuben. Shadows. Dim outlines. Buttons that couldn't be pushed. Parts that no longer worked, bits of him failing to make a whole.

Broken.

He looked at them looking to him.

Maybe there was a way. Scour the shadows, find DI Peter Kalus wherever he's hiding. Turn whatever stones he lies under. He was there somewhere - lost, damaged, broken - but he was surely still there. Somewhere.

***

Detective Chief Superintendent Frank Ridgway put the phone down and considered the fates that had dealt him such a hand. Less than four months away from retirement, the nice chocolate box cottage in Wiltshire that he and his wife had their eyes on, and here he was contemplating a can of worms that looked ever more unappealing by the minute.

Ridgway was a lifer, a career *bobby* who'd worked his way up the promotional ladder, a career spent cultivating the image of a man who '*gets the job done*'.

Starting on the beat he'd made his reputation as a Detective Sergeant in the aftermath of the Birmingham Pub Bombings. In the late-seventies the then Detective Inspector Ridgway had been a significant player in the *West Midlands Serious Crime Squad*, a unit where many of his current superiors had built their own meteoric careers.

It was a unit now increasingly the subject of complaints about their methods and ideology. Methods going back to their very inception, ideologies touching the careers of all those who had served in it. They cut corners. They constructed cases on flimsy evidence and dubious confessions. Ridgway saw it in simple terms: they put criminals away. They got the bad guys - dependable evidence or not.

But he wasn't stupid. The signs were there that their future was time limited. The media were sniffing around, stirred up by a kaleidoscope of liberal lawyers and civil liberties pressure groups championing the cause of what they claimed were '*insecure*' convictions. Within the West Midlands Force itself there was growing pressure for an investigation into the Squad's work - not just their current cases, but convictions going back to its inception. There were new brooms sweeping clean.

He planned to be long retired before that happened.

The local press liked him. He gave them headlines, ensured they were well served with choice quotes and the inside track on investigations. In return they gave sympathetic treatment of policing work. The nationals were a different story. They liked their crime raw and preferably bleeding. The tabloids liked sex and sensationalism. The broadsheets, whilst alluding to a certain above it all aloofness to such things, had similar circulation urges to titillate their readers with political scandal.

The murder of a striking miner in the middle of a police operation aimed at controlling picket lines had the makings of a story to suit all possible tastes. The death that summer of a picket at Ollerton had created shock waves and a period of intense violence. The fact that his death had later been found to be the result of a traffic accident that could have happened anywhere meant the story had quickly abated. A picket beaten to death was altogether different.

The media was a hungry beast. It sought fresh meat each day. Once the first details had been reported, they would seek new angles to pursue, new ways to keep readers interested. After that summer's shock of Orgreave, the images of bloodied and broken heads filling TV screens and front pages for days, the news of a picket's murder would surely tear the scab off those stories. It would lead to a widening of the narrative, one that would be impossible to contain. There would be stories of improper policing, stories that would lead to pressure for the West Midlands Squad to be investigated. It was a dam cracked and ready to burst.

He stood, walking to the office window. The view was pleasant, almost rural with its trees and the fields beyond. He'd come a long way from Birmingham with its scars of economic depression. A long way from racial tensions, of rioting and the IRA. He'd come far, further than the young policeman on that first beat of a war-damaged Birmingham of the late fifties could ever have imagined.

He had the nice house, the nice car. He had kids at university and a wife planning their move to idyllic retirement. He had much to be thankful for; much to lose, much to protect. His reputation meant a great deal to him, maybe everything. A case like this could be damaging to those it touched, damaging in ways that could scarcely be imagined. The ripples of a serious crime investigation spread far and wide. Once in motion, no one could predict where they might lead.

Containment was essential. Control. In all things it was control.

Control from the outset. Seize the high ground. Seize the initiative. Tell the waiting world what you wanted them to hear. Give the waiting media what they craved: a story.

A simple story. *Heroes. Villains.*

He turned back to his desk, contemplating a day of meetings and phone-calls. Local politicians, national government, the Home Office, the Staffordshire Police Authority, his immediate superiors. Each of them anxious for news, signs of progress, *something to make the whole thing go away.*

A simple story.

What did he have to work with?

Kalus. Kalus was good, one of his own. *His boy.*

What happened to Kalus in Handsworth - *the Rueben matter -* had damaged him. *Christ, it would have finished most men.* But it was months ago. He'd seen all of the reports on him since his return to duty. The official ones of the medical doctors, the GPs. Those of the psychiatric therapist and the police board. The unofficial ones of colleagues. Kalus was fine. Maybe he was wounded, but he had resolve, an inner strength. He wasn't the kind to crack. He was his man. *His boy.* He knew him better than any of them. He'd fast-tracked him. Shown faith in him. Kalus had never let him down.

Whatever Kalus' demons might be, he needed him.

There were matters at work beyond the death of a miner. Shadows reluctant to be brought into the light. He'd already had a courtesy call from Whitehall. Another from Number Ten. Both had reminded him what was required of him.

Expediency. Official Secrets. Matters of State. *Silver Fox.*

He knew little about *Silver Fox* beyond the outline of its ambition and some idea of its methods. He knew that to begin with it had required assistance at a local level, but its details had always been strictly need to know. His only knowledge had been that should the need arise, his position placed him as someone who would be called on to ensure its secrets were protected.

The death of Stephen Jackson was seemingly just such a need.

He thought about the calls. The opportunity. A *get out of jail* card.

It came down to one thing. The need to show a watching world that the investigation was above suspicion. That DCS Frank Ridgway ran a clean unit. That Frank Ridgway and His Masters were clean.

And that was Kalus' greatest asset. Despite Handsworth, despite Rueben; Kalus was clean. A misjudgement was one thing, corruption something else.

He sat back in his chair.

From what he could deduce, everything was textbook. Kalus was going about things just as required. Just as expected. All that remained was for the channelling of what would soon be a rabid media interest onto those paths where Ridgway had control.

He sat forward, picking up a pen and tapping it on a pad of paper.

And, if Kalus should slip up?

Well, DCS Frank Ridgway would have shown faith in an officer he trusted. It was a quality playing well with the media, his superiors, and the rank and file alike. With government, too.

He took the phone off the hook, drawing a sheet of the paper towards him.

It would be a simple story. A compelling narrative.

Kalus could be its hero; if not, necessity dictated he could equally be its villain.

Three

The second key proved to be the one Kalus was looking for, the scarred red front door yielding stiffly to his push. The door juddered as it opened, damp having swollen the frame it sat in. The short hallway was a stump of a room, stairs straight ahead and a door to the left giving access to the living room.

'Cosy,' Mallen commented. They had knocked loudly for a few moments before trying the keys retrieved from the body of Stephen Jackson, but Mallen still called out, 'Hello! Anybody at home?'

The silence that greeted them provoked a shrug from both detectives. They stepped inside, closing the front door, and took in their surroundings.

Personnel records from the colliery had supplied the address, one of a row of terraced properties on a small road off the A5 about a mile from the colliery. The lounge was situated at the front, net curtained windows providing some privacy from those walking past. Beyond the lounge was a smaller room. Kalus was familiar with the layout, he'd visited many such houses as part of his duties. The back room would originally have been a parlour, but Jackson or someone had made it into a dining room, a pine table necessitating a body swerve to access the galley style kitchen. Beyond that, a bathroom extension had been added. Upstairs would be two rooms, the front and back bedrooms.

The house felt damp, cold.

Mallen knelt to turn on the gas fire in the front room. Finding its ignition system clicking uselessly, he used his lighter. The soft thud of the released gas catching fire drew Kalus' attention.

'Might be here a while,' Mallen said. 'No point in freezing.

My feet still won't warm up from standing in that bloody field.'

Kalus said nothing, instead turning his attention to the room itself.

It was small, window to the front, and a door to the rear. The gas-fire was mounted on the wall surrounded by grey plastic sheeting moulded to give the appearance of a rustic stonewall. The whole construction was topped with a stained wooden mantel. Next to this, in the corner by the window, were a TV - a rental by the look of it - and a record deck with a built in amplifier, and a pair of wood grain speakers. The couch took up most of the wall opposite the fire; cheap, velour covered, with sagging springs – the whole fronted by a cheap glass coffee table. By the door to the rear room was an armchair of matching decrepitude.

Kalus picked up a pile of letters stacked on the coffee table between an overflowing ashtray and a line of empty beer cans.

'*Stephen Jackson,...Stephen Jackson,... Stephen Jackson*,' he read as he flicked through each envelope's address.

'Right place then,' Mallen observed. 'Anything interesting?'

Kalus shook his head, grimaced. 'Just bills. Bills and circular letters.'

Mallen picked up a magazine from the settee. '*Hetero* then,' he said, waving a well-fingered copy of *Playboy* in the air. He opened it to the centrefold and spun it round, dangling it at arm's length. 'Nice.'

'Well, another piece of the puzzle found,' Kalus commented.

Mallen turned the magazine so that it faced his colleague. 'Might be a vital clue. Maybe I should follow this one up with *Miss June*.'

Kalus shook his head. 'I'll check the kitchen and bathroom. Take a look upstairs.'

After one last lingering look, Mallen threw the magazine back on the settee. 'Fine by me,' he said standing by the hall door, hand cupped to one ear. 'I think I hear *Miss July* calling... *Richard, oooh...Richard!*' performed whilst rubbing his chest, his face contorted into an approximation of sexual pleasure, tongue lolling out.

Kalus smiled. 'You look like a simpleton.'

'Jealous!' Mallen pouted.

The two men laughed and went about their work.

There was little for Kalus to discover about the man and his life. The dining room table had a vase in the centre, but no flowers. The kitchen yielded little beyond the fact that he'd had Weetabix for breakfast and that he'd have needed to go shopping that day if he'd wanted to eat anything beyond an out of date bottle of salad cream.

The bathroom yielded even less. A mirrored medicine cabinet contained a razor, shaving foam, and a deodorant. On a higher shelf were a variety of medicine bottles, mainly aspirin and a tube of salve for grazes.

Kalus closed the cabinet and caught his own reflection. 'Tell me something I don't know,' he asked of his mirror image.

'That's worrying,' Mallen stated from the bathroom doorway. 'Any answers from your spirit guide?'

Kalus smiled. 'Not a bloody thing. How about you, anything?'

'A well-made bed, very crisp. Tidy, very much so. Chest of drawers has a few tee shirts and undies. Back room's a study of some kind. Well, it's got bookshelves and a desk and chair in it. Nothing out of the ordinary from what I can see. Double bed but no sign of any women's clothing or anything.'

'An ordinary bloke.'

Mallen nodded. 'Seems that way.'

Kalus shook his head in reflection of what they'd found. 'Hardly seems lived in at all. As if he was never really here. That he was already a ghost.' He shifted the bathmat with the tip of his shoe, wondering just what he was finding so troubling. 'You know, one of my uncles' died last year. Cancer. He'd been expecting it for some time. But even with all those months to prepare and get his affairs straight, he didn't leave everything so… empty. Cleansed.'

'A very quiet bloke who lived simply,' Mallen suggested.

'There's nothing personal here at all apart from a couple of records by the stereo. No photographs. No ornaments or bits and pieces. Empty.'

Mallen shrugged. 'What with the strike, he might have sold off everything just to get by. Or maybe he had it re-possessed by the men from the never-never. The bailiffs. Lot of folk round here have.'

It was Kalus' turn to nod. 'So, we're back to a miner going picketing and ending up being beaten to death. No other apparent issues or motives.'

'A stash of drugs or some diamonds would have been good.'

Kalus smiled. He looked around the room. 'No suicide note.'

'What, ... *I can't stand it anymore I'm going to go out and stove my own head in with a big stick...* That sort of thing?'

'It would certainly make our life easier than what we've got,' Kalus snorted.

'A crazed copper?' Mallen asked.

'A crazed copper,' Kalus confirmed.

'Next step?'

'Catch the killer.'

'What are you thinking? Murder? Manslaughter?'

'Probably an accident... A beating gone out that went beyond the necessary. The red mist coming down. A thumping going too far. Maybe whoever did it didn't even realise he'd killed the bloke. Handed out a pasting and then moved on. You know what it's like.'

Mallen knew. Like Kalus, he'd seen the pictures, the TV news footage of the picket lines. The pent up, pumped up aggression: the hails of missiles. The bricks, the stones, the bottles. He'd watched officers led white-faced and bleeding from the line, heads cracked open. Seen miners, their heads dripping blood from gaping wounds after the baton charges. The cavalry. They'd watched in disbelief the *Battle of Orgreave*. Fellow officers running rampant, cornering and beating miners, pickets, anyone not in uniform. It was like football hooliganism. Men let off the leash and encouraged to attack. Some of the officers, like Kalus and Mallen himself, had seen a lot of previous action – the football every Saturday, the inner city riots of 81. Both knew only too well the reigned in frustration of having to take it and not be able to respond.

Sometimes, something just had to give. Frustration. Rage.

'But they'd know by now,' Mallen stated flatly.

'Yeah. They know now,' Kalus agreed.

'And would have come forward?'

Kalus shrugged. 'You'd expect so. But fear, uncertainty. Powerful emotions.'

'What, the…*maybe it wasn't me, maybe it wasn't the bloke I battered into unconsciousness*…reaction?'

Kalus smiled at the sarcasm. They both knew what they were dealing with. 'When you put it like that.'

'Why else wouldn't they come forward?'

'That it was intentional. That Stephen Jackson was marked out by someone. Marked out for a beating. Marked out for murder.'

* * *

Karen Terry sank down into her favourite armchair, felt the welcoming sag as the cushion formed itself comfortably around her. *The best part of the day?* Possibly. Kevin had left for the picket, Ricky had been deposited at school, Michelle at the nursery. There was still plenty of work to be done - the ironing lay ahead as did the rest of her chores; the shopping, and later the daily load of washing to sort and get out on the rotary dryer. But that was ahead, not yet.

She shifted slightly in the chair to look out of the window. The weather looked a little more promising, the overnight rain had passed and the garden was drying out.

She picked up the mug of coffee she'd just made and took a long re-assuring sip. Made with hot milk – her little luxury. *Christ, she deserved something.* Things were hard. The strike had been going for months. Kevin's pit had started their walkout in May, and it was tough. God only knew how the Yorkshire women were coping with their men having been out since March.

Five months.

Five months she'd had to cope with no money coming in, other than some meagre strike pay. Their savings had just about gone, as had the holiday abroad it was going to have paid for. Two years they'd been saving for that.

Two years. At times it had been all that had kept her going.

The trauma of Michelle's birth had begun it. The complications, the back and forwards to hospital. The depression, the sense of being alone, no understanding. They'd come close to splitting up. She'd had nothing to dream of. Nothing making it worthwhile. Oh, she loved her children. Ricky was a joy, though every day he grew more and more like his dad – close, morose, and demanding. And Michelle was a picture-book daughter. Two years old and already everyone could see she was going to be a looker, *'break all the boys hearts'* they said, *'just like her mom had'* they said.

Had. Was.

Maybe that was it. Maybe that's when it all began.

She'd confronted Kevin a few times. They never went out, never did anything, never had any fun. That's when they'd decided to go to Spain. She hadn't been abroad since she was a kid. Spain – the sun, the beaches, the chance to buy tight-fitting swimming costumes and new summer clothes. A reason to get in shape and show off her figure. *A white bikini.* She remembered a white bikini. *Sixteen.* Remembered the looks' of the local Spanish boys. *Her white bikini.* Her body tanned dark brown, the white bikini setting off her figure. *Like a model. A star.* She wanted to feel that way again. Like when she was sixteen. A year before Kevin. Two years before their marriage and Ricky coming along.

So they'd saved. At least Karen had. Kevin still went out on his weekly drinking nights with the blokes from the pit. She'd scrimped and saved whilst he went out and blew so much more, pissing it up the wall. Her resentment had grown, but what do you do? What options did she have? Her dad and mom would have killed her if she'd said she was thinking of leaving him. *'What's wrong with her – he's a lovely bloke, got a good job, puts money on the table each week, loves his kids. What's wrong with her? She don't know when she's well off, that one, never has done... head full of dreams.'*

And then the strike.

No money. No food on the table. No escape. No dream holiday.

Nothing.

Nothing, apart from Stephen. Stephen, who'd been kind, attentive to her at the workingmen's club when they'd staged the benefit concert for the strikers. Stephen, who'd called around from the union with the boxes of tinned goods they'd collected from local shops to help the strikers. Stephen, who'd sat at her kitchen table interested in her, making her laugh, making her feel special. Making her nervously brush the hair falling in her eyes whenever he was there. Making her think about what she would wear on the days he was due to come round. Making her feel alive when he did come. Coming round more and more until the time when he came round without the tins, without the reasons, without the excuses; nothing, other than to admit that he came to see her.

Wanted her.

Had her.

For months now he'd visited twice a week whilst Kevin was away at the picket line or canvassing support in the town. For months Stephen Jackson had been her lover, her dream. Her escape.

Sitting in the chair, coffee cup in her hands, she shivered at the thought of him inside her. She squeezed her thighs tight together in anticipation of the tremor she knew would run through her just from that thought. That's how he made her feel. Even when he was no longer there she could imagine him, feel him inside her, hard and powerful.

She wanted him. Wanted him every night.

When Kevin made love with her each week, every Saturday like clockwork, she thought of Stephen. It was him she felt inside her, not Kevin. It was Stephen she imagined when she closed her eyes in the dark feeling her husband go about his business.

Like clockwork.

A wind-up lover, mechanical, predictable.

It was Stephen's hard body she wanted against her, hard like the military man he told her he'd been, hard like the coal he hewed each day. Not soft with the beer gut of her husband. Twenty seven years old and he was flabby, an imitation of his father and of her own.

She clasped her hands tight around the mug, sipping deeply.

She had no idea where her life was heading. A future that had always been so clear was clouded with uncertainty. Kevin offered little other than the fact that he would always be there. Stephen offered something else, something intangible yet unarguably better. They hadn't talked of any future, not yet. There'd been nothing beyond their next meeting, their next time. But she believed they would. That like her, Stephen wanted more - more of her, more than just the furtive meetings, the fucking. He would want her and her children. He would want to make a future for both of them, all of them.

Soon. She knew it would be soon. It had to be.

She looked at the clock. He'd be here soon.

She took the mug into the tiny kitchen stretching out at the rear of the house and made her way to the bathroom beyond it.

She looked in the mirror and flicked her hair.

No lines, no wrinkles. Eyes still blue and clear. Blonde hair still shining from the conditioner she'd used earlier in anticipation of him, conditioner she'd saved from her birthday. She smoothed the sides of her sweater and stepped back. She had a good figure. Two children hadn't taken away the firmness of her waist, her tummy. She'd been religious in her exercises after each birth, putting all of her energy into regaining her shape. She'd been determined; images of her mother - belly distorted by childbirth - repulsed her. She would never allow that to happen to herself. Never. The dream of Spain had given her all the incentive she needed. The dream of the white bikini.

And now it was Stephen. Stephen, who would soon be running his hands over her body; standing behind her, resting his palms on her stomach, feeling the tautness of her hips, the firmness of her breasts. Stephen who would hold her, feel her wetness as he slipped his hands between her thighs.

She tingled at the thought of him.

She heard the door.

She flicked her hair once more, then rushed out towards the lounge, and the passageway that led to the front door.

She stopped in shock, her mouth moved but no sound came from her.

Kevin.

Kevin stood there. Kevin, his back to the door. Kevin not Stephen. He looked strange, distant.

'What...' she began, but her words stopped short of any meaning beyond intention.

Kevin shook his head. 'There's been an accident... a dreadful accident. On the picket line.' He looked to the floor. 'Someone we know... one of the union committee. Christ, he's been here. Brought food round. Stephen. Stephen Jackson. He's dead. He's been found battered to death.'

Karen staggered. She put out a hand towards the wall to prevent herself from falling to the floor. She stood, struggling for breath, and began to sob.

'Karen,' Kevin called, reaching out an arm towards where she stood propped against the wall.

'Keep away!' she screamed, flapping her arms in his direction. 'Keep away from me!'

He stood there, arms outstretched, helpless. 'Karen, what is it?'

'You killed him,' she screeched, a sobbing broken wail. 'You killed him!'

Kevin looked bemused at the madness appearing to engulf his wife. 'What are you saying? I just help organise the pickets. Stephen was my friend. It's not my fault he's dead.'

'You killed him!' she screamed. 'You killed him!' She slid

slowly down the wall; falling to the floor, hunched, foetal, wracked by sobbing.

'Karen, I don't understand what you're saying.'

'You know,' she sobbed. 'You know.'

Four

The crowd of reporters outside Tamworth Central police station was in most respects little different to that gathered at the colliery. The same mix of TV, radio, and print press. The local, the national. The TV crews had gathered some time previously, corralled in pockets of cables and temporary lighting. They clustered around outside broadcast vans and radio cars, earnest men with eager assistants flicking at their hair.

The print boys were more familiar faces, faces that today registered scorn, resentful that their vigils of countless, numbing cases of burglary and petty crimes counted for nothing as they were shoved to the side to allow the temporary glory boys of TV and radio the space they voraciously consumed.

The assembly was however more restrained than that at the colliery. At least here they knew they were going to get something to satisfy editors hungry for whatever facts were out there. In the absence of facts, everyone knew it would be whatever they could glean that they could pass off as such, spinning it to suit the political preferences of their audience. The police here at the station would be anxious to throw them something to feed on and they circled in anticipation.

For the most part the journalists stood in clumps, sheltering from the wind that blew around the hunched presence of the central police station. They huddled against the grey pebble-dashed concrete of the building, the regulars warily sharing what they'd heard from their particular sources. Some retreated to the more inviting space of the nearby car-park. A couple of camera crews had set up further down the road, finding the old alms-houses presented a more interesting backdrop to their filmed reports than the squat brutalist concrete of the station.

Inside, Kalus and Mallen found Ridgway in Bailey's office hunched over the press release they were about to present to the gathered media.

'Looks okay,' Bailey observed, assuming the air of one used to running a critical rule over such things.

'Then this what we'll give them,' Ridgway confirmed.

'I'll get Betty to run it off.' Bailey rose and made his way towards the door to his outer office, Kalus and Mallen stepping aside to allow his passage.

'Hope you two have got better news,' he said waving the press release in their general direction as he passed.

'Not much. One or two tit-bits of information about our man but, other than that...' Mallen shrugged his shoulders. 'You know...*tragic death... awaiting coroner's report on causes... early days, proceeding with enquiries.*'

Bailey shook his head. 'Is that it? *Platitudes?* Christ, I'm glad I'm not fronting this one alone,' he said to Ridgway as he left the room.

'So am I,' Ridgway said, waiting a beat after the door closed. 'Can you imagine what the nationals would do to him?'

The officers shook their heads in mute agreement.

Ridgeway sat back in the chair, opening his arms expansively: the sage old headmaster in his study with his favoured prefects. 'OK, so I wing it with our friends from the media. The straight bat. Where are we in reality?'

Kalus and Mallen outlined the progress of each element of the enquiry, ending with the union's reluctance to co-operate beyond confirming the basic details of their now dead member and his presence at the picket.

'One of you needs to get over there. Try and persuade them of the benefits of co-operation.'

Kalus and Mallen exchanged glances. 'Toss you for it,' Mallen said.

Ridgeway grunted. 'Short straw I know. However, neither of you are getting off lightly. Whoever doesn't get to visit with our union friends will have to get to grips with interviewing the senior officers in charge of the riot squad, see if we can narrow down how many uniforms we have to interview from this morning's picket. Three hundred interviews...' Ridgway shook his head. 'As for your request for additional bodies for interviewing them... I'll see what I can do. We're pretty thin on the ground as it is. The picketing won't stop. Unless one of you has powers of persuasion verging on the divine with the Miner's Union this afternoon.'

'Maybe you can get *Thatch* to give King Arthur a ring,' Mallen joked.

Kalus smiled, 'I can't see those two moving an inch to help each other.'

'On our own then.' Mallen stated. 'With everyone waiting for us to stumble so they can put the boot in.'

'Speaking of which,' Ridgway put in. 'I've had a call from the Home Office. Seems they're preparing for you to find it's one of our own involved. They're sending up Complaints on a watching brief. They want to be in a position to step in quickly if it looks as if it's going that way. Officer called Riordan. John Riordan. Know anything of him?'

'Complaints? He's a wanker,' Mallen stated.

'You know him?' Ridgway asked.

'No. But he's Complaints. He's a wanker.'

'Well, he's your wanker, unless of course you can prove that it wasn't one of our own who killed this picket. He'll be over with you at the pit later today.'

'It just gets better and better this one,' Mallen opined.

'That's why you've got it,' Ridgway said, offering a bone. 'Every faith in both of you to get us through this. To find the killer. But I tell you this: whoever it is, get it done quick. If it's not one of ours then the sooner we get this shit off our backs the better. If it turns out to be one of ours then the quicker we sort it out and get it off the front pages, the sooner we can get on with the job.'

'You make it sound so appealing, sir,' Kalus observed.

Ridgway stood up, moving towards the door and the waiting press conference. Kalus and Mallen rose with him. 'Make no mistake, I'm out front on this one with my ass in my hands, along with the Chief Constable and the whole of the force - maybe even the government itself. There are eyes all over it. Everyone involved is looking to dump it in someone else's lap. Make it someone else's mess.' He paused by the door. 'Richard, would you just pop ahead and check they're ready for me?'

Mallen hesitated, looking from Ridgway to Kalus and back again. He nodded.

Once he'd left, Ridgway turned to Kalus. 'Everything okay, Peter?'

Kalus nodded. 'Fine.'

Ridgway scrutinised him. 'It's just that, well.... you know. After everything that happened. Handsworth. Reuben.'

'I'll be okay.'

Ridgway stood in silence. After a moment he relented, some unspoken decision made. 'Counting on you, Peter. You know that don't you?'

'Yes, sir.'

'No margins for error on this one. No screw-ups.'

'I understand sir. I'll be fine.' He let a beat go by. 'I-'

The door opened cutting him off. Mallen pushed his head back in the room. 'Everything's ready,' he said.

Ridgway looked at Kalus.

Kalus forced a smile. 'It's fine.'

Ridgway made to go, then stopped once more. He turned in the doorway, a parent wanting their meaning clear with no room for misunderstanding. 'Pass the parcel's got nothing on this. Our friends in the media have got the whiff of blood in their nostrils, and they're baying for flesh. Most are hoping it's one of ours they'll get, but at bottom they don't really care who it is just as long as they get something to feed on. Make sure it's not you. That it's not us.'

They watched the Detective Chief Superintendent leave, making his way to the assembled press conference.

Mallen turned to Kalus, drawing a hand through his hair, exhaling a slow, resigned sigh. 'Tell me. Why do I suddenly feel like I'm a big juicy bone?'

Five

Angus McKinnon and Brian Terry gave little away. They sat *zen-like* in their expression, unrevealing. *Poker faces*, Kalus thought, feeling that he was holding a pair whilst they most likely held a flush.

'You see our position,' McKinnon growled, the serious intent of his words crumpling his face. A face pale, almost grey in places, highlighted by the flecks of broken veins, blue and red, that ran through it. A drinker; for sure. A worker; for certain. Angus McKinnon was a man who bore the scars of his trade, a life etched across his face for all to see. *Angus McKinnon; Miner.*

'And you, no doubt, understand ours,' Kalus returned.

'Aye. In the shite.' The smile that accompanied the judgement, the smile that gave McKinnon's features the appearance of a concertina, lacked all trace of humour.

Kalus dipped his head in acceptance. 'But your own's not that much healthier.'

'How d'you reckon that, then?' The burr was pure West Scotland. Fife, Lothian Kalus thought, a man who had no doubt followed the coal all the way down the spine of his own country to finally come up in the alien land of the Midlands. He wondered if McKinnon used the accent as part of his arsenal. He had seen his own father do it, the descent into native tongue and dialect, the thickening of the Polish accent accompanying his growing anger, covering his uncertainty. He had the feeling that McKinnon would long ago have discovered the advantage of accent as a weapon, a dark Scots tones intimidating all opposition. Certainly, in the ten minutes since they'd met, the accent had decidedly thickened.

Kalus spread his hands wide, a gesture of the obviousness

of what he was saying. 'You need public opinion. You're dead without it. How long do you think they'll keep filling the strike boxes left outside the shops once they find out that you're obstructing the enquiry into the death of one of your own? How would they react if they thought you'd decided there was more mileage in playing politics than getting to the truth of a killing? A murder?'

McKinnon fixed Kalus with a long stare. His eyes never flickered. *Poker face.* 'You're very confident, Chief Inspector. Are you sure of that?'

He wasn't. His head ached. For the last hour a dull pain had centred behind his eyes. When he spoke, the firmness in his voice surprised him more than it did the other two. 'Are you sure they won't?'

A pause. A hesitation. 'The people round here are very strong in their support of the strike. They'll stand by us.'

'Mr McKinnon, *I'm* from *round here.* My father's on a pension. He's disabled. But, like a lot of people from *round here*, he has food tins put in the miners' strike box every week. He's done so for months. He may not believe in what you are doing or how you are doing it, but he supports the miners. The men. I can't see him carrying on putting food in those boxes if he believes their leaders care less about them than he does.'

'Disabled, you say.'

'Pneumoconiosis'

A flicker. A reaction. '*Black Lung*? He was a miner.'

'Poland and here.'

Brian Terry leant forward. 'What we're fighting for. This government -'

Kalus turned to Terry. He was a small man, wiry where McKinnon was stocky, hair thin where McKinnon's was thick, face shining where McKinnon's was pale and white. Eyes narrow, Kalus spoke directly to him. 'My father may have been a miner, but like a lot of the people around here he voted Thatcher last time. Part of the landslide. I'm not here because of my politics or yours. I'm here investigating a murder. And you and your members, like it or not, are part of that enquiry.'

Terry half-turned towards McKinnon, mouth opening as if to speak. McKinnon inclined a hand slightly, a gesture holding him as surely as if he'd grabbed him by the collar or shoved him up against a wall. McKinnon spoke to Kalus. 'You make a powerful case, Inspector. I hope you're as good at making a criminal case, especially against one of your own.'

'One thing I've discovered about a murder investigation is to never go into one with pre-conceptions about its possible outcome.'

Terry could contain himself no longer, when he spoke particles of phlegm and spittle formed at the edges of his lips. 'Oh come on! You must know it's one of your own that's murdered him!'

'Like I said, I never have pre-conceptions.'

'Sounds like the beginnings of a white-wash!' Terry spat the words, spittle pooling ever larger on his lips.

It was McKinnon who Kalus fixed with his attention. 'If that's what you truly believe then the best way to ensure that this investigation gets to the truth is for you to give my officers what they want.' He held his left hand in the air, flicking up thumb and then fingers as he enumerated the requirements. 'Who was there, what they saw, what they know about Stephen Jackson.' There was a pause as both men examined Kalus' hand, took in the scope of his demands. 'The alternative is that I start making a series of arrests around here, starting with both of you for obstructing a police enquiry. Apart from putting you where you will have no influence over the rest of the strike, all that arresting you and any other miners will do is tie up men and time that I don't have to spare.'

McKinnon's burr grew a semi-tone deeper. His words were a beat slower than Kalus', his words stressed for emphasis, each sentence separated by a pause for intent to be weighed and understood. 'Chief Inspector, you need to understand what's been happening here, what's been happening all across the country during this strike. We've got injured miners. Men beaten, bones broken because they're standing up for what they believe in. Men who just want a job for tomorrow. A job for their children. This government may or may not be killing men, but they're killing the pits, killing communities. They're killing hope. No matter what this government says, what we're fighting for isn't a fatter wage packet. We want a future. We want to work. If this government has its way there will be no work. There will be no future.'

Kalus dismissed him. 'At the risk of repeating myself, I'm not here for politics.'

McKinnon leant closer; the desk separating the two men taking on a sudden sense of its fragility. 'But you are. You and your force. It's all politics. People are taking sides. You need to choose where you stand, Chief Inspector. Choose what it is you're fighting for.'

'I'm clear what I'm fighting for. Justice for Stephen Jackson. I want to find whoever killed him. Whoever and whatever they are. Miner, policeman… it makes no difference. What about you? What do you want for Stephen?'

Terry scowled. 'You know who killed him. What miner would want to kill a picket, a fellow miner?'

Kalus' exasperation seeped through. 'There have been threats, beatings even. Miners who want to return to work are being attacked, strike-breakers are hospitalised. Just look at the protection that's necessary to get the coaches into the pits each morning.'

'Scabs,' Terry hissed.

Kalus gestured in Terry's direction, the man's reaction proof of his point. 'There's anger in this strike. Not just between the police and the miners. Miner and miner.'

'Anger's not the same as killing someone.' Spittle; white and foaming. Kalus found the thought *mad-dog* form from somewhere. Terry stabbed his fingers. 'I'll say it again, what miner would want to kill a fellow miner?'

'What miner would want to impede the finding of his killer?'

Terry laughed. 'What miner would want to help police

that are trampling over the democratic rights of its citizens?' *Stab.* 'We've had police barricading motorways, turning cars back because they want to get into areas where there are picket lines.' *Stab.* 'Police stopping the right to protest.' *Stab.* 'We're becoming a police-state. And you,' *Stab.* 'You, Inspector,' *Stab.* 'Are becoming the instrument of this government's desire to destroy trade unions. The rights of the working man. This is a war, inspector. A war. A war has casualties.' *Stab.*

Kalus hesitated. *We're counting on you, Peter. No screw-ups.*

'I'm investigating a murder,' his voice replied.

'Are you sure of that?' McKinnon asked. 'Are you so sure you're not part of a cover-up. A white-wash? Let me ask you a question, Detective Chief Inspector. How many men have been assigned to this investigation?'

'A dozen.'

'A dozen. And that's detectives?'

'Total.'

'So, a dozen men in total.' McKinnon sat back in thoughtful contemplation. 'Hardly seems like the numbers you'd need to thoroughly investigate a case with so many suspects. Not when every morning there's a few hundred of you lined up at the colliery.'

'It's early days. The force is stretched thin.' He smiled grimly. 'There's a strike on.'

McKinnon pursed his lips. The expression ran like a slit across his face. He nodded an acceptance of his own decision. 'Inspector, we'll get you the records you want.'

Terry turned, mouth opening to form a protest. McKinnon for the second time stifled his words before they could be spoken. 'Brian here will see to it that you get the names of all the stewards, and as many of the names of the pickets as we can find. It gets pretty confusing out there. We have supporters from all over the country, not just miners. Hard to keep a track of who's turned up, but most of our own colliery do. We'll get you the names of those who knew Stephen. Those who might be able to tell you what they saw of him this morning.'

'Good.' Kalus stood to leave.

McKinnon rose, offering his hand across the desk. Kalus hesitated then shook it. McKinnon's grip was firm. He held Kalus, one hand cupped over the handshake, binding them together. 'Tell your daddy…we wish him well. If there's anything we can do for him….'

Kalus nodded. 'Thanks. I will.' McKinnon released his grip. Kalus turned to go and then paused. 'Tell me, what made you change your mind?'

McKinnon half-smiled. 'To be honest, Chief Inspector, after what you just told me about your team and the support you've been given by your superiors, it seems to me that you're going to need all the help you can get.'

* * *

The Minister closed the folder. Running a manicured hand through carefully trimmed hair, he settled into the dark red leather chair behind an imposing desk of English oak.

What he'd read troubled him.

He steepled his fingers, elbows resting on the arms of the chair. He gazed across his Whitehall office, deep in introspection. The paintings, the walls, the lush green drapes, all faded from his mind as he focused on the report he'd just read and its implications.

He was part of what the papers dubbed *True Disciples*, those whose allegiance to Thatcher was unquestioning. Acolytes like himself had been key in delivering the landslide victory that had brought a second term of office, and with it the mandate for the ever-greater pursuit of her vision. *Thatcherism*.

She had been clear in her first address to the new cabinet. There was much to do. The time had come to confront all who stood against them. The welfare state leeches who took but never gave; Brussels and the bureaucrats of the common market; Ireland and its catholic militants. All would be targets of her reforming zeal.

But, above all else, it was the unions whom she declared would be first to feel the power of her New Britain. She had been clear; the militant power of the Unions was the greatest threat to the fabric of the nation. They were the enemy within. Their power was a dagger aimed at the heart of the democratic process. It had to be restrained and it had to be brought to heel.

The miners had been carefully selected. The miners, the shock troops of the militants, would be destroyed. A lesson would be taught, cowering the rest. In this plan the key role lay with Cabinet Group Twelve. An elite within the Cabinet. Government within government. The spearhead of *Thatcherism*.

Throughout the previous summer, stocks of coal had been amassed at each power station. Stocks ensuring the lights would be kept on and the wider economy unaffected by the anticipated miners' strike that her plans for pit closures was sure to provoke. An early act of the new government had been legislation extending the power of the police to deal with the excesses of civil unrest and strikes. They would neuter the strikes at their source, the picket lines. It would not be like '74. This time they would win.

Cabinet Group Twelve were charged with managing the strike. Within this, his own role was specific: co-ordinating the police response. Such a remit stretched far and wide, not just the policing of the inevitable picket lines but the disrupting of the so-called Flying Pickets. He was a cog in an operation involving economic planners, media specialists, and financial experts. There were military planners too. Should a crisis point be reached and the troops have to be deployed to keep the docks and the power stations running, it was through his office that civil order would be restored.

But within this group was an even more clandestine operation. The use of the intelligence services to penetrate and disrupt the miners' organisation. Deep lying agents. Intelligence gathering *agent provocateurs* provoking the violence that would split the strikers and turn public opinion against them. At the very summit of their work, their prime asset, a mole recruited deep within the leadership of the NUM: *Silver Fox*.

Eight months into the strike, there were rumours of the group and its remit but these barely touched on the actual scale and ambition of the operation, the daring of their plan.

He was clear, like all *True Disciples*, that they were fighting for the soul of the nation. The NUM was attempting to bring down an elected government. Scargill and his communist cronies were hell-bent on destroying democracy. They wanted Socialism. Communism. Revolution. MI5, Special Branch, and all of the other intelligence assets had been mobilised to break them.

The miners had been ill-prepared and divided from the outset. The dragging out of the strike and its growing impact on mining families had further divided them. The operations of his agents had worked on such splits, a crowbar levering them ever wider. The whole country was divided. Those who saw the confrontation as the necessary battle for future economic prosperity ranged against those who believed they were witnessing the dawning of a police state. A state where the curbing of trade union power was but the first step towards stifling all dissenting voices.

She had been clear. The police must do their duty. Miners had to be arrested, prosecuted. Early in the strike *She* had railed against the attitudes of the police, castigating Chief Constables for dithering when action was required of them. *She* had been clear in her instruction to Cabinet: they were to stiffen the resolve of the Chief Constables. Show them what was wanted.

The Cabinet were mesmerised by her, and he shared much of that. This was the leader who had pushed the nation to victory in the Falklands. The leader providing the electoral landslide. The leader of vision. Her certainty, her belief, percolated through the ranks of government, galvanising it at all levels. *True Disciples*.

It was why the report regarding Tamworth troubled him.

The killing in Staffordshire was a complication; one that would have to be quickly dealt with. That the truth surrounding this man's death might be revealed was too awful to contemplate.

Whatever else happened, Stephen Jackson's secret had to be buried with him.

He looked at the wall opposite. The wooden oak panels, above it the portraits of the good and great. More likely those who had succeeded in promoting the deceit of that fact whilst keeping hidden their true natures and ambition. The truth could not come out. It would destroy them.

Jackson's secret would cost them the strike. It would bring down the government.

He was a *True Disciple*.

It would not happen. Not on his watch, whatever the cost.

* * *

'It's a complication. But that's all it is. A complication.'

The men gathered around the table adopted a variety of poses. Some stared hard at the tabletop, some into the middle distance, their eyes unfocussed. One or two looked up to the ceiling. None of them looked the speaker in the eye. Three of those gathered took drags on cigarettes, watching their exhaled smoke drift away. To a man they were uncertain, at least, lacking the certainty that the speaker had in his own words, his own assessment.

Confirmation. That's what they sought, what they needed. They sought the sense of security that some outside verification would give them. If they knew that the series of events that had just been relayed to them was nothing more than a *'complication'* they would be satisfied. Complications were unwelcome, but at least they could be dealt with, solutions found, ways forward agreed. Complications simply required a plan to surmount them, and the men gathered around the table were strong on planning. They had been selected for that very reason.

The room they were sitting in was like many of those used for such meetings. Ordinary. Today it was a room above a shop. Last time it had been a clothing warehouse. The time before that it had been inside the grounds-man's hut in a local park. They had friends everywhere. Sympathisers, those prepared to put themselves at risk because they too believed.

'Believe me,' the speaker said, seeking to stir the vacuum of uncertainty that clung around the table. 'Our people on the ground say it's a complication, nothing more. Sure, it's caused some immediate problems, but they say they can ride these out. In the long run, nothing's changed. Nothing.'

'Police, crawling all over the colliery? Special Branch no doubt everywhere. TV, newspapers, radio, the government - all of them turning their attention to the murder of a striking miner? Nothing's changed?' The thin man's tone conveyed some measure of his scepticism, which was just this side of incredulous.

The principal speaker remained secure in his manner as well as his words. 'As I said, it's a complication. Nothing more.'

'I hope you're right,' one of the smokers put in, arching his eyebrows. 'We've got a great deal riding on this. All of us.'

The men around the table, though their eyes remained distant, nodded in agreement. There was a great deal riding on this.

Some of them believed that everything rode on it.

Everything.

Six

Mallen picked up a dozen or so sheets of paper from the stack on the station counter. He yawned, dog-tired, overwhelmed with reviewing yet another set of interview notes that had posed the same questions and provoked the same angry responses.

The sheets he chose were loosely clipped together, slipping in his hand like wet fish. He put the mug of tea he'd been carrying down on the counter, slopping some of it onto the dark wood. Most pooled around the mug's base, but the majority coursed towards the main stack of interviews and began seeping into it. 'Shit!' he cursed.

The WPC behind the counter reached out an arm, plucking the papers from disaster. She settled them further along the counter before moving the mug and mopping the counter with a tissue produced from her pocket.

Mallen looked at her, the gratitude obvious in his face. 'Thanks,' he said.

'No problem, sir,' she replied, returning a now wiped mug to the counter.

'Bloody disaster that would have been. Re-typing all that lot again,' he gestured towards the secured stack of forms. The statements were among the first gathered from interviews of officers present at the morning's picket. They told little other than where they themselves had been, how they had been deployed, and how it was impossible to comment on anything other than what had been happening right in front of them. There had been no time for *'fucking sightseeing'* as one particularly resentful uniform, weary of Mallen's questions, had told him.

'Not that they're of any great significance,' he admitted.

'No?'

He shook his head, smoothing a hand through his hair. 'No-one wants to break ranks. Everyone's scared of saying something that might put them or one of their mates in the frame. Some unthinking remark, some small observation.'

'I can understand that.'

'Sorry, you're…?'

'WPC Lawrence,' she replied.

'Lawrence. You know a lot of these officers?'

She nodded. 'The local force, yeah, and one or two of the rest. You know, the ones that have been seconded from neighbouring areas. I've met some of them on courses at the academy. Most of them are based out at the local barracks towards Lichfield. Some are up in the caravan park. We don't get to see them much. They're pretty much just faces, some not even that, what with the helmets and visors. Faceless.'

He nodded. Constables had been bussed in from Northampton and Nottingham. Most had been barracked at the army base at Whittington with others housed in a caravan park near Lea Marston. It made sense; the duty rosters were harsh, the shifts long and frequent.

He'd started by interviewing senior officers from the local force, those who had faced the picket line that morning. Tamworth first, then Staffordshire, before moving onto those seconded from outlying areas.

They were commanders with knowledge of where officers had been deployed. However, as the violence developed, those placements had changed in response to the circumstances that the second tier of senior officers, those actually at the colliery, had encountered. These too had fragmented as the police lines had been charged and their Snatch Squads had rushed the pickets, leaving behind holes in the line that other uniforms had been forced to fill.

What began as a careful plan had soon degenerated into something else, something quite different. '*Organised chaos*' as one of them had it. Impossible to plot. They had '*moved like waves*', according to another. An improvised dance to a jagged rhythm: movements difficult to make sense of from outside and impossible to understand for those inside.

He found that what might on paper appear to be effective positioning was in reality something altogether different. The ground might be boggy or undulating. It might be overlooked, making it vulnerable to the pickets' assaults of bricks and bottles. From the start there had been adjustments to the deployment of officers, forces moved *en masse*, by group, or even as individual officers.

And, of course, once the coaches of '*scab*' miners arrived at the entrance then all hell had broken loose.

The gates had proved an obvious hot spot, with most of the police and pickets attention focussed there. Once the coaches were in, the violence had spread along the driveway, spilling into the fields surrounding it.

The Snatch Squads were faceless. Their visored helmets anonymised them. Officers could have been standing and struggling next to their brother or a total stranger and - behind the helmet, beyond the shield - would never have known the difference.

Lawrence had it right. Faceless.

He stared at the sheets in his hand, the stack on the counter. It was late and he was tired. Tired of the questions; tired of the suspicious looks; tired of the barely concealed contempt of the string of officers parading before him all afternoon.

The senior officers were, for the most part, more concerned with their careers, keen to assign blame away from their own actions. According to each of the Inspectors he'd interviewed, they had *gone by the book, played it straight*.

Communication. That was the issue for the sergeants he spoke with: equipment that failed, frequencies that became overcrowded - a gabble of noise and static that few of them in the heat of the conflict could make sense of. Decisions had been made under stress, their actions improvised. They were responding to pickets who weren't working to the formula so carefully worked out by those back at HQ.

What emerged was chaos, each group trying to survive the pounding onslaught of pickets whilst desperately seeking some sense of purpose to guide them in their actions. None of the ranking officers, none of the command structure, could give a meaningful account of where the men they commanded had actually been during much of the morning's action. Nor could they see any way of how they might now trace where officers had been. Not one of them could offer any sense of how Stephen Jackson could have been beaten to death in the midst of it all with no one apparently seeing a thing.

'*Medieval*' had been the comment of the last sergeant he'd spoken with.

Mallen picked up his mug of tea and sipped.

'Messy business,' Lawrence offered.

For a moment he was uncertain whether she was referring to the tea he'd slopped or the enquiry. He opted for the enquiry. 'That's some understatement you've got there.' He sipped more of the tea, then gestured with the mug towards her. 'And don't call me sir all the time. Makes me sound bloody ancient.'

'Sorry, s-' She stopped short, smiling.

'Christ!' Mallen observed, flicking stray hair back across his head. 'That's the first smile I've seen since I walked in here.'

'Everybody's tense.'

'Especially around me.'

She stopped smiling, uncertain whether to respond. 'Well, they see you as sort of... the enemy, if you don't mind me saying so. Like Complaints. They think you're out to get them.'

He waved the mug around. 'It's a murder enquiry. What do they expect?'

'It's not easy. We've had weeks of hostile press. Some officers have been spat at by their neighbours. Some of the constables here live in the mining villages around the town.'

He wanted to impress, be cool. Instead, he snorted. 'And some of them have been waving their overtime sheets at the pickets.'

She shook her head. 'Not us, not the locals. That's those lot from down south. That lot from Northampton and the like.'

'Whoever it is, it's hardly likely to make for good relationships between the pickets and us. To them we're all the same. One uniform. One target.'

She fixed him with a look. 'If you don't mind me saying sir, we didn't ask for any of this. No one wants to spend their time toe to toe with strikers. I joined to do some good.'

'Put bad men away?' his intended tone was light, but it came out as mocking.

She picked up on it, bridled. 'Actually, yes, I did. Didn't you?'

He considered a smart reply but rejected it. 'Yeah, suppose I did.'

'And that's what you do.'

He nodded, flicking at his hair. 'Most of the time. Some of them get away.'

'What about this one?'

He considered the dregs of tea remaining in the mug. He swirled them round, draining the mug and placing it on the counter. 'As you so rightly observed, WPC Lawrence, it's a messy business.'

***

The house was bright. All of the lights were on, even those in the rooms where no one went.

Just in case.

God knows how much it cost him in bills. For the past five years or more the lights had burned continuously throughout the night, seemingly only switched off once the summer came. From three o'clock each afternoon, when the first edge of darkness came creeping towards the house, until the following morning, the lights would burn.

They'd tried to talk him out of it, tried to reason with him. The cost, the futility of it. Nothing would shift him. He was immoveable. At times like that he became stone, like the rock he'd hewn all his working life.

Kalus put his key in the latch, calling out as he opened the door. 'Dad, it's Peter.' He shut the door, stiff and catching on the carpet like it had ever since it had been lain just weeks before his mother's death. He scooped up the post from the floor: bills and flyers. 'Dad, where are you?' He knew where he would be. *The lounge; his chair.*

He walked the few paces down the hall and entered the lounge.

Andrzej Kalus sat in his chair. Same shirt, same dark grey flannel trousers, same faded slippers, the ones his mother had bought him that last Christmas. The TV set flickered in the corner, the colour garish and poorly set, the volume a thin whisper in the background.

'Dad?'

He turned towards him, a great block of a head, the silver hair swept back and shining, lying in strands, the pink flesh showing like water glimpsed through reeds. 'Petr.' He breathed the name more than spoke it. It was confirmation, recognition as much as greeting. 'Petr. Good boy.' The accent, the pattern; the rhythm thick and unchanging.

Kalus lifted up the carrier bag. He held it at shoulder height for his father to see. The emblem of the ferry line was stamped across the bag - three blue wavy lines giving the impression of sea, and a V- shaped wedge cutting through it. The words *Stenna Line* stamped in red across the top of the graphic.

'Cigarettes?' Andrzej breathed.

Kalus shaking his head, fishing inside the bag and withdrawing the bottle of clear liquid. 'Vodka. *Stochkoi*, like from home. Bloke in the drug squad went to a conference in Stockholm. Duty free.'

Andrzej turned his head back to the television. 'No cigarettes,' he said to the presenter.

'You know they're not good for you.' His tone was exasperated. He couldn't stop himself. Chided himself for it.

'Lady from social welfare. She brings me cigarettes.'

'Because you ask her to. Because you pay her to. You know

what the doctor's said. Especially with that thing around.' Kalus nodded his head in the direction of the blood red oxygen cylinder that stood next to his father's chair. A clear plastic facemask was draped over it, its elasticated ties hanging limply down. 'Go up like a bloody light if you smoke around that and get careless.'

His father shook his head but didn't breathe any reply. The cylinder, at first a strange and alien presence, had long since become a familiar landmark in the room. Kalus remembered how his mother had tried to domesticate it, at first tucking it behind his father's chair, then covering it with doilies, even placing a standard lamp in front of it. Eventually she had given in as several times each day his father had struggled to reach for the mask, turning the taps, seeking release from the struggle to breathe. Each year the struggle grew more desperate. The turning to the cylinder more frequent. Now it stood next to his chair with no effort made to disguise it. It was a part of Andrzej. It would be with him until his last breath. It would be his last breath.

Peter pushed the bottle back down into the carrier bag. 'I'll put it in the kitchen,' he said.

***

By the time he got home it was late. Andrew and Katrina were in bed and Anna was busy in the kitchen. He kissed her on the cheek.

'Hey there,' she said. 'Busy day?' she asked, returning immediately to her emptying of the tumble dryer.

'Pretty much.' He noticed the washing machine clicking into another thunderous cycle, the water cascading and foaming inside. 'Looks like you've been pretty busy yourself.'

'Hmmm,' she murmured by way of agreement. 'Been over to your dad's.' She nodded her head in the direction of the laundry basket into which she was dragging the contents of the dryer. 'Collected this lot whilst I was there.'

'I stopped off on my way back. Dropped off that vodka.'

'How was he?' she asked of the basket.

'Hard work.'

'I meant was he okay?' She stood up, hauling the basket to waist height in front of her. 'He seemed to be a little bit more distant today. Not so chatty.' She manoeuvred her way across the kitchen towards the radiators in the hall, the normal winter dispersal point for washing in the house. 'He was using his mask a lot.'

He turned, examining the kitchen, the remains of Andrew and Katrina's tea: bread board, ketchup bottles, sauce filmed plates. 'He just grumbled about me not bringing him any ciggies,' he said.

Anna shuffled the children's dry pants and socks along the top of the radiator, turning one or two items to ensure they would dry. 'That bloody woman from welfare sees to that for him. I told her last time I saw her there. They're killing him. And it's not safe.'

Kalus walked out of the kitchen, stood behind his wife of eight years. He watched her shuffle the washing. 'I know.'

'If only your mom was here,' she said.

His mom had been a rock. The stone even Andrzej could not break. She had been his strength, his reason, his love. They had met at a dance during the war. He a soldier in the Polish Free Army. She a land girl, her family refugees from Estonia. He'd had the cigarettes, she the light. Within months they had married. Within a year their first child had been born. Later, after the war, had come Peter. For the whole family his mother had been the enduring point of safety. As they'd grown and left home, having families of their own, she had remained that point. The family rotated around her. They gravitated to her at Christmas and Easter, family occasions. She *was* the family.

And then, within months of falling ill, weeks of her diagnosis, she was gone. January five years ago. Their last Christmas, a cold and bitter one. His mother encouraging them all to be happy, to smile, to laugh. And then she was gone. And all that was left of her was Peter and his sister. Their children. All that was left to mark her presence. A good woman, a good life.

'Maybe you should talk with them again, Social Services. See if you can get through to her. Those cigarettes he gets her to bring are killing him. She needs to know. What she's doing... she's killing him, you know. You should tell her,' Anna stated fixing the waistband of a pair of pyjama bottoms behind the radiator.

'What? Show her my warrant card? Take her in for questioning?'

Anna moved further along the corridor. She held a tee shirt to her cheek, testing for warmth, damp. 'You know what I mean. He's your father.'

'He thinks more of you.'

'That's not true. You know that. He loves you.'

'No. No, he doesn't. You and the kids, not me.'

'Peter, that's a horrible thing to say.'

'You don't know him the way that I do.'

She raised a towel, draping it over the banister rail before moving up a step or two of the stairs. 'He's always been good to me. To us.'

'That was mom, not him. She was always the best part of him. He knew it, so did she.' He moved to the foot of the stairwell, watching as Anna worked her way up laying out washing as she went. 'She knew it would be like this, with her going first,' he called up to her. 'He can't cope. Can't cope with people. Can't cope with the loss. Can't cope with life.'

'All I know is that he took her death badly.' She paused near the top step to lay out a pillowcase. 'He's certainly not been the same. But lots of old couples are like that. He's still grieving for her.'

'He's dying.'

'He's been ill for years.'

'He's dying. And he's scared. It scares him.' *Scares me.*

She'd had turned the corner, standing above him, separating bed linen along the balustrade. 'That's natural.'

Kalus stood part way up the stairs. 'He won't admit it. Won't let on that he's scared. Won't talk about it. Won't ask for help in dealing with it.'

'God's always there. God's with him.'

Kalus sighed to the banister rail, to the children's tee shirt with the Postman Pat logo. Anna's religion had always been a comfort to her. It was an area of her life, her being, that he accepted, accommodated. When they'd first married he went to church with her, mainly because it pleased his mother, pleased her that he was *'coming back to God'*. Since the children he'd gone less and less. A high-holiday church-goer. These days she took the children, bringing them into the faith, her faith. The daughter of immigrant Estonian refugees from the same war, the same forces that had brought his own father and mother here. They had met at Saturday school, their courtship encouraged by sets of parents still clinging to some of the old ways, the old beliefs. Anna had her faith just as his mother had. Anna and his mother: one God, one faith, one belief. Catholic. Orthodox.

'Yeah, there's always God for him to talk to.'

'He doesn't need to talk with him. He knows. He knows everything.'

He shook his head. 'Well I just wish He'd let me in on one or two things. Bit of *His* help in sorting out the killing of that miner this morning wouldn't go amiss.'

'Peter…' she walked down the stairs, squeezing past him, leaving her admonishment unfinished. The issue of her religious beliefs and his scepticism was never grounds for argument or disagreement between them, but every now and then his frustration with the world and its depravities would grate up against her fundamental belief in the existence of some grand plan giving shape to everything that happened. Someday *'It'* would be revealed, she held. Sometime Peter wished *It* would come quicker than *It* was.

'I know, I know.' He watched as she disappeared back into the kitchen. He stood on the stairs, Postman Pat and Fireman Sam gazing back at him. 'Think I'll go and look in on the kids.

Have a shower before I help you sort out dinner.'

He went to the children's room, tugging the duvet up around Andrew, placing a kiss on his head.

He stood looking around the room. *Dark. Silent. No sound.*

Innocence. Sleep of the good.

When had he last slept like that?

He had no idea. Weeks, months.

When? When had it begun?

He knew the answer.

Two months, one week, three days and… how many hours? What time was it? Seven fifteen. Nineteen hours. Midday, Saturday August 4th. A sunny day. A hot day. The sun burning. The sweat oozing rivulets down backs. The hair where it met bare skin soaked and dripping. A line, wet and cool. Sweat on bodies, heat burning through uniforms. Hands swept across brows, a pulsing tiresome monotony, like wipers.

Then he had known. Known it all. There was nothing he could be told about the Job, about leading men, about decisions. Invincible. Certainty. He was top of his game. King of the world. There was nothing beyond his reach Everyone listened when he spoke, everyone took note. He was The Coming Man. By thirty he would be Detective Superintendent, he was Ridgway's chosen heir. His boy. He was the next Stalker, bound for greatness.

They'd listened when he spoke. No-one contradicted. Why would they?

He'd told the squad to wait. There was no doubt in his mind. The man had already been locked in the kitchen of his flat for five hours. Five hours in that heat. He had had his son and daughter with him: nine years of age and four. He wouldn't hurt them. Not his kids. He wouldn't put up much resistance. Not after the heat. The waiting game.

Early on they'd heard his sobbing. His crying. Soft, gentle, almost a whisper. There was no rage from the man called Rueben.

Simple.

Walk in the park.

On his instruction they'd turned off the water. Routine. Force him out. There had been no dissenting voices.

They waited. Three more hours in that heat. That kitchen.

The man would be a soft target. An easy scoop up.

No violence, no storm-trooper tactics. No complaints on his record.

A notch. A success. A triumph.
Rueben.
Two months, one week, three days, and nineteen hours.

Seven
Day Two

The sense of anticipation was palpable. Their lines were tightly packed, stretched out, gun-metal blue against the grey-white misty smudge of the morning air, the horizon broken and distorted by their undulating shape.

Kalus looked to his left, then to his right. On each side the line tapered into the distance; shields raised, visors shut tight. Only the rising steam of their breath gave substance to them. These were men, not mannequins. Flesh and blood not machines.

Opposite, separated by no more than fifty paces, were the pickets. They stood close to the colliery entrance. They stood in silence.

'This is fucking eerie,' Roberts whispered into the gloom.

Kalus merely nodded in recognition of the Detective Sergeant's comment.

Kalus, Roberts, and White had been at the colliery for over an hour. They'd wanted to get a feel for what it was like, what it had been like twenty four hours earlier when Stephen Jackson had been bludgeoned to death on a picket like today's. The problem was that today's picket was unlike any other. The silence was merely the outward sign of something much deeper.

McKinnon had contacted the colliery manager Gordon Craig late the previous night. 'The picket will be there, but there will be no trouble. Guaranteed,' the miners' leader had said. The morning newspapers were not yet available, but the word was that the picket today was to be by way of a tribute to the dead miner.

The indication from the journalists covering today's picket was that their papers were all leading with a press release from Angus McKinnon, a copy of which had been sent to Kalus and the Chief Constable.

You'll see that the miners are in control of themselves. That miners do not give vent to mindless anger, do not strike out unthinkingly. The miners are not the ones striking out with clubs and batons regardless of who stands before them. The miners in Staffordshire are peaceful in their picketing. We seek only to make a point about the closure of pits.

Stephen Jackson was murdered because he chose to protest. Stephen Jackson chose to make known his willingness to raise his voice for the life of this pit and the life of the villages around it. Chose to speak out for the livelihood of his fellow miners and, more than this, spoke out to secure the future for their children. Stephen Jackson raised his voice. The police raised their batons and cut him down.

Stephen Jackson was bludgeoned to death because he dared to say to this unfeeling government, this unfeeling, cold and cruel prime minister; 'No more. This far and no further.'

Stephen Jackson deserves all our thanks. More than this, Stephen Jackson deserves our respect. Tomorrow morning, on our picket, we will show the world and the Thatcher government our respect for a fallen comrade. A worker. A fighter. A miner.

The first indication of the imminent arrival of the coaches containing the working miners - the so-called *scabs* - was as ever the sweeping glare of headlights as the vehicles turned from off the A5 onto the colliery approach.

The police stepped forward to their mark, anticipating the pickets' surge. The miners, to a man, stepped forward three paces and stopped. Abruptly, on the blast of a whistle, they turned and stood with their backs to the coaches and to the police lines. The coach drivers, not fully believing their reception, accelerated and swept rapidly through colliery gates that were quickly slammed shut behind them. The metallic clang of the gates echoed in the silence left by the departing noise of the coaches' engines. As they'd passed, their lights had picked out a graphic stencilled on the back of each of the front row of miners' jackets – a police visor with a hammer dripping blood. Each of the first row had red paint daubed in their hair, as if they had been beaten around the back of the head. The red paint was splattered down their coats and dripped onto the graphic. At the same time, the rear rank of pickets had raised high banners pinned to poles, the words smeared across them like blood. *Justice for Stephen Jackson. Justice for Thatcher's hired killers.*

'Jesus Christ!' Craig offered up.

'Fuck me!' Roberts responded.

The camera bulbs flashed as the news photographers captured tomorrow's front-page image. The TV station cameras zoomed and panned back and forth across the scene. The lunchtime editions would all be led by the same images.

Kalus watched as McKinnon stepped forward from the ranks of pickets and walked slowly up to the colliery gates. He carried a small bouquet of flowers which with great deliberation he secured to the gate. He stepped back, standing for a moment in contemplation, head bowed. As he stood there the cameras flashed and whirred once more. He was framed against the line of sombre pickets, the gates, the line of faceless menace that was the police. It was an image beautifully and knowingly constructed.

After a moment of silence and further picture opportunity, he turned from the gates and approached the throng of reporters who'd been held back during the arrival of the coaches. He moved towards them. In their eagerness for a defining shot or to get the first words he spoke, several of them tried to break the agreed line. A number of uniforms stepped out in front of them, shields automatically raised, blocking their path. It was the cue for the cameras to flash into action once more. McKinnon held his hands up, waving them in the air. 'No! No, no. Stay where you are. Don't give them an excuse to hurt you or to break this gathering.'

The media stopped and stood still. The police officers looked around, uncertain what to do. Shields raised, visors down, more than ever they appeared to Kalus and everyone else more like automatons than men. '*Get them back into fucking line!*' Kalus heard Bailey spluttering into his radio. A moment later, the sergeant in control of that section of the operation emerged from the police line gesturing for his officers to return to their original positions, which they did.

'I hope,' McKinnon began his address, 'that you are witness to the restraint of the miners. Under extreme provocation and intimidation we have gathered to show our respect for Stephen Jackson. Our picket is peaceful. Our cause just.'

'Thinks he's fucking Ghandi,' Roberts said. 'Look at them. Look at those journalists. Lapping it up.'

'It's a hell of a story,' Kalus commented.

'Easy enough for them,' Roberts muttered. 'All they've got to do is spell it right and write it up. It's us who's got to sort the bloody thing out. Find the killer.'

Kalus turned his attention away from McKinnon and his speech. If he said anything interesting he would be sure to catch it later on the news or in the papers. Instead, he focussed on taking in the scene. The crime scene. His crime scene, he reminded himself.

How many were there? Three hundred police? Maybe three fifty? *How many miners?* Similar numbers? Maybe more. And then there was the media. More today than ever, but many of them had been there yesterday covering the picket.

'Mick.'

'Guv?'

'Get someone to contact all of the media. The papers and the TV. Anyone who was covering things here yesterday. We need to talk to them. See if you can get any pictures they took, any footage at all whether they used it or not. I want someone to look at it. See if there's anything there. Anything at all.'

'Got it, Guv.'

Roberts slipped away through the line of police, making his way towards the TV trucks. Kalus turned his attention back to the scene in front of him.

'Piggy in the middle,' Kalus muttered to no one in particular.

'Sorry, guv?' White asked.

Kalus shook his head. 'Nothing. Thinking aloud.'

Kalus scanned the crowd. Whoever killed Stephen Jackson had stood here, maybe many times, maybe now. His killer was familiar with the landscape and the deployments of police and pickets. He tried picturing the scene: the dark and the rain. Imagined the cold, the noise, the tension, the hate, the fear, the rush of adrenalin. He had shared such things, felt them grip his instinct to lash out. To fight back. The football violence. The anti-war parades. The riots. He knew the power, the crazed sense that gave distance to actions. The adrenaline that flowed, a moment removing conscience and reason from survival and instinct.

That was what the training was for. To instil control, to preserve that sense of responsibility. To maintain the civilising link between action and consequence. The training was about the heat of the moment. But it was just that: *training*. Not the real thing. He knew only too well that once action began then all of the training in the world could not be guaranteed to hold against the surge of adrenalin-fuelled power. Could not prevent the swinging arm, the levelled baton.

He took it in.

The pickets. The police.

Lines of battle.

Immovable objects. Unstoppable forces.

Nature unleashed. Genie's leaping out of bottles.

He took in the visored figures of the police, the bandanas of the pickets. Alien and faceless. But behind them were men. Flesh and blood. They were prejudice. They were anger and hate. They were fear. They were jealousy and envy. They were repression and loathing.

They were men. Flesh and blood.

And someone here was a killer.

***

'Look, constable, I don't like this any more than you do, any more than the three hundred or more others I've got to sit down and ask the same questions. But we've got to do this. And the less of the attitude I get and a bit more of the co-operation that I should expect, then the quicker we'll be finished and we can both go and get on with what we're supposed to be doing. Am I clear on this?'

The figure opposite Mallen shrugged; his agreement mumbled to the desktop he sat at.

'Are you clear on this?' Mallen persisted.

'Sir.'

'Right.' Mallen flexed his arms ahead of him, retrieving the biro that in his frustration he'd tossed onto the desk, and returned to completing the *Record of Interview* form in front of him. 'Again, can you tell me about your actions on that morning.' He shoved the map of the colliery and surrounding area towards the uniformed officer. 'You can use this map to refresh yourself of the deployment and to indicate where you were and what you saw.'

'It was a mess.'

Mallen placed the pen on the desk. He sat back. 'Constable, if you can restrict yourself to actual details rather than any personal field evaluation then I'd be more than grateful. Everyone who's sat in that seat over the past twenty-four hours has told me it was a mess. A *fucking mess* seems to be the preferred adjectival descriptor.'

It was the start of his second day in this room and at the present rate he was looking to at least another day here, possibly two. It was early, but he'd already removed his jacket, rolled up his shirtsleeves, and was on his third coffee. The interviews with the senior officers and sergeants had been completed the previous evening. Today was the turn of the constables, both here and out at Lichfield and Lea Marston. Men like the one in front of him.

PC David Jones was five years in the force and a member of one of the Snatch Squads deployed at the colliery. The squads were elite five man teams forming human wedges that would plunge through opposing lines of pickets or rioters to swallow up and drag back to their own lines those identified as key agitators, or as being particularly violent. The premise was to arrest them so that the courts could later suitably punish them. It was also designed to disrupt the rioters' immediate lines of communication and action. The key qualification for the squads was a strong sense of teamwork and an almost unthinking ability to react to orders. Mallen would personally have added '*bollocks of steel*' to the list. The job was tough and fraught with danger. Each snatch laid them open to being dragged into greater harm to themselves. They depended on each other to hold their position in the shape. The training was not to look after yourself but the man next to you, trusting that someone else was in turn doing the same for you. It was modelled on the Spartan and Roman system.

Jones hunched himself forward, half-turning in his seat so that the map could be shared. 'Here,' he pointed to the field to the side of the access drive. 'That's where we were deployed. We were held back waiting to see how the picket went. If they'd charge, where they'd charge. Their favourite tactic is to wait for the coaches to be spotted on the A5 and then one of them rings through to one of the phone boxes near the pit. Then they signal with torches. That way they're already pushing up to our line as the coaches arrive. Then they push, trying to bash the side of the coaches, slow them down so that they can brick them and smash the windows. Once they've gone through, then the lines fold back. Some hang around, but most get off home or wherever until the next shift change is due. Start all over again.'

'And yesterday?'

'Yesterday was one of those days when things got a bit… well…messy.'

Mallen gestured acceptance of the maligned description. 'Okay. *Messy*. In what way? What happened?'

Jones sat back, pursing his lips. He looked back to the map, tapping it where the gates were. 'Some days the coaches go through but the pickets don't stop. Maybe the push has been a little bit more physical than usual. Maybe some of our boys have used the batons a little more to hold them off. Then it just keeps going. The coaches, the dispute - it all becomes less important than hitting out. The confrontation becomes a fight, a scrap. Bit of a free for all. Some days it just gets out of hand. Personal.'

Mallen looked at the officer hunched over the map. 'Like what happened at Orgreave.'

Jones looked up. 'I'm not sure what you mean.'

Mallen inclined his head towards Jones. 'You were there, weren't you?'

'Orgreave? Yes. Yes, I was. There were forces from over ten counties deployed there. It was a big do.'

'A big do. Yes. Yes, it was, wasn't it? So you know more than most how these things can go.'

'I'm still not sure what you mean.'

Mallen sat back. His fingers played with the pen, twirling it slowly between them. 'Well, like you said, things can get a bit out of hand. From what I read that's what happened there. Started with the miners playing football and lying around in the sun and ended with cavalry charges and street-to-street fighting. Some said it was like the Wild West.'

Jones smiled. He sat forward, leaning in towards the detective opposite him. 'We made over 90 arrests that day. Last time I looked we had 72 officers injured, the pickets had 51. Strikes me that the stone throwing, the burning cars and all of them barricades they built suggests they were the ones looking for trouble. Scargill knew what he was doing that day.'

It was Mallen's turn to smile. 'Come off it! We both know that pickets seeking treatment for injuries are liable to arrest. No-one really knows how many pickets were beaten by the Snatch Squads that day. The mounted police charges. I saw the TV pictures. Brutal.'

'Like I said, sir. Everybody has their view of what happened. I was there.'

'Yes. I see that.' Mallen flicked through the officer's

personnel sheet. It recorded training and attachments to other forces. 'You were in some of the first groups trained in short shield tactics.'

'After Toxteth and Brixton in 81.'

'And you were in Handsworth during 81. You were on the lines.'

Jones nodded. 'Dustbin lids against petrol bombs.'

Mallen flicked through more of Jones' sheets. 'Seems to me you're the closest we've got to being an expert.'

'Suppose you could say that.'

Mallen closed the file, moving it to the side. 'So, what happened yesterday? Did it get out of hand?'

Jones shrugged, despite himself appearing to relish the conferred status of *expert*. 'Look, sir, it's like I said. Sometimes it gets a little more than '*business*'. Like Orgreave. That day from eight until after nine, there were four pushes by the miners. Four times we held them and drove them back. Then Scargill gets to parade around between the lines, like he's defying us to arrest him. It was hot. Some of the miners are stripped off and sunbathing. We're standing there in full riot kit – boiler suits, helmets, the lot. Some fuck up means we've had no drinks for hours. Then they start rolling lorry tyres down at us and the bricks start flying. So we advanced, pushed them back over the railway line. Then, we're told they've taken up positions in the village, barricaded the streets. So we're sent in to shift them. Highfield Lane, Rotherham Lane. There's burning cars, all kinds of shit they'd taken from the scrap-yard. The horses went in. Then us. It got ugly. Hand to hand. But we shifted them. Made sure they didn't come back.'

'And yesterday was like that?'

'Yesterday we did what Orgreave taught us.'

'Which is?'

'Hit them hard. Hit them so they don't come back.'

'How many of the men with you at Orgreave were there yesterday? On the lines?'

Jones shook his head in uncertainty. 'Hard to say. The

helmets. The visors.'

'But some.'

'Yeah.' Jones nodded. 'There's a whole load from Nottingham out at the barracks. They'll have been there for certain. They're good lads.'

'Yeah. Good lads,' Mallen repeated.

Eight

The canteen was relatively quiet. Holding the police interviews in Tamworth or out at the Lichfield barracks or Lea Marston caravan park meant there was little in the way of the previous day's activity. In its place was a steady rhythm of work; the pulse beat of procedure that the team were imposing upon the investigation.

In Kalus' experience each investigation found its own tempo, its own variation on a theme. Underpinning each enquiry was a basic measure, a rhythm to be understood and tapped into. He knew opportunities had to be seized whenever they presented themselves, but proceed too quickly and things were missed, significances not grasped. *The Yorkshire Ripper Enquiry* was evidence of that. On the other hand, proceed too slowly and events faded, became distorted in witnesses recall, opportunities disappearing never to return. He hated to be the officer that *did it by the book*, but he he'd developed a manner of proceeding an investigation that worked, one he insisted his team adhere to.

He was the conductor. He could cope with invention, the virtuoso. But, too much improvisation and it became jazz, free-form and out of control. After Handsworth - after Reuben - form, shape and pattern was all he had left to cling to.

He sat at the table that had become his desk, scanning the pile of notes left there for him. Among them were scribbled phone messages asking for him to contact Bailey or Ridgway. They would want updates, progress reports. *The powers that be* whom they answered to were no doubt anxious for crumbs of comfort. They needed words and scenarios. Things to cling to. Signs. They demanded predictions, as if he possessed some spiritual contact line to the dead. Most of all they would demand an estimation of the time-scale for the completion of his investigation, a promise that would hold the press at bay, offering them some respite from the gathering media storm. Like feeding new-born chicks, the media were ever hungry, their mouths ever open for rich titbits of news to fill their columns, their screens and their air-waves. If there were none, they would make up their own.

If he offered what Ridgway wanted, he would be hostage to it.

He considered what he had.

Very little. *Proceeding with enquiries…Hopes of early breakthrough… etcetera…etcetera.* Add it all up or boil it all down and it still meant nothing. But you couldn't say that, you couldn't offer up *nothing yet* as a marker of progress.

He rang Ridgway.

The DCS's reaction to his progress report was self-evident. The response 'Shit!' more a measure of his disappointment than any sense of anger. Despite his hopes, the DCS knew the game too well to have formed fanciful notions of an early breakthrough. His comment that 'I was hoping for something a little more,' was one more accurately reflecting his position: *Hope*. 'The media are camped outside the ACC's door. He's getting jittery, to say the least.'

'You think his nerve will hold?'

Ridgway exhaled deeply. The Assistant Chief Constable's well-known political ambition meant he was rabid in his insistence of there being early breakthroughs. 'I doubt it. Still, at present he's got no choice. He'll have to be made to see that.'

'We're going as fast as we can. The problem's man-power. We've interviewed the senior officers down to sergeant, but that still leaves us with nigh on three hundred uniforms and a similar number of miners and pickets.'

'I'll speak with the ACC again, see if he can rustle up some more DCs for you.' Ridgway's tone suggested he was less than hopeful.

'Experienced men would be useful,' Kalus persisted.

Ridgway snorted. 'At the moment you're going to have to settle for whatever we can get you.'

'Surely this investigation's about as pressing as one can get?'

'You'd think so. However, it seems that the whole force is stretched to breaking point. The picket lines, the IRA, those fucking Libyans. There's also the small matter of security at the Party Conferences. Not to mention the usual run of the mill crime and domestics and murders. Be lucky to get two or three detectives, let alone anyone with experience. As for unforms…' Ridgway let the silence speak for itself. 'Far as the Home Office is concerned you're already up to your eyes in them, what with that lot stationed at the barracks and those out at the caravan site.'

'Don't they realise that they're not part of my team. That technically they're suspects, witnesses?. There's no-one there I can call on.'

'I'm sorry, Peter, but it appears that the nature of the officers assigned to the strike is of little concern or consideration to Our Masters.' With that the conversation ended.

Kalus fiddled with the memo pad notes in his hands. The early work in an enquiry was always that of sifting. He had a dead body and a probable means. They had no witnesses and no clear motive other than the political or plain and simple rage. What concerned him was the fact that they had little else because everything about the victim beyond his name and occupation was little more than sketchy.

There appeared to be no family - no parents, no siblings, no aunts, no uncles, no nephews, not even cousins twice removed. Nothing. Employment details prior to the colliery were being sought by officers sent to the National Insurance and tax offices, but at present all they could say was that in terms of any documentation beyond his birth certificate it was as though he'd sprung up fully formed a year ago. No school records. No exam records. No tax returns. No employment beyond his arrival at the colliery after a military discharge. The Ministry of Defence were notoriously coy about sharing military service records whilst the IRA were so active, and as yet they were not returning their calls. It was on the to do list, but for the present on a backburner awaiting the paperwork. The chance of an IRA killing seemed a long-shot. At present it was not one fitting their mode of operation on the mainland.

All the idea did was show that there was too much to do with too little manpower. The prioritising was down to him. Decisions, always decisions. A heartbeat away from getting it wrong. The case review team months or years from now dragging up every mis-step and wrong turn he might make.

Handsworth. Rueben.

He turned his mind back to what he had, to what was possible. They were still awaiting the autopsy results, but the injuries he'd seen hadn't been caused by a stray lobbed brick or a carelessly swung club. They were deliberate. They were sustained. They were blows dealt with a clear sense of the outcome.

What did that leave? A frustrated officer who'd snapped. A personal vendetta by a fellow picket.

Decide.

On balance the investigation had to centre on the former, and that meant the interviews. Jackson's life history and any possible vendettas he may have accrued were secondary to that line of enquiry.

He picked up the roster sheet that White had put on his desk, scanning the list for some movement, some flexibility in deployment.

His head ached. He tasted metal in his mouth, at the same moment conscious of his heart beginning to race. Palpitations. He stared at the sheet, a growing pixelation blurring the vision in his right eye. He looked across the room. The pixelation was still there. It followed him, looked where he looked. His heart began to beat faster.

He squeezed his eyes open and shut, but the blurring remained. It was a watery haze, a splintering of glass. It was as if a kaleidoscope had been placed in front of his line of sight.

He felt his grip tightening on the sheet of paper. Palms sweaty.

The third time.

The first had scared him to death. A month ago. Ridgway easing him back. Admin. A Case Review. A missing schoolgirl whose body had been found mutilated and shoved in a shallow grave on Cannock Chase. He had been sitting, like now, alone, late at night in the middle of the enquiry room. He'd found it hard not to shout out in shock at the sudden loss of sight in one eye. Thirty long minutes of uncertainty and confusion before it had phased away. Relieved, he'd told no one, certainly not any colleagues, certainly not Anna. Dismissed it. What could he have said? They would have side-lined him for good.

The second time he knew what to expect. Two weeks of long shifts staring at paper and screens and his dad rushed into hospital. He'd sat rigid in his car at a set of traffic lights, immersed in the honking horns of other drivers at his failure to pull away. He'd pulled the Maestro to the side of the road and waited for it to pass.

'Guv. There's someone to see you.' White stood in front of him.

Kalus stirred. 'Who's that?'

'A DCI Riordan. Home Office.'

Kalus looked towards White's desk. A tall man, dark hair cropped close to his skull, stood flicking through the Murder Book.

White followed Kalus' gaze. 'Who is he, Guv?'

'Complaints.'

'Shit!' The young DC exhaled.

'Only to be expected. They can't spare any detectives but they can send over someone to check up on us, someone to see that we're doing everything by the book. That we aren't cutting corners or showing favouritism.'

'Do they really think that?'

Kalus smiled. 'Public accountability. It's Thatcher's new thing; *Justice must be seen to be done*. No one wants any of this to come back and bite them in the bum. It's party conference time, remember? Labour this last week, Thatcher's lot next week down in Brighton. Lot of points to be scored on both sides. Better show him over.'

White hesitated. 'Guv?'

'Yeah?'

'Are you Okay? It's just that you seemed a little… You don't look well.'

'Nothing. A cold. Standing out in that field yesterday.'

White nodded and went to tell Riordan.

Kalus rubbed his eyes, tidying up the scrum of notes and stacking a few files to the side of the table. Riordan was quickly over. Kalus half-rose, reaching out a hand. Riordan's grip was firm. 'DCI Kalus,' Kalus stated.

'DCI Riordan. John.' He smiled, polite as required and no more. Close-up, Kalus realised Riordan was taller than he'd estimated, well over six foot. He had a faint tan, so he'd clearly either holidayed somewhere hot that summer or was a fan of sun-beds. With his white teeth and healthy glow he was far removed from the grey pallor of Kalus' team. Based on the evidence of his build, his grip, and his general demeanour of good health, Kalus thought it a good guess that under the business suit and crisp white shirt was a muscular torso. Not the usual Complaints profile of pale-faced bureaucrats. He signalled for Riordan to sit opposite.

'Hope you don't mind,' Riordan indicated back over his shoulder towards White's table. 'Thought I'd get up to speed by taking a look at your Murder Book.'

Kalus shrugged acceptance. 'Not at all. Absolutely fine.'

'Good job by the way. It's a model. Textbook.'

Kalus accepted the compliment with a nod. 'White's first time. He's got a good officer mentoring him, DS Roberts has done it a few times.'

Riordan nodded. Preliminaries, rules of engagement were being set out.

'Anything you want to know?' Kalus asked.

Riordan considered for a moment. 'Where the investigation's at. Some sense of where you see it going'.

Kalus nodded. 'And your role?'

Riordan smiled his best diplomatic smile, tight-lipped, one not flashing the pearl-white teeth. 'Observer. You know how it is.' He waved a hand in dismissal of his role, its inconsequence. 'Home Office are pretty jittery. No need to tell you just how politically sensitive this is right now. A dead miner in the middle of Party Conference season isn't good news for anybody.'

'Especially the miner.'

'Especially the miner,' Riordan repeated, corrected.

'Well, let me tell you where we are and then we can find out whether you might be able to shine a little light onto it, shall we?'

'By all means, Chief Inspector. After all, it's your case.'

'Yes,' Kalus affirmed. 'It is, isn't it.'

Nine
Day Three

She waited for the sound of the door closing before creeping to the bedroom window. She stood by the half-drawn curtains, carefully tugging at the sides, forging a slit through which she could look out and down. She watched him walk away along the street waving to a neighbour, pausing in his stride for the man to catch up with him before they headed towards the main road.

She crossed the room, dragging the chair from its place next to the dressing table. She placed it in front of the wardrobe and kicked off her slippers. Gingerly, she stood on the chair, the upholstered pad shifting under her stockinged feet. Reaching up, her fingers scrabbled in the dust seeking the edge of the book she'd secreted there. Finding it, she dragged it towards her, lifting it carefully up over the lip.

She sat on the edge of the bed, hands fumbling nervously as she pulled at the hinged clasp that bound it. The book had been a present from Angie. Angie had been her best friend at school and the journal was something she'd brought Karen back from Cornwall after the CSEs. It had a pink and white cover, a pattern of intertwining flowers and stems – honeysuckle, she thought. The gold coloured clasp held the pages tight together. She opened it, surprised to find her hands were trembling.

The book was her secret. Until recently it had been her only secret. A book in which she kept her treasures; a poem from the strange long-haired boy in her year who'd gone on to college and so she'd later heard to university; pictures of the boys she'd met in Spain; a Valentine's card with a romantic message she knew hadn't come from Kevin; locks of her children's hair. On some of the pages in her strong, florid handwriting were thoughts she'd written down. Secret thoughts. Nothing to be ashamed of. Nothing to be suspicious of. But secret thoughts. Thoughts about her world. Her life. Thoughts she found comfort in writing but ones that she would be embarrassed to explain. The book was a private world, her world. It was hers, something that didn't have to be shared.

She had been careful not to write anything about Stephen - that would be stupid. But she had kept one thing, a token of one particular day. A token from the day of his visit after they'd first made love, when he'd stood at the back door holding a flower picked from a neighbour's garden. Blushing, she'd taken it from him, standing it in a vase next to her bed whilst they'd made love once more. It had stayed there for a week, unquestioned by Kevin, before she'd pressed it between two sheets of toilet paper and later placed it in her book.

She turned to the page where it was kept, heart in mouth, barely daring to breathe. *Still there. Nothing changed.* She skimmed through the rest of the pages, searching for some sign of disturbance. *Nothing.*

She sat staring into the middle distance.

What did it prove? What did it tell her?

She chewed her bottom lip. *Nothing. Nothing had changed.*

She placed the book back on top of the wardrobe and returned the chair to its place.

She sat back on the bed.

Ever since he'd announced the news of Stephen's death, Kevin had been attentive to her. When she'd collapsed he'd taken her up to bed, told her to get some rest, brought her sweetened tea for the shock. He'd even taken care of the kids.

She knew he'd found her reaction to the news extreme, but later that evening she'd overheard him talking on the phone to his mom, heard him saying that she was under stress *what with the lack of money and everything. It had been a shock for everyone, especially as Stephen had been so helpful to Karen and the other miners' families in the street.* Heard him say that he thought Karen's hysterical accusations were *her way of saying she holds me and dad and the others that organised the pickets responsible for Stephen's death.* She wanted him to return to work, wanted the strike over. Somehow, *in her mind,* he'd said, he thought she saw him as being responsible for the death of a picket because *in her view* none of them should be out there.

She could tell from Kevin's reaction what his mom would be saying. His dad was a union organiser, a staunch supporter of the strike. His mom would back her husband to the hilt. They saw Karen as weak, '*a flippity gibbet*' she'd once overheard her father-in-law describe her as to his wife. Maybe they were right.

She stood up and moved back to the bedroom window, looking down the street at the row of terraced houses, the long line of net-curtained windows. *Had they been seen? Had someone noticed Stephen's calls, the length of his stays? Had someone spoken - gossip, whispers that had found their way to Kevin or one of his mates? Had he found out? Had he acted? Had Kevin killed Stephen?*

She tried to think of what his reaction would be to news of her adultery. Shame, ridicule - a blow to his pride, to his masculinity. She knew he had a temper, admittedly not as bad as his dad's who'd been in countless pub brawls as well as being arrested on a picket in Nottingham that summer for assault. Kevin was different to his dad, but he had a temper all the same.

She had to find out. She had to know.

But how to go about it? If she was wrong and he knew nothing then she risked him discovering what had been going on. If she was right, then she was sleeping with a murderer, the man who'd killed her lover. How might he react to her betraying him once more, this time to the police? *How could she get the police to investigate him without having to tell them what she thought his motive might be? To investigate him without them telling him why he was a suspect?*

What could she do?

Whatever she did, whatever happened, Stephen was dead and her hopes for any sort of happiness had died with him.

What future was there for her now?

***

Brian Terry scowled. To Kalus it seemed to be his default reaction. As arranged, he and Riordan had arrived at the union offices to collect the details of those who'd organised the picket along with the names of those miners who'd been there.

'Angus said that you were to have these,' Terry stated, unable to conceal his contempt for the decision to co-operate with the enquiry.

Kalus inspected the contents of an old supermarket cardboard box. *Kellogg's Cornflakes* stencilled in blue. A number of folders slopped around inside separated by sheets of lined A4 paper on which there appeared to be handwritten notes.

Terry nodded his head towards the box. 'The home addresses and phone numbers of the union stewards organising the picket yesterday. Some of them have already written statements.'

Kalus nodded.

'Won't be of any use. We'll have to speak to all of them,' Riordan stated flatly.

Terry eyed him with suspicion then looked at Kalus. 'This your minder?'

Kalus followed Terry's glare, allowing himself a half-smile. 'DI Riordan's casting an eye over the investigation. He's representing the Home Office.'

Terry barely stifled a guffaw. 'He's here to keep an eye on you then! See that you do it properly. Don't they trust you anymore Chief Inspector?'

Kalus allowed himself the other half of the smile. 'Procedure.'

'My ass.'

Kalus hefted the box up. 'Be sure to thank Mr. McKinnon for these.'

'Oh, I will.'

Riordan stood still. Terry looked him in the eyes. 'Anything else I can do for you, officer?'

'Terry. Brian. Employed at Birch Coppice colliery since 1979. Before that, Nottingham. Arrested for assault three times. Cautioned each time, but no conviction. Last time was, what… two months ago. Nottingham? Assaulting a fellow miner, wasn't it? You and a few mates going round to his place, sorting out a scab?'

'There was no conviction.'

'There was no evidence. The miner who bought the charges dropped them a day or so later. Said he couldn't identify who'd attacked him. He's since quit mining, but I suppose that you know that. Scared for himself. More scared for his wife and kids.'

'Like I said. There was no conviction. I don't know why you're telling me this.'

'Let's say it's in the way of a reminder. It's just so you know, Brian, that we keep records too. That the case in Nottingham hasn't gone away. Never know, if you were to be charged with something putting you out of circulation for a month or two maybe that ex-miner might be persuaded to give his evidence after all.'

'I've got nothing to hide.'

Riordan smiled. 'Glad to hear it, Brian. Glad to hear it. Just wanted to be sure you have things straight. You see, we know that there's miners attacking miners out there. Working miners attacked by strikers. The only innocent miners getting hurt in this strike are those that you and some of your members are hurting.'

'I've hurt no-one.'

Riordan nodded. 'Like I said Brian, glad to hear it. Man like yourself, man of violent actions, man with form for attacking fellow miners with pickaxe handles. Man like that is sure to be a person of interest in an investigation like this.'

Riordan turned and walked away leaving Kalus to follow.

The two officers made their way to Kalus' car. Catching up, Kalus pushed the box into Riordan's arms whilst he himself fumbled for the boot keys of the Marina. 'Mind telling me what that was about?'

'Just letting Mr. Terry know that miners aren't the only ones with pertinent records or information.'

'Nice of you to let me and my team in on it. When were you planning to tell us about that one?'

Riordan shifted the weight of the box cradled in his arms. 'Be fair, Peter, I've just got here. Hardly had time to say hello.'

'Time to read up on one of the main men involved in leading the strike.'

'Well, as you say, he's one of the leaders. I looked him up. Be prepared and all that. Just surprised your team hadn't uncovered that already. Public record and all that.'

'Pretty good records at Complaints, then.'

'Has to be. Goes with the territory. We need to get it right,' Riordan stated.

Kalus hoisted open the boot, steadying the lid with one hand as it rose on its springs. 'It's a murder enquiry. We have to get that right too,' Kalus replied, stepping forward and taking the box from Riordan and slipping it into the boot.

Riordan dusted his hands. 'Absolutely.'

Kalus slammed the boot shut. 'Any other surprises I should know about?'

Riordan shook his head. 'Not that I know of.'

'Good.' Kalus locked the boot and stood upright. He pointed the keys in the direction of the boot. 'In that case, let's get back to the colliery and get this lot sorted.'

***

Matthew Brody pulled down the green leatherette case-lid of his Olivetti portable, snapping the catches into place and pushing the whole to the back of his desk. Job done, he let out a sigh, spending a moment or two contemplating the space around him. His bedsit. Finding nothing of inspiration, he picked up one of the spiral bound reporters pads and started flicking through the pages of the shorthand notes he'd made.

The police conference yesterday had given little. The usual round of points about *officers doing their duty under difficult circumstances*. The routine denial of those questions he and a few others had tried to ask about breaches of civil liberties, denials of violence, denials of political manipulations. Just a group of well-intentioned men doing their duty.

The polar opposite had been the previous night's miners' press conference. *Intimidation...police state...conspiracy theory... death of the pits...death of communities*. Little actually about the actual death itself. Little about the man who'd died, one Stephen Jackson, a miner. It was tantalisingly little for a man whose death was now the centre of a murder enquiry.

He tapped his pencil on the edge of the pad, sliding it up and down the spiral of metal. Somewhere there was a story. An angle. The national media had been all over it for the first twenty-four hours, but already their interest was waning. There'd been news of a major drugs haul happening a few days previously on the Norfolk coast, the result of something the Home Office dubbed *Operation Bishop*. Today's well-timed press release of news of that seizure had begun to occupy the tabloids whilst the broadsheets had already moved to the politics of the dispute - the Labour Party Conference that had just finished in Scarborough, the Conservative one coming up the following week in Brighton. The Big Boys were also chasing the fall-out from the previous week's High Court ruling that because there had been no actual ballot the strikes in Yorkshire, Nottingham, and Derby were illegal.

As a freelance, he was sickened by the state of the press. The nationals were gadflies, supping here and there with no real intention of sticking with an issue. Of seeing it through. The crusading journalism of a Pilger in the sixties and early seventies was dead. The great campaigns of the *Daily Mirror*, the ones that had fed the developing political minds of himself and his generation had long ago been lost in a rising swell of bingo and tits. There were no causes anymore, just circulation.

He flicked over the rest of his notes. The neighbours had added little to the story of Jackson. Most of them were as hostile to the press as they were to the police. The coverage of the strike had done little to make anyone feel the media were impartial. Even the BBC had screwed up over Orgreave, transmitting an edit that suggested the pickets had attacked the police rather than the correct sequence of that day's events. All he'd been able to gather about Stephen Jackson, miner, twenty-nine years of age and single, was that he was *'a quiet man'* who *'kept himself to himself'*.

He slapped the pad down on the desk. Not enough. Not nearly enough.

He'd been part of Militant Tendency for some time, regarding himself as something of a doyen of the political magazines and free press spawned from it. His experience was that though they talked a great deal about taking the dispute to the streets there'd been little evidence of it ever happening. Jackson's story was one that should be stirring not just the miners but the community.

He needed human interest. He needed something to make people care. The big stories of the strike had eluded him. Nottingham, Yorkshire, and Wales were the areas that had seen the real action.

For himself, steeped in Union history and the persecution of the workingman, Jackson's death was *the* story of the strike. It was the stuff of myth: the *Tolpuddle Martyr's, the Suffragettes*. He wouldn't let go. He'd pursue it wherever it took him.

Ten

'Tell me again. From the start.'
'The start?'
'From the moment he told you what he knew.'

Brian Terry wiped a hand across his brow, a gesture of thoughtful consideration of exactly where *the start* was. He puffed out his cheeks, released his breath. 'Like I said, he knew about the arrests. Knew the charges. The outcomes. He knew details. The beating we gave Tindall.'

McKinnon thought about questioning the use of the word '*we*'. Brian Terry was a brutaliser, a man known for his willingness to use violence in pursuit of any grievance, real or perceived. McKinnon knew of the beatings already handed out during the dispute in Nottingham and Yorkshire. That Terry's willingness to use violence verged on pleasure. That at times he found the man uncomfortable to be around. He also knew that men like Brian Terry were a necessity to be tolerated and whenever required used.

He pursued a different tack. 'You think he's more than just a detective?'

Terry nodded enthusiastically. 'Certain. The other detective, that Kalus bloke, he said he was from the Home Office, keeping an eye on things. But he knew stuff. You could see it in the eyes of the other bloke – that Kalus - that he was shocked too. Like he didn't know any of the stuff this Riordan bloke was coming out with.'

McKinnon picked up the letter he'd retrieved from the file in the union safe. The logo of the NUM was stamped in the corner. Scargill's office title was emblazoned across the top, along with the caution CONFIDENTIAL. It warned local union leaders to be on their guard against infiltration by police and security forces. It warned of the existence of moles relaying details of union plans to the police and government. The traps they'd laid at Orgreave.

He tapped the letter, 'They say there's army intelligence working the strike. Yorkshire reckoned that some of the police up against their picket lines were army. It was the way they charged, the way they operated in the villages. Fitzwilliam, places like that. They were more interested in breaking up the pickets, in handing out beatings rather than arresting folk. They charged through and left them bleeding at the side of the road whilst they chased after others. No attempt to make an arrest. No coincidence that most of the police they've brought in from outside the area have been put up at local barracks. That they have their police numbers covered up.'

'Army then?'

McKinnon tapped the letter once more. '*SAS*. Military Intelligence. Special Branch. Take your pick.'

Terry leant in. 'What do you think they want?'

McKinnon knew Brian Terry loved moments like this. Although an elected union executive, Terry held little interest in conference resolutions, welfare and pensions, or in improved benefits to miners. Terry craved action. He wanted conflict, a class war. He'd been there in '74 and at every other picket line that had formed since then – dockers, rail-workers, teachers, nurses. He was engaged in his own personal struggle against those forces he believed were ranged against him and his class. McKinnon distrusted him, but the fact that Terry believed the war needed to be fought on the streets rather than the ballot box didn't necessarily make him wrong. In some matters they were absolutely aligned. It was a war they were now fighting, and like any war it had casualties. Miners had already died and pit villages had been ravaged. Women and young children had been terrified. Property had been burnt. Bones had been broken. They were fighting for the future, for what they believed in. At such times brute strength as much as a just cause was necessary. If it was a war, then it was one they had to win. In that objective, men like Brian Terry had their uses.

McKinnon looked at the headlines of the local papers scattered across his desk. The previous day's tribute to Jackson had been effective in capturing the morning headlines, but he knew that the truth was struggling to make itself heard. 'They want to break us. Not just here, this picket, this pit. The lot. The pits, the railways, the Dockers - everything. They want to break us. They've not forgotten '74. *She* wants revenge.'

Terry knew who '*She*' was. They all did. 'But, this Riordan. Why's he here? What's his game?'

McKinnon tossed the letter from the NUM onto the desk. 'Pin it on a miner. Stir the shite. Hide the truth; manufacture the evidence to what they want. A cover up.'

'So what do we do?'

'Keep a watch on what the police are doing. We stick together. Support each other, no matter what. At the same time, maybe we look for ourselves. If the police have no interest in discovering the truth about who killed Stephen Jackson then we'll do it ourselves.'

Terry looked dubious.

'What's wrong? He was a good friend of your Kevin's wasn't he?'

'I don't know as I'd describe him as that.'

'But he knew him. Knew him better than any of us. Maybe we should start there. You have a talk with him, with your Kevin. He might know something that could be useful about Jackson. His background. I mean, he must want to find out who killed his mate.'

'Like I said, they weren't mates,' Terry snapped, shuffling in his seat. 'But I'll see what I can do.'

'Do that. Maybe we can get a jump on whatever this Riordan's got in mind.'

***

She was a metronome. Back and forth. Reminded of when she was eight, a Christmas treat. Taken into Birmingham, gazing into a shop window bright with lights, white with snow that dazzled. At the centre, a clock. Special, a Swiss clock. Two figures emerging. A dark haired boy and a blonde girl. Emerging from separate doors, pacing up and down across the ledge of the clock face, back and forth. Back and forth. A metronome.

She had cried then. Not out of any selfish desire for the clock - though she truly had wanted it – but wanting to see the figures once more. Wanting them to come back out of their separate doors, their separate houses. Wanting to see them parade back and forth. Wanting them to find each other. Knowing even in her childish heart that they were forever alone, forever lost, forever waiting for that which would never come.

She stared at the phone box. She had stood there for what, ten minutes? *No, stupid talk, more like five. Maybe two at most. What was she waiting for? What was she expecting? Some sign? Some divine act of intervention to guide her?*

She had paced back and forth in the rain. Walked past the box - two, three times - continued past to the end of the street and then cursing herself, her weakness, retracing those same steps. *Back and forth. Back and forth.*

She was a metronome.

She twitched the handle of the umbrella. The slight jerking movement spiralled the rivulets of rain across its surface, cascading them over the brim to fall in front of her face, their spattering a staccato backdrop to her thoughts.

Time was getting on. Soon she would have to be at the nursery to pick up Michelle. It was her one opportunity to make the call. If she didn't - couldn't - do it, then she would be faced with later having to make some excuse to Kevin as to why she was going out. She couldn't just '*pop up to the shops*' anymore, they had no money for anything. The local shop offered credit to the strikers for necessities, but as the months had dragged on they were finding it harder to keep going themselves when most of their custom was miners' families.

She had decided on her way back from dropping Michelle at nursery to make the call. The idea had been on her mind since last night but it was seeing the phone box that had finally decided her. She knew enough from TV that the police could trace calls. She didn't want police turning up at her door asking awkward questions about a call made from her home phone.

She would be anonymous. A concerned citizen. *The phone box.* Anyone could have used it. Anyone who knew Kevin could have made the call.

She had sat at home planning the call. At first she'd tried writing things down but had quickly abandoned the idea, fearful that Kevin would find her notes. She had torn and burnt the paper in the kitchen sink, watching it turn and writhe as the flames consumed it before washing the grey-black ash away.

She had sat at the small drop-leaf kitchen table, staring at it until the speckled blood-red Formica top had swum before her eyes. She had nothing but vague ideas of what she wanted to say. She formulated words, phrases, selecting what she felt best suited the outcome she desired. Repeating them over and over to herself to get them straight.

'I'm calling about the murder of that miner, Stephen Jackson. I've heard that one of the picket organisers had a grudge against him. That he wanted to harm him. You need to investigate him. You need to investigate Kevin Terry. Investigate him. Find out where he was during the picket. Why he wanted to kill Stephen Jackson.'

Grudge. It was a good choice for her purpose. More than *a falling out.* It suggested something deep, something powerful and fierce. It meant she did not have to be specific. The police would have to pick him up. They would pick him up and interview him. They were professionals; they had clever ways of making people talk, finding things out, things people wanted kept secret. Kevin would be scared, worried. If he'd done it, if he knew about Stephen and her, then it would come out. They'd find out. They'd know.

She'd left the house early to collect Michelle from nursery, allowing herself plenty of time to make the call. The rain that had been falling for most of the morning was good, it kept people off the streets. Less chance she would be seen using the phone-box, less chance others would be out using it. Turning into the road, she'd seen the red box of the booth from some distance away. Empty. She had drawn nearer, words rotating round and round in her head. *'I'm calling about... grudge... you need to investigate...'*

And then, somehow, she'd found herself walking past. *Past the box. Walking on, her feet taking her away. Every step betraying her intention.* She walked, hands gripping tighter the handle of the umbrella, the tears forming in her eyes. She cursed herself for her weakness, finally forcing herself to a halt some twenty paces away from the box on the opposite side of the road.

And here she stood. Staring.

* * *

'What do you mean, *'he's more than he appears'*?'

Kalus frowned, uncertain himself as to what he meant, or what he wanted from this call to Ridgway about Riordan. What was it? *The air of certainty he carried with him? The sense that he was privy to information, to secrets that were not to be shared with Kalus? The lean fitness and glow of health that marked him out as 'different'? The way that the man had so carelessly intimidated Brian Terry? The suggestion of menace that his words and demeanour had carried, that implied a man used to threatening others? The fact that he knew so much more about this case and about all those spinning in its orbit, than Kalus or any of his team?*

What was it? Professional envy or the belief that an already difficult case was becoming ever more treacherous?

The more he thought about it, the more certain he was that there was more - so much more - to the man than his remit of observer, his role within Complaints. The more he thought of about it, the more confused he was as to precisely what those issues were, what that role might really be.

So disposed, he murmured. 'It just doesn't feel right.'

'What are we today, Peter? *Russell Grant? Doris Lessing?*' Ridgway asked.

The reference to the well-known astrologer and the

spiritualist who convinced so many that she was in contact with departed souls, stung. 'I know it sounds...'

'Fucking stupid, Peter. Fucking stupid is what it sounds.'

'It doesn't ring true, sir.'

'Peter. It's a murder enquiry. It's an enquiry into the brutal murder of a miner on a picket line. One with the very real possibility that it was one of ours who did it. A copper. The Home Office, the cabinet, even the Prime minister are all over this one, waiting for us to find the bastard who did it. They want to know. *Now*. Not tomorrow, not next week. *Now*. Given that, and given all the other pressures we've already spoken about surrounding this whole enquiry - is it any wonder that they want eyes of their own on it? Is it thus any wonder that they send us their '*boy genius*' briefed up to the eyeballs on the case? Is it any wonder that he in turn with his bright career and shining reputation riding on it, has ensured that he knows as much about this case as anybody else, including you?' There was a pause. A beat. A moment. 'Listen... I hate to say this, Peter... But... let's remember, you're still the SIO. That's a given as far as I'm concerned. But after Handsworth... well, it can't be a surprise to you that there's some here at HQ and in Whitehall with... well, questions over your state of mind. I trust you, Peter, you know that. But this is government. Politics. The Brighton conference is next week. They want a result by then. The right result. There's a great deal at stake for all of us.'

He could think of nothing. He knew what Ridgway was saying was right. It was nothing more than what he'd already told himself again and again the past few hours whilst he'd mulled over his reactions to Riordan and the nature of the man's presence on his case. *His case*. Was that it? Was it all traced back to the man's comment to him as they'd stood in the canteen. Kalus, claiming his right as SIO - marking out his territory like a dog pissing on the ground. '*It's your case after all*,' Riordan had said. And when Kalus had confirmed it - '*Yes, it is, isn't it*' - Riordan's smile had made his statement more like a question that Riordan himself had for the moment deigned not to answer.

***

'*Idiot!*' she admonished herself, the door of the phone box creaking slowly to a close behind her, the woman's voice calling after her. She ran down the street towards the nursery, the rain now increasing in tempo so that within a few moments her hair was soaked. She opened her umbrella, raising it over her. *How could she have been so stupid? How could she have messed up something so simple?*

She had entered the phone box; finally summoning the conviction to do what she'd spent all morning planning. She'd opened her purse, carefully laying out coins for the call onto the cold metal shelf. She had decided upon the local station rather than *999*. An emergency call would want details of her business before putting her through. She was sure they recorded calls like hers, she'd read about it somewhere, heard it on the telly. *Crimewatch.*

She had dialled the number. A voice had answered. '*South Staffordshire Police, Tamworth*,' much of the identification being lost in the insistent pips of the call box urging her to put in the money. She did so, the whirring of the coins dropping in the slot giving way to the voice at the other end completing its sentence, 'How may I help you?'

She began her recital '*I'm calling about the murder of that miner, Stephen Jackson. I've heard that-*'

'Hold on caller, I'll put you through,' the voice had said.

'But-.' Before she could protest, before she could continue with her prepared message, she had been put on hold. She waited, looking at her reflection in the mirror above the phone. Tired. She looked tired. She looked at her watch. *How long? How long had she been on? How long before her money ran out? Had she anymore change? Had she the right money? Would they right now be tracing the call, keeping her on the line so they could work out where she was? Send a car to get her?*

'WPC Lawrence speaking.'

'It's about the murder of that miner,' she began, trying to get back on the track of her learnt statement.

'Stephen Jackson?' The voice of the officer asked.

'Yes, Jackson. Stephen Jackson. I've heard that-'

'Just a moment, you need to speak with one of the detectives on the enquiry team.'

'No, I just want to leave a message. *I'm calling about the murder of that miner, Stephen Jackson. I've heard that one of the picket-*'

The WPC cut across her. 'You really do need to speak with CID. I'm just manning the phones here at the station. They're all out at the colliery. You could call them there, but some of them are here doing interviews. I'll get one of them.'

She tried to protest, but again the line went quiet, the sound of the WPC moving away and calling someone.

She'd turned from side to side, restless, anxious to get out. The box was small. She'd repeated her mantra *I'm calling about the murder of that miner, Stephen Jackson. I've heard that one of the picket organisers had a grudge against him and wanted to harm him. You need to investigate him. You need to investigate Kevin Terry Investigate him. Find out where he was during the picket. Why he wanted to kill Stephen Jackson.*

Her thoughts were broken by the sound of the receiver being picked up. 'CID. DC White.'

'I'm calling about the murder of that miner, Stephen Jackson,' she began her message once again.

'Did you know Mr. Jackson?'

'What?'

'Did you know the victim? Did you know Stephen Jackson?'

'Look.... I just want to say something…let you know about what happened to him.'

'Okay, that's' great, but I need to know some details about you in case we get cut off. What's your name?'

Karen turned. *Someone standing by the phone box. A woman. A face she knew. From where? A young child standing by her side, tugging at her shopping bag. Nursery. She knew her from nursery. Michelle. They must have begun to let the children home.* She turned back towards the mirror above the phone. Her face was pale; all colour gone, eyes scared, fearful. This was not how it was supposed to be.

'Caller, what's your name?'

'It's not important.'

'Did you know Stephen? Are you a friend?'

'What? Yes. No. I mean… look, just listen. *I'm calling about the murder of that miner, Stephen Jackson. I've heard that one of the picket organisers had a grudge against him and wanted to harm him.*'

'And how do you know this?'

'What?'

She caught her reflection. Fear. She saw her fear looking back at her. She turned her head away, turned towards the door. The woman standing outside looked up from her child and smiled at her.

'You say someone had a grudge against him?'

She turned from the woman. She felt trapped. The booth was hot, steam creeping up the tiny panes of glass. 'Yes… they do… did.'

'Who is this?'

The pips started to beep. She tried to open her purse one-handed but succeeded in simply pushing it around the shelf. She tried to wedge it in a corner so that she could gain some leverage. She forced the clasp partially open, only for her action to spin the whole purse awkwardly towards the edge. She grabbed it.

'I said my names not important. It's not about me… not really.'

The pips louder. Pounding. Incessant. Demanding. Everything demanding. Demanding of her. The phone, Kevin, her children, the voice on the phone, Stephen… even the dead demanding. Shouting at her. Shouting.

'Caller put some more money in. We'll get cut off.' The voice urgent.

'I said my name's not important.'

'No, I meant the name of the man. The person who you say had a grudge against him. Is it a man? What sort of grudge?'

'Yes, it's a man.'

The pips stopped.

'Give me your number, I can call you back,' the voice said.

The line went dead.

She looked into the scratched and pitted surface of the mirror, the dead eyes that looked back at her.

'Kevin. Kevin Terry,' she whispered into the mouthpiece, the silence of the line. 'It's Kevin Terry.' She pulled the receiver away from her face.

She felt trapped. The heat. The closeness of the walls. Slamming the phone down, she'd scrabbled for her purse and shoved at the door. She'd flown out of the box. The woman waiting there had to tug her child close to her to avoid Karen stumbling into her.

'Sorry... I'm sorry,' Karen stammered. She breathed the cool air, running as fast as she could from the phone box. The rain pounding down. The woman's voice calling after her.

'Late, Karen? Don't worry! Michelle will be fine! I was just a little bit early,' the woman called after her. Called her. Called her name.

She knows my name, was all Karen could think of. *She knows my name.*

Eleven

He sat silent in the room. Darkness had fallen. How long he'd sat there, he wasn't certain. Often, at times like this, aides would magically appear to turn the lights on. Not today. Today they kept a distance. Today, the passage of afternoon into evening had been marked by the lights in the windows of the buildings opposite, fluorescent stars of yellowed-white pinned to a murky backdrop of slate grey. Soon it would be Daylight Saving and the clocks would be going back. More demand for power. More electricity. More drain on the stocks of coal so carefully amassed.

Pressure.

He stood and walked to the sash window with its view across to other similar Whitehall windows behind which, undoubtedly, stood others such as he contemplating their present situation.

The afternoon Cabinet meeting had been its own exercise in power and character. Those, the sheep that attached themselves to such things, had urged caution, concerned for their reputation. Worried over careers and the possibility of knighthoods. They'd called for negotiation, an ending of the strike. Her withering glare had silenced most, though some secretly clung to the idea. The miners were reeling had been her judgment. Now was not the time to settle. Now was the time to push harder, finishing it for good. The miners had to crawl back. There could be no return with heads held high. No romancing of their struggle.

The rain drizzled down. The streetlights were on, the haze of yellowed light reflected in the oily sheen of wet tarmac. The pavements were busy. Commuters scurrying home, briefcases in hands; shoppers, designer bags clutched against the bruising passage of the crowds.

He turned, gazing back across the room to his desk.

The business of government in the late twentieth century lay not in making the great decisions or in wielding the power of armies or finance. It lay in managing the message. In making thinking - or more pertinently making *not thinking* - easier. Reassuring the great mass below that as they went about their lives there was nothing to be troubled about. Nothing to see.

He walked back and sat in the chair.

He saw it every day. Constituency meetings, party conferences - even here in his own office, his own civil servants. Faces, minds, all of them blank, waiting to be written in. Waiting to be told.

The business of government was to see that nothing stirred them, that nothing troubled their minds. Shielding them from thoughts that might turn their attention to matters best left unconsidered by those not qualified to understand them, those unaware of the bigger picture. Better that they think about the bingo and the breasts and the TV funnies. Not matters like this.

He looked down at a copy of that day's *Guardian*: *POLICING ACTION LINKED TO DEATH OF MINER*. The Telegraph: *MINER'S DEATH PROMPTS LABOUR LEADER'S CALL FOR ENQUIRY INTO POLICING OF MINERS' STRIKE*

He sat, leaning in so that his chest almost touched the edge of the desk. He suddenly swept an arm in front of him scattering the newspapers to the floor. He looked down at the chaos of newsprint surrounding the desk, white leaves at the foot of the tree.

No matter what *the Guardian* or others might say, they were winning.

Bit by bit they were winning. The strikers were crumbling. In Nottingham and in Kent, even in parts of Wales, there was a steady return to work. What the media were calling *a drift*, was actually crack, a deftly engineered ever-widening fault line in the dispute. Soon it would become a torrent, a flood washing King Arthur away forever.

It all hung on the police and intelligence services doing their part. It was what he'd told them in the post-cabinet meeting.

Group Twelve, the true believers. Those that would ensure the triumph *She* demanded.

The voices of protest had been diminished. The violence of the miners at the collieries was playing into government hands. The violence stoked by his operatives - the *agent provocateurs*, the undercover men - swamped the TV news. *She* had called the miners *the enemy within* and each night their carefully orchestrated actions offered proof of all that she claimed.

Hearts and minds.

The public were unconcerned about pits closing. No matter what the Left might say, the crocodile tears wailing about civil liberties, there were no tears shed by the great masses over violent yobs getting a truncheon to the head. They wanted their streets safe, their factories to be working, and their lights to turn on when they wanted them to.

In this regard, everything had been moving *Her* way, months of planning materialising into reality.

Until Tamworth.

Now the media were on alert, sensing a story. They had grown tired of human interest features focussing on the hardships of striking miners or the struggles of those returning to work. They'd had their fill of stories of scab miners living in hostile communities that shunned and despised them, harassed them and drove them out. The details of the back to work negotiations lacked any sense of movement. Thatcher and Scargill were the story of the strike, but even that battle was becoming less interesting as each day they repeated unchanging mantras. A trench-war of propaganda.

The meeting had been clear: they could not afford for this murder enquiry to drag on and offering comfort to those ranged against them. They could not allow it to be the lever by which those on the left might yet undermine the policing of the strike.

The story had to go away. More than that; it must end with a miner held responsible for murder. A culprit demolishing forever the reservations of those who questioned the policing of the strike. They were creative men. Resourceful. They could make it so.

But beyond even political expediency, there were more pressing matters. Whoever was held to blame for the murder, Jackson's connection to the wider intelligence operations entangled in his life had to be sealed. There could be no loose ends. No strand compromising something bigger. *Silver Fox.*

He steepled his fingers, elbows on the desk, chin resting against his hands. Given the nature of Jackson's death, they had to proceed on the assumption that *Silver Fox* may have been blown, that its existence had somehow been discovered, its work compromised. A leak to be sealed.

It was the puzzle he'd wrestled with all day: if that were so, then why had nothing come out? On top of that was the question of why Jackson would have been murdered rather than his secret exposed, especially when killing him undermined their cause. Miners murdering an undercover policeman muddied the waters of guilt and righteousness that they would wish be kept clear. His death offered them nothing.

Could it be something else? Could he have been killed because someone had discovered another secret he held? *Bishop's Mitre.*

Was that operation why he was murdered? Would that explain the silence? Was it possible that one intelligence operation might be blown whilst the other remained secure? It was unlikely, but possible. His part in *Bishop's Mitre* might better explain his murder.

He stared into the darkness that had slipped deeper into the room.

Whatever else happened, knowledge of those operations had to be contained. *Bishops' Mitre* was sensitive but could, should its details emerge, be something the government might survive. But *Silver Fox*, the truth of what the intelligence services had been doing these past months, would be the end of the government.

His remit was clear: *tidy up the loose ends. Find what could be salvaged.*

There was still the chance of success. At the very least of any failure being contained and despatched to the footnote of history.

He reminded himself he'd been placed here for just such reasons. He had *Her* trust for a reason. He was a man who got things done.

Capable.

Ruthless.

* * *

The pub was hot, crowded. It was good. The more people the less likely the chance they would stand out.

Brody made his way through the throng, nudging with his shoulders; standing aside as a customer moved away with a clutch of full glasses in his hands, he eased his way to the bar. He waved a pound note attempting to attract the attention of busy staff. A young woman, her white blouse pulled tight revealing a deep cleavage and dark coloured bra, was ringing up for the man standing next to him. As she returned with his change Brody took the chance to leap in. 'Whiskey, love. Lots of ice. Have one yourself.' To the annoyance of those further down the bar who'd been waiting longer, she served him.

Having used the optic, she turned, standing in front of him shovelling in the ice.

'Busy,' he said.

Her look suggested that she was as much used to punters stating the obvious almost as much as she was used to them staring at her breasts. 'Hadn't noticed,' she replied.

He smiled. 'Oh, yeah, right. Good one.'

She placed the drink in front of him. He proffered the pound note, which she plucked from his hand. She rang it up on the till, the change slapped into his palm, and she was gone, immersed in the attempts of others to gain her attention.

Cyndi Lauper finished on the jukebox. A pause before it shuddered back into life. Madonna. *Borderline.*

Brody turned away, lifting his glass above his shoulders and extracting himself from the crush of those waiting to take his place. A pace or two away from the counter the crowd thinned and he was able to stand still for a moment and take in the room. At a booth by the rear wall he saw his man smiling at him. Closing the ground between them he saw that the smile was in fact a leer.

'No chance there Matthew, my man. No fucking chance.' The accent was thick Brummie, nasal and tight throated. Some said it had more the quality of a whine than an accent. Unkind, but with some degree of accuracy.

The man himself was thin, wiry, lank blonde hair worn in dirty dreadlocks tied back in a ponytail. He wore a black Tee-shirt with the logo of a band on it. Brody was unsure which band it was - the folds of the shirt making it almost an anagram - but he was certain they would be loud. He wore blue jeans with flares that completely concealed whatever footwear he was wearing, though Brody was equally certain it would be trainers. A brown leather jacket, blouson style, was laid across the bench seat next to him. On the table was a half-finished pint, a tin of Golden Virginia, some Rizla cigarette papers, and a box of matches. Tim Plant was a man defined by his style. If clothes truly *maketh the man*, then Tim Plant was walking testimony to the character reference of his outfit.

'She's fucking the licensee. Everyone knows. Everyone apart from his missus.'

'This your current local, then?'

'One of them.'

Madonna filled the room. *Borderline feels like I'm going to lose my mind*. *Borderline*, the biggest record of the summer just passed, hit its chorus.

Their meeting place had been decided upon by Plant. He lived locally, spending every night in one of the pubs in the area - *The Fighting Cocks, The Bull, The Prince of Wales* - drinking and selling dope. He was small time, a kilo or so a month. He was your friendly local dealer, a remnant of the late sixties. A dealer who knew his customers by name. Part connoisseur: part counter-culture revolutionary, Plant insisted on smoking whatever he was selling with his customers. Scoring off Tim Plant was a commitment to a night of getting high. A night of listening to reggae music, Led Zeppelin, and a host of other bands, most of whom had split-up long ago.

Whatever else he was, Tim Plant was no businessman.

What he *was*, was ears to the ground. A man who knew what was happening in counter-culture. Plant attended those meetings advertised on low level handouts stuck to telegraph poles and phone box windows. Plant was political on a social revolutionary level, and it was during a Militant Tendency meeting that they'd first met. Plant believed in local action, a low level revolution. It was the politics of the Militant Tendency that had eventually turned him off; *they* were *Stalin*, he *Che Guevara*. But he believed in change, in social equality, in breaking *The System*. Brody had always liked him, a friendship enduring even Plant's leaving of Militant. For Plant such things were no big deal. He'd lost count of the number of counter-culture groups he'd joined and left. The hundreds of marches he'd been on since Grosvenor Square in '68.

'So, what do you need?'

'Information.'

Plant laughed. 'Fuck off! Do I look like Bamber Gascoigne?'

'Local stuff.'

'How local?'

'I'm looking into the death of that miner out at Tamworth.'

Plant scoffed. 'Tamworth. Fucking shit hole. Really fucking uncool place.'

'Yeah, well, that's as maybe. I'm trying to get an angle on it.'

'Angle?' he asked, intrigued.

'What precisely happened. How he died.'

'Ain't the tabloids got all that covered?'

'You know what they're like. They'll print whatever the police tell them. They just want the juicy bits. There's more to it, I'm sure. Corruption, police violence. Stuff like that.'

'I went out there, you know early on. We had some collections in the *Traf* and the *Prince*. No good asking in the *Cocks* or *Bull*, all fucking *bourgeois* wankers in there these days. The picket was pretty good. Some cool people. We tried to stir it up a bit. Some of the Militant lot were there. You know, Griggsy and Smithy. Lot of us who'd been at Handsworth in 81.' He broke off from reminiscing, 'Anyroad, what do you expect I can do?'

'Well, that's it. You know people. You know the agitators. I want to get some sort of inside drift.'

'Well you're still in Militant, ain't you? What about asking them lot?'

Brody screwed up his face. 'I want something a little more local than that. A little deeper. People who know the local situation. Feet on the ground if you like.'

Plant giggled.

'What is it?'

'Well, there is this one bloke I know. Bit of a laugh, really.'

'Yeah?'

'Bloke scored off me a couple of times while I was over there.'

'Yeah?'

'Yeah. He might be able to help you. Might be just what you're looking for.'

'Yeah?'

'Yeah. He's a pig of some sort. Undercover. *James fucking Bond stuff.*'

* * *

Kalus studied the latest of the NUM stewards' statements provided by McKinnon. Like each of the fifteen or so others he'd read, it was a litany of the details of their arrival at the picket and the arrival of the '*scab*' miners coaches. It had continued with detailing the '*brutal and unprovoked*' attack on pickets by the police and ended with their hearing of the '*murder*' of Stephen Jackson and the subsequent dispersal of themselves and the miners they'd been organising.

He tossed the sheet in the direction of the cardboard box it had come from, watching as it drifted gently to a halt half-in and half-out of the battered container. He sat back in the armchair, cupping his face in his hands, fingers massaging his forehead.

His father's house.

Twice a week he visited. Twice a week either he or his wife taking it in turns with his sister to sit and wait for their father to sleep. Waiting to be sure he'd finally settled. They were there to reassure him. Waiting for him to call out, to know that despite the ever burning lights he wasn't alone in the dark. When Kalus was working a case like this it became difficult. That was when Anna would take a turn. With the children growing it was increasingly difficult for her to do so, but it wasn't worth the aggravation of asking his sister to change the schedule or for her or her husband to take on an additional sitting because of his case.

So he sat here and worked whilst Anna stayed home looking after the children. It was easier, if somewhat limiting. His wife was good with his father, good with his sister who could, when the mood took her, make life awkward. At times he thought she enjoyed doing so, exerting that little piece of power over him just for the sake of it, just for her own satisfaction. Anna knew how to deal with it. She knew how to approach her, get the best out of her. He found it hard. It grated, went against his own grain of stubbornness.

He sat in his father's chair. Around him, his father's life. The grey misty photographs of the young soldier, grinning with his squad, berets at rakish angles, arms entwined around shoulders. *Musketeers. Strangers in a strange land.* The wedding photo. The uniform. His mother's white dress, veil pulled back revealing her round open face, her smile; shy, unassuming. The pictures of grandchildren and of their children's' own weddings. Images held in dark brown mounts and framed in pine and silver. The treasures: paintings bought on holiday, the plates, the vases, the figurines. All his mother's touches and flourishes.

The TV. The remote control. The lamp. The red cylinder. The tablets. The medication. The oxygen mask.

He laid his arms along the arm of the chair, hands grasping

the roll of the edge.

What did it feel like? To sit each day surrounded by all that your life was? Surrounded by all that your life would be? To sit each day confronted by what you would leave behind. To see how you would be seen. To know what you had amounted to. To see all that you would be.

He stood, walking away from the chair, away from the moment, the thought, the fear. In the hall he picked up the phone. It was old, heavy duty, a dial rather than the push button of their own new Trim-phone. He dialled, each whir of the mechanism bringing his focus back to now.

'288871'

'Katrina?'

'*Daddy!*'

He could hear the sound of the TV in the background. 'Hey, shouldn't you be in bed by now?'

'Mommy's busy sorting Andrew's bag for school. She's let me watch *Postman Pat*. Are you coming home soon?'

'Soon. I'm at granddad Andrzej's.'

'Is he asleep yet?'

'Yes. And so should you be. Can I speak to mommy?'

'Yeh.' The phone clattered to the table, Katrina's voice moving to the distance '*Mommy! Daddy's on the phone. He wants you.*'

Muffled responses. Anna's voice, muted. Andrew's voice. Disagreement. Instructions. Warnings. Anna's voice nearer, picking up the receiver, her concern evident. 'Peter? Is everything okay?'

'Fine. Everything's fine. Dad's asleep. Just wanted to talk.'

'Talk? Now?' Concern shading to exasperation. 'Peter, I'm in the middle of getting the children off to bed. How do you expect me to talk?'

'Sorry, it's just that… I'm sitting here, looking round at everything. You know, the pictures and that, and I was thinking about dad, his life.'

Voices in the background – Andrew shouting, Katrina giggling. Anna her voice distant, turned from the receiver, '*Katrina* turn it off now *Now*!' Her voice closer, returning to him. 'Look, Peter, I'm in the middle of everything. I haven't got time for this right now. We'll speak when you get back. Oh, and don't forget to bring back that casserole dish I left there the other day.' Voice turning away once more, '*No. Bed! Now*! Voice then full, close and rushed. Dismissive. 'Peter, look I've got to go! I'll see you later.'

A click.

Silence.

He put the phone down. Stood in the hall; long, narrow and warm,

The hallway. Narrow. Hot.

They had waited in the hallway. Long, narrow, hot. They had waited in that heat. Waited as late morning had turned to afternoon.

Five hours passed.

Should we be waiting so long, guv...? The SWAT team leader wonder's what we're waiting for... He says it's too quiet in there, sir... Shouldn't we go in....? He's not asked for anything for a while... The kids are quiet... Maybe we should rush him... Get in there, finish it... We ought to take him down soon, guv... It's not right... Something's wrong.

No. Give him time. He'll come out. A sheep, not a lion.

At one point Reuben's wife had appeared in the passage screaming for them to do something. Begging. Sobbing. Why's it taking so long? What are you doing? Why haven't you got them out? You don't know him... It's too long... Get them out! Save my children!

She'd been restrained. Comforted by his words.

We know what we're doing. He'd said. Trust me. He'd said.

Trust me. We know what we're doing.

Finally, when he'd decided it right, they'd gone in. SWAT team first.

The door had broken with a crash.

Splintering wood. No sound like it. A crack, a tearing.

Then the silence. A call. A shout.

Guv you'd better get in here. There's a problem.

Twelve
Day Four

PC David Vaughan hated nightshifts. Hated the disruption brought to the order of his life. Hated the dark, preferred to get up with the sun rather than the moon. Hated not being able to watch his favourite TV shows. Some of his neighbours had just got video-recorders and as well as watching films that they rented from the local shop they were able to record the football and stuff. At the moment they were too expensive, but with a bit more of this picket line overtime they might soon be able to get one. See the look on his dad's face then when he came round to theirs and saw it. A Toshiba or a Phillips.

Vaughan swung his torch in an arc. *Grass. Hedge. Wire fence.*

He tried to think of night shift as something positive.

The extra money was undoubtedly the big plus but Alison hated them. They had been married for just over two years and she still found it hard to accept that he had to do them, let alone that she had to get used to them. The birth of their daughter had if anything made it harder for her to accept. During the pregnancy she'd read a book that had become her guiding voice over all aspects of their daughter's life. They were going to be the perfect parents for their perfect child, and night shifts for the father didn't figure anywhere in the pages of Alison's manual.

Despite the extra money buying the best cots and toys, she still voiced her complaints that the cost of him being away from home was too high. He knew she had ambitions for him. Sergeant... Detective... Something with a desk. An office, plain clothes not uniform. For his own part, he had no real issues with it, with any of her plans. He lived life in the present, the here and now. He had ambitions, but he had never really sat down and worked out a schedule for them to happen in the way his wife had. Organisation, that was her forte, even when it came to her dreams.

'There's nothing wrong with having a plan, David. Plans are what help you make decisions about what to do.'

He couldn't disagree with her. He didn't even resent the jibes aimed his way at family get-togethers about *'can see who wears the trousers in your house'* when she would outline for his brother and sister-in-law and his mom and dad what he and Alison and baby Sarah were going to be doing. *David's Fantastically Planned Ambitious Career*; the big new house with *ensuite*; the new car; the holidays abroad.

He loved her, had wanted to please her from the moment they'd first met. He'd do anything for her. All she had to do was to accept that as a policeman he had to follow orders, and that part of that involved night shifts. He had no say in the matter. It wasn't as if he could take in a note from his mom asking to be excused night shifts, not that he'd even jokingly say that to her for fear that she would ring his shift commander and ask.

Still, nights like this he wished he did have a note.

The wind was stronger than ever. A Siberian wind he'd heard the weatherman say – though Christ knows they knew sod all about what the weather was likely to be doing. Stick a wet finger in the air be as good. Better still, stick their heads outside their bloody windows at Pebble Mill and have a look. Siberian or Timbuktu, wherever it was blowing from it was bloody cold and his standard issue raincoat was next to useless. Kept you dry but gave no protection from the cold. Bad enough around the streets of Tamworth, but out here exposed to the elements whilst patrolling the colliery, it was a joke.

He checked his watch, tugging the cuff back and exposing a band of flesh between sleeve and glove to the bite of the wind. *Four a.m.* The shift from the barracks would be arriving in under an hour. He'd met one or two of the blokes from Warwick who were billeted at the caravan site at Lea Marston, decent types he'd thought. The ones from the Met pretty much kept themselves to themselves. Stationed out at Whittington army barracks there was bugger all else for them to do apart from shifts and sleep. Anyroad, they seemed to know what they were about. The way they'd gone into those pickets over the past week was brutal, hardly surprising that one of them died - amazing that it hadn't happened earlier to more of them.

He knew most of his fellow officers had little sympathy with the pickets or their cause. For his own part, he'd no real thoughts about the closure of pits or the rights and wrongs of the dispute. Whatever happened to pickets happened because they chose to be there throwing bricks and breaking the law. Whatever happened, they'd brought it on themselves.

He swung the beam of his torch a little further ahead. *Grass. Hedge. Wire fence.*

The fencing appeared secure. He'd little doubt that it wouldn't be. The pickets had little choice about where to gather and how to picket the arriving shift of miners. This fence was at the far side of the colliery and it could only be approached with difficulty over a series of fields and wooded areas that at this time of the year were more bog than pasture.

It came as a surprise to see a group of three men in donkey jackets and work clothes standing around the foot of the fencing some distance ahead. They had a series of what appeared to be metal toolboxes gathered around their feet and about fifty yards beyond them was a parked transit van with the NCB insignia on its side-panel. Maintenance was still being carried out by pit deputies, and the security of the fencing was at present as high on their list of priorities as checking the winding gear.

Vaughan saw no need to do anything other than to continue his approach to the men, who in turn continued with their work with seemingly little interest in his own presence there.

'Morning lads,' he called.

A desultory response was offered by one of the men who appeared to be supervising the work.

'Keep it secure. Don't want none of them pickets getting in.'

'That's for sure,' the supervisor replied.

Vaughan paused, glad of something to break the monotony of his patrol. He watched the two men squatting and wrestling with the wire. 'Fucking freezing. Weather forecast's shit. Siberian I heard.'

'Yeah,' the supervisor muttered.

'Glad when this lot's done and we can all get back to somewhere warm. Bad enough in the summer. Don't fancy spending the winter out here.'

'That's right.'

'Any sign of a breakthrough?'

The two men stopped working and looked to the supervisor. 'Probably a fox,' the supervisor said.

Vaughan laughed. 'No, I meant the strike, not the fence. Any sign of an agreement?'

The supervisor gestured for the men to continue their efforts with the wire. He smiled at Vaughan, amused at his own misunderstanding. 'No. Nothing at all.'

Vaughan blew out a long breath. 'Ah well. Better be getting on with it.' He turned to continue his patrol, only then noticing the open lid of the larger of the toolboxes. He saw screwdrivers, pliers, and cutters lying inside but glancing around became aware that there was no sign of the wire to make the repair. He turned back to the maintenance crew. 'Don't you–'

The lump hammer smashed onto his skull with great force. The first blow stunned him, dropping him to his knees. The second turned the world black.

***

This time the push was hard. Harder, PC David Jones thought, than any of the previous weeks. The sweat beneath his visor threatened to blind him. The salt stinging his eyes caused him to screw them closed, shaking his head violently from side to side to clear them. The crush of bodies pressed against him.

He planted his feet and pushed, the bottom ridge of his riot shield cutting across the top of his thighs as he leaned against the top of it in an attempt to force back the group of pickets who had placed themselves firmly in front of his section of the line.

Hands reached over, scrabbling for his visor, his helmet. He pushed his head back, aware of the danger of their gaining a grasp on the strap and choking him. He thrashed wildly ahead of him with his baton, alternating vicious down-strokes with short jabs and swings. He felt contact but was uncertain which part of his assailant he was striking, aware only of the moments of success where the attack on him lessened as the crush of bodies became limp. The front wave of pickets, reacting to his blows, were now shoved against him by the waves of pickets behind them rather than any active pressing by those in the front row themselves.

Hurt men couldn't fall, the press of bodies keeping them upright. The injured, aware of the danger of falling beneath the feet of pickets and police, could do nothing other than allow themselves to become part of a human wall of flesh, their battered bodies carried back and forth like flotsam breaking on the shore.

The noise was overwhelming. The clatter of rocks on plastic shields; the staccato crack of hurled glass bottles breaking; the shouts and cries of pickets and police; the exhortations of section commanders. '*Hold!*' '*Push!*' '*Move!*' The chaotic shouts of pickets, the cursing and screaming of abuse. It was medieval in its chaos, its movement, its pitting of foot-soldier against foot-soldier, hand to hand, toe to toe, face to face. Clubs and stones, bottles and fists. Helmets. Shields. Masks. Blood. Gashes. Wheals. Broken bones.

The first indication that it was over came with the slow sensation of give in the wall of flesh. An easing of the pressure against his body that suddenly became a lurch forward, that in its turn became a stumbling shift as the line of pickets collapsed in on itself as those at the rear stopped pushing forward.

It was at this point that men fell, the sudden lurch taking them by surprise, a drunken stagger followed by the removal of the very pressure that had been keeping them upright. They stumbled like drunks in search of a wall to hold onto, like falling down the stairs whilst blindly flailing for a banister to hold. Those with gashes, concussion, and broken bones were the casualties of such movement. Unable to hold their footing from a mixture of confusion and pain, they fell to the floor where they were kicked or just plain trodden on as the lines moved over them. The cries changed, becoming pleading and fearful. The wave broke; the noise subsided.

Jones looked along the line. The gap between police and pickets resolved itself. The line of blue became fixed, purer. The line of black donkey jackets of the pickets firmer. The plastic shell of the shields locked into line. A carapace of resolve; a plastic skin of shelter.

The picket line fell back. It was over.

On command Jones lifted his visor, shield swung aside. Men looked at each other. There were smiles, laughter and relief. Some had pain etched across their faces, fingers dabbing at wounds that would be requiring treatment.

Jones looked at the shields around him, scratched and splintered. He looked at his own shield. It was covered with the smear of bloodstains. He raised his baton in front of his face, fascinated by the lines of blood running along its shaft from a daub of dark red blood at its head.

He turned to the PC next to him and tentatively waggled it back and forth. The PC smiled and gave him the thumbs-up. Jones smiled widely in return.

Raising his baton higher, he twirled it above his head. Those around him began to cheer, a sound that rippled down the line growing in its frenzy.

***

They knelt at the base of the wire fence. The three of them, the two dressed as colliery maintenance workers and the smaller third man dressed as their supervisor. The unconscious figure of

PC Vaughan lay in the ditch where the two big men had dragged him. The smeared trail of blood from the head wounds shone dark like melted chocolate in the growing light of dawn.

'What the fuck do we do now?' The bigger of the two workers spoke, his voice gruff, large and direct. His fellow worker wiped the sweat from his own brow, black curly hair even darker in the slowly lifting shadows of daybreak, eyes shining bright and blazing with adrenalin. He was a good man in a fight. He was a good man in a tight spot. He was a man who would shirk from nothing. A man known to have killed to prove it. He in turn looked to the third man in the Supervisor's jacket who considered the question.

'We carry on. Do what we came to do.'

'We didn't plan on this,' Gruff Voice said.

'Plans change. We have to adapt,' the Supervisor stated.

'Won't he be missed?' Bright Eyes asked.

The Supervisor cocked his head to the side, inviting Gruff Voice and Bright Eyes to join him. 'Can't you hear?' he asked.

Like a distant train the sound rolled over the colliery and the fields, the sound arising somewhere to their left. A dull rhythmic slap and thump. A beat, a roar like a football crowd or the noise of engines humming.

The Supervisor returned his head to the upright. 'That's the sound of 300 pickets and the same number of police. I think you'll find that they'll all be a little bit too busy to think about searching for a constable minding the fence so far from the real action.'

Gruff Voice nodded. He understood the Supervisor's calm manner, his reputation as a man not easily panicked.

'That's why we're paying our friends so much money,' the Supervisor stated. He held up a fob. Two large mortise style keys hung from it. 'Providing copies of the keys to the store containing what we want and a map of its location and layout are one thing. Their organisation of such a powerful distraction quite another.'

'But they'll know what we've done,' Bright Eyes stated, his concern switching from the imminent fear of discovery to the wider threat posed to their plan.

The Supervisor waved his hand in dismissal. 'What will they know? That some policeman came across some pickets who were attempting to breach the site.' He shook his head, his Cork accent more prominent, 'Sure, that's what's been going on for months. They'll find him, see the gap and that's it. They'll see it as revenge for that dead miner.'

'Won't they search the site?' Gruff Voice asked.

'Search for what? A bunch of pickets? If they decide to mount a search it won't be for hours, by which time we'll be long gone. And they'll be looking for people. Miners. Pickets. They won't be aware of what they should really be searching for.'

Gruff Voice and Bright Eyes smiled. 'That's for sure,' Bright Eyes agreed.

The Supervisor returned their smiles. He was a motivator of men. A leader. That's why he'd been chosen. 'And even if they do find out what we've done, by then it'll be too late.'

There were nods. The plan was good. Given that it had been hastily put together over the past few days, it was brilliant, a testament to their leader's skill. 'Besides,' he added, 'should they stumble onto what we've taken, they'll be looking all over the country for it. No doubt, given the limited imagination they usually apply to such matters, they'll look in all the usual places on their lists. But thanks to our new friends we're going to be stowing it right under their noses. Inside the cordon. Inside a ring of police. In a few days' time we'll use the means that our friends have also procured to move it to where it's needed. After that, others will see to it that it's put to good use. We're going to make history, lads. History.'

He looked in the direction of the prone policeman.

'It might be that it even works out better than we thought. A copper in the hospital or the morgue will send them off in every direction but ours.' He weighed the hammer in his hands. 'Trust me. Nothing's changed. Nothing.'

***

'Can anyone tell me precisely what this morning's debacle was all about?'

The wall of silence dividing Chief Inspector Bailey from his senior officers remained securely in place.

He scanned the room. One or two faces met his glare, but for the most part the assembled watch commanders averted their eyes. He let the silence lie, considering its meaning, weighing its significance. These were men he knew. Men he trusted. Men who could be counted on. They were men most of whom he had appointed himself, pushing for their promotions. Something had happened, something obscuring the bond between Commander and men. It was happening outside. It was happening across the force. Now here it was inside this very room.

Bailey shook his head. He was tired, maybe more tired than he had realised. He rubbed at his face, massaging fingers into his brow. When he spoke it was with exasperation rather than venom. 'This fucking strike!'

He looked down, picking the newspaper up off his desk. He lifted it from where he had earlier tossed it whilst barking into the phone the orders that had summoned his Watch Commanders here before him. Summoned them from the colliery, the barracks, and the caravan site. He held the front-page towards them, shaking it for added emphasis, demanding their attention.

'I take it you've all seen this?'

The photo of PC Jones waving a bloodied baton in the air adorned the front page of the lunchtime edition of the Birmingham Evening Mail. *'Bloody Victory'* was the block lettered headline. *'Miners' Demonstration Beaten Back'* proclaimed the strapline beneath.

'A protest about the battering to death of a picket is stopped by this...' Bailey waved his free hand angrily across the page, '... This display of... What would you call it? Joy? Triumphalism?'

No one said a word.

'John?' All eyes looked with relief at Inspector John Bennett, the commander of Jones' squad. 'He's your man isn't he?'

'Yes sir,' Bennett confirmed.

'And?' The question hung.

'He's a good officer, sir. He's been on the line at Selby and Orgreave. The riots before that. He's proven himself time after time. The rest of the squad look up to him.'

'John, the issue isn't about whether he's a good officer or not. It's not even about whether he's regarded by the rest of the squad as a good bloke or not. It's not his manhood that's in question, it's his fucking lack of judgement.' Bailey tossed the paper back onto the desk. 'His lack of fucking common sense. What the fuck did he think he was doing? Was he fucking thinking at all?'

'They'd had a hard time of it sir. This morning in particular.'

'I don't need to remind you, John, that these are trained men. They're supposed to handle tough situations. It's why they are there.'

'Yes sir.'

'Instead, we come off looking like yobs. Yobs.' Bailey scooped up the paper, brandished it once more. 'And as for tough times… I don't know about you, but he looks as though he's enjoying it. Given what's happened, the picket beaten to death, it hardly plays well for us, does it?'

The line of men, looked to the floor.

Bailey shook his head, releasing a long sigh. He was tired. His men were tired. Mistakes happened when men were tired and pressured. He knew that. But this was more. Things had altered, something had changed these past weeks, shifted in ways he barely understood. Shadows under the surface, barley glimpsed. Feelings without names. He had the abiding sense that he was losing control, but of what or how, he could not have said.

There had been change before. The social revolution of the sixties and seventies had shuddered up against the young PC Bailey on his beat. But the line of order had held because the police were seen as representing the law of the land. Not now. Not anymore. The strike was changing all that. He saw it. Felt it. The police had become figures of menace rather than respect. And to his shame the men of his command were acting as if they themselves were the law rather than its defenders.

He was a Conservative, loving Thatcher and all she stood for. But he was too much a policeman not to be apprehensive as to where the policing of this dispute was taking them. Where it would finally leave them.

'I can assure you Chief Inspector-' Bennett began.

'Can you, John? By the looks of this you can't assure me of anything. Miners and pickets out of control is one thing. Police officers rampaging around with batons and shields is something entirely different. We've got a dead miner lying in the morgue. We don't need this. We don't need images of officers out of control or revelling in confrontation. That includes your men out at Whittington, Peter.'

Inspector Peter Bradley nodded acceptance of Bailey's admonishment.

'No more of this waving of payslips that we've all seen. No more provocations. We've got enough on our hands without the press and politicians shoving their noses in even further. Am I clear?'

The heads all nodded. There was little to be said.

'From here on, it's by the book. By the book.'

He watched the nods along the line. 'Now, what about this incident this morning over at the other side of the colliery?'

Bennett leant forward, relieved to be on surer ground. 'It appears that one of our men was clubbed by a group of pickets. He's in a bad way. A coma. We think we caught them trying to get in through the wire.'

'Bastards,' Bradley muttered to a murmur of agreement from the rest.

'What do you think were they doing there?' Bailey asked.

Bennett shrugged. 'Trying to find a back way in. Trying to get through our lines. Probably intending to confront the working miners when their coach got into the pit head area.'

'And did they?'

Bennett shook his head. 'No. That's the funny thing about it. They got through the wire but they don't appear to have seen it through. Probably scared off by attacking the officer.'

'But he wasn't found for how long?'

'A couple of hours or more as far as we can tell.'

Bailey's irritation stirred once more. 'Why so long?'

'We're not sure. We think the picket might have been in full throttle when the attack on Vaughan happened. It took a while to realise he was missing and that he hadn't reported in. We initiated a search and found him by the hole in the fence. He was rushed to Good Hope. Wife's with him. Poor bastard.'

Bailey sat back, somewhat mollified. 'So where are we with it?'

'I've asked for CID, but they're all busy with the Jackson enquiry.'

Bailey nodded. 'I'll speak with Ridgway. See if he can get Kalus to spare a Detective or two. I want whoever did this. I want that attack on the front page tonight. Let the public see just what we're dealing with. See how long they'll be supporting their precious miners then.'

Thirteen

Brody alighted from the platform of the bus, looking around and gathering his sense of direction. Checking his watch, he moved off into the stream of commuters making their way towards the station. Out of habit he stopped and looked into the window of the small tobacconists that sat at the corner of Corporation Street and New Street. Amongst the packs of imported cigarettes and pouches of tobacco and Zippo lighters, he watched the reflection of those passing by, checking to see if anyone was paying more attention to him than they were to the throng of people around him. He'd once interviewed an active member of the IRA for an article commissioned by one of the left wing magazines. Before agreeing to the meeting the man had given Brody a crash course in avoiding surveillance. They were lessons that he still periodically employed, especially when meeting someone like his current assignation.

Satisfied, he slid into the phalanx of bodies moving across the busy intersection and up the ramp towards the station and the shopping complex that sat astride it.

There was something comforting about being part of the slow wave of bodies sweeping up the long incline. A togetherness. A sense of belonging he found re-assuring, part of the herd.

Marx had it right – bread and circuses, the opium of religion. People wanted to belong more than they wanted to be free. Wanted to believe more than they wanted to think.

His platform was busy. Suits and suitcases, and the train was late. The loudspeaker spluttered something about rain or leaves or repairs, the distortion leaving everybody none the wiser to the cause for the delay. The journey to Tamworth would take 30 minutes or so. He checked his watch, grateful he'd allowed plenty of time to make the meeting.

Once on board, the journey took its allotted path through the backyards of the city. The walls of hotels and stores merged to fly-blown yards of factories and warehouses that in their turn yielded to the fixed pattern of streets and roads and the brief strip of green fields fleetingly separating the city from the encroaching overspill sprawl of Castle Vale. Then it was Chelmsley Wood before finally Tamworth itself.

The arrival platform was the High Line. Alighting, he took the series of steps down to the Low Line platform before emerging through the ticket office area and out onto the taxi rank that curved around the front of the station. Consulting first his watch and then the torn page of scribbled directions, he headed in the direction of Albert Road and the centre of the town.

He paused to consult the reflections in the window of an off-licence, scanning the faces that passed on both sides of the road. *Three people from the train. A woman and a young child. A man in a business suit.* No one looked his way. As they disappeared ahead of him, Brody turned, re-tracing his steps towards the pub he'd passed moments before.

The outer door led into an internal porch area and a passageway that opened into a public bar. He took it in. Red leatherette, dark wood bar, cigarette scorched tables, ring marks of glasses, framed pictures of huntsmen and dogs. The counter was lit from a rack of glasses above it that cast an unworldly glow over the two men standing close by and a bleached blonde barmaid. Under the artificial light the woman's hair took on tones of yellow and red, her lipstick glistening like a scar against the powder of her rouged face.

I'm in a cartoon Brody thought to himself. *A postcard of a pub.*

The three occupants eyed him with differing measures of appraisal. Seeing nothing of great interest or distraction, the two men went back to their discussion. The barmaid spoke out of obligation. 'What can I get you?'

'Pint.' He scanned the pumps. 'Pedigree.'

She flipped a glass from the shelf and heaved on the Marston's pump. The swoosh of the amber liquid swirling into the straight glass held Brody's attention for the time it took to fill it and the barmaid to top off the glass.

'Anything else?'

'No thanks.'

He handed over a pound note. The barmaid rang up the cost and returned with the change. Brody sifted through it for some silver. 'Phone I could use?'

The barmaid pointed to a door at the side of the bar. 'Down the passage. By the fags machine.'

He nodded, inclining the glass in thanks towards her, a gesture completed to a back already turned as she swung her attention back to the two customers and their conversation. 'Cheers,' he muttered to the glass.

He took a swig of the beer and made his way to a small table close to the side-door she'd indicated. Putting his cigarettes out next to his pint, he settled to wait until the time he had been told to make the call.

He smiled. '*James Bond*,' he whispered.

* * *

She considered the sharpness of the knife, held it loosely in one hand, the chicken breast in the other. She pushed; slowly, firmly, feeling its progress into the flesh, the glancing to the side where it met bone. A resistance. Then, a slow withdrawal, followed by a more solid push, the sudden progress through and out the other side. The emergence of the blade surprised her, cutting into the cushion of flesh across her palm. She dropped the knife clattering to the floor along with the chicken that fell to the work surface. Shaking her wounded hand, she held it up in front of her for closer examination.

'You alright, Karen?' Kevin called from the lounge.

'Yeah,' she called back.

'What's going on?' He appeared in the doorway holding

Michelle in his arms. She was giggling, reaching for the foam giraffe toy held out of reach in his free arm. 'Eh, you cut yourself?'

'Yeah. Stupid. Not thinking.'

He moved closer, examining the cut. 'You want to be careful. Does it need a plaster or summat?'

Karen moved the hand to her side. 'No. It's okay.'

She bent down, picking up the knife from where it had clattered to the floor. He nodded his head towards it. 'Them knives are lethal. Dad sharpened them the other day. You need to watch what you're doing with them.'

'Yeah. I'll be careful.'

'That chicken looks good.' He hunkered the giggling and squirming Michelle higher in his arms, wrapping her a little more firmly. 'Dad gets it from that bloke with the farm over Hurley way. Ex-miner he is.' He jiggled Michelle up and down. She giggled joyously. 'Known dad since they both worked at the pit together. He's like everyone else around here, they all want to help out. See us win.'

Karen picked up the chicken portion and washed it under a running tap. Kevin moved closer. Michelle reached out an arm, tapping her mother's shoulder, pulling at her hair.

'We're doing better than most,' he said, his voice softer.

'Yeah, I know.'

Following his daughter's example, he used his free arm to reach out, rubbing his wife's shoulder. A gesture of comfort, of togetherness. 'Dad always manages to find stuff. Tries to help out.'

Her back stiffened under his touch. 'I know,' she said.

It was true. Everyone else had turned their gardens over to vegetables, but Brian Terry had an allotment which she assumed to be the source of the extra food that found its way to their table; that and his farmer friend from Hurley.

Kevin continued to massage her shoulder, seemingly unaware of the growing tautness under his touch. 'He's a good man. I know you and him don't always get along... see eye to eye like. But he's just doing what he believes is best. She'll destroy the mines, you know.' *She* was she who did not have to be named. *She* was Thatcher.* 'She'll do it too unless she's stood up to. It's like what dad says, what Scargill says. This is the line, the moment when we have to take a stand. Not just for us, but for Michelle and Ricky. Their future, their kids.' He instinctively smoothed his daughter's hair from her face. She snatched the giraffe from him, cooing with delight. 'We have to. We owe it to them.'

Karen kept her back turned. 'I want better for them than the pit,' she said. 'I want more.'

She pushed the knife once more, this time deeper into the breast of chicken. This time there was no hesitation, no resistance.

'Steady on,' Kevin said from over her shoulder. 'You could hurt yourself again.'

* * *

The phone call had taken just a few seconds, a cryptic series of call and response. Nothing more than a place, a time. Returning to the bar, Brody had finished his drink followed by a second, before once more consulting his watch and walking outside.

It was Plant's contact, a man he'd at first hinted was police. Later, he'd backed off that idea, suggesting that his contact was rather a man who *'knew stuff'*, a man he'd advised was someone not to be crossed. As he stood waiting, Brody speculated as to precisely what that meant.

Within two minutes of his standing on the street a dark green Austin Marina car pulled up. The rear door opened, and Brody climbed inside, the door barely closing before the car accelerated away.

The hands that pushed him back in the seat and, so he supposed professionally frisked him, belonged to a large man with the build of a boxer. He'd broad shoulders, a stocky neck, and muscular tendon-ribboned arms. The man's age suggested he'd seen his last bout some years ago and for some reason Brody thought *army*.

'Clean.' The man reported to the two in the front seats of the car. The front passenger nodded in confirmation, exchanging glances with the driver. The car suddenly swept first left, then right, passing the central police station before turning back onto itself and following the main road out beyond the cinema, past the old hospital and the F.E. college and finally out into the country roads beyond.

They travelled about two miles before the front passenger, having assured himself through several looks into the rear mirror that they weren't being followed, indicated that they pull into a lay-by. The driver switched off the engine and turned off the headlights. He turned in his seat so that he half-faced Brody and the Big Man.

'Out,' he said.

The Big Man leant across Brody and opened his door, a commanding nod of the head ushering him out into the lay-by. Standing upright, he looked across the roof of the car separating him from the front passenger who had also exited the vehicle. The man moved down the length of the car motioning for Brody to follow.

They walked a few paces to a hedge separating tarmac from field. The passenger leaned against the fencing and produced a pack of cigarettes.

'Quite an operation,' Brody observed.

'Precautions,' the man stated, a voice flat and clear, one not easily ruffled.

Brody accepted the proffered cigarette. 'Is all this supposed to impress me?'

'No,' the man replied matter-of-factly. 'It's to keep me clean. Meeting with journalists, particularly those with sympathies like your own, isn't the sort of thing I'd want to get around.'

Brody nodded. 'Our mutual friend said you were a man of principle.' Brody took a light from the other's match. He drew in a deep lung full of smoke. Exhaled slowly. 'It's unusual to meet someone like yourself, someone in your line of work who supports what we believe in,' Brody continued.

The man lit his own cigarette and, in the glare of the match, Brody was able to discern something of the man's features. Smooth shaven, slight pock-marking in the cheeks from childhood illness. The nose was large, thin and hooked. The eyes were dark, deep set, seeking shelter under a brow that was angular, almost square.

'My line of work?'

'You know. Intelligence. What is it, Special Branch?'

The man shook the match dead, plunging them back into darkness. He blew a thin trail of smoke out, examining Brody, maybe searching for some sign of whether what the journalist had said about '*principle*' was genuine or if the man was a flatterer out for his own ends. 'Listen,' he finally said. 'You know nothing about me. Nothing. And I want it kept that way. I was told there was information you wanted about the picketing. Information I can help you with.'

'I just wondered about your... motives. Whether Tim Plant is your dealer or your grass.' Brody smiled. 'You know, whose pulling whose chain.'

The man's movement was sudden. The cigarette one moment idly at his side, the next millimetres from Brody's eye with the man's other hand holding Brody's head immovable. His palm was across Brody's face, thumb spread wide and gripping the eyelid to pull it hard up into the socket, exposing the eyeball. The weight and position of the man's body held Brody tight against the fencing.

Brody saw nothing but a red glow; felt nothing but intense heat. The man leant his own face closer to Brody's. His voice, a whisper, remained flat. 'My motives are just that. Mine. As far as you're concerned I'm doing a favour for a friend. Understood?'

The moment was held, Brody's understanding allowed the time to descend to his rational mind. His eye felt dry, hot, burning. His tears were sizzling dry in the socket, the heat-pain unbearable. There was a sense of dread, a fear of the consequence of any struggle, any sudden movement. For a long moment he anticipated the fierce pain that would be the consequence of any movement, any decision by the man that this was a cause not worth his time, his trouble.

The man stepped back, loosening his hold, releasing Brody as quickly as he had held him. The man took a slow drag on the cigarette, the ash glowing red.

Freed from the pressure, Brody staggered upright, reflexively rubbing his eyes. He pushed himself off the fence, looking out at the world through the curtain of his parting fingers, hands held either side of his face like blinkers. His vision was blurred. Fireworks. Staring at the sun. He shook his head. 'For Christ's sake!' he shouted. 'What was that for?'

'That was me, making a point.'

Brody rubbed at his eyes. 'Point? What fucking point?'

'Too many questions. Too much speculation about me, my motives. You don't need to know anything about me. That's not part of the deal.'

Brody squeezed his eyes alternately shut tight and wide open. 'For Fuck's sake, I'm a journalist. It's what I do.' He bent double, squatting back on his haunches. He pulled a handkerchief from a coat pocket and flicked it open. 'I'm supposed to ask questions.'

'You know what they say about curiosity. Killing the cat.'

Brody scrabbling his hands around, picked up his cigarette from the floor where it had dropped in the attack. He drew in a long comforting lung full of nicotine. 'Yeah, well you know what they say about cats. Nine lives.'

'You might need all of them on this one.'

Brody tentatively rubbed at his face with the handkerchief. 'Whys that?'

'After Tim called me I asked around. Seems there are a lot of people anxious about the outcome of this investigation. Powerful people. People with a great deal at stake. People who don't like losing. People who don't like anyone interfering where they're not wanted.'

Brody rubbed his eye. 'So who are these powerful people?'

The man grunted. 'Who do you think? Government.

Security Services. Politicians. High-ups in the police. Take your pick.'

'Hardly news. The broadsheets are full of editorials about the government's desire to beat the miners. Police being manipulated by the government. It's nothing new.'

'I'm talking about something more than twisting the arms of a few Chief Constables on the look-out for a knighthood. I'm talking conspiracy. I'm talking about the sort of things that get people like you hurt, badly hurt.'

Brody shook his head clear, wiping at his face, tentatively dabbing with the handkerchief at the corner of his eye. 'So what is it? You're saying Jackson was battered to death in a baton charge and his senior officers are planning a white-wash? Again, nothing new. Nothing that the miners' haven't been claiming.' He looked at the man, his outline thick and impenetrable against the darkening sky. 'What are you offering? If you're *the Job* - a copper - what do you know? Bit of canteen gossip? Someone boasting about beating a miner like that wanker on today's front page? What do you know that I can use? Something new. Something worth my time.'

'I know a great deal Mr. Brody. For instance, I know a great deal about you. I know you're looking for a big story, something more in keeping with your sense of your own political credentials than what you've been given lately. Local council elections, meetings of little people plotting for world socialist domination. The *apparatchiks* who think their meetings and their motions and petitions and rulings will change the world.'

Brody levered himself upright. His eye was sore, the socket tender, certain to bruise. 'So what are you giving me? Police brutality? Over-reaction. Lack of leadership and restraint from senior officers? Is that it, because, if it is, it's not a fat lot more than everybody else on this story has got.'

'What I'm offering, is that Stephen Jackson was a great deal more than some poor miner killed on a picket line. Stephen Jackson was a lot more than a miner.'

'I know. He was an activist. He was one of the local militants.'

The man smiled.

'What?'

'Stephen Jackson was army. Records say he was discharged nine months ago.'

'Army?'

'Army. Three years' service. Queen and country.'

'Is this common knowledge?'

'That rather depends on whose asking the question,' the man responded.

'The police must be aware. You're aware.'

'Some of them.'

'Some of them?'

'Those who need to know.'

'I don't get it. What relevance is the fact that he was once in the army? Lots of men were once in the army. Probably more than a few miners were at one time or another. What are you offering? A man who served his country killed by police? A human interest story. It's not what I was looking for.'

The contact nodded, at the same time dropping the stub of his cigarette and scraping it into the gravel. 'You ever heard the phrase *to hide in plain sight*? Give an investigator something that they'll likely find out anyway, something genuine, something that stops any further enquiries.'

'Like a false wall?'

'Exactly. A false wall. A wall around a truth you want to keep hidden. Like the real story of Stephen Jackson's army career for those who might want to ask. The story according to his records is that he was dishonourably discharged.'

'Okay. So the man killed in the baton charge was an ex-soldier. A disgraced one at that. I'm still don't see a story worth all this cloak and dagger.'

'Ah, Mr. Brody, there you have it.'

'Sorry?'

'Cloak and dagger.' The man considered the phrase. 'You wanted to know my background. It's ex-service. I now ply my trade in what I like to call the independent sector. My current employer is a local businessman, a club owner and property developer seeking to expand his operations. In return for certain favours, say from those in a position to advance his planning applications, he's happy in loaning some of us out. A little bit of free-lance security work during the strike. So you see, I know what I'm saying when I tell you that Stephen Jackson was more than just a picketing miner. More than just army. Prior to his discharge, I knew him. The man, that is. You see, up until his discharge he had another name. Another identity. The man you know as Stephen Jackson was Army Intelligence, Special Ops. He was working for Special Branch. They loaned him to the police. Special duties. A unit they call the SDS. You see, Stephen Jackson didn't die in that field for the simple reason that Stephen Jackson never existed.'

Fourteen
Day Five

Brody sat in front of his typewriter considering the story he could write: an army special operations soldier killed on a picket line. Why had he been there? *Answer: he was under orders.* What had his orders been? *Answer: to provoke violence and undermine the strike.* Jackson was an *agent provocateur*. A soldier on loan to the police. A soldier working for the security forces with the aim of discrediting the pickets. He was there to break the strike.

A unit created to infiltrate the left. A unit charged with gathering intelligence, the evidence to prosecute miners for acts of violence that they themselves would instigate. They were deeply embedded according to his contact. Deep in the communities and organisations they sought to destroy.

There was some irony in this. He knew of several attempts by militants to instigate violence by placing their own activists amongst the pickets to provoke police attacks so that the miners in turn would wish to retaliate. Workers uniting against the forces of suppression. Workers against the state. The spark for a revolution. It would have been like Paris in 68. Prague in 69. But it had failed. The confrontations had been bloody and violent but hadn't drawn in other workers or other industries. The leaders of the big trade unions were scared of losing control. Scared over losing their positions, their peerages.

But evidence of security forces employed against strikers? Evidence of the politicisation of police actions? Evidence of a well-planned and co-ordinated state conspiracy to destroy workers' rights? If he could get it in the majors, the credible ones, it could bring down the government.

Jackson may be dead, but there were others. It was a can of worms.

Plant's contact would never go public with his evidence, he was a criminal a gangster. Whatever his previous employment, he was certain that he worked for Robert Faulkner, crime lord of this parish. The Brummie crime family that was the city's own Reggie and Ronnie Kray.

He needed corroboration. No one on the majors would publish a story without it. Without corroboration it would be dismissed as the ranting of the 'loony' left. He needed evidence of Jackson's military career and of his deployment to this unit.

He needed to talk with someone on the investigation team. Plant's contact had told him that there were some in the police who knew of the operation, the question was who. Was this DCI Kalus in the dark about Jackson or part of the cover-up? Did he know about his military service and his deployment in the strike? Whatever else, it pointed towards a motive for Jackson's death. A motive indicating cold murder rather than an accidental killing. Stephen Jackson was killed because of who he was, what he was doing. But by who?

But a miner would want to expose him, not kill him.

So who? Answer: his own. Special Branch. The SIS. The Spooks. But why? Why kill one of your own?

He picked up a biro and doodled on a notepad.

Maybe Jackson was about to tell his story. Maybe whilst undercover he'd gone native, switching sides to the miners, the men he'd worked alongside. Maybe living so long in their community he'd come to sympathise with their cause.

Then again, maybe it was just an accident, coincidence. That he happened to be the wrong man in the wrong place. A baton charge gone wrong. Maybe his death was one with no reason other than police brutality. He was an unlucky victim with a secret that now had to be veiled by his masters.

Too many *maybe's*.

He looked at the scrawled mix of names and question marks he'd made on the pad. Whatever else might be here, Jackson was the story. His death, whatever its origin, was a trigger and he was going to pull it and take his place in journalistic legend. Woodward and Bernstein. Fleet street. The Big Boys.

He spent ten more minutes scribbling on the pad. It was a series of words, names, ideas, and organisations. Some of them he circled and then linked to others with a series of arrows and lines. He circled one last idea before finally tossing the biro down and sitting back.

He stared at the pad, teasing out the sense of what was there.

The detectives on the investigation couldn't possibly know. If they did, they would be intent pushing their investigation into just the miners and the pickets. He knew that wasn't the case. That they were pursuing an investigation of the police on duty that day told him they hadn't a clue as to the real reason for Jackson being on the picket line let alone that they might be aware of his fake identity.

And, of course, the security forces couldn't possibly tell them the truth because that would mean they would have to admit that they were using *agent provocateurs* on British picket lines. That British security forces, under the direction of the government, were attacking the very constitution they were supposed to be protecting. That they were breaking the law.

Special Demonstration Squad.

A conspiracy.

It was a revelation that could bring down Thatcher. There would be demands for the curbing of intelligence operations. The murder of IRA suspects in Gibraltar had already led to media scrutiny and the questioning of their activities, of whether they were out of control. Such an action on British soil would see them leashed for a very long time.

It was the story of a lifetime. A series of stories. He would become a leading figure in investigative journalism, feted amongst the left.

All he needed was corroboration.

If the investigation team were unaware of the man they

called Jackson's military service, then maybe in return for inside information and an exclusive, he could educate them. Blow it apart from the inside.

But who was in on it? Who could he trust to approach in the Staffordshire force? Who in the investigation team? He had no contacts within the police. Politics, not crime, was his particular beat.

He picked up yesterday's local paper, flicking through the pages to find the by-lines for reports on the investigation.

Eddie Kramer. Crime reporter.

He picked up his biro and circled the name. Maybe this Eddie Kramer could be persuaded to extend a little professional courtesy to a fellow hack. Provide some background on this Kalus and his team.

He knew about Handsworth, Rueben, but it was sketchy. There'd been no need at the time to pay too much attention to the story of an operational blunder by the police, even one that had led to such a tragedy.

With help from Kramer he could write the story that he knew was there. His future was calling, and its name was Stephen Jackson.

* * *

'So you're saying there's nothing at all. Nothing we can use.'

Mick Robert's voice crackled back down the line, '*No guv.*'

'Right. Okay, get yourself back here. See if you can lend Jimmy a hand with the Book.'

'*Okay, guv.*'

Kalus dropped the receiver back onto the cradle. He scribbled out a line from the sheet of A4 paper cello-taped to the table. It was a list of options for progress in the investigation.

'Bad news?' Mallen asked.

Kalus tossed down the biro. 'Roberts. Nothing doing with the video stuff.'

'Well, it was a bit of a long shot.'

Kalus studied the list. The number of scribbled out lines were growing. 'We don't seem to have much more than those at the moment.'

Standing next to the table, Mallen twisted his head, scanning the list. 'What about your man Riordan? Any insights from him?'

'Not much. Ever since that day at the union offices he's kept pretty quiet.'

'The lads find him a bit... creepy.'

'Creepy?'

'Yeah, the way he's always hovering around. Listening. Watching. Bit like a ghost.'

'What do you make of him?'

Mallen considered the point. 'After the riots in '81 we had visits from Complaints. You know, the usual stuff. Accusations of assaults and aggression by the locals. I mean, yes people got hurt – after all, it was a fucking riot. But you know the Complaints boys, they came and stuck their noses in, just breezed in and lauded it over us. They made their judgements and then pissed off again. You know what they're like.'

You know what they're like.

'So your point is?'

'They had a ... way, a manner, an air about them. But Riordan doesn't have that. I mean, don't get me wrong, he's an arrogant prick all right, but just not in the way of Complaints. They sort of... put it on, like it goes with the job. Like wearing a hat or a coat. Riordan's not like that. With him it's more natural. On top of that, he doesn't seem to revel in his work like the rest of them. It's like... well it's like it's not really of interest to him. It's like he's got something else occupying him. Something more important. Something beyond the likes of the rest of us.'

'Such as?'

Mallen held up his hands, 'Hey, you asked what I thought of him, not for *Gypsy Rose Lee's Fortune Telling*. What about you?'

Kalus sat back. 'Me?'

'What do you make of him?'

Kalus moved his head rhythmically in thought. 'I know what

you mean. He just stands there, a presence. Apart from the do with Terry and McKinnon, he's not said or done a great deal.'

Mallen tapped a pencil he'd picked up from the desk, letting it fall up and down in a staccato movement. 'That's what I mean. Shouldn't he be asking questions? Investigating? So far all I've seen him do is look at our records, looking at what we've been doing.'

'Yeah, well I suppose that's what Complaints do. Paper Policemen. Records, files, transcripts, reports.'

'White says he checks the Murder Book all the time.' Mallen dropped the pencil back on the table. 'It's like he's looking for something in particular. Like he's waiting to see it there.'

'White say anything else?'

'He says Riordan's particularly interested in Jackson's private life. Always scribbling down details from the Book about anyone who knew him. White says he seems more interested in investigating what we know about Jackson than the details of the picket-line that day or how he was killed.'

Kalus shrugged. 'Maybe he's getting background.'

Mallen shook his head, face creasing in considered dismissal. 'What for? I just don't see it. What is it about a dead man's life that so interests Complaints?'

It was Kalus' turn to shake his head. He knew Mallen to have good instincts. 'What do you think?'

Mallen scratched the back of his head. 'Well, for one thing, I don't think Riordan is being honest with us about why he's here.' He looked Kalus in the eyes. 'I don't think he's Complaints and, if he is…' He widened his arms in an expansive gesture of uncertainty, 'Then it's more than just this one miner's death he's interested in investigating.'

Kalus found himself unable to disagree. There was more, surely much more to DCI John Riordan than met the eye. More to his sudden appearance on the case. If that were the case, then it meant that there was more to the killing of Jackson. That there were things they hadn't been told. Things that Ridgway wasn't letting him in on.

He felt a growing headache, a tightening band around the top of his skull. He massaged his temples, concentrating hard on breathing, on slowing the rising palpitations in his chest, the growing desire to run from the room. He stood up.

'Are you okay?' Mallen asked.

'I'm fine. Just a bit... Too much coffee. Not enough sleep.'

'Amen.'

Kalus went to the toilets, entering the furthest cubicle and latching it shut. He sat on the pan, resting his head against the cool of the cubicle wall. He held a hand up in front of him. It wavered.

He tore off a length of toilet roll, wiping a brow that was wet with sweat.

What the fuck was wrong?

* * *

Karen sat back on her haunches surveying the array of items she'd scattered around her.

She'd dropped Ricky and Michelle at school and the nursery play group. Returning home, she'd spent the last two hours emptying cupboards, draws and folders in the search for something that would give substance to her suspicions about Kevin.

The suitcase dragged from under their bed had been the latest object of her search. It was its contents that was now spread across the carpet as she sat on the bedroom floor mired in frustration. Nothing. A pair of old beach shorts and a few bits of memorabilia from a holiday over eighteen months ago along with a few envelopes and folders full of old gas bills and receipts.

In terms of evidence, proof of Kevin's guilt, proof that would persuade the police to provide her with the protection and new identity she craved, there was nothing. One thing, just one thing - a letter, a note, maybe a plan scribbled on a scrap of paper - and she would have him. With Kevin arrested and charged they would surely have to move her. They would understand that she couldn't be left in the midst of his family, not with a father in law with a history of violence, a man regarded as a leading figure in the wider community who would present her actions as a betrayal.

But there was nothing. Not a scrap.

She sighed, pushing her hair back over her ear and setting about dragging the contents towards her and stuffing it back into the case.

There had to be something. Some evidence that he'd had known about her and Stephen. She knew Kevin was a man of lists and notes. His union work meant he'd become almost obsessive about keeping details of phone-calls and minutes of meetings. The strike and the distribution of welfare meant that it had become even more of a necessity to keep a record of who had been spoken with - what they wanted, what they needed, what they had been given. He had notes of strikers, details of scabs and suspected scabs. He had details of votes and the directions from NUM organisers as to how to progress the action. There were pickets to organise, plans of protests to be held. Meetings to book, flyers to be created for them and then printed and distributed. Letters to MPs. His life had become a series of lists and details. Somewhere amongst it all there had to be something. A doodled note. A plan. Something.

She glanced at the clock. Time to fetch Michelle from her nursery playgroup.

She went downstairs and gathered up her coat. She looked out of the back parlour window, checking if the morning rain had stopped. She looked down the garden, overrun with weeds. No one had time for gardening now apart from the patch that Kevin, like so many miner's with families, had begun converting to vegetables. Everyone had dug up their lawns and planted them. Kevin's efforts had ceased at the digging up of her flowerbeds. Too busy with the strike to finish it. As far as she knew, the seeds for the crop provided by the Miner's Welfare were still in his shed.

The shed.

The shed, where he'd installed an old kitchen table and chair so that he could work on the organisation of the strike without disturbance from the kids, without them messing up his papers. His papers. The one place she hadn't looked. Hadn't looked because he kept it locked and he always took the key with him.

Fifteen

Late lunchtime, the bar still crowded; office workers stretching their break, a few loud students who seemed to be celebrating something, along with the regulation barstool inhabitants that frequented such places. Brody scanned the room even though he knew from what he'd heard about the man that the only place he'd really needed to look was the stool at the far corner of the bar.

Eddie Kramer. *Fast Eddie* as he liked to be called after a character in a Paul Newman film, was in his late thirties. He had tightly curled brown hair, a pronounced 5 o'clock shadow and pale skin. In all things, he was average and inconspicuous, a face easily forgotten except for the fact that most days it could be seen adorning columns of print in the *Birmingham Post* and the *Birmingham Evening Mail*.

Fast Eddie, like his film namesake, had risen relatively young. Starting as an office junior, he had quickly shown a keen eye for self-promotion and a willingness to ingratiate himself with those who could best serve his career. A temporary posting to cover the holiday leave of the then established crime reporter had coincided with a massive drugs bust. Eddie had proven adept at toeing the party line, in using the press releases of the West Midlands Regional Crime Squad as the basis for his reporting. His series of articles on the case and the *'heroic'* exploits of the WMSCS had prompted positive feedback to his editors from the squad, alongside their guarantee of exclusive inside knowledge should he be allowed to continue in the role.

The years since had been productive. Eddie maintained his inside link to the WMSCS by providing a stream of articles lauding their contribution to the safety of the city. His work had helped in deflecting some of the more awkward questions concerning police integrity now gathering like a storm cloud around the squad.

Brody crossed to sit on the stool next to him. Kramer glanced sideways, appraising him. He removed the cigarette from his mouth, placing it on the lip of an overflowing ashtray. He half-turned, awkwardly extending a hand in greeting. 'You must be Brody,' he said, a perfunctory shaking of the hand before turning and retrieving his cigarette.

'Thanks for meeting. Drink?' Brody inclined his head in the direction of Kramer's glass.

'Very kind. Whiskey. Double.'

Brody waved his wallet in the direction of the white-shirted barman. 'Whiskey, a double and a pint of M&B.' The two watched in silence as the barman poured the drinks, took their money, and finally wandered away down the bar.

Kramer raised his glass, dipping it in Brody's direction. 'Cheers.'

'Cheers.'

Kramer set his glass back on the bar, savouring the taste. He half-turned back towards Brody. 'So, you've got information for me.'

Brody inclined his head to the side. 'Sort of. A story I'm working on that might be of interest to you. A collaboration.'

Kramer gave a look of distaste. 'I don't do collaboration.'

'Of resources,' Brody put in quickly. 'Information. You use it to write your story and I write mine.'

Kramer dragged deeply on his cigarette. 'And what would your story be? Strikes me someone like yourself wouldn't have a lot of interest in crime.'

Brody placed his glass down. 'I see you've done some research.'

Kramer half-smiled. 'Look, no disrespect, but some bloke rings me up and wants a meeting, says he's got valuable information for me… I look him up, I make a few calls. This line of work, I've got enemies. I need to be careful who I meet.' He picked up his glass, waving it in front of them to take in the bar, 'And where I meet them.'

'Crowded bars.'

'Always. Somewhere nice and public anyway. Careful, see?'

Brody nodded. The dialogue was already a negotiation. *What to give; what could be achieved; what price.* 'I understand. I've had some run-ins myself.'

'Yeah?' Kramer scoffed. 'But if I'm not mistaken, yours were with the police, the authorities. Not quite the same as the mobs that run around my turf. Then there's the Irish.'

'The Irish?'

Kramer turned, facing Brody full on, the glass now jerked back and forth between the two for emphasis. 'Look, just because they have some cause, something your lot on the loony left would no doubt express sympathies with, doesn't mean that they have some holy or political righteousness on their side. How do you think they get the money for the guns and the bombs? Not from sending a bucket around the *Irish Harp* or the pubs in Dale End or Moseley. We're talking serious money, serious crime. That drugs haul the other day, that *Operation Bishop* or whatever bloody codename them Special Branch and Customs wankers gave it. Four tons of dope. Ten million quid's worth of hash from Pakistan on a boat from Cyprus, boarded off Essex by Special Branch and customs with eight Irish smugglers baby-sitting it. What do you think the paddies are smuggling dope for? They're not bloody hippies seeking cosmic enlightenment or a good high. The IRA don't want dope, they want what it brings. Cash. Funding for Semtex, Libyan guns. Irish muscle; Paki drugs.'

'Yeah. Suppose so.'

'No suppose about it.' Kramer tapped the side of his nose. 'I've got sources. There's more IRA in Brum then there is in Belfast. The amount of bloody Irish around Brum... Easy pickings. It's a crime-wave all by itself. Putting the screws on shopkeepers, pubs and businesses for protection. Where do you think all of that cash ends up? I tell you, it's a story and a half.' He leant forward, squashing the butt of his cigarette in the ashtray, a small flow of ash spilling over the bar. 'But write it and it'll be the last story I do.'

'Yeah. Well it's not a story about the Irish I'm writing. It's about the miners.'

Kramer laughed. 'Fucking miners!' Shook his head, downed the last of the whiskey. 'Sorry pal, not my beat. You want Dave Ensor. He does all the industrial and political stuff.'

'It's about the death of that miner out Tamworth way.'

'Yeah, I read about that.' He took another cigarette, waving the pack in front of Brody who refused. 'Johnson or something.'

'Jackson. Stephen Jackson.'

Kramer flicked his lighter. 'Yeah, Jackson.'

'The police are investigating it. I wanted to write something about him. Tell his story. I'm told by someone in the know that he was ex-army, that he more than likely did a tour in Ireland. No-one's mentioned it. Right wing press you see, they more than likely want to keep it quiet. You know, military man on the picket.'

Kramer lit his cigarette, inhaling deeply, blowing the smoke up and across the bar. 'What, so you want to make him a martyr for the commies?'

'I want to tell his story. You know, what makes him act. What makes someone like him, a man who served his country, stand on a picket line. What made him face the batons.'

Kramer flicked ash towards the ashtray, 'Made him toss the bricks. Beat up the scabs?'

Brody nodded, accepting the point. 'Maybe. Yeah, warts and all.'

'And what do you need from me?'

'A contact. A name on the police side investigating it. An introduction.'

'And in return?'

Brody, shrugging his shoulders, leant closer. 'Well, you said yourself, there's a story to be written about the IRA and crime. Maybe you'll get around to writing it. Maybe then you'll need a link to the *loony left*, the *commies*. And I'll be there. A contact, your inside man.'

Kramer screwed up his face in contemplation. He smiled, half-turning back to the bar and raising a hand to catch the barman's attention, which he then circled over the two glasses. The barman pulled the pint, poured the whiskey, took the money.

Kramer turned back to Brody. 'What are your credentials for this then? For delivering on what you say you can?'

Brody accepted the drink. He sipped slowly. 'Well, we've established that you've done some research. I've got to think that if you've done that, then the chances are that you've already checked out my track record, otherwise we wouldn't be here, would we?'

Kramer smiled. 'And you need my contact for what?'

'A few more details about Jackson. There's precious little out there. I need to know what the police have.'

'What about your chums in Militant or the local Labour Party? What about the miners? They worked with him. They must have more stuff than the police.'

'Yeah, well, I'll be talking to them, but you must know that Militant and the Party don't exactly see eye to eye on a great deal. The police might be a little more forthcoming in supplementing what I've got.'

Kramer considered Brody's response, weighing it. He grimaced. 'You're probably right. But it's a little more complicated than whether I believe you or not. How do I sell it to my contact in the Force? I don't think they'll feel too happy about providing bullets for someone with your political leanings to shoot them with. All this bollocks about the Crime Squad being investigated.'

'That's why I need to use you. A kind of guarantee that they'll talk to me.'

'And how do I look if you stitch them up with some story about a heroic martyr of the left?'

'We both know that no major newspaper would touch a story like that. Certainly not one from me. Look, I'll be frank with you; Militant's run its course. The way that the print industry's going, I need to get a piece into the mainstream. This could be it, my ticket to the Big Boys. I'll give you full approval.'

Kramer lifted an eyebrow. 'Full approval? Fuck, you are desperate!'

'I won't include anything that you or your contact don't give approval to.'

Kramer pursed his lips, looking carefully at the man in front of him, studying his face. 'Alright. I'll talk to a couple of people I know. Ones I use. If they're okay with it, then we'll put something together in the next twenty-four hours.'

'That's great. You won't regret this.'

Kramer shrugged. 'Maybe. Maybe not. But a word of warning. Professional courtesy if you like. Mess with these blokes and you might be the one with the regret.'

Brody nodded acceptance of the risk. He was in the game. Soon the rest of the media, hacks like Eddie Kramer, would be beating a path to *his* door. Begging him for *his* story.

How I brought down a government.
How I changed Britain.

***

Night. Always night. Such things always happen at night.

Midnight.

Comforting blanket-warm routines and rituals torn open by the incessant ringing of the phone in the hall. Sleep-dizzy stumble down the stairs. The heavy phone cradled, hand trembling. The voice - unfamiliar, distant and uncertain.

'You need to come as soon as possible…. Not certain what it is… He's okay but it's difficult to tell at the moment.'

The dash in the car.

Rain.

Always the rain. Pre-cursor of bad news, of tears.

Wipers slapping, headlights smeared.

The sprint from car to house. Fumbling at the key latch. The door opening, falling in. Turning, rain dripping on red raddled tiles. Shaking the collar, shaking the discarded coat. Flecks of water shed like tears.

The voices, the hushed tones. *'An event… gave him a scare… gave us all a scare… resting… don't be alarmed if he doesn't seem to recognise you… to be expected really… a difficult time.'*

Kalus sat staring at his father, the shape propped in the bed. The closed eyes, the slow unsteady rise and fall of his breathing. The rattle of lungs, a wet murmur of sound underscored by the rain spattering against the window.

A call from the District Night Nurse had summoned the locum doctor who in his turn indicated a call be made to Kalus and his sister. Kalus, being closest, arrived first. After talking with the doctor he'd rung his sister, passing on the medical opinion: *false alarm*. She, deciding that her presence wasn't necessary.

He had rung Anna. There was a spare bed; told her he'd elected to stay but would be back early in the morning before the children were awake. Her tired voice offered nothing in resistance.

He had sat for almost an hour. His legs ached; his back ached.

He stretched, pushing each shoulder forwards and back in turn, twisting his spine, then dipping each shoulder once more. He pushed each leg out, tentatively stretching first heel and then toe. Restless, he stood, moving to the window and pulling back the curtains, at the same time smoothing and lifting the nets up and to the side. The brightness of the room meant he could make out little other than the dull reflected glare of the bedroom lamp. He raised a hand, placing it against the glass to shield it from the shimmer of the pendant lightshade. He didn't really need to see. It was a landscape familiar to him, one that, apart from new streetlamps and one or two gardens being made into parking areas, had changed little in forty years. His memory filled in the details.

He let the nets, damp with condensation, slip back into place, tugging the curtains tight.

He turned and surveyed the room.

Bed, bedside tables, dresser, wardrobe - all matching; all wedding gifts. His mother's parents; proud of their daughter. Doing their part in seeing them off on their way, their new life together. Like his own mother; proud of her son, proud of his career, proud of his wife and proud of her grandchildren.

Her touches were everywhere. Even now. Looking round, nothing had been changed. He doubted whether some of these things had even been moved since her death. It was his father's very own Taj Mahal her memory. A way of keeping her alive, keeping some part of her here, still part of him helping in keeping the dark at bay. The blackness. The end.

He returned to the side of the bed, picking up the small silver framed photo of his mother. She was young, a dark ribbon in her hair, bow tucked out of sight. She smiled, an expression open, warm and full. Her eyes danced and blazed with life, eager with desire for all that lay ahead. She looked at the camera with what he could only see as the certainty of youth. She was carefree, a life lived thus far without consequence, without guilt or the weight of expectation.

He placed it back on the bedside table.

He stood looking at his father. Her husband. Her man. It was he who had held the camera and taken the picture. It was his eyes she had looked into beyond the lens. It was desire for him that shone from her, a desire captured forever, frozen in the frame that now looked out at his wheezing husk, watched his fight for breath, the dry carapace, the remains of a life. Past and present; the bookends of Andrej Kalus.

Was that how it happened? Those certainties of life, the things that you assume will be there forever slowly ebbing away. The things you never question, the things that you accept: love will never die; passion will never dim; the truth will always be known.

The curse of age was not just the slowing of reactions - the ache of muscles, the loss of energy - but the recognition, the darkly growing awareness, that things could be lost. That love could be lost, that passion dulled, and that a truth once so certain was now elusive - a changeling, a chimera, the ghostly outline of shimmering illusion. Certainty gave way to doubt; sharply drawn lines became ragged edges of compromise. Leadership, once so easy to slip into became an ill-fitting costume, harder to wear, harder to convince yourself that it remained possible for you to still carry it off. The idea taking hold that others recognised it too, saw what you saw: the costume was tattered and torn, worn-out beyond repair.

He shivered and looked down. His arms hung at his side, fists clenched. He screwed his eyes closed, taking deep breaths that helped still the tremors in his legs.

He sank back into the chair he'd dragged to the bedside.

He rubbed his eyes, grimacing once more at the light that filled the room, aware he would get little sleep.

He pulled his notebook from the jacket draped over the back of the chair. Flicking through the pages, he pushed his thoughts to nothing but consideration of the investigation.

It was proceeding on the lines sketched out for it, but it wasn't enough. They needed something to break; they needed some shift in the landscape they were trekking through that would show them the direction to go in. At present there were too many paths to follow with too few men to take them.

If they continued at their present rate it would be months before they had interviewed all of the officers and pickets. They were trying to filter them into priorities, but even here they had found difficulties. The key players such as the Watch Commanders and NUM leaders had never been at the sharp end of a picket. All they could offer amounted to nothing more than a broad backdrop to that fateful day's picket.

The identification of key junior officers and constables was difficult but possible. The role meant that had been visible leading others, showing their men a presence. The pickets were by contrast anonymous, mere shadows.

No one had seen Stephen Jackson leave the picket. No-one had seen him cross the field or be assaulted. No one had seen anyone dragging him, chasing him, or assaulting him. No one could verify that he had even been on the picket line standing next to them that day.

The time of death gave a two-hour window. It meant

he could have been lying there dead in that ditch at least two hours before he was found. Over an hour before the main confrontation had begun. If that were the case, then why had he been there? *What had been his purpose? Who had he met? Why had they bludgeoned him to death?*

Mallen had finished with the senior officers. His feeling was that all he was doing was going through the motions. For most of the day it had been a sequence of daisy-chain dolls, each interview mimicking the pattern of the one before and the one to come next. The officers had struck him as grim and resentful.

The miners' interviews were yielding similar results, just with more hostility.

And there was Riordan. Since his intervention at the NUM offices, the man had been as good as his word and hadn't interfered with anything the team were doing. Like Mallen, Kalus found this lack of intervention, the lack of any obvious forensic analysis of what they were doing, disquieting. Mallen was right; Complaints by their nature were all about interfering and questioning. Their very *reason-d'être* was pissing off working detectives who were trying to get the job done. Riordan appeared almost disinterested in the line of their enquiries. Kalus had checked with White, who'd confirmed Mallen's suggestion that Riordan had instead what appeared to be almost an obsession with the Murder Book and any personal information they unearthed concerning Jackson.

There appeared to be another game inside the investigation, one that Ridgway claimed to have no knowledge of. If Ridgway was genuinely in the dark then it could only point to Special Branch or one of the sister services. *Spooks. Spies. Cloak and dagger.* But why? What was the interest?

He wasn't naïve. He knew the stories circulating inside the force of security service action in the strike. Scargill was seen as a threat to national security. The strike of the seventies had brought the country to its knees. The three-day weeks; the blackouts. For some it was vital that the miners didn't win. Some said that they wouldn't be allowed to win, that there were troops on stand-by. He'd heard of plans for martial law if the strike should spread to the trains or the docks. What with the external threat of the IRA, the PLO, the Libyans and the Russians, there was little tolerance for the internal chaos of a Militant element stirring social unrest.

The police remained a bulwark, a bastion against civil disorder, but only if people saw them as a force of law rather than the muscle of government.

Special Branch had no such remit. If Riordan had been placed in the enquiry with a security agenda, its purpose wasn't yet clear. If it was a watching brief, then it surely concerned the extent to which the killing of Stephen Jackson could be turned to political advantage.

The problem he had was knowing that Special Branch rarely limited itself to merely watching.

Sixteen
Day Six

Brody watched the morning rain form into rivulets that snaked down the window, puddling at the base. He placed a finger on the pane, idly tracing the movement.

Drawing on a cigarette, he inhaled deeply, allowing the nicotine to do its work. He needed to focus on the piece he was writing, his interview early that morning with Kramer's contact. He picked up a spiral notebook, scanning his own variation of Pitman shorthand.

He read the notes once more and found himself coming to the same conclusion. DS Mick Roberts appeared to be exactly what he was: a jobbing police detective. In Brody's assessment, Roberts, like so many other detectives he'd met, had assimilated the traits of TV coppers. He was to Brody the embodiment of the Denis Waterman template of CID, an extra from *The Sweeney* all blonde hair and brawny physical presence. Officers who in the questioning of suspects played heavily on intimidation rather than underlying intelligence or any subtle plan.

He'd approached him using Kramer's reference.

Roberts had been remarkably candid. Police who spoke to the press were interested in two things: how much they were going to get for their information and concern that they would be protected from identification. Roberts had asked for neither. There had been none of the usual discussion about payment and no demand for covering up those details that would shield him as the source.

'I know what you people are like,' he'd stated when Brody had commented on it towards the end of their discussion. 'Any agreement with your sort isn't worth the breath it takes you to say it. You'd do me over and think nothing of it. All you want is a good story. Something to satisfy your editors and the thick bastards that buy your rag and thinking that they're getting the truth.'

Shortly after he'd left. But not before Brody had burrowed into his knowledge of the investigation. What they knew. What Brody realised they had been kept ignorant of.

He sat back at the table, balancing the cigarette on the rim of the ashtray. He scrolled the paper up above the bar of the typewriter to glance over the paragraph he'd just typed.

After speaking with sources close to the investigation of Stephen Jackson, it is clear that they have been given little idea as to the true nature of the man whose killing they are investigating. Whilst they spend time and resources interrogating miners and those close to the victim, I discovered evidence that not only indicates that Stephen Jackson was a government agent on assignment for the security forces, but that this may have been the motive for his murder.

He scribbled a few pencil notes around the text before scrolling it back down.

He took a long drag on his cigarette. Two things were clear: Roberts was close to the core of the investigation and they had no idea as to the true extent of Jackson's military record. They were aware he'd once been a soldier, but that was it. As far as they were concerned it was simply a detail on the man's CV along with his education and employment. What was it that Plant's contact had said to him? *Hide in plain sight.* Plant's source had told him that it was a fake. That it was the doctored military record of soldier who remained in special ops. A soldier loaned to the *Spooks* of Special Branch. So why was it being kept from the police, and by whom?

Again and again he came back to the same answers. *Military intelligence; operational reasons.* Jackson was active and therefore on assignment. He been at the mine for months. He'd been involved not only in the strike but in its planning. He'd been in a position to direct the picket line to the orders of the security services. Seen like that, an unhindered investigation of his death would precipitate the revelation of his operational role: *agent provocateur*.

Jackson's death was a problem for his controller, *His Masters*. They needed to direct the investigation into his death, bury his role and hide their wider operation. They needed to be sure that the investigation kept to the track planned for it. It meant having someone on the inside. Someone to guide it, someone nudging it back on course if it should seem to be moving towards a broader investigation of the victim and his background.

Roberts had mentioned an officer from Complaints. An officer who had arrived unusually early in the investigation. An officer sent from the Home Office. He thumbed back and forth through his notes to find him. *Riordan*.

He stubbed out his cigarette. Someone in a role like that was ideally placed to monitor all of the strands of the investigation. Placed to intercept reports at their source and spin them in a direction suiting Special Branch's operational needs.

The story was coming together. All he needed was access to this Kalus, the chance to reveal the depth of duplicity suffocating his enquiry. The chance to get in close. The chance to reveal the real reason for Riordan's presence, possibly his murder. The chance to show the government's intention to hi-jack and manipulate the investigation.

He spooled the paper out of the typewriter, rolling in a clean sheet, and began to compose a message. He needed a meeting. What could he say that might persuade this Kalus to grant access to a journalist at the height of a major murder enquiry?

Kramer had provided him with the details of another contact he felt might prove of use. A man who could pull strings, so Kramer had said. A man who could get things done. An officer helpful to the media and one close to retirement. A man whose back might be scratched. Detective Chief Superintendent Frank Ridgway.

He'd heard the name. An officer with a past closely connected to the dubious practices of the West Midlands Crime

Squad. It was far from unusual. It was a unit whose grubby tendrils were known to reach into many senior officers career paths. The key point was that he was Kalus' boss, the only man with the ability to instruct a meeting to be taken. Used wisely, Ridgway's name might prove to be the conduit he sought. After all, a message copied into his immediate superior would surely force Kalus to take a meeting.

He tapped the keys of the typewriter. It had to be a message telling the DCI and his boss that he was in possession of important information about the victim, information crucial in breaking the case.

Whatever his reservations about two officers both of whose pasts he'd learned to be flawed, they were his way into the story. If he could meet with Kalus, he was certain he would prove to be the lever by which he would break open the greatest political conspiracy of the age. It would be Watergate all over again.

He checked his watch for the post. If he was quick, by tomorrow morning Kalus and Ridgway would read his request for a meeting. By tomorrow afternoon Kalus would have the lead that would set him on his way to finding the killer they sought whilst he himself would have found the missing links of his story.

He began to type.

* * *

The rain beat against the window. Pushed by the wind it pulsed rhythmically, a drum-beat pattern, maddening in its irregularity.

Karen lay still, eyes wide open. Kevin lay on his side, his breathing deep and regular. She raised her head, looking at the luminous dial of the clock. He had been in the same position for over twenty minutes and his breathing had been settled for most of that time.

She slid a leg from under the duvet before easing the rest of her body out of the bed. Turning, she arranged the bedding back into position. She paused, holding her breath as she listened for any change in the pattern of his breathing, any stirring. She sensed movement, a shifting of position, but nothing more.

Re-assured, she tugged her dressing gown from under the bed where she had earlier hidden it. The last thing she'd wanted was the creaking of the wardrobe. Slipping it on, she crept out of the room, cushioning the door behind her.

His jacket was hanging on the hook by the backdoor. A quick rummage through the pockets yielded the key ring. The padlock key for the shed was on it, easy to identify being so much smaller than the Yale or the even larger mortise lock keys.

She slid the whole bunch into her dressing gown pocket.

The door to the garden opened easily. She'd pretended to check it as usual whilst they'd readied themselves for bed but had left the top and bottom bolts as well as the mortise itself unlocked.

Slowly, she made her way down the garden towards Kevin's shed. The moonlight was sufficient to make out Ricky's scooter and Michelle's abandoned bucket and spade. The path was slick with rain, but at least the reflected light made avoiding those obstacles easier.

Reaching the door, she fumbled in her pocket for the keys. She fingered through them until she found it again, small and stubby. She raised the padlock up and towards her, brushing the key backwards and forwards across it probing for the tumbler. She knew this operation might be noisy, but there was little she could do other than hope that she was far enough down the garden for the noise not to travel back to the house, back to the window where the children slept.

The lock snapped open. She twisted the horseshoe of metal, rotating it clear of the block until she was able to slip it out from the eye and hook fixed to the door.

She looped the bar of the lock back into the hook-eye and pulled the door open. It was lightweight and opened easily. Stepping inside, she pulled the door closed and waited for her eyes to grow accustomed to the gloom of the interior. As her eyes adjusted she became aware of a dim shaft of light coming in through the small window at the gable end. Beneath it stood the old kitchen table now serving as Kevin's desk.

Tentatively, she reached her hands out either side of her, anticipating sharp tools, cobwebs. With slow sliding steps she edged forward finding the edge of the table.

From her pocket she took out the children's pencil torch that she'd picked up from the coalbunker where she'd placed it earlier in the day. She pressed the button. The beam of light was intense in the confines of the shed, more than she had thought. In a panic she pointed it towards the floor, anxious for it not to be seen by the children or a neighbour. In the process, it somehow slipped from her hand, rolling across the makeshift desk, its beam swinging wildly searchlight style, back and forth, knocking a pencil pot and Kevin's letter tray to the floor. Scrambling, she grabbed the torch and punched at the button until the beam extinguished. '*Shit! Shit! Shit!*' she cursed. The last thing she wanted was to disturb the desk or any of his papers. She dropped to her knees and reached out with her hands seeking the pot, the pens, and the papers that had been scattered.

After a few moments scrabbling she was sure she'd retrieved everything, at the same time re-assured that no one had seen the torch beam or heard the noise.

She took off her dressing gown, draping it from a nail so that the pane of glass was covered. She switched the torch back on, now careful to aim it on a downwards angle.

She checked the floor, immediately finding a pencil and a sheet of A4 paper missed in her previous search for scattered stationery.

Confident that everything was back in place, she scanned the beam across the cork notice board hanging from the wall at the side of the desk. Charts. A wall calendar with a few dates circled in biro. There were sheets of A4 paper crammed with names and locations, each one something to do with marshalling the pickets at the mine. Pinned in one corner was a sheet with the address of the local coach companies that were being used to ferry in the miners. There were printed sheets, clippings from local papers detailing events with the names of the journalists and their bye-lines circled in red biro.

She lifted some of them; letting them fall back one at a time, each one similar to the one proceeding it. Lists. List after list of names, dates, times or places. Nothing. Not a thing about Stephen. Not a thing that might prove Kevin's involvement, suggest a link to murder.

She stood staring at the wall. Nothing. All that remained were suspicions, her doubts, nothing other than blind intuition. They were thoughts sensing the outlines of things, of truths and half-understood motives. But she was unable to give them definition. Knowing there was something there ahead of her, helpless to see what it was, she had stumbled towards understanding.

She looked back at the improvised desk. She'd already checked everything that was on it. The old kitchen table that had been her mother's, passed on when she and dad had refitted their kitchen. It had been moved out here before the strike when Kevin had finally built the breakfast bar she had so wanted. *'Faddy'* was how her mother-in-law had described it, one more example of Karen's desire to *always be better than those around her*, always wanting something more, *things she saw in those magazines of hers*. All she'd commented on was the loss of useful larder storage.

Storage. The old knife drawer. The kitchen table had a knife drawer. She looked down below the tabletop. Where was it? *The other side.* The table had been set with the drawer facing to the wall. *Why?*

Carefully, she dragged the table away from the wall, creating an angle from which she could reach round and ease out the drawer. But something was stopping her. She felt along the recessed handle and found what seemed to be a hasp and hinge with a small padlock attached. *Why lock the drawer?* All those years it had stood in first her mother's kitchen and later her own there had been no padlock. *Why now? Why face it to the wall?*

She pulled Kevin's keys from the pocket of the hanging dressing gown, shuffling through them, searching for one small enough to fit the padlock. Finding one, she returned to the table, leant around it, and slotted the key home. Turning it, the hoop sprang open and with a twist she was able to free it and open the drawer.

She slid her hand inside, fingers searching.

She touched what felt to be an envelope and dragged it towards the front of the drawer. It was large, A4 in size and bulging. She pulled it out, only for the front flap to open and the contents begin spilling back into the open drawer.

Quickly tugging it fully out, she looked back into the drawer itself.

Money. Wads and wads of money. Bundles of £20 pound notes. Some eight or nine in the drawer and bundles more still in the envelope.

She stood there unable to take in what she was looking at. Thousands and thousands of pounds. Tens of thousands. She took a step back. *How?* *How did Kevin come by so much money? What was it for? Where was it from?*

She sat on the stool.

More money than she had ever seen. More money than Kevin could possibly have earned in ten years, twenty, let alone to have saved or put away. So where was it from? How long had it been here?

She knew they were questions that would have to wait. She had to return it, put everything back where she'd found it. Wait, consider her options, work out what it meant.

She began stuffing the money back inside the envelope.

Doing so, she turned it over in her hands. Across the top corner, handwritten in black ink, was a name. *Robert Gordon.* The name was unfamiliar. *Who was Robert Gordon? What did he have to do with Kevin, with this money?*

She shook her head, continuing replacing the cash, her mind worrying away at what she had discovered.

If she hadn't found a link between Kevin and the murder of Stephen, then what had she found?

More importantly, what was she going to do with it?

Seventeen
Day Seven

He had been marked for great things.

He was part of the New World Order, the new orthodoxy; *Thatcherism*, the end of society, at least a society that was all about suckling welfare scroungers. The New Britain would be built by creating opportunities for those with the nerve to grab them. The rest would learn that there were no longer any free rides, no more free tickets. Everyone must pay.

They stood on the cusp of a great future, and it was his hand wielding the sword that was despatching to the margins of history all who opposed it.

All that was required was resolve.

He checked his watch, knowing the message had been sent, wheels set in motion. There had been no need to sit awaiting a response, the order would be relayed, followed to the letter. Yet still he'd lingered waiting for the new day to tick around, the change tolled out by Big Ben.

Already the sound of the city had shifted in anticipation. The Chimes of Midnight. Falstaff's notion of fortunes fading and of eras ending. Outside his window Whitehall was now a murmur, a wash of sound pinpointed by the odd blare of a horn or the screech of a siren rather than the bustle of early evening or the clamour of late night. He sat in his office, his war-room, the great leather topped desk comforting him with thoughts of those who had sat here before him. The great line of history. The torch passed from one to the other. The chimes of midnight.

Resolve.

A copy of Riordan's last report lay open, a white winged

bird fanned across the desk open at the pages where he'd finished reading. It had arrived late afternoon. It was the report that had clinched things. Riordan was clear. The miners' knew nothing of Jackson's role. The pertinent issue was the SIO, this troublesome DCI Kalus who appeared intent on finding the killer wherever it might lead and whatever its consequences. Riordan was doing a decent job of side-tracking him, but now there was the complication of some leftie reporter whose communication had been intercepted, its contents passed on by Ridgway.

The Minister sank deeper into his chair. He had been brought up on tales of family honour and daring-do. His father had served in war-time, a role requiring tough decisions, matters of life and death. He knew the stories. Those moments where the good of the many had been weighed against the necessary sacrifice of the few. Men and women had died on such decisions. The consequences could be lived with because they had been made of necessity. Some were sacrificed so that higher causes might be achieved.

The situation facing him was clear; should the true identity of Stephen Jackson become public knowledge it would bring down the government. It could not be allowed. Action had to be taken to prevent it. Leaks had to be plugged, loose ends tied up. There could be no equivocation. No room for doubt.

Silver Fox was a secret yet to be shared with the wider Cabinet. It was a card that Cabinet Group Twelve must now play. It would bind them together, each minister inextricably tied to the plan to not merely keep the nation running in the face of the strike but to its wider ambition of destroying the unions.

The lessons of '72 and '74 had been learned. Then the miners' had not only blockaded the pits but had succeeding in starving the steel plants and factories of supplies. This time the Government had been ready. Stockpiles of coal had been in place; months and months of careful logistics. Months and months of calculated planning for a fight to the finish. A fight to the death.

In 1974 the pickets had been bolstered by the sympathy

of the wider public. Everyone had wanted a chance to hit the bosses, to take a punch at the fat cats. In '74 the Three-Day week had been difficult, but some had almost come to see it as a welcome break from the monotony of the working routine. The brown-outs had been irksome, but some had romanticised them. Crucially, the violence had been limited. There had been scuffles here and there, but there had been little in the way of lasting physical confrontation. The miners had retained public sympathy.

Not now.

From the outset the *agent provocateurs* had been in place. The Special Demonstrations Squad. Men whose remit was to insert themselves into mining communities. Once there, embedded, they'd stirred the strikers to violent action. Their remit was to get miners out on the streets, convince them that something more than placards was necessary if they were to stave off the threat to their pits. They'd played on their deepest fears: the threat to their way of life, the threat to their families and to their communities.

The agents had traversed the nation from pub to pub, working men's club to miner's club. There they bought drinks, spreading tales of grievance that sparked anger and a clamour for action. They took names. Gathered intelligence. During the early months of the strike they had formed 'hit squads'. Transit vans of ex-police, ex-army. Boiler-suited men with boots and clubs, travelling the pit villages and the mining towns - Hattersley, Hemsworth, Orgreave. One night attacking the homes of striking miners, stirring the anger, stirring demands for retribution. The next night, attacking the still working miners' homes, the daubing of *scab* on walls and cars prompting those miners to a greater determination to work, a greater desire to oppose King Arthur.

They had been on pickets. Inflaming situations, throwing bottles and bricks.

They had stood on the lines inviting the police charges, inciting the melee.

They had been well briefed, making certain that the cameras

were there catching every detail, that the news each night was full of the violence of the miners. They ensured there were bloodied images of police officers led from the picket. They saw to it that reporters were attacked by *'miners'* hostile to the stories they told, the pictures shown.

Agitation. Disinformation. Bile. Hatred. Sticks and Stones. They infiltrated. They listened. They watched. They acted.

Their intelligence was fed to uniformed police, seeing to it that the motorways were blocked and the side roads patrolled. County forces stopping flying pickets from getting to the working pits. Later, under guidance from their intelligence, funnelling them to the pits where they wanted them to be, those where the police waited for them. Laying traps. Nottingham, Derby, Hemsworth. Finally, critically; Orgreave. The battle plans had been laid in advance. The ground selected. The measures directed to punitive effect. Shields and batons. Snatch Squads. Dogs. Horses.

Charge after charge.

The police knowing what would come.

When it would come.

Violence organised by men like Stephen Jackson. Army intelligence. Men at times themselves victims of police beatings, all adding credibility to their standing, their capacity to extract yet more intelligence, incite yet more violence from miners who held them as friends.

And at the sharpest point of the plan *Silver Fox* himself. A figure at the top of the NUM. A figure so close that King Scargill thought him a confidante, a trusted member of his inner cabinet. A man persuading them not to put matters to a vote, an action putting the strikers beyond the law and alienating tens of thousands of his own members. The revelation that such a figure existed would be more than enough to whet the appetite of the rest of the Cabinet. Once they knew that fact, then the idea that the truth of Jackson's death - *after all, such a small cog* - would destroy the operation they had created would be as unthinkable to them as it was for himself. They weren't fools. They would see the cost of such a secret getting out.

With that knowledge the Cabinet would agree to whatever was asked of them. After all, they would be deciding under *Her* watching glare. There would be no desire among them to look any further under the stone, to see what else lay there. *Silver Fox* was a hero, essential to everything. She had declared it so. He must be protected.

Jackson was an asset, a chess piece moved at the direction of those who understood the game they played. He had been a pawn, part of a bigger plan. The King was *Silver Fox*. Anyone knowing the game knew that a King must always be protected, no matter the sacrifice.

All that was required was resolve.

* * *

She lay in bed. She felt him next to her. Felt his heat. Aware now, more than ever, that she hated him. Hated him more than she ever had. More than during her post-natal depression. More than when she'd discovered the money he wasted in the pubs. More than when he lectured her about the strike and how it would *all be worth it in the end*.

She looked at the alarm clock, the luminous dial of fold-up travel clock they'd been using since selling the *Teasmade*. She'd watched, waiting for the new day to tick round, lain for hours unable to sleep, knowing it was the end now. Knowing that when it came just what the new day would mean. She couldn't go on living the pretence. Living the lies of love and care for her husband or her own family. She had a newly gained understanding that there was better. That she and Ricky and Michelle would be okay. That they could find a future better than anything they had here.

Since her discovery of the envelope with the cash the previous night she'd spent the day turning over the options available to her, resisting the urge to simply go back to the shed and take the money and run. Running meant preparations.

Where to go was least among them. How to travel? What to take and what to leave? How to find the opportunity to pack her own and the children's things without Kevin finding out.

To work, she needed Kevin to be arrested. To be taken away. For that to happen, she would have to tell the police. This time she would tell them what she knew and what she suspected. To work she would have to tell them who she was. How she knew that Kevin was guilty.

And he was. She was sure of it. It had been a week now and for all their interviewing of miners and police the papers said they were no closer to finding the killer.

It was because they were looking in the wrong place. They lacked a motive. A motive that only one man had. Given that motive, they would surely arrest him, break him. He would confess. She was sure of it.

Kevin had known where the pickets would be. Kevin had assigned them their places, assigned them their roles. It would have been easy for him. Using the confusion he would have separated from the main picket and attacked Stephen. She had seen the reports on TV. Seen the chaos. How easy it must have been for him to deliver the blows and then slink into the crowd.

But she was his wife. He couldn't hide it from her. She knew the tone in his voice, knew it when he spoke to her. Knew the way he looked at her. Somehow, she had given herself away. Somehow he'd found out about Stephen and had taken his revenge.

She would tell the police. Tell them all that she knew, all she suspected.

She had to make her plans. *How to get away?* How to get clear from Kevin, clear from his family and her own, the whole mess that was her life here. She had to think of a way to make certain that he could never find her. She needed assurance that once she'd told the police what she knew that they would take care of her. Witness protection, like in the films.

She would demand they give her a new identity. A new life. A fresh start.

And there was the money. The envelope with the name of the mysterious *Robert Gordon*. Were they clues? If so of what? The more she'd lain there thinking about it, the more certain she'd become that they couldn't be linked. Stephen had murdered for love, for jealousy and anger, not for money.

The question was did she have to tell the police about it. Was there a way in which she could turn Kevin in and keep that money?

To do so, she would have to do more than point a finger at Kevin. She needed proof, something solid proving that he'd murdered Stephen. If she could find it, she would get her new life, the life that had been denied her for so long.

* * *

Midnight chimed, a buzz of his watch. The rain had been falling for hours. Against the light of the waning moon, the drizzle created a silver haze shimmering the landscape. Not that from where he stood Riordan had a view of anything other than the empty car-park of the pub.

He flicked the stub of his cigarette into a puddle. It hissed briefly. He watched, mildly distracted from his vigil as it floated on the trembling rainbow-hued surface. He tugged back the cuff of his coat, twisting his wrist so that the glow of the lamp some ten yards away caught the face of his watch. He was late. Lateness unsettled Riordan. He knew the man's reputation. Lateness didn't figure anywhere in it.

A car turned into the parking area, lights bouncing as it negotiated the dips in the cinder. It stopped twenty paces from where he stood. The lights flicked off. He moved towards the vehicle, the passenger door opening on his approach. He climbed in, shaking the rain from his hair.

'So, what have you got for me?' the driver asked.

Riordan took an envelope from his inside pocket. 'This'

The Specialist took the proffered envelope, sliding out the folded paper.

Riordan studied his face as he read. It gave away little of his thinking.

The Specialist lowered the paper, pursing his lips. 'Genuine?' he asked.

'I think so.'

He passed it back. 'Who else has seen it?'

Riordan shrugged. 'Not sure. After Ridgway's call, I picked it up off the pile in the canteen, the desk they call the Murder Book. Maybe one of the other detectives might have seen it. From what's in the letter, this Brody's clearly got a source. I made a couple of discreet enquiries of my own with a contact in West Mids. I found out that he spoke to their tame reporter, bloke called Eddie Kramer. My contact tells me that this Kramer says he gave Brody a lead to a copper on the enquiry called Roberts. I've met him. He's the DS who was sorting through the media footage out at Pebble Mill. This Brody used him as a way to verify what the police know. He sent two copies of the letter. One to Ridgway and this one to Kalus. It's why I sent the report.'

The man nodded. 'It appears to have left us with few options.'

'Options?'

'He read your report. The Minister. I've had word. Instruction. We end it. We do it as quickly and discreetly as possible, but we end it. Too many loose ends. Clearly, we have to eradicate the source, Brody. He's the imminent threat, and this letter only confirms it. We deal with anything that flows from that as we need to.' He shrugged in thought. 'Maybe this Roberts, though I can't see that he knows anything about what's really going on. Low level. Containable. But Kalus.' He shifted in his seat. 'We may also have to neutralise that particular situation.' He looked Riordan in the eyes. 'If we do, then it needs to be done in a way that leaves no room for doubt.' Riordan nodded. It was expected. Built into his assignment here.

Decision made the Specialist moved on, considering the means. 'You say you made enquiries. What do we know about Brody?'

Riordan produced a second sheet of paper. 'He's Militant - the organisation, not his thinking. Bounced around the fringes of activism. Known to the *Branch* and *West Mids*. Writes for small-time journals and the like.'

'A believer, then?'

'Seems so. Though one with ambitions according to Kramer. Fleet street. The Big Boys.'

'Where's he live?'

'Moseley. That's in Brum. It's a student area.'

'Immigrants?'

'Yeah, pretty much from what I can make out.'

'Irish?'

'Yeah. It's where The Six came from, round there anyway.'

'Lives alone?'

'Yeah.' Riordan scrutinised the paper. 'Second floor flat.'

The man nodded towards the letter. 'Okay. The letter goes back. We don't know who knows he sent it or if its already been logged on the enquiry system. Bury it; lose it for a day or so whilst I make some arrangements, see if we can turn matters to our advantage in resolving the bigger problem. Handled the right way it might yet be the answer to whatever prayers our Masters have been offering.'

Riordan handed over the second sheet of paper. The man tossed it on the rear seat. Turning back he indicated the door.

'That it?' Riordan asked.

'For now. You know how these things work.'

Riordan nodded. 'What do you need me to do?'

'Everything that you've been doing. Eyes, ears. Distraction. Disinformation. Whitehall says keep this DCI Kalus on his toes. Dance him around.'

Riordan got out. He stood in the rain for a moment watching the car pull away.

He knew how things worked.

His Masters' had decided.

This man, his contact, had a reputation. Even amongst the very few who shared his rather specialised field of work he was a talent. Once he was called in everything else became subordinate. All other ideas, the different approaches and solutions were now redundant.

He was a fixer. A Specialist. A problem solver. His solutions final.

Eighteen
Day Eight

The knock at the door, though they had been expecting it, still managed to startle Karen sufficient for her to slop her cup of tea onto the carpet.

'Easy, babes' Kevin offered as he rose to answer the knock.

The voices murmured down the hall, the ritual of introduction and apology. Karen busied herself scrubbing at her spilt tea with a tissue. When the officers entered they found her crouched down on her haunches.

Kevin stood in the doorway behind them. 'These are the officers who've come to ask about Stephen.'

'Sit down,' Karen said rising, crushing the tissue in her hands. 'Bit of an accident with my tea,' she said, arms sweeping down in a gesture of revelation. 'Stains terrible if you don't get it out straight away.' She blushed at her meanderings.

'My mom swears by soapy water,' WPC Lawrence said, smiling.

'Can I get you some?' Karen asked. 'Tea, I mean... not soapy water.'

Lawrence smiled. 'That's kind of you.'

'They'll not be wanting a drink,' Kevin put in. 'I doubt they'll be staying that long. There's not much to tell.'

'Kevin, there's no need to be rude. They're doing their job. Stephen died.'

Kevin moved to the centre of the room to stand a few feet from the officers. 'Murdered. Murdered for standing his ground. Murdered for doing the right thing.'

'It's okay, Mrs. Terry. Mr. Terry,' Lawrence intervened. 'We understand. This is difficult for everybody, Mr Terry. No matter what you think of the police, your wife is right, there's been a death, one in circumstances that need investigating. We need to talk with everyone who knew him.'

'So you come here. Interrogating miners, his work mates.' Kevin sneered.

Lawrence maintained her composure. 'We're interviewing all of those that were at the pit that day, those officers on duty along with everyone who knew him. We understand that you were at the pit that day, Mr Terry. We also understand that Stephen Jackson delivered food parcels here to you Mrs. Terry, and to others on the street. We're just trying to get a better picture of him and of any possible motives for his murder.'

'Other than being a miner, you mean?' Kevin's words were loaded with obvious contempt.

'Kevin. It's not them you should be having a go at.' Karen wrung the tissue in her hands. 'It's a terrible thing. He was a lovely man. I can't believe that anyone would want to harm him.'

Kevin jumped in. 'That's why you lot should be looking at those who *would* harm him. Your own lot. Police. The soldiers dressed as police. The bloody security service.' Kevin stepped closer to PC Cummings who'd thus far remained silent. The distance narrowed to an arm's length. 'That's where your killer is. That's who murdered Stephen Jackson.'

Karen shook her head, moving in between her husband and Cummings. 'You can see we're all a bit upset by what's happened. Perhaps it might be easier if you interviewed the two of us separately. Maybe it'd save time.'

Lawrence exchanged looks with Cummings who was intent on focussing his attention on Kevin. 'That sounds the best,' she said.

'Perhaps you and I should have a chat in the kitchen,' Karen said, indicating the way out of the parlour to Lawrence reluctantly leaving Cummings and Kevin standing a few feet apart exchanging hostile body language.

'Maybe it might be better if I speak with your husband,

rather than PC Cummings,' Lawrence re-considered as Karen closed the dividing door.

'Kevin will be okay. I'd rather talk with you,' Karen responded whilst moving towards the cluttered work surface. She took a packet of cigarettes from off the worktop and pulled one out. She proffered the pack in the direction of Lawrence who shook her head. 'It's been terrible. I can't believe that he's... gone,' Karen stated. She lit the cigarette, drew in deeply.

Lawrence looked around the kitchen. The terraced house was old but had been updated. She was looking for a place of her own, so was as familiar with the style of older properties like this as much as those outlined on the glossy sheets picked up for the new builds going up around the town in places like Wilnecote, Glascote, and Fazeley. The kitchen was what they were lately describing as *galley style*; long and thin with little in the way of room. A small PVC covered table, what they termed bistro style, covered with brown and cream gingham check with two matching chairs tucked underneath stood opposite the outside door. A recently fitted breakfast bar meant it was where the room was at its widest.

Lawrence indicated the table. 'Is it okay?' Karen nodded.

Lawrence dragged out a chair. She sat and placed her notebook on the table. 'Were you close then?' she asked.

Karen exhaled slowly, allowing the smoke to float away. 'How do you mean?'

'Well, I understand your husband worked with Stephen.'

Karen nodded. 'He was on the committee.'

'Committee?'

'The strike welfare. That's why he was delivering food and stuff.'

'And that's how you met him?'

'Yeah.'

'What sort of man was he?'

Karen looked at the WPC bewildered, confused. 'He was... kind.'

'Kind to you?'

'Yes. I mean... kind to everyone. He delivered welfare stuff to the whole street, at least those who were miners.' Karen pushed herself away from the worktop where she had been leaning. She fiddled with the mugs sitting on the drainer next to where Lawrence sat.

'So you knew him well. Better than most, what with your husband being on the committee.'

'Suppose so.'

'Did he ever talk about any problems he might be having? Any threats, anything worrying him?'

'No. Nothing.'

'When did you last see him?'

'A few days ago. He came round to see Kevin.'

'What did they talk about?'

Karen hesitated. *What to say?* Her mind raced ahead of her. A jumble of possibilities pulled at her, tugging her one way then another. *Keep calm. Think. Think.*

'Kevin wasn't here.'

'Did Stephen say what he'd come to see him about?'

'No.'

'How long did he stay?'

Karen shrugged. 'I'm not sure.'

'Did he and Kevin meet after that? To discuss whatever it was Stephen had come round for?'

'I don't know. They might have done.'

'Not to worry, we can ask your husband and sort that out.'

'No. Don't... don't ask him.' Lawrence looked up from her notebook. Karen's body had visibly stiffened. She half-turned, holding the WPC's eyes before looking away, lowering her gaze. 'He wouldn't know... I mean... He didn't know Stephen had called round.' She turned back to the drainer, shoving the tea-towel on a vacant hook, tugging another cigarette from the packet. She lit it, sucking the smoke greedily down. She moved round, dragging out the other chair to sit half-facing the window at a right angle to Lawrence. 'He... Kevin, he's jealous. He gets worked up if he thinks a man's... looking at me, like interested.'

'And was he?' Karen screwed up her brow, so Lawrence clarified the point. 'Was Stephen *interested*?'

Karen inhaled again, her head resting on the steeple of her arms, elbows propped on the table. She chewed at a nail, cigarette smoke drifting across her face. She looked out of the window. The edge of the garden wall, the clothesline that led to the shed. *Kevin's shed. Kevin's secret.*

'Yes. Yes, I think he was.'

'And Kevin knew this?'

Karen was suddenly filled with the realisation that she was now where she wanted to be. Somehow she had got there. She had power. She had someone in front of her who would listen. Someone who would look. Someone who could change everything. *What to say?*

'You have to understand…' Karen's words petered out. She looked at Lawrence. Her eyes sought understanding, some response to the uncertainty she knew sat in her own. 'He's like his dad. His dad's a powerful man. He's a miner too, big in the union. He can be... aggressive, violent. He's been convicted for assault. You know, after a drink… there's been a fight in a pub. Some incident with the union too. An argument that got out of hand.'

'And you think Kevin takes after him?'

Karen considered her response. 'Maybe. At times.'

'Times like when he's jealous?' Karen drew on the cigarette, inhaling deeply before crushing it in the ashtray. 'Karen, did Kevin have anything to be jealous of? You and Stephen.'

'He spent time here. Whenever he came round with the welfare. You know, we talked. He was... like I said, kind. Interested in what I thought.'

'About the strike?'

'About everything. He was interested in everything I said.'

'And Kevin? Did Kevin know about Stephen's interest in you? About the time he spent with you?'

Karen weighed her words. 'I don't know. It's just... he's been odd with me, especially since Stephen was killed.'

'Odd?'

'Different. Secretive.'

'Secretive?'

Karen thought hard. A moment. A chance. *Now. Now*, she told herself. *Tell her. Tell her what it is you found. Tell her what you want.* 'A man called around to see him a few days ago...when he wasn't in. He wouldn't leave a message. I had to push him to get him to leave his name. Robert Gordon. Later, when I asked Kevin who he was, he got angry. Told me it was none of my business.' Karen looked Lawrence directly in the eyes. 'Do you know who he might be? What his connection could be to Kevin? Has anyone else talked to you about him... Robert Gordon?'

Lawrence shook her head. 'Robert Gordon? Doesn't ring any bells. I'll ask.' Karen watched as she made a note of the name. Watched the two words form on the page. Watched as Lawrence flicked the pages shut. 'I shouldn't worry. Could be nothing. It must be difficult for both of you. The strike. The worry.'

'It's more than that. It's like I said, Kevin's changed. He's distant. Cagey. Secretive. He spends a lot of time in his shed. His *office* he calls it. It's where he does his union business. He keeps it locked all the time.'

'Well, there's a lot of thieving going on, especially with the strike. A lot of people have been tempted,' Lawrence smiled.

'Yeah. I suppose you're right. It's just odd though.'

'Odd?'

'He keeps that key with all the time now. Since the killing, that is. And he's stopped letting me in there to clean. I just wonder why. What's he got in there that's suddenly so secret?'

***

'Many more left?' Cummings asked, huddling close to Lawrence. The short canopy of the door of the terraced house offered meagre shelter to escape the drizzling rain. She held the typed list of names and the addresses of Jackson's contacts clutched between them. She shuffled slightly to the side, away from her colleague. 'One or two.'

'How was Mrs. Terry?'

Lawrence wrinkled her nose, considering the question. 'Not sure. Distracted, maybe.'

Cummings nodded. 'To be expected. Not every day you get interviewed in a murder enquiry.'

'What about the husband? Did you two play nicely?' she asked.

Cummings ignored the sarcasm. 'Jesus, what an aggressive bastard! Didn't get more than a two word answer to any question. He looked like he was grinding his teeth for most of the interview. Don't think he unclenched his fists the whole time.'

'Do you think he's the violent type then?' she prompted.

'Not much doubt there. He hates the police with a real passion.'

'Don't most of them round here?'

'That's as maybe. A lot of frustration. There's many looking for something to lash out at. That's why the pickets been getting so tasty the past week or so.'

'So you think there's nothing in it, then?' she pursued.

'In what?'

'Kevin Terry being violent,' she spelled it out, words evenly spaced.

'I think Kevin Terry has been violent all his life. His dad has form for it. This strike's just an outlet for men like him and Kevin.'

'So you think he's capable of murder?'

Cummings looked at his partner, shocked. 'Blimey, that's a hell of a leap!'

'Someone killed Jackson. I don't suppose it's someone who does that sort of thing for a living. Whoever did it, I'm certain that their neighbours would go *Bloody hell! You'd never have guessed*! Isn't that what a murder is all about? I read at training college that most killings are committed by people who are known to the victim. Kevin knew Jackson. Knew him well.'

'So did his wife and thirty other families around here,' Cummings responded. 'Anyway, what's this about training books at the college? I didn't read that anywhere in the manual.' He tutted scornfully, 'You know, it's what some of the others were saying back then, you spent too long in that library.'

Lawrence knew precisely what Cummings was referring to. They had been graduates together, a cohort that had been a mix of men and women but predominantly men. A proclivity for spending free-time in the library rather than the bar had acquired her nicknames - *Miss Marple, Agatha, Nancy Drew*. A year later, here she was in Tamworth; tired, wet, confused, and still finding her ideas provoked male ire.

'She thinks her husband was jealous of the time Jackson spent coming round, that he suspected Jackson of having an interest in her,' she continued.

Cummings found it hard to hide his irritation. 'Christ, Helen! Most women think their bloke's jealous of them speaking with other men. If you ask me, they *want* their men to be jealous. Hardly a motive for killing someone.'

'I think you'll find it's one of the most common motives,' she offered.

'And what book did we read that in?'

Helen chewed her lip. It irritated her that she still fell back on such an adolescent trait, a remnant of her inability to follow through in arguments like this, the ones she'd learned some time ago didn't get her anywhere. Officers like Cummings were decent enough but saw their role as doing the shift, putting in the hours in the hope of sergeant's stripes. They wanted a cosy berth in the station, the steady 9-5. Solving crime was the remit of CID. Which was much the way that CID and her superiors saw it.

'Forty-two. The Robinson family,' she stated flatly reading off the list. Cummings turned up his collar and pushed his helmet strap more firmly under his chin. Helen stuffed the list into the pocket of her police issue gabardine raincoat and followed in his wake.

Miss Marple. Agatha. Nancy Drew.

Nineteen
Day Nine

Kalus sat at the table in the converted canteen reading through the notes of the interviews Mallen had typed up. The coffee someone had some time ago placed in front of him was cold. He swirled it around, exploratory, considering the merits of cold caffeine against no caffeine at all. He came down on the side of no caffeine at all.

The morning at his father's had been difficult. The care woman had been late again, so he'd been forced to kick his heels waiting. The call home had given little respite. Anna had been brusque, the children shouting in the background. She'd asked him when he'd be back, a question whose indeterminate answer had provoked a silence followed by a sigh and finally the inevitable *I have to go.*

What to say? His father was ill, verging on crazy. There was a madness overtaking him, a madness Kalus was powerless to stop. The progress of his father's obsessions was relentless and it would soon overwhelm what little was left of his sanity. His grip on reality, on what was happening around him, was loosening. Soon whatever Kalus knew as *his father* would cease to exist. He would be lost forever. Lost even to himself.

Kalus' head swum with it. His eyes began to blur, the now familiar metallic taste seeping into his mouth. He swallowed. Screwed his eyes shut. Focus.

Focus.

He had to push it away. Musings on death and sanity, the real and the hallucinatory, would have to wait. He had a murder enquiry to lead, a challenge where right now he felt further and further out of his depth.

'A good read, eh?' Mallen called out making his way to the table and tossing a wet raincoat across a nearby chair.

Kalus pulled himself out of his downward spin, forcing out a smile. 'Gripping. Can't wait to find out how it ends.'

Mallen slumped into the chair opposite. 'Personally, I have it on good authority that *it was the butler what did it*. If not him then the maid. Maybe Mrs Scarlett with the candlestick in the colliery.'

Kalus focused on a response. 'Any suspect would be good.'

'Nothing?' Mallen asked, flicking a hand through wet hair.

'Nothing.'

In the face of Kalus' responses Mallen's apparently good mood evaporated. 'Pity. I was hoping we'd be finished early so I could catch the football. Not got to a Villa game yet this season.'

Kalus dropped the sheaf of paper onto the table. 'The way this lot is going we'll both be getting plenty of time to watch the footie. We'll be on crowd control.'

'That bad?'

'Worse than bad.' Kalus leant forward, tapping the folder on his desk. 'Your report is the last of the principal interviews. We've spoken with all of the senior officers on duty: the squad leaders, the miner's leaders, and the stewards responsible for organising the picket. We're now down to interviewing the lesser union officials and people who knew Jackson from his welfare runs. After that, it's any junior ranks who we believe - and I stress the *believe*, not the *know* - may have been operating in the area close to where the body was found. Beyond that... I haven't a clue where we go.'

'Worse than bad.' Mallen echoed.

'You want some more?' Kalus dredged a bulky manila folder from under a pile of similar ones. He waved it in the direction of his DI. 'The coroner's report. Preliminary draft. *Blunt force trauma. Several blows from a heavy, blunt wooden instrument such as a pickaxe handle, base-ball bat or baton. Precise time of death still to be determined but between 4 am and 7am. Death occurred in the place where* the body was found. *The victim was probably kneeling for at least one of the blows, as some of the blows suggest a pattern of being struck from behind and above by a right-handed perpetrator. There was considerable force employed in the blows.*'

Mallen shook his head. 'Christ, that's thin. When will they have a precise fix on the actual time of death?'

'You know Doyle, he won't be pushed. Later today. Tonight at the latest. Until then...' Kalus tossed the folder back on top of the pile, '...Everybody's still in the frame.' He sat back in his chair, sweeping his own hands through his hair. 'Five days and we're no further forward. No prime suspect, no one eliminated, no progress. We are simply treading water, running and standing still both at the same time. We have nothing. And that's all we've got for our report to Ridgway later this morning. Nothing to report. Proceeding.'

Mallen found the mood of despair contagious. He leant back on his chair; the shift of weight tipping it backwards to rest on the rear legs. Rocking school-boy-like, he cast around the canteen. 'Any ideas about him?' he asked, nodding towards Riordan who had just entered the room and made straight to the desk of DC White. The Murder Book.

'Looks like he's updating himself on the overnights,' Kalus offered.

'And why would that be? Keenness to lend a hand? Seeing if he has any startling insights we've overlooked?'

'Possibly.'

'Or just checking to ensure that we've not beaten our suspects to an inch of their lives to extract a dubious confession?'

A half-smile escaped Kalus. 'Be the thing to have a suspect to beat.'

'Maybe you should ask Ridgway about that.'

Kalus felt his smile slip away. 'Careful, Richard.'

Mallen's chair snapped back to the ground. He leaned forward across the trestle table separating Kalus and himself. 'Talk of the canteen. And I don't mean this place. Tamworth, Stafford, Brum. Everyone's aware of what's been going on.'

'Allegedly.' Kalus cautioned.

'Allegedly my ass. West Midlands Regional Crime Squad have been banging up suspects for years, and I don't mean putting them away. I mean literally banging them up. Beating them.' He sat back. 'Verging on torture some say.'

'Some say a lot. Point is, when push comes to court case or statements, they say nothing. Frank Ridgway's a good copper. End of.'

'You think so?'

'Frank Ridgway's a lot better than me at this. Better than all of us.'

'In that case, maybe he can tell us where we're going wrong. Not heard much at all from that quarter. Maybe he can tell us what to do next.'

'Amen, to that. Amen.'

* * *

PC David Jones tossed his helmet onto the cot-bed and flopped down next to it. Shift finished he could relax until early afternoon when, along with the rest of his squad, he would be required to secure the exit of those miners still working the colliery's early shift.

He slumped back, focus coming to rest on the fluorescent lamps that hung in regimented lines the length of the bunkhouse. Lichfield barracks. *In the army now*, the refrain trumpeting through his mind, a memory from somewhere.

He turned his head, taking in the footlocker and the small table next to the bed. Christ he was glad this was temporary. Some years ago he'd entertained thoughts of joining the army, a life of travel and good money, all found. His dad had been army and his uncle too. They'd seen service in Aden. Christmas get together stories of action. Tales of foreign women, cheap fags and booze. He'd never followed it up. The police had been his choice. Looking round the bunkhouse it appeared more and more to have been a good one.

He sat up, shuffling around the bed and opening the padlock on his locker. He took out an envelope. It was large, A4 size. He tipped the contents onto his bunk.

Pay slips. Six of them, covering the six weeks he'd been based here. Six weeks of enhanced shift pay, of overtime and accommodation allowance. The hazardous duty allowance and all of the other allowances that his presence here meant. He had thus far resisted the temptation of following some of the other officers stationed here and taking his pay slips to wave at the pickets.

He had nothing personal against them. He knew they were doing what they'd been told to. The NUM leaders, men like Scargill, were the issue. They were the ones responsible for the mess. Men desperate to hold onto power, whatever the cost. The miners were being used.

The ones he held in contempt where the leaders. The ones he wanted to punish were the Militants, the ones who turned up at the marches, at the protests and the disputes seeking to turn them to violence. They had their own agenda, their own desire for a fight. A class war. Those were the ones he wanted to beat, the ones that he wanted to break.

The DI that had interviewed him had it right. He'd seen their work at Handsworth and Orgreave. The Militants. The bottles and the bricks and the petrol bombs. That was the difference; the miners, the local ones, were hand-to-hand, feet, fists, and elbows. It was the radicals, the Militants that threw the bottles. They were the ones hurling the bricks, the ones making the petrol bombs. They stayed to the back, urging others forward, pushing others onto the shields and into the batons. They were kids thrusting a stick into a wasps' nest, twirling it round to see what happened but all the time knowing full well the consequences, the outcome.

It was why he'd volunteered for the Snatch Squad. Sick and tired of standing there taking it, he'd wanted to get out and get at them. He wanted to show them, wanted to punish them and to make them pay.

He couldn't deny that he liked what he did. When the Snatch teams went in the leash was off. There was no restraint, no voice holding them. They were free to do what had to be done. Reasonable force was a boundary that stretched. In reality it meant they could do whatever they liked to those they targeted. The first time his baton had found its target it had shocked him at just how resistant and resilient human bone could be. He had struck the man three times, textbook style. First the collarbone to paralyse the arms, denying the target the ability to retaliate; then the back of the legs to compel the target to drop, make them easier to drag back to police lines as they lost resistance to being pulled; then across the side of the head, behind the ears to deny the target the ability to comprehend what was happening until it was too late and they were behind police lines, cuffed and ready for the custody van.

He had hit the man across the collarbone, nothing. The picket had continued to raise the lump of wood he'd been using as a club. Jones had struck him again, harder, the dawning realisation that training was one thing but a target pumped full of adrenalin, alcohol, or drugs was something else. He'd struck him a third time, full force, sensing the crack rather than hearing it as the man's collarbone had smashed, his arm dropping and finally letting go of the club as he sought to grasp and support his damaged arm.

It was only as he looked up - swearing at Jones, baring his teeth, reveaing the venom that defined him - that Jones had brought the baton down for a fourth time. It had been a massive blow, a blow across the face, a blow splintering teeth and splitting lips, smashing nasal bone. It was a blow so shocking to Jones himself, that he'd stood for what seemed minutes staring at his work, dimly aware of arms rushing past, grabbing the target, dragging him back to the police line. He'd felt the tug of colleagues at his own arm, shields up deflecting the hail of stones and bottles that reigned down as they retreated. The police line had closed, forming up once more after the snatch squad had passed back through.

He'd stood looking at the figure lying at his feet. The blood that had spread through the target's fingers, the hands clamped across his face, horizontal for the mouth, vertical for the nose. The blood had poured from his mouth, soaking his shirt, spurting in bubbling streams from the soft pulp where his nose had once been.

The hands of colleagues patted Jones on the back, slapping his shoulder. He'd felt the taste of satisfaction. A job well done. A purpose realised.

He sifted through the slips of paper on the bunk. Six weeks. And, from the news, there would be more to come. A lot more. The party conferences had upped the stakes for both sides. But, it wasn't the money that motivated him. The money was secondary. It was the chance to hit back. To strike at the rot he felt was eating away at law and order. He was putting the fear back into the nation's policing. The fear that people needed in order to be good, to make the right choices. Punishment and retribution were a necessary part of the system. Checks and balances.

He'd struck many pickets over the past few days. He'd struck many pickets the day the miner had been killed. Hit them hard, watched them fall.

No longer did the Snatch squads set out to bring back targets. The orders hadn't changed, but the nuance of the briefings was clear. Like the squads of soldiers that he knew were secretly being used, many of them from the very barracks where he currently sat, the snatch squads intention was to strike down the target, take them out of the action. The objective was simple: make it impossible for them to get back into it. Deterrence.

He'd no conscience over the death of a picket. He had no idea if he or another of those officers on duty that day had struck the blow that had killed the man Jackson. He'd heard he was an activist, part of the union strike committee. As far as he was concerned whatever a picket got was necessary, part of the balance.

Law and order. Checks and balances. Crime and punishment.

Later today he would be on the line again. He would not be deterred from striking the blows necessary to get the job done. It was his role in the equation.

* * *

Kevin Terry sat in the gloom of the late morning rain that was battering at the window of the small café. The morning's newspapers were laid out across the table. A half-drunk mug of tea sat next to the remnants of a half-eaten breakfast alongside an already overflowing ashtray.

The door opened. A customer flicking the rain off his collar staggered in, closing the door behind him with a *'Bloody hell!'* as accompaniment.

Not him.

Kevin returned to his pre-occupation of the past thirty minutes. Brooding. Staring at the rain running down the glass next to his window table.

The interview with the police had troubled him. Not so much his own with the copper who'd seeming more intent on eyeballing him than in the questions he was undoubtedly supposed to ask, but Karen's. *What had gone on in the kitchen?*

The WPC had emerged with a strange look on her face, as had Karen. He'd found it hard to know what to make of the WPC's look, but he was certain of Karen's. He had seen it twice before. Once, when she was 17 and he knew she'd been with Billy Dodd; the second, when he'd told her about the death of Stephen Jackson. Guilt.

But guilt of what? He'd asked her what she'd said, what she'd been asked, and she'd just made some comment about… nothing… *you know, how well we knew Stephen. Did we know of anyone who might have a grudge.* But she'd turned away as she said it. Like she had about Billy Dodd.

The steam emerging from the kitchen that was tucked behind the café's counter began clouding the window. It was a mist wreathed in fat, a blurring haze of smoke mixed with the vapour trails from a boiling urn of water. He reached out, rubbing at the window with his sleeve, and peered onto the side street.

There was something she wasn't telling him. It had nagged at him all morning. It had finally drawn him out into the wet, tugging at his mind until he'd phoned, knowing only too well the reaction he'd get.

'What do you mean you need a meet?' the voice had asked, angry and impatient.

'It's important.'

'Fine,' the irritation clear. 'An hour. *The usual place.*'

And here he was. *The usual place.* The corner window table. Privacy, back turned against the peeling walls, that living membrane of oil and grease and grime layered onto flaking paint slopped on top of peeling wallpaper. A table with a view. Who came in, who went past. Who might be watching, waiting. At the moment there were three other patrons, each either staring unthinking into the distance or head down into their fry-ups. A place where nobody knows your name. He thought of the *Cheers* episode that had been on TV the previous evening. Her favourite show, and she hadn't even raised a smile. *Was it the effect of the strike?* No. It was something else, something that had lain between them ever since he'd told her of Stephen's death. *You killed him.* That's what she'd said that day. Straight away. No long drawn out mulling it over. Straight out. *You killed him.*

He'd told her she was mad. Didn't know what she was saying. Insisted it was just the shock making her say things. *Stephen was a friend. My friend. Why would you believe I'd killed him?* It was his job, nothing more than that. He assigned pickets their places. He'd directed the picket that day. But there were things he'd left unsaid, unsayable things, things she'd picked up on.

He'd told his dad what she'd said. Assured him that she was simply in shock. She knew nothing. She blamed him because of his union work. There was nothing more to it. That was it. *She didn't know what she was saying. She's okay now, it's forgotten. She doesn't know.* His dad's response had been clear. *She needs to be told. She needs to keep thoughts like that to herself*, he'd said.

Despite what he'd told his dad, the worry pulled at him like an undertow in the water. It was dark and deep, like the water in the rivers he fished. The riverbank where his dad had first put the idea to him. The morning's fishing that had changed everything. The day that had led to everything that had happened since.

You killed him. And in many ways he had.

The door to the cafe opened and he was there, but not alone. The man called Loach was with him. Collins offered not so much as a nod of recognition or greeting, instead walking to the counter and ordering teas. It was Loach who came over to where Kevin sat. Loach who slid the chair out rotating it so that he sat in a manner Kevin's mother would have called *like an American*; legs straddling the chair. With its back now nearest the table, it offered itself as a rest for Loach's long arms that dived into his coat pockets, returning with matches and cigarettes. He wafted the pack in front of Kevin, who shook his head. Loach's face wrinkled into a *'please yourself'* grimace as he placed the pack of cigarettes and matches onto the table. As he spoke his hands continually re-arranged the stacking of the two.

'So, I understand that you've had a visit from the coppers.'

'That's right.'

'Only to be expected.' Loach scratched distractedly at an ear.

'Bloody shock, I can tell you,' Kevin offered, filling the empty silence.

Loach examined his finger, rolling the wax between finger and thumb. 'Nothing these lot do can come as a shock after a while. Here... there... Birmingham, Belfast. The same. Always the same. No imagination, you see.' Elbows now resting on the table, Loach held his hands out in front of himself, parallel and facing each other, fingers pointing forward like blinkers. He moved his hands steadily across the table towards Kevin. 'Straight lines. That's how they are.' He rocked his hands back and forth in emphasis before returning to shuffling the matchbox and cigarette pack.

Kevin looked across at Collins standing by the counter. 'It was Michael that I rang.'

'Yes,' Loach agreed.

'Yes,' Kevin repeated. He watched Loach fiddle with the cigarette pack. 'I just wanted to let him know. That they'd been round.'

Loach, shuffling the boxes, nodded.

'So what happens now?' Kevin asked, falling into the silence.

'Now?' Loach echoed.

'Now. Next.'

Loach sat back. A breath of a sigh escaped. 'How do you mean?'

'What do I do?'

'What you've been doing.'

'All I've been doing is going to the union offices and organising the pickets.'

'Exactly,' Loach stated.

'But that's what I've been doing for months.'

'Exactly.' Loach leant in. 'We want you to keep doing what it is that you've been doing for months.'

'But I thought–'

'Ah, you see, that's the problem right there, Kevin. We don't want you thinking. We want you just *doing what you've been doing for months*. That way, there's no suspicion. No grounds for anyone to ask any awkward questions. Questions about you and what it is that you've really been doing. D'you see?'

'Yeah, but–'

'There you go. You're forgetting what it is that I've only just been telling you.'

Kevin stared at the mug of tea. This was not the conversation he'd expected. It was not the conversation he wanted. He looked across at Collins chatting animatedly with the owner.

'It's just…'

'Just what, Kevin?'

Kevin drew in a breath, considering his words, found all

of them wanting in different ways. He sighed, 'It's difficult… at home. Karen.'

'How do you mean, *difficult?* You not getting any?'

Kevin looked up, eyes glaring with hostility. 'I'm not saying that.' But it was true, when had they last had sex? Was that it? Was that what was getting to him?

'Whoa, fella! A joke.'

Kevin looked back down. He pushed the mug absent-mindedly around the table, the spilt tea scattering ahead of it. 'I think she knows.'

'What do you mean?'

'Karen. I think she knows that there's something going on.'

Loach halted his stacking and shuffling. 'What have you told her?'

'Nothing. Nothing at all. She just seems… different. Not there. Vacant. She looks at me… strangely. She said thinks I'm to blame for Jackson's death.'

Loach forced a smile. 'The dead picket? Why would she think that?'

'She knows I assigned him that morning. She thinks he'd be alive if I hadn't sent him out on the picket.'

Loach considered the situation. 'Listen, Kevin, women are a law to themselves. They don't act like blokes, they're wired different. She's maybe thinking about the strike and feeding the babies. The death of someone she knew, someone she was close to… well, it's bound to affect her. Women get screwed up by stuff like that. Give her a while and you'll see.'

'I wish I could take her on holiday. Her and the kids. Get away from all this.'

'Listen. That is the very last thing that you're going to do. You need to stay here with your head down. You're a striking miner. Just where are you supposed to have got the money from for a holiday all these months into a strike?'

Kevin felt the tears coming, the dam bursting. 'I feel like I'm losing her… maybe already lost her.' The mucus bubbled from his nostrils, mixing with the tears that trickled down his cheeks.

'It's like, I don't know who she is anymore.'

Loach leant across the table. 'Look at me,' he hissed. Kevin rubbed a hand massaging his brow, dragging it down across his eyes, his focus on the table. 'I said look at me,' Loach repeated, the command insistent. Loach looked around the room, across at the owner, at Collins who had clearly heard the rise in voices, the change in tone. Loach shook his head at him, returning his attention to Kevin. 'Listen, you get a fucking grip! You understand? The last thing any of us need now is for you to fuck-up over your wife. I don't care what it is that you're thinking about her, you stay focussed. Jackson's death caused problems for us all. Deal with it!'

Kevin wiped a hand across his top lip, finger and thumb pinching at the pooling of mucus and tears. Collins came over, pulling out a chair and sat down. 'What's the problem?'

Loach looked at Kevin, considered the figure before him. He shook his head. 'Nothing. Nothing at all. Young Kevin here will be just fine. Won't you, Kevin? He knows what he's got to do, don't you?'

Kevin nodded. What choice did he have.

Twenty

She'd been clever.

The interview with the WPC had given her an opportunity, and she'd taken it. Now she had to think about what to do next. She knew that she couldn't always count on chance or good fortune. She had to take control. She had to make things happen.

She patted the stack of notepaper into shape, pulling it closer. The note had to be right. She had to say the right things. To explain.

Angus McKinnon had been easy. She'd had time to think through her words to him. Careful. No more hesitations, not like at the phone box. This time, with McKinnon, she had been clear in what she'd set out to do.

The meeting with the police - her interview with the WPC - had been the turning point. The moment when she'd emerged from the kitchen and lied. She'd lied to Kevin, lied with ease, lied with no sense of panic or fear. He was becoming aware of something having changed in her and she knew that she couldn't conceal it for much longer. At some point he would confront her, challenge her. It was why she had to act now.

She'd met McKinnon at the union offices. It had been easy. *Kevin not here? Oh I thought he was going to be here all day. Out on picket and then meeting with union stewards? Never mind, nothing important that won't keep until later. How am I? Oh, you know, fine, yeah, the kids too... Oooh, there's just one thing, though, if you've got a minute...*

The door to the office had shut. They'd begun with the usual pleasantries - the kids, his wife, her dad, her father in law, the strike, the pressure. The killing.

They had soon got to the killing.

'He was a good man,' McKinnon had nodded in emphasis

of his assessment of Jackson.

'And still nothing about who did it? How it happened?' she had asked.

'Oh, the police have their ideas, but nothing they'd share with the likes of me.' Leaning forward, intimate. 'Between you and me Karen, I don't think they have a clue. They're running around interviewing everybody they can think of, but they've got nothing.'

'And what do *you* think?' Flattering, attentive.

'I think some rotten *polis* with a short fuse took a chance to hand out some rough justice, some payback that went too far. Now he's more than likely sitting in some army barracks, terrified to come forward, shitting himself that he's going to get caught... if you don't mind my saying.'

She'd waved it off. 'But, if that's what happened, why haven't they got him yet?'

'Because it's not the killer they want.'

'I don't understand.' *Naïve, innocent.*

'They want a miner. A picket. A rabble-rouser. If they can't get that, then they'd rather find no-one at all.'

She chewed at her nails. 'So what'll happen? Will they just give up?'

'Wouldn't surprise me. If they can't find a miner to frame for it then once all of the hoo-hah has died away they'll just let the investigation splutter to a stop. Move on. Like that miner in Yorkshire that got killed. I mean, who remembers him, eh? Ach, the local *polis* are decent enough, this Kalus that's heading it up seems okay to me. But the Regional Crime Squad lot? They're bigger bandits than the buggers they arrest.'

'Really?'

McKinnon scoffed his assessment of the merits of the Crime Squad. 'The last thing the police round here want is some investigation into one of their own. Turn over that particular stone and who knows what might come crawling out.'

She'd considered what she'd heard. 'What if it's not a policeman? What if it is a miner?'

'Who would want to kill Stephen?' he'd almost tutted at her naivety.

She'd measured her way through what she wanted to say. 'Maybe he was involved in something. Maybe someone thought he was stockpiling union food... or money. He had access to the welfare funds, didn't he? Maybe they might have suspected he was robbing the union. The strikers.'

'Stephen Jackson stealing from the union? And killed by an angry miner?' He laughed. 'I'm sorry, but you really should be writing some fiction, Karen.'

'Isn't it possible?' she pursued.

McKinnon shook his head. 'For one thing, Stephen had no access to the welfare fund.'

'No? I thought he did.'

'No, there's only three people have that.' He held up a large hand, fingers like sausages, a thumb distorted with arthritis. He ticked off the trio. 'Your father-in-law, Brian. Your Kevin. And me. Hardly the James Gang.'

'So Kevin has access to the welfare fund?'

'Aye. I thought you'd have known that.'

A shrug. 'He doesn't talk much about work. Spends a lot of time in his shed - the office he calls it - doing his union work. I don't get to see what it is that he does in there.'

McKinnon had let out a bellow of air, a gust of surprise at the priorities of the young. 'A canny lass like yourself, and those lovely bairns waiting? I'm surprised he can drag himself away to work. Surprised he's got so much to do at home, even with the strike.' He mused for a moment before snorting dismissively, 'He's no doubt keen, you see. He wants to get on. Provide for you all. Be better. He's a good man, Karen, a good man.'

'Yes, that's what everybody says. A good man.'

She rose to leave, stopping part way up as if suddenly remembering a triviality. 'Oh, I almost forgot,' she rummaged in her handbag. 'You talking about union business reminded me. There's some miner. Kevin asked me to drop a note round to his house.' She plucked out a crumpled envelope. 'Union stuff, I suppose. It's just I forgot to ask for the address. I was wondering, as you've got all the details here...'

'Sure.' McKinnon went to the dull green filing cabinet and tugged open the second draw. 'What's the name?'

'Gordon. Robert Gordon.'

McKinnon paused and shook his head. 'There's no miner of that name works here. I know all of them by name. Gordon. Are you sure you've got that right?'

'I think so.'

He scanned the files. 'No. No Robert Gordon.' He slid the draw shut.

'Maybe I've got it mixed up.' she suggested. 'Maybe he works in the colliery offices.'

'No. There's no one of that name works there. I'd know.'

'Maybe I've just got the name wrong.'

'Maybe. Well, don't worry, whatever it is, I'm sure it'll wait.'

'Yeah, I'm sure you're right. I'll speak to him tonight.' She opened the door.

'Karen. I meant what I said. He's a good man.'

She half-turned, her face held low, looking down and away from his eyes, frightened that her own might betray her. She nodded. 'I know. They all say it.'

* * *

The man looked innocuous enough. Kalus estimated that he was thirty but could have been older. A tanned face, youthful but earnest, a face passing for anywhere between mid-twenties and mid-forties. His hair was cut short, tidy but not fashionable. The suit was dark grey, a charcoal pinstripe matched by the tie, striped blue and grey, a classic. Shoes, freshly polished, black oxfords that spoke of function rather than style. The smile seemed to have similar origins. It was formal, necessary and useful, but a long way from warm or spontaneous. It was the type practiced in front of mirrors each morning. A carefully measured routine, one ensuring that it was honed to the necessary impression of professionalism and available on demand.

His briefcase - brown tan, supple and expensive - sat on the edge of the table. He'd placed it there whilst extending a hand towards Kalus. The shake had been short, as measured as the smile. It was the shake of a man who delivered it many times each day, a gesture conveying little beyond a healthy respect for the laws of ritual rather than the recipient. It was a nicety to be observed. A means to an end.

'James Harper.' A voice surprisingly pleasing and of a higher register than expected.

Kalus nodded. 'DCI Peter Kalus.'

Harper fished a card from the inside pocket of his jacket, proffering it to Kalus who took it. Crisp. A clean white board, the print dark and firm; *James Harper: Harper, Cauley, Janes; solicitors.*

Kalus indicated the chair opposite. 'Mr Harper, I understand from one of my team that you have some pressing information regarding the investigation into the death of Stephen Jackson. Information that you would only talk about with myself.'

Harper sat legs crossed, a man at ease, sure of himself. 'Death. Murder. Killing. We do have to be careful in our choice of words these days, don't we Detective Chief Inspector? However, I'm not here to debate semantics with you. I'm assuming a busy man like yourself would prefer it if those who seek your time make good use of it.'

'As you say Mr Harper, I'm a busy man with an investigation to lead.'

'I feel you've more on your hands than an investigation into the death of a miner, Chief Inspector. I'm sure we both know that there are bigger fish being fried here than that.'

Kalus smiled. 'I'm not certain what you mean by that, but I can assure you, Mr Harper, that the death of Stephen Jackson is more than enough for myself and my team to be getting on with. More than enough.'

Harper waved a hand, a gesture intimating wider concerns. 'I'm getting at the fact that this investigation, before it's finished, will find itself having to go way beyond a simple killing. Providing of course, that it's handled properly. And by that, I mean with due diligence by those charged with pursuing it. That's of course if you are able to slip off the very tight leash that your Masters' have presently got you on. One they've had you on from the very start of your investigation.'

Kalus stared at the man, unwilling to rise to whatever bait was being floated. 'Just exactly what is it that you want, Mr. Harper?'

'I work for the National Council for Civil Liberty. I'm sure that you've heard of us and of our work. You probably know that we're interested in any case touching on the work of serious crime in the West Midlands. The West Midlands Regional Crime Squad in particular.'

'I'd hope that any citizen, let alone a solicitor, would be interested in the work of the police in our region. But I'm still left uncertain as to the reason for you asking to meet with me. We're Staffordshire. We have nothing to do with West Mids apart from local co-operation as required.'

'DCS Frank Ridgway, your superior here in Staffs. He's of *interest* to our organisation.'

'Interest?'

Harper placed his hands on a knee, fingers interlocking. 'We've followed Frank Ridgway's career with some interest ever since he was first attached to the Serious Crime Squad.'

'That's over–'

'Ten years,' Harper interjected.

Kalus nodded. 'Ten years. You must find him very interesting.'

Harper smiled. 'His career was somewhat spectacularly launched to its current heights by his time at Serious Crimes. A time we're now very much interested in. A time he's quite coy about discussing.'

'You've spoken with him?'

Harper shrugged. 'My colleagues at Liberty have at various times approached DCS Ridgway and others with links to the Serious Crimes Squad to talk about their work. Notably, the work that resulted in serious miscarriages of justice.'

'Frank Ridgway-'

'- *is a damn fine copper*,' Harper interjected. 'Yes, Inspector, we know. We've been told the same thing by every officer we've approached.'

'Doesn't that tell you something?'

'Yes. Yes it does,' Harper agreed. 'Unfortunately it's not what you'd like us to conclude. Certainly not what Frank Ridgway and his former colleagues at Serious Crimes wish us to.'

'It strikes me that you're not going to be satisfied until someone tells you what you want to hear. I think that both you and your organisation are guilty of what it is that you're trying to charge Frank with. That you've already come to your conclusions about him, about Serious Crimes. That they're guilty. And now you're simply fixed on finding some justification for your conclusions. Isn't that the sort of 'fitting up' that you accuse them of?'

'You're right. We do believe that Ridgway and quite a few others who've worked in that Squad are guilty. But it's not a conclusion based on prejudice or bias or trusting the words of a colleague. It's witness after witness. Victim after victim.'

'Crook after crook. Scumbag after scumbag.'

Harper leaned forward. 'Is that what you believe, Inspector? Really believe? *All crooks are scum? All suspects are guilty?* Surprised you even bother to collect evidence yourself. Surprised you even feel the need for a trial.'

'Due process.'

'Ah, due process. And what does that mean? In reality?'

'We gather evidence. Present a case.'

'And if the evidence isn't there? But you're sure the suspect in front of you is guilty. Sure as sure can be?' Harper quizzed.

'Due process.'

Harper waved a hand, a small gesture of his acknowledgement of a simple, obvious truth. 'Which in Frank Ridgway's book means fitting them up. Creating the evidence. Sealing the deal.'

'Now whose relying on hearsay. On assumption.'

'The first time, the first accusation, you're right. The second, maybe coincidence. But case after case, year on year? The same story, each of them variations on a theme of abuse, stories of violence and corruption. Perverting the course of justice. Different victims, different causes. Irish, black, gypsy, poor. But always the same process, the same outcomes. It all adds up. It all points in one direction, and one direction only.'

'Look, Mr Harper—'

'James,' Harper interjected.

'Mr Harper. I'm not certain what all of this has to do with me, or my investigation.'

Harper exhaled. Another small gesture of the hand. 'Everything. Your investigation is rubbing up against a number of very important issues, important causes. Important people. Should you turn this enquiry in certain directions, then some very important people are going to get very uncomfortable. Frank Ridgway is one of them. Frank and his friends. Powerful friends. I'm offering you a hand of friendship, Inspector. Support from some equally very powerful people interested in seeing Frank Ridgway and his like brought to account.'

'Politicians,' Kalus stated flatly, his distaste self-evident.

'Among them. More pertinently those who see the actions of DCS Frank Ridgway and others still at Serious Crime as a stumbling block to a wider political accommodation.'

'Ireland. You're talking about Ireland.'

Harper nodded. 'There's no doubt that the Birmingham Six are seen by many here and abroad as a symbol of the prejudices of the British government. Their innocence and the fact their trial was based on the evidence of Serious Crimes is a miscarriage of justice. It means that the legal system, the Crown, and this Government's credibility is compromised. There can be no peace in Ireland until things like this are put right. Only then can peace talks begin, the path to peace get started.'

Kalus sighed. 'Again. What has this to do with my investigation?'

Harper stood, laying a hand on top of his briefcase. He smiled his charming smile. 'I sense that I've outstayed my welcome Inspector. I do appreciate that you're a very busy man.' He picked up the case. 'But, just consider the fact that Frank Ridgway has interests in the outcome of this case that might well go against the line of natural justice.' He paused. a manner suddenly hesitant. New ground. Wary. 'We know of your... situation. Your standing with colleagues. Your problem in Handsworth. We believe you to be a man of integrity, Inspector.' He waved a hand, like wiping a mirror, a blessing being given. 'I followed that case with great interest. A bad decision, yes.... But anyone could have made such a misjudgement.' He examined Kalus' face for a response. 'So, let me be very open with you, Chief Inspector. Frank Ridgway put you on this case when others might not. He knows you will be grateful. That you are indebted to him. There are those of us who feel that he might use it as a lever. All we want of you, Chief Inspector, is that if and when he tries to push you in a certain direction... When he goes beyond what he should, what's regular.... Then talk to us. You'll see that we're right.'

Kalus stood. Harper reached out a hand that Kalus ignored. 'Mr Harper. You're right. I do believe that you've outstayed your welcome.'

Kalus watched the man leave.

Your situation. A misjudgement. His hand a blessing, a wiping away.

Could you wipe it away? Start again?

He knew the answer. Deep inside he knew.

The silence.

The men standing there. Arms at their sides. Batons hanging. Loose. Deflated.

They had formed a corridor, a path for him to walk down. Between them.

None of them looking at him, none of them.

The room. Silent.

No crying. No shouts for justice, no cries of brutality.

Reuben sat there on the floor his back against a cupboard.
A cup sat on the draining board. A child's cup. A drinking mug. A tippy cup.
He cradled them. One in each arm.
They sat slumped against him. Throats slit.
Rueben looked up at him. There were tears in his eyes.
Why didn't you stop me? He'd asked.
Why didn't you come?
Why didn't you stop me?

Twenty-one
Day Ten

She'd dropped the envelope off. The officer on duty reassuring her that WPC Lawrence would receive it as soon as she came on duty. For a brief moment Karen had stood there, still gripping one end of the envelope as the officer had held the other. She had faltered before finally letting go.

Letting go.

Despite the rain starting up again, she stood on the kitchen step staring down the garden towards the shed. Madonna came on the radio. That song. *Borderline.*

Their song. That's what Stephen had called it. All about Mexico she'd thought. Stephen had laughed, said it was about the madness of love. *That's what Borderline means. A state of madness. The line between sanity and insanity.* He'd sat in her bed, arms around her. *It's what my life is* he'd said. A madness. *The whole world*, he'd said. *All of it. A madness.* And he'd lain next to her and stared at the ceiling. *Listen to the words,* he'd said. *It's about losing your mind; of being driven too far. Crossing a line.*

She hadn't understood what he'd meant. She'd thought he was talking about them. His love for her. Now it was a different line she'd crossed. One with no going back.

Madness or not, she was committed.

Once that WPC read what she'd written, telling her about her concerns over Kevin's increasingly strange behaviour, then it would start. Telling her things she said she'd heard him shout out in his sleep. Lies setting it in motion. They couldn't ignore it. They would have a suspect. A motive. The papers said they had nothing. She was offering something.

They would come for him. Take him into custody. They'd interrogate him and get to the truth. They'd find out what he'd done. They had ways to do that, she'd read about them, ways that could prove what she knew: Kevin was Stephen's killer.

She shivered.

Rubbing her arms, she stepped back inside and closed the door. From the kitchen, she looked out down the garden, longing more than ever for the sun. Longing for he summers of her youth. The White bikini. A future full of possibilities.

She reached out a hand, tracing the path of the rain down the glass of the door.

Once he was in custody they would want her statement. She would volunteer to give evidence, evidence that would help them convict him. They would have their man, their killer. Knowing the history of violence of Kevin's father, they would give her the witness protection she needed.

A new life. Somewhere different. Somewhere warm.

In the background Madonna finished her song. *Borderline.*

A line crossed. A madness that had taken hold.

***

Things had to move fast. Everything was instinct.

Ever since the meeting a few mornings ago with Riordan in the carpark he'd tussled with the logistics of it. It required thought and precision, time to consider the options. The very things now denied him.

The original plan had been compromised. Plans often were. That's why a man like him was part of the team Someone to adjust situations, someone adapting operations to fit changing circumstances. Someone to fix things.

The original plan was *Silver Fox*, an operation in which the man he knew as Jackson had a role that was simplicity itself. Intelligence. Like a dozen or so others in Nottingham, Yorkshire, Wales and Kent, he'd forged a new identity, a dead man walking, infiltrating the union to gather information on plans and intentions. Later his objective would have been to agitate for violence, foster those conditions where the police could respond with legitimate force.

The least of his objectives had been gathering evidence for possible trials.

The third objective had always been contrary to the other two. A redundancy. His role and that of others in *Silver Fox* would remain closed forever. At the end of the strike he and his fellow SDS were to slip back into the shadows. They would disappear back into the graves where they'd been taken from. Their identities would be sealed forever. As the old poem had it, sent back *where all the dead men lie.*

In some respects it was a shame that such effective undercover work should be unknown. From what he knew, off all of the operatives, Jackson's work had been among the best.

His infiltration had been deep, a tribute to his skills and commitment. His fearsome pursuit in instigating violence, the beatings he'd inflicted on the police and they on him were so fulsome that there was little doubt amongst those he sought to infiltrate as to his loyalty. Of course, it now transpired that Jackson had taken the idea of penetration quite literally; his fucking of one of the union leaders wives, which, whilst frowned upon might be seen as yet further proof of his 'undercover' role. If anyone suspected his actions, they could be put down to his furtive sexual liaisons.

But he'd stumbled across something unforeseen.

Early in October, an operation designed with disrupting IRA funding had resulted in the seizure of a ship off the Essex coast. Along with the expected 4 tons of cannabis they had found known IRA gunmen babysitting a shipment of Libyan Semtex.

One of the Libyan crew had broken under questioning. He'd told his interrogators he'd overheard one of the gunmen saying the explosives were destined for a major operation on the UK mainland. *History making,* he'd heard another of the Irishmen say.

The police had trumpeted *Operation Bishop* as a drugs haul, a major boost in the Customs and Excise war against drugs. The Semtex haul and its ramifications had been smothered for fear of alarming the public.

A few days later, at a drunken gathering of militant pickets, Stephen Jackson had picked-up what he thought to be crucial intelligence regarding a possible IRA operation. It was the rumour of a plan for something bigger than the strike. One of the picket organisers, the worse for drink, had boasted of his own involvement. He'd confided to Jackson how he was deep in something that would *'show Thatcher and her cronies the price of a class wa*r'.

He'd told Jackson that a shipment had been lost. That their *'friends from across the water'* needed it replacing. These *'friends'* were desperate. It was so urgent that they were willing to pay a small fortune for what they wanted. The man was *'going to be rich.'*

The conversation had been brief, ended by the appearance of others in the group whom the talkative picket had been wary of. Jackson had later relayed the conversation to his handler. *What should he do?* The answer had been easy: *pursue the link, press the contact, infiltrate deeper.*

The discovery of Jackson's body had prompted two concerns. The first was that his death was proof that he'd stumbled onto something more than just the drunken boasting of a militant picket. That the crewman had told the truth. A major terrorist attack on the mainland was imminent.

The second concern was that Jackson's death instead arose from the discovery of his subterfuge. That he and the wider operation dubbed *Silver Fox* might now be exposed.

He closed the file.

Two problems. Each carrying its own particular threat.

A major terrorist attack like the one the previous year at Harrods, or the attacks at Hyde Park and Regent's Park in the same year would mean carnage on the streets. Whilst awful to contemplate, in itself it posed no threat to government. It might even strengthen it.

Terror was a threat to law and life. It struck at the heart of democracy. This government, like the ones before it, was waging a war on those who threatened democratic ideals. Should these monsters succeed in carrying out such an attack, it would only strengthen the government's cause, uniting the nation. It had happened before; ten years previously the Birmingham pub bombings had driven public support for the war against terror. It had legitimised almost any action the intelligence services might wish to take.

It was the second threat that could prove disastrous, its impact far more widespread. Should the government be caught with its hands on the stick stirring civil unrest, it's actions would be judged to be as anti-democratic as those of any of the terrorist groups it sought to destroy.

The exposure of *Silver Fox*, of a government provoking violence against its own people, would surely bring it down. It would be the end of Thatcher. The end of *Thatcherism*. The end of the Tories.

It was, in the end, all about politics.

He was not a political animal. He was a servant of the state. The actions of governments could not be judged in the same way as those of men. Wasn't that what Nixon had said? In the end it wasn't about motives but about who won.

He tossed the paper in the grate. The outline of his plan. The plan to save The Minister. To save Thatcher. To save the country from itself.

The flames of the coal fire ate it hungrily, forcing a grim smile. Maybe there was irony here. It was coal that had begun it, and now it was coal that consumed it.

Everything could be fixed. Every problem had a solution.

That was why he was here.

They had been clear.

Protect *Silver Fox*. No matter the consequences.

* * *

'So, Father, what do you think?'

Father Rodgers shook his head. 'Fear is a terrible thing, child. Terrible. It's the time when we most need our faith to show us the way. Faith in god gives comfort, offers us succour. Your father-in-law is facing a terrible thing.'

'Dying is awful.'

'Contemplation of death, the inevitability of it, is something that challenges us all. You and I have our faith to support us. We are never alone. Your father-in-law... It seems he has lost that.'

Anna Kalus nodded agreement with her priest's assertion. Her father-in-law had lost his faith and it concerned her. 'To be honest, Father, he never truly believed. It was always his wife who had the faith. He believed for her. She held the faith for both of them. She prayed for both of them. Her greatest fear was that without her his faith would not survive.'

'Her death was a blow for him.'

'It destroyed him. He's never recovered. Everything has piled in on him.'

'His illness.'

'For one thing.'

The priest held her hands in his. He patted them in comfort in the face of the inevitable. 'What do the doctor's say?'

'He's dying. A matter of months, weeks.'

'And he knows this?' The priest asked gently.

She nodded.

'A terrible thing,' the Father added.

'He's scared, Father. Scared of everything, particularly the dark. He sits in the house with the lights on day and night. He thinks if he can keep the dark away... It comforts him.'

'Surely that's okay? If he finds comfort in it.'

'It's just that it's... not normal.'

'Normal?' Father Rogers conveyed his mystery at what such a thing meant today.

'He clings to it. If he wakes and the lights are off then he screams out, screams and cries until they're switched on. It's like... he believes that the light is keeping him safe.'

Father Rodgers patted her hands. 'What about your husband? What about Peter? How is he dealing with all this?'

Anna chewed her bottom lip. 'He's busy. A big case. He does all he can. His mind's on the case. I know he worries… he just…'

'Carries on?' the priest ventured.

'Carries on,' she repeated.

'And his faith?'

Anna paused. *Peter's faith*. 'He believes. In his own way.'

'His lack of faith still troubles you,' the priest suggested.

'With what he does, all he sees. The awfulness of the world surrounds him, Father. More than any of us. He knows the evil of men. He lives with it every day. He needs strength, something to help him see that there is good. To see what he's doing this for.'

'You feel he doesn't?' Father Rodgers pushed.

'Not anymore. Once. Not anymore.' She looked into the eyes of her priest, the man who kept her soul in his charge. 'Is that wrong, Father? To have no faith that what you are doing has any meaning?'

Father Rodgers side-stepped. 'And this affects you.'

She considered the matter. 'To have no faith…' She shook her head in confusion. 'I don't know how to find him, Father. Sometimes… when he's with the children, there's a silence that suddenly comes over him. It's like he's seen something. That he's suddenly realised something. Once or twice, at those moments, I've looked in his eyes and …'

Father Rodgers squeezed her hands tight, 'And?'

'There's nothing there. It's like he's empty. Gone.'

***

He stared at the folder. Where he could still make them out, the words stamped across the cover swirled and danced before him. Where he couldn't was a mosaic of shattered glass splintering his sight. Temporary. A selective blindness. A thing that he knew would pass, yet still unnerving. The print appeared as seen through a child's kaleidoscope, the text pixelated. Stress, the doctor's had warned him. He could return to duty but be careful of the stress. Know your limits.

He rubbed at his eyes, screwing them tight shut. Flares soared. He opened them.

Across the room, Riordan sat watching, that day's witness forms stacked in front of him. *What was he searching for? What was it he wanted? What was he doing here?*

Kalus' head ached. A tightening band gripping the top of his skull.

He took out a sheet of paper. He stared at the notes he'd scrawled there, aware only of the patterns it made. Knowing that there had to be an approach that was currently eluding him. Something that metaphorically as well as now literally he just wasn't seeing. There had to be a way to carve out some sense. He just couldn't find it anymore.

Not since Handsworth. Since Rueben.

He shook his head.

Go back to basics. *Motive*: the building block of any murder enquiry. If there was no motive, then Jackson's death had to be an accident, manslaughter. A baton swung too hard. But repeatedly? He recalled the photographs of the dead man's head pinned to the file. This was no accident. This was no errant blow, no mis-directed aggression. Pre-meditated or not, the objective of this attack had been to kill.

The Snatch Squads were highly trained. They were drilled. But no one really knew the consequences of prolonged exposure to such violence. They had been trained for short skirmishes: football hooligans, parading protestors, the occasional outbreak of street riots. These men had been the front-line of violent picketing for five months. Orgreave, Pontefract, Hemsworth and the rest.

He rubbed his temples. He'd read somewhere about the consequences of sustained front-line pressure on soldiers coming home from Vietnam. *Where was it? Mai-Lai?* Men who had been trained to attack, to use violence in a controlled situation, had suddenly gone crazy. It had been a dam breaking, an outpouring of violence.

Was that what had happened here? Was that possible?

Who would be taking that message to the government? To Maggie?

Was that why Riordan was here? Whitehall already assuming that the culprit must be an officer. A uniform. If so, then what was Riordan's brief? To find the culprit and then be sure that he's branded a renegade, a freak, the exception that proved the rule. The guilty man that would allow nothing else to change. To shape Kalus' own findings? To ensure his own stamp of approval?

The band around his head tightened. His eyesight dimmed. The ache behind his eyes blazed. Know your limits.

Not his problem. Not his concern. Know your limits.

His job remained simple: find the killer.

The rest was politics. Not his concern. He knew his limits.

Twenty-two
Day Eleven

WPC Lawrence hesitated. The silence that had fallen on the room when she had first spoken was so thick she could feel it lying on her shoulders.

At first she thought it was courtesy. Then realised it was shock. Roberts was the first to break it. 'It's usually just *CID* that *talk* in these, love,' he'd told her.

'Sorry,' she stumbled out and started to sit back down.

Her chair was in the corner area of the canteen where Kalus had decided to hold his impromptu updating session. Lawrence's presence was happenstance, she was there going through the latest batch of interview reports with DC White for the Murder Book. It was paperwork. Filing.

Halfway down to her seat, she suddenly stood back upright. 'It's just...' The heads turned towards her once more. A first interruption might be put down to a naïve unawareness; a second unsolicited intervention, merely brazen. 'Well...You said you were looking at motives.'

Kalus nodded. 'That's right.'

'Yeah, it's something we Detectives do a lot. Detect.' Roberts put in, the emphasis on *detectives*.

Kalus held up a hand quietening him.

Lawrence continued. 'Well, you said anger and greed.' A pause, a heavy silence. 'That if it wasn't an officer that did it, then it would have to be one of the pickets. And if they didn't do it accidentally - and the pathology suggests it couldn't ever be an accident-'

'Not unless he fell into a threshing machine,' Mallen interjected.

She carried on, knowing that if she paused she would lose the nerve to finish her point. 'Then it has to be personal, it has to be an argument over money and the like.'

'We know what personal means,' Roberts commented.

'Well, from what I can see, there's no evidence of Jackson gambling, or of him ever being short or owing money. But equally there's' no evidence of him being wealthy. So not greed.' She stumbled on, aware her words were falling into each other but too nervous to stop. 'And everyone says he was a nice bloke, someone who was unlikely to be killed in a fight or because of a grudge.'

A pause. 'So?' Mallen asked, arms now spread wide in a gesture of expectancy. 'For someone who's *a nice bloke* he seems to have more than held his own on the picket.'

'Well, what about sex?'

The silence grew heavier. Finally broken by Roberts' perfect Leslie Phillips' *Carry On* take-off. '*Ooh I say! Ding-Dong!*'

'I mean…' She flushed, the tips of her ears turning deep crimson, 'I meant to say…. What about a lover?'

'What? A woman did this?' Mallen asked incredulously 'Have you actually seen the autopsy? Peter and I saw the body. No woman did that. Not unless she was a Russian shot-putter or something.'

'No. No not a woman, her husband.'

'What, he was a queer?' Roberts' gasped.

'No. Jealous. The jealous husband.'

'Her husband?' Kalus turned the words around in his mouth, testing them.

'Whose husband?' Mallen asked.

'Karen Terry. Her husband, Kevin Terry,' Lawrence managed to get out.

'Bollocks!' Mallen passed judgement, a chorus of agreement moving round the group.

Kalus raised his hands, gesturing for calm. He appraised the

WPC, who stood with such unexpected certainty. *When had he last had that?* 'Why so sure?' he asked her.

Encouraged, she attempted to find a response. 'When I interviewed her, she was nervous. Agitated. But more than that, she was frightened. She's not coping. There's something going on that's she's afraid to talk about. Earlier today she dropped a letter off at the station. In it she says her husband Kevin is shouting out in his sleep. She says that something's changed. That he's not himself. He hides himself away in his shed.'

'Isn't that stuff all a…woman thing,' White suddenly said. 'You know, her seeing stuff when it's just a bloke…I dunno… worried about his football team? Maybe worried about money or work. Providing for his family. I mean, it's a tough time to be a miner.'

'No, it's more than that,' Lawrence pushed back. 'She's scared. Scared of him. Not just of what he might do to her. It's more like she's scared about what she's beginning to think that he might *have* done. What he's *capable* of doing.' She scanned the faces, knowing what they were thinking: *woman's intuition.* 'Jackson was a frequent visitor to the house. She says nothing happened. But her husband's a violent man. Old school. Old values. A dinosaur,' she couldn't help but add.

'Like his dad,' Mallen said.

Lawrence nodded. 'And, according to Karen, one of his roles in the strike was being in charge of the deployment of the pickets. Doesn't that mean that he'd know better than anyone where Jackson was. That he'd have known where to find him. He could even have arranged for him to be in that field, alone.'

Kalus raised his brow quizzically. 'Lads?'

White shook his head. 'Don't know, guv.'

Roberts offered a non-committal shrug, 'Suppose.'

'Richard?' Kalus asked of his DI.

Mallen had clearly decided that the meeting's shrug account was approaching overdrawn. 'Brian Terry's a known agitator with a history of violence. Maybe his son's a chip off the old family block. Who knows?' He looked at Lawrence, considered the point. 'To be honest, we've little else. Yeah. Why not give him a tug? See what happens.'

'Piss the miners off is what'll happen!' Roberts offered.

'Yeah,' Mallen agreed. 'But at the same time it might boost our own boys. You know, let them see that we're not just focussing the investigation on them.'

Kalus agreed. They had precious little else to follow. Maybe Mallen was right too, the idea that it might take some pressure off, generate a little breathing space. Whether there was anything in it or not, jealousy was an old school motive. One they all felt comfortable with. 'Okay. But remember, we're bringing in a miner, a leading figure in the strike. For us it's not about the politics, it's about the policing. But folk out there may not see it that way. Richard, I need you to take point on this. Take a couple of uniforms. You get in and you get out. Quick as you can. Low profile. No messing. Don't want to attract a mob. Don't want you having to fight your way out.'

'Right you are.'

'And nothing gets to the press. I don't want them spinning it either way. Anyone asks, then he's helping with our enquiries, like the rest of them. There's nothing to be read into it.'

As the group dispersed Kalus raised a hand to Lawrence, beckoning her over. 'I know that took a lot,' he said. 'Whatever happens. Good work.'

'Thank you, sir.'

'And, WPC.'

'Sir?'

'Keep hold of that certainty. Sometimes it's all you've got.'

***

They came for him with no warning.

The knock at the door. The muffled voices in the corridor. Then they were in the room, standing in front of him. The words *'accompany us to the station… connection with the killing of Stephen Jackson… anything you say…'*

The decision to run had not really been a decision. It had been more an urge. An instinct.

He had knocked one of them to the floor, his sudden upward surge from the chair where he'd been sitting when they came in the room taking both officers by surprise. The second officer had staggered under the shove but had managed to stay on his feet, his hand reaching out for Kevin who had shrugged him aside and lunged for the kitchen door.

He was out and part way down the path before the second officer was out of the door. A few more strides and Kevin had leapt for the top of the wall, his hands scrambling for leverage, his legs flailing for purchase.

He felt hands grabbing at him. He kicked out blindly, thrashing his legs around seeking any available contact with the arms that sought to drag him back down. He managed to get one arm over and one leg, finding himself momentarily almost prone astride the wall. By now the other officer was upon him. Both uniforms reaching up for him.

He kicked out once more, before dragging his trailing leg over the wall and tumbling down on the other side.

His neighbour's cold frame smashed under him. Splinters of the glass dug deep into his right leg and his arms. He pulled himself upright, aware only of the wetness of the blood on his inner thigh rather than any pain as the adrenalin coursed through him. He tripped over the wooden runners of the smashed frame, arms flailing for balance before staggering half-upright across what was once his neighbour's lawn. As he stumbled forward, his arms became entangled in the bamboo canes supporting a crop of broad beans where the grass had been turned over to growing vegetables.

He tried shaking free. A few of the canes were twisted, tied together in a makeshift tepee entwining him even further as he thrashed around, desperately trying to shed them. He fell, feeling a sharp pain where his side thudded against the stump of an ornamental tree sacrificed to the demand for yet more crops. The fall at least freed the last of the canes. Pushing himself upright, he took off in the direction of the gate that led out onto the road.

He slipped the bolt, pulling the gate wide. To his left, two uniformed officers were racing around the corner of the road. Kevin sprinted in the opposite direction, legs pumping as fast as they could, the blood from his groin wet and sloppy, conscious that he was losing blood and would have to do something about it as soon as he could. The sounds of the two officers closing fast told him there was little chance of stopping and tending to the wound any time soon.

His head was returning from the backward glance over his shoulder when he stumbled down the kerb and into the road. He staggered on, looking ahead, planning the best path to take when the car hit. Blindsided, he felt the impact against his right leg followed by a sudden lift into the air; the strange other worldly sense of spinning - ground above, sky below - before his mind recognised what was happening.

He landed across the bonnet, head against the windshield which cracked under the impact. Coming to such a sudden halt, his body seemed to freeze for a moment before the reverse momentum, Newton's cradle like, knocked him back and he slid off the bonnet, finally coming to a rest slumped to the passenger side of the car.

'Fuck!' Mallen swore as he climbed out of the vehicle. He stood in the road staring at the collapsed miner and the shattered windscreen. 'My fucking no claims!'

***

Brian Terry stared at the telephone receiver trying to take in what he was hearing.

'They've arrested your boy.' *Your boy.* Kevin. 'You still there?' The voice was thin, metallic.

Terry pulled the receiver back towards his ear, cradling it at his chin. 'You're sure?'

'Course we're fuckin' sure.' Loach's tone suggested he was always sure.

'When?'

'An hour ago, maybe longer. They've taken him to the hospital.'

'Hospital? Why? What happened?'

'Seems he did a runner. They chased him down and he got hit by a car.'

'Is he okay?'

'Well, Brian, that sort of depends on your definition of *okay*. You know, your terms of reference. He's alive, he's in the hospital. Physically it would seem he's okay. As for the rest... well, that's what we're anxious to find out.'

'He won't say anything,' Terry stated.

'Well, that's reassuring to hear, Brian. But my colleagues are looking for something rather more than a father's words. Something a little more solid than a family testimonial.'

'He'll be okay I'm telling you.'

Loach's tone hardened. 'My colleagues are powerfully sceptical men, Brian. They'll want convincing.'

'I'll go and see him.'

Loach snorted. 'Well that's great too, Brian. A father should be with his son at a time like this. But the point is, you may not be able to get to him. He'll be under guard. Soon as he's up to it they'll be shipping him off to Burton or Birmingham. If it's Birmingham and Steelhouse Lane then we'll know they're on to us for sure.' Steelhouse lane. West Midlands Crime Squad. Where they held all regional IRA suspects for interrogation.

'Karen. I'll see Karen. She'll know. They'll let her see him. His wife.'

'What does she know?' Loach's manner was suddenly direct.

'Nothing,' Terry put in quickly.

'So what's she going to tell him? What fucking use will it be to us, her seeing him?'

'She can take a message. Something she won't make anything of herself. You know, cryptic.'

'It's not a fuckin' crossword we're doing here, Brian.'

'I know, but he'll get something out. He'll let us know what's happening. You'll see.'

'Just see that she tells him. See that she gets something out. And whatever it is, make certain she knows the consequences if she lets on to the *polis* about any of it.'

* * *

'So he ran?'

'Like a greyhound. Slippery fucker. A right Roger Bannister.' Kalus nodded. 'So what's he saying?'

'Nothing.' Mallen slumped into the chair opposite. 'He was sedated at the scene by the ambulance guys, and once they got him to the hospital the doctors were all over him. They say he needs rest before he can be seen. He's all drugged up at present.'

'What's the damage?'

'Broken arm. Fractured ribs. Usual sort of stuff when a car hits you.'

'Nothing that'll stop him being questioned once he comes round?' Kalus asked.

Mallen shrugged, 'Probably not.'

'So, what have we got?'

'Well, we know that he knew Jackson. Knew him well. They were on the Miners' Welfare Committee along with his dad Brian. We talked to a few neighbours. It's like the WPC said, seems he called round at Kevin's house a few times. Delivering food and that. Maybe more according to some.'

'Why didn't Kevin take it himself?' Kalus asked. 'The Welfare stuff. Why send someone round when he could just take it home himself?'

'The committee wanted it to look honest. Above board. You know, show everyone he wasn't slipping in the odd tin of beans or something. In the end, seems the neighbours think Jackson might have been slipping something else in.'

'And Kevin?'

Mallen shook his head. 'Don't know what he thought. It's a motive though, guv.'

'A classic of its kind,' Kalus agreed.

'What do you think?'

Kalus sighed. 'Like we said earlier, we've precious little else. It's worth pursuing. If it's that, it wraps it all up nice and simple. Motive. Opportunity too, even if we haven't a weapon or a witness.'

'We've put them away for less, guv. Circumstantial.'

'Yeah. True enough.'

'Frank would be okay with it,' Mallen encouraged.

'I'm not Frank Ridgway,' Kalus responded more aggressively than intended.

A silence lay between them.

'Confession?' Mallen asked.

'Would be good,' Kalus agreed. 'What about alibi?'

'Seems he was on the picket. He was there early, organising it.'

'An alibi that places him at the scene of the crime at around the time that Jackson was killed.'

'Catch 22,' Mallen stated flatly.

'What?' Kalus asked, puzzled.

'A book.' Mallen stated. 'Mate leant me. Weird. All about how you had to be mad to get sent home from the last war. But if you wanted to get sent home from the war, then that proved you were clearly sane because only a madman wouldn't want to be sent home. He called it Catch 22.'

Kalus studied his fellow DI. 'Didn't have you penned for a reader, Rich.'

'Like I said. Weird. Like this. Everything about this case points in every direction at the same time. We're not exactly short of suspects or motives. If anything, the problem is we've got too many. It's the fact that none of them get beyond being suspects. You know, the plod on the picket lines, the miners themselves, the left wing militants. And now we've got the age-old jealous husband to consider. All we need is Jackson having a ton of money secreted away and we've got the set. Anger, envy, jealousy, fear, and greed. Woods and fucking trees.'

Kalus nodded. Woods and trees. *Can't see the wood for the trees.* One of his mother's sayings. A thought was prised loose from some inner recess. 'Anna and I went to Hampton Court last summer. We took the kids. Nice day out. They've got this maze. Enormous. Standing in the centre of it... Well, you know that there's a way out, you know it. But trying to find it... it near drove me and Anna crazy.'

'But you did find it,' Mallen stated.

'Actually little Andrew did.'

'Maybe we should send for him. How'd he do it?'

'Turned out that what looked like a hedge was an illusion. There was an exit there all the time. We just couldn't see it. He just walked up to it and went through.'

'So you're saying... what? It's the husband who did it? That we just couldn't see it for all of the shit pushing us to investigate our own?'

'Maybe. Either that or maybe he's just put there concealing the real path out.'

Twenty-three

The blow across the face took her by surprise.

Brian Terry was a violent man, she had known it for some time, but she had never expected her father-in-law to slap her. She shrank back into the chair, knees tucked up foetal style under her.

He advanced. Stood over her. 'Do you understand what I'm saying, Karen? You're clear on what's to be done?'

She nodded. She wanted this man out of her house. Wanted him gone.

'You're to find out just what the fuck is going on. Why Kevin's been arrested. What they've said to him. What he's said to them.'

She nodded. 'I'll try.'

He sat on the coffee table and leant forward, blocking any movement she might make to get up from the armchair. 'Karen, trying is no good. I need you to sort this.'

'I said I'll try. There'll be police there. In the room. I'm not sure I can. They'll hear.'

His hand snaked out towards her, causing her to flinch and bury her head in the wing of the chair. Instead of the anticipated blow his huge hand caressed the side of her face, stroking the hair away from her cheek. Already the weal where he'd struck her was swelling. There would be heavy bruising. 'Karen, there's a lot at stake here. Things you don't know.'

'Like what?'

'Things you don't need to know. Things that are best you don't know. All you've got to do is to get whatever message Kevin has for me.' He stroked her hair, brushing it back over her ear. 'Understand? We need to know why he's been arrested. What the police are thinking.'

'*We*. Who's *we*? What are you two involved in?'

He tugged at her hair, violently pulling her face away from where she'd buried it against the chair. She felt exposed, vulnerable. 'Karen, all you need to know is that the others involved in this, they're men who won't think twice about hurting you.' He tugged more tightly, pulling her head back, exposing her throat. 'Really hurting you. Hurting Kevin. Hurting me. Maybe the children, too. Believe me, if we don't get this sorted, we'll all be joining Kevin in that hospital. Worse.'

He let go. She pulled back and sat looking at him. 'What's he done?'

'You don't need to know anything more than you know now.'

'Did he kill Stephen?'

Terry lunged forward, grabbing her chin. He held her face tight in his grip. 'What the fuck makes you think that? What's been said?'

She struggled to get the words out. 'Something one of the police said. They said his arrest was about Stephen.'

'What else?'

'They said another name. Robert Gordon.'

Brian Terry slackened his grip, his face turning ashen.

'Who is he? What is he to Kevin?' she asked.

Terry's grip tightened. He held her face even more firmly. 'Just get me that message.'

***

'Can we trust him?'

'How the fuck should I know?'

'You recruited him.'

Sean Loach slid open a draw of the desk where the two men sat and took out a small can of oil, placing it on the table. 'Recruited? Fuck you make it sound like some James Bond comic book. I found him. I found a man in a position to help us secure what we need. A man who would do pretty much anything for money. That he was sympathetic to the cause just made it easier for his conscience to accept the offer we made him. I doubt that it makes him any the more resistant to interrogation. Or the son either.'

The second man tugged the upturned collar of his jacket tighter. The room at the rear of the carpet shop was cold. Their breath hung cloud-like between them.

'So how much does he know?' he asked.

'Enough.'

'Enough for what?'

Loach tugged an oily rag from the draw. From the back of the draw he produced a long thin brush, laying it out next to the rag and the oil. 'Enough to fuck us.'

'So what do we do?'

'Getting to him isn't the issue. That can be done anytime. He knows that. It's the son that's the problem.'

'How so?'

'He's the one in custody. Right now, I've no idea exactly why he's there or how much his *da's* told him about the plan. Brian knows nothing of the target or the place, so the son can't tell them that. At best he knows where the stuff's hidden. Maybe how we intend to move it.'

'That's enough to fuck everything. There's no time for finding another source.'

'That's why we need Brian Terry to find out why his son's been arrested. Once we know that, well then we can make the judgement as to how to proceed.'

'So you're telling me that we do nothing.'

'No, we prepare. Like always.'

'Prepare?'

From the deeper bottom draw of the desk Loach removed a Smith and Wesson. It was a 29-2. It had an eight inch barrel, army issue. Loach had seen the film *Dirty Harry* and sometime after that the gun had found its way to him. It was a gun he liked. He liked the weight of it. Liked the fear that a sighting of it provoked in those he pointed it at.

'Prepare for what?' the man repeated.

Loach slid open the chamber, spinning it round with the palm of his hand before flicking it back into place. 'For all eventualities,' he said.

***

'Karen, thank god you're here.'

Karen Terry stood impassively at the end of the hospital bed. Kevin's left arm was held in a cast strapped across his chest. Beyond that, he had a series of scrapes and bruising to his face and neck.

The officer sitting on a chair in the corner of the room indicated that she should sit at the wooden chair by the side of the bed. Prior to being let in she had been told that there was to be minimal contact between herself and her husband. There could be no whispering.

Kevin leant towards her. 'I have no idea what the hell is going on,' he stated accompanied by a meaningful glance at the seated officer. 'Fucking outrageous!'

The officer, unimpressed, looked back at his newspaper.

'What have they said?'

'Nothing. They're planning on interviewing me later this evening or tomorrow morning. Apparently they need the doctor's permission to go ahead with it.'

'They must have said something,' she persisted.

'Seems like they want to interview me about Stephen. They think I know something about his death.'

'Have they said what?'

'It's crazy. They think that he was having an affair with you.'

'Why do they think that?'

'Some information they received. I thought it was just neighbours or scabs trying to stir the shite. But then I thought about it. I started to wonder just what the fuck you might have said to that WPC who came around.'

'Nothing. I said nothing.'

'Well you must have said something. Gave them some cause.'

'Why, have they said something? I didn't say anything. Nothing at all. Not like that. What have they told you I said to her?'

'They're not telling me anything. That's why I'm asking. I'm lying here wracking my brains for some reason as to why they've arrested me… and that's all I can think of. Are you sure you didn't say something?'

'What? That I was having an affair?'

'I don't know.'

'Is that what you think? Is that what you thought?'

'No. No course I didn't… don't. It's just…'

'Just what?'

'Well, why would they think that?'

'I dunno… Maybe because he came round with the food and that. Maybe like you said… one of the neighbours has said something when the police came round doing all those interviews.'

'Yeah. Suppose.' He leant forward, his voice reduced to a whisper. 'It's just, well… you did act weird that day. When I told you he was dead. You said I'd killed him, that's what you said. Did you say that to them… to that WPC?'

'Course not. Like you said. It was the shock… I was hysterical.'

'No whispering,' the officer interjected.

Kevin leaned back onto his pillow. 'What have they told you?'

'Nothing. Just a load more questions.'

'About what?'

'All sorts of stuff. Where you were the day he was killed. How you behaved.'

'What did you tell them?'

'The truth. You were at the picket that day. You'd left early to organise it. Like you always did. You came home and told me what had happened. I was shocked. Upset. The truth.'

Kevin looked ahead. His mind racing, sifting everything that was coming at him.

Karen looked towards the officer, checking he'd returned to his newspaper. When she spoke, it was soft. 'Your dad came round.'

'What's he say?'

'He said he needs you to be strong. That he needs you to do the right thing. Said you had friends who'd visited him. People who were interested in your health. He said they'd asked for some sort of a message from you. Some reassurance that you would be fine. Be strong with what's happened.'

'Fuck!'

'Kevin, I don't understand. What's going on? What have you got us involved in?'

'Nothing. Everything's fine.'

'I'm scared.'

She dabbed at her eyes. Kevin sat looking at her, for the first time noticing the swelling under her eye. The bruise on her jawbone. 'What happened?'

She reached a hand to her cheek. 'Your dad.'

'What?'

'Your dad. He was concerned that I delivered his message. Made sure that I got it right. Said he had to make sure that I understood the gravity of it. The consequences.'

'Karen. I'm sorry. I...'

'Just what have you gotten us into? Me. The children. What the hell have you been doing?'

'Keep your voice down, love. I'll make things right.'

'How?'

'This will all work out okay. Thing's will be okay. You'll see. Just tell dad to tell the committee that I'm strong with this. That the charges are about you having an affair with Jackson. It's a misunderstanding. There's nothing else that they're interested in. Nothing. Its personal, not about business. Make sure he knows that. Make sure that he passes it on to the committee, his mates. There's nothing in it. I get out of here and we're finished with it.

The union, the mines, everything. We'll go away.'

'How?'

'Don't worry, I've been working on something.'

'What?'

'Something big. A deal. A big deal. We'll be okay. I promise.'

'Does it involve your friend Robert Gordon?'

'What? What did you say?' Kevin stared at her, his mouth open, his eyes widening.

'Robert Gordon. The police asked about him. I told your dad. He went the same colour as you. Who is he? What is it that you're doing with him?'

***

Brian Terry's head was spinning. An endless stream of thoughts. Everything swirled around him. There was no pattern. No way forward. There appeared to be no solution.

Brian Terry, the man of action, the good soldier, the foot soldier. The man who asked few questions. The man who followed those paths laid out by others. The muscle. The sword. The arrow. The man of violence. The soldier without conscience.

Despite what others thought about him, he had his vision of the world. It was Marxist but filtered through the simple human trait of jealousy. What the bible referred to as covetousness. Put simply, Brian Terry wanted what he believed was his due. It meant that he would fight for any cause that put within his grasp what he believed was his entitlement. He believed in what he fought for. The violent commitment he brought to a march, to a picket line or a demonstration, was total and deeply held. But it was underpinned by a deep-rooted sense of embitterment.

Commitment to the cause was his strength. He was an arrow, a spear: precise and effective in its destructive power but a weapon essentially directionless. His bearings came from others. His willingness to align himself with Loach and the Irish cause was based on the offer of a quicker and richer return, riches beyond his wildest dreams.

He knew that Loach's approach for help in securing explosives from the colliery had been made from a position of urgency, of desperation. The seizure off the Essex coast of a boat from Libya with its cargo of Semtex had been a far greater loss to the IRA cause than the millions of pounds of cannabis found on board.

The major operation they had planned had a time-scale, a schedule that brooked no deviation. He knew nothing else and didn't want to. He knew enough to understand the possible consequences of Loach thinking him a weak link. A loose end.

The payment offered was enormous. The risk, minimal.

The cause to which the explosives would be put was of no concern.

The plan he'd executed was simple. He'd had similar ideas in his head for years whenever he thought of the day when the revolution would require resources such as those his job gave him access to.

He knew the colliery routines. He knew the security and he knew the location.

It had been his idea to recruit Kevin. He needed someone he could trust, someone who was *his* man not one of *theirs*. The payment he'd demanded had been increased to accommodate his son's involvement. Loach had agreed. They were desperate men, and Brian Terry the union negotiator understood only too well that such needs gave him unsurpassed bargaining power.

Down payments had been made, gestures of good will. Twenty thousand pounds for Brian, ten thousand for Kevin. A further fifty thousand had been made when they had extracted the explosives a few days ago. With his oversight of the secure explosive stores, it was a theft that the impact of the strike meant might remain undetected until the next stock check in two months' time. If the strike continued as it had, it might be later even than that. The explosives would have long done their work and the final payment of over two hundred thousand pounds would have been made. They would be set for life.

And then Kevin had made his mistake.

The money had been secreted away. Loach cautioning the danger of any sudden spending drawing unwanted attention on them, especially during the strike. But Kevin had not been able to resist. His big night out at the club. Flashing his money. The last of his holiday savings he'd told them. The Big Man treating his friends. An oasis in the dry desert of the strike. Chatting. Talking. Joking. Opening his mouth. Most had ignored him. Most had taken his drink and moved on. But not Jackson. Jackson had encouraged him, urged him on with his stories.

Brian Terry knew that his son had envied Jackson. Envied his easy manner, his commitment to the picket. Jackson had quickly become a hero. In that moment in the club, Kevin had been unable to resist the temptation of boasting of his own coming *special moment*. Of him, Kevin Terry, being selected as a key player in something special. *We'll be heroes. Making history.*

Jackson had listened. Listened too well.

Brian had pulled Kevin away, cutting him short. But it was soon clear that it had been too late. Over the next few days he'd watched Jackson take a growing interest in Kevin. Stalked him. Encouraging him to talk.

Brian had grown nervous, caught between too many decisions: *Should he tell Loach? What would Loach do? Would they pull out? Would he and Kevin lose all of the money? Would he and Kevin be seen as a risk? Should he confront Jackson and if so, what would he say to him? What would he do?*

Eventually, inevitably for a man like himself, it had led to only one path, one decision. Jackson had to be removed.

Kevin had been less than reliable in that.

He'd agreed to lure Jackson to the field with the excuse that they were checking for weaknesses in the police lines ahead of that morning's picket. The promise of talking alone. The promise of revelations. Jackson hadn't had a clue.

Brian had moved quickly from behind the hedgerow. The first blow had hit Jackson before he'd realised what was happening. The second blow had probably finished him.

Kevin had stood there, open-mouthed. Aghast.

That was probably why Brian had swung the third blow and the subsequent ones.

Kevin. Kevin needed to be shown how it worked.

You acted. Committed.

Kevin said he'd thought they'd wanted to talk to Jackson, to reason with him. Brian knew such a course to be unreliable. Jackson knew too much. He was a threat.

Jackson died because of Kevin's inability to do what he was told. Kevin had to see that. Kevin had to learn that there were consequences for his weakness. Brian was his father. He had to show him. It's what any father would have done; he'd protected a son from the consequences of his own foolish actions.

When he'd heard of how Karen had reacted to the news of Jackson's death - screaming, breaking down and blaming Kevin - he'd worried how Kevin would handle it. He'd offered to talk to Karen himself, but Kevin hadn't wanted that. In the end Kevin had seemed strong, he hadn't wilted. Maybe he was learning.

But now Kevin was in custody, and he had no way of finding out why. No way of finding out how he was coping. How he was holding out.

They were back to where they were before he'd killed Jackson.

Loach was not a man of understanding. He would eliminate loose ends. The only thing in Brian and Kevin's favour was that before he could act Loach would want to find out just what those ends were, where they led.

Karen was the key to surviving and to securing the money. And that worried him. She was weak, like her own mother and father. He knew why his son had married her; she was a slag. A pretty one, but a slag all the same.

He'd preyed on that weakness to get her to deliver the message to Kevin. Scared the shit out of her. She'd understood. A slap or two and she had come round. All he needed now was to discover what Kevin had told her. Find out just what the police knew. Once he had the facts he could formulate a plan. Things could still work out.

For now, his head spun. A centrifuge.

Twenty-four
Day Twelve

Brody massaged his brow. Calling in a favour, he'd spent the first part of the morning sitting in front of a micro-fiche screen in the clippings library of the *Evening Mail* researching the key players in the story he planned to write.

Thus far, there had been no response to either letter. From what he'd learned from Kramer's source and what he'd pieced together for himself, it seemed more than ever that there was a conspiracy of silence, one involving policing at the highest level.

The more closely he'd looked into it, he realised his error of judgement. During his check in the clippings library, the name DCS Frank Ridgway appeared again and again in connection to demands for a probe into West Midlands Crime Squad and corrupt practices. If Special Branch were involved he felt certain Ridgway was in their pocket. In which case, Ridgway knew of Brody's suspicions and of his claim to have information to share with the Enquiry.

On top of that, a few phone calls to former sympathisers now stringers on the nationals had also produced a sketchy outline of the officer from Complaints Roberts had talked about. Riordan, an officer shrouded with whispers of covert operations.

It was during a coffee break that he'd first seen the Reuters information come through with news of the arrest of Kevin Terry. Although Kevin himself was unknown to him, Brody knew Kevin's father by reputation.

In the solitude of his booth, he'd soon realised that the arrest was all wrong. Even if Brian's son had suspected his wife of having an affair with Jackson, it didn't read right for murder.

Given what he knew, and what he could surmise, it smacked of being a cover up. The police were going to stitch Kevin Terry up for the killing. Jealousy and passion made it palatable to both sides of the accusations, to police and miners alike. Certainly it the inclusion of illicit sex offered a story that would be leapt on by the tabloid Red Tops and their waiting readership. Case solved, move on. It would be classic West Midlands Crime Squad tactics. Ridgway's prints all over it.

From the point of view of his own theory, the arrest served only to add weight to the idea that Jackson was an alias of an operative working as an agent provocateur. Brody's narrative held up: that his sudden death was forcing a hastily organised cover up of his identity by the very security forces that had been running him. Jackson was only the tip of this particular iceberg. There would be others like him, operatives all over the country doing the bidding of Thatcher and her government.

Brody stood and scooped up pad, pens, and the small sheaf of photocopied articles into his shoulder bag. Speed was now of the essence. By now Ridgway would have alerted others involved in the conspiracy. Whitehall. The *Spooks*. Special Branch. Probably this Riordan. Maybe Kalus.

He'd call Brian Terry, leave a message that he was onto a story that would not only clear his son but vindicate the wider objectives of the strike.

If Kevin could be cleared of Jackson's murder, then no matter what Ridgway and the rest might do, the investigation would have to continue. That being so, the greater his own chance of finding the evidence that he knew to be out there. Evidence confirming all those dark secrets that the government were clearly growing ever more desperate not be exposed.

* * *

Riordan sat alone in the colliery canteen flicking through the pages of the latest entries into the so-called Murder Book. There was little beyond the mundane, the routine. The log of detectives assigned to which duties and the cross-reference to their reports. To his trained eye, there was little taking them anywhere other than the questioning of Kevin Terry. He was a suspect with motive and opportunity, and one certainly with the means.

It was good enough.

There was no indication of any link to *Silver Fox*. For the moment, the fact that Jackson had little in the way of any existence outside his paperwork prior to his arrival at Tamworth had drawn nothing in the way of suspicion. The man was simply a loner. A man who kept himself to himself. A drifter.

As far as he could see, there remained just one fly in the ointment. The journalist Matthew Brody. In the last hour he'd been intercepted on an MI5 phone tap contacting Brian Terry, telling him that he had proof that his boy Kevin was the victim of a cover up.

Brody had formed a key part of his report of a few days ago. He was a known rabble-rouser, but according to Eddie Kramer he was a revolutionary who wanted to come in from the cold. His Big Story was seen as his means to do so.

At first, he'd suggested bribery, but the Specialist had rejected it. Such things would only offer the man certainty that he was on to something worth pursuing. Whitehall's confirmation of the Specialist's plan had been clear. The Specialist had been sent for just such an outcome.

Brody's persistence meant he had to be eliminated, and they had planned accordingly. But now, with his call to Terry, circumstance had conspired to offer an even better resolution, one resolving each of the threats to Silver Fox.

It had been the Specialist's idea. Finessing the plan. Riordan had to admire its genius. Its simplicity. Its finality. If they acted swiftly, Brody's death offered an outcome satisfying all of their requirements.

The Specialist would control this part of the operation, Riordan would assist. Brody would not be the first man whose death he'd played a part in. Three in Ireland, two in Gibraltar. Severed brake pipes in Gibraltar. An electrocution and an explosion in Belfast. Each judged to be either tragic accidents or the work of person or persons unknown. Terrorism was after all a dangerous business.

The Specialist had been clear in what was needed. Brody's death must be untraceable back to *Silver Fox*. From the start, they'd sought a suitable perpetrator to take the blame for Jackson's murder. A man like Brian Terry had been one of several in the frame. Terry, a man Brody had contacted and with phone records to prove it. Brody, a journalist very publicly looking into the murder of Stephen Jackson, had this morning contacted Brian Terry, a violent man whose son was currently the prime suspect for a brutal murder.

Circumstantial. But men had been imprisoned or executed on less. Just ask Ridgway or West Midlands Crime Squad.

To work, they required Kevin Terry out of hospital and out of police custody.

The Specialist had been unperturbed. Strings would be pulled. Accommodations made.

* * *

The journey from the hospital had been completed in silence. Both Brian and Kevin wrapped in thoughts they were reluctant to share.

For Kevin, the fact that his father had threatened Karen, struck her, lay between them. The violence he'd witnessed throughout his life seemed to be making up a greater share of the man he knew. It had become the default action to anything troubling him, anything that he found hard to deal with.

The brutality of the killing of Stephen Jackson had shocked Kevin to his core. It wasn't just the sheer horror of what he saw that morning - a man's head reduced to pulp - it was the cold detachment of his father as he had reigned down the blows.

More than that, he couldn't shake the fact that his father had been looking into his own eyes each time he'd brought the hammer down on the recumbent body of his friend, his hero,

Stephen Jackson.

From that point on he had known the extent to which his fate was tied to that of his father. They were set on a path with no perceivable way of stepping off. They had to see through to the end the plan that his father had pulled them into. Survive. After that, a year or so from now when no one was interested in the death of a miner on a picket line or the source of explosives for one IRA bomb among many, he would take Karen and the children and disappear forever.

'Fantastic stroke of luck, eh son?'

'What's that?'

'That lawyer. Harper. The civil rights people getting you out.'

'Yeah. Amazing.'

'Sound like you mean it. It's a get out of jail free card having that lot on your side. No prosecutor will want to take them on, not now, no matter what they might suspect. There's no proof. No witnesses. Nothing. You being arrested might just be the thing we needed. Nothing'll stick! *Teflon*!'

'Yeah, sure. It's great.'

'Fuck me, Kevin, it's the first decent break we've had since this whole thing started.'

Kevin's silent stare ahead frustrated his father. 'For fuck's sake, Kevin! You know I wouldn't have done it if it weren't necessary. I'd never really hurt her.'

'That right? You see, I'm not so sure.'

'Kevin,' Brian protested.

'Don't, dad. Just don't. You've never liked her.'

'What? You think I've been looking for a chance to slap her? Your wife? That's crazy. What kind of bloke do you think I am?'

Kevin bit back the words he wanted to say; *I don't know anymore*. Instead he opted for silence.

'We need to get word to Loach. Let him know things are okay,' Brian stated.

'Okay? When you told me about your plan, this great opportunity that had fallen into our laps, you made it sound so simple. A way of getting back at Thatcher and all she's done, at the same time making serious money. And look at it. Where we are. Jackson is dead, killed because you thought he might be a threat to the plan. And where's it got us? A shit load of police asking questions of everybody, forcing them to recall what they've seen over the past few days - days when we've been seen talking to Loach and his lot, something I'd rather people forgot about. And, because of all that snooping around and asking questions, I've got a team of detectives thinking that I might have killed him because some busy-body nosy neighbour told them they thought he was fucking Karen. Meanwhile, there's a batch of explosives to shift, and shift soon. And now, because of the killing and all of the attention on the picket, the police have stepped up their stop and search of every car travelling around the area. Now they're looking not just for flying pickets, they're searching them for murder weapons. Great, dad. Fucking great!' He paused, mind scooting off in a more pertinent direction. 'And from what I've seen, Loach is not a man to be disappointed. He's not going to let us miss his deadline. Fuck up his plan. If we do, he'll kill us as much out of spite as much as to keep us quiet.'

'I thought I'd brought you up with a little more balls than this.'

'How's that then? Because of all the beatings?'

'I never-'

'Never what? Gave me a beating unless I deserved it? Jesus, dad, I must have been a very bad boy! All those beatings. You had your work cut out with me, didn't you?'

'For God's sake, Kevin! You're my boy. I love you.'

'Yeah.'

'Yes. Yes, Kevin. You're my blood.'

'But you wish I wasn't.'

'That's not true.'

'No? Maybe not. You certainly wish I was more like you, though, don't you?'

The car stopped outside Kevin's house.

He tried opening the door but his sling got in the way. He

reached across himself with his good arm, yanking the handle up and down in frustration. He smashed at it; beat it with his fist.

His father leant across to open it.

'Leave it! Leave it!' Kevin screamed, knocking his father's hand away.

Brian Terry pulled back.

The door sprang open and Kevin awkwardly scrambled out, slamming it shut behind him.

***

'Christ what the fuck's happened?'

The house was in disarray. The armchair overturned, the coffee table smashed. The sofa was covered with the same blood that lay pooled on the carpet in front of it.

'Jesus!' Brian Terry uttered.

'Karen! Karen! Where are you?' Kevin dashed into the kitchen. 'It's me, Kevin! Where are the kids? What's' happened?' He raced through the lounge and up the stairs. 'Karen! Karen!'

Brian Terry stared at the wreckage that was the parlour lounge.

'I can't find her. None of them. What the fuck's happened?' Kevin asked, picking up the phone that was lying on its side, the tone a steady *burr*. 'Explains why she wasn't answering,' he said. He pumped the reset button and began to dial.

'What are you doing?' his dad asked.

'Ringing the police.'

Brian Terry stepped forward, slamming a paw down on the reset button.

'What did you do that for?' Kevin demanded.

'Why the fuck are you ringing the police?'

'She's gone. She's not here, nor are the kids. Look at it. Something's happened.'

'Something's happened sure enough. The question is, what?'

'What do you mean? *What?*'

'Kevin, who the fuck do you think's done this?'

'Robbers... A maniac. How the fuck do I know?'

'Kevin, maniacs and robbers don't do this... They don't take the people they've robbed away with them.'

'Loach?'

Brian nodded. 'Loach has got her. Got to be.'

'Why would Loach have taken Karen and the kids?'

'He would have come looking for re-assurance.'

'About what?'

'About you. That you weren't going to say anything untoward about their plan. About the explosives.'

'Why would I do that?'

'Because you were arrested and about to be interviewed by the police as the prime suspect in the murder of Stephen Jackson. No-one knew what the fuck was happening. We couldn't get to see you. That's why we got Karen to go. She was supposed to find out what was going on. To bring answers back.'

'But why would they have taken her? I told her. I told her it was all a mistake. They thought I'd killed Jackson because some neighbour or someone had said she was having an affair with him. I told her it was crazy, that we'd get it sorted. I'd be out. That's what I told her to tell you.'

'She never said.'

'What?'

'She never said. I came round last night to find out what you'd told her. There was no answer. I just thought...'

'You'd slapped her around. She wasn't going let you in if she was here by herself.'

'I thought she might be asleep or at her mother's.'

'Fuck, dad!'

'I should have seen it. Loach. He was... doubtful. He must have come round before I got here and not liked what she told him. Maybe he thought she knew more than she does.'

'So what's he done with her? With the kids.'

'He'll have taken them all as security.'

'What? A hostage?'

'Maybe. I mean if... Maybe he didn't' trust her to keep

quiet. Didn't like what he heard. Maybe she said something. She's got a smart mouth on her at times. Thinking she's better than the rest. Maybe she upset them Maybe he just wanted some extra leverage for you to keep quiet whilst the police interviewed you.'

'But he must know I'm out. Didn't you say he had some source at the police station? They'd have told him. He'd know by now that I'm in the clear.'

'So maybe he decides to keep her to make sure that we go through with the plan and hand over the explosives.'

'Why wouldn't we?'

'Like you said, police operations have tightened up. He's on a deadline, we know that. It's a tight one, after which the explosives are pretty much useless to them and whatever it is they're planning to do with them. Them holding Karen and the kids ensures we get on with it. Make the drop.'

'Then contact him. Let him know what's happened. Tell him to let Karen them go.'

'I can't contact him. He does all the contacting.'

'So what do we do?'

'Get the stuff and make the drop as planned. Tonight. We get Karen and the kids back, and he hands over the rest of our money. We can do this, Kevin. It's still there for us. Everything we planned. We just need to be strong. Like I showed you.'

Twenty-five
Day Thirteen

'What do you mean he's been sent home?' Standing in front of his temporary desk in the colliery canteen, Kalus could barely contain his agitation at the news he'd been handed of the release of Kevin Terry.

Richard Mallen blew out his cheeks. 'Seems like your man Kevin had friends in high places. Higher than any of ours at least.'

Kalus tossed his coat on the desk, scattering files and paperwork. 'How?'

Mallen shrugged his shoulders. 'Some civil rights lawyer, that Harper, got on the case. Appears the powers that be got jumpy. Phone calls to Ridgway. Seems Ridgway caved. No doubt worried his involvement might set the hounds off in the direction of *West Mids. Crime Squad* and his own track record. He said there was no evidence. He said that we were throwing dice with no hope of success.'

'Christ!'

'Yeah, I thought it a bit rich. You know, *physician cure they self*. All the ropey things he's got his name attached to. End of the day, word is that he was all for letting Kevin go. Said it couldn't wait till the morning. It had to be done right away. He called off the security. Hospital said that Terry's dad picked him up late last night.'

'And no contact with us?'

Mallen shrugged. 'Seems like Ridgway didn't feel the need.'

'Fuck that!' Kalus reached across the table and dragged the telephone towards him. He dialled the number for Burton HQ, and within moments was through to his DCS.

'Frank, what the fuck is going on?' Kalus demanded.

'Steady Peter,' Ridgway advised.

'Fuck steady!' Kalus put equal emphasis on both words. 'The one suspect we've got, and you put him back on the street before we've a chance to even ask him his fucking name.'

Ridgway's tone was calming, matter of fact. 'You said yourself he was a longshot. Looks bad if the media think we're just chucking sticks up in the air and seeing where they land. We look desperate. I mean, a letter from a wife who herself is under immense emotional pressure from months of striking, of making do. A letter where she says he's *different* and has *bad dreams*. Any half-decent defence QC would make us a laughingstock. And that's something no-one here or in Whitehall is going to allow. Not as things are.'

'Longshot or not, he was *my* suspect,' Kalus snapped. 'Interviewing him, charging him, releasing him - that's *my* call, Frank. Mine.'

'Actually, Detective Chief Inspector, I think you'll find that it's my call,' he cautioned.

'What? You gave me this case. Told me to get to the bottom of it. Told me to follow my instincts. Not be deflected by the pressure. What happened to that?'

'We're coppers, Peter. Bobbies. We follow orders, all of us. We're not politicians. Things change. Circumstances.' Ridgway's voice had an edge, that of a superior officer resenting a challenge to his authority.

Kalus felt his frustration spill over. 'Who the fuck has got to you, Frank?'

'No-one has *got to me* Detective Inspector,' Ridgway responded, voice clipped, terse. 'Strikes me you've been watching too much TV. Too much *Sweeny* or *Professionals*.'

'Tell me, Frank. At least do me the courtesy of not treating me like some naïve rookie. What have they got on you? Just what have they got?' He was in no mood for being side-tracked. 'What were you doing all those years in the Regional Crime Squad? Is that it? Is that what they've got? Harper puts some pressure on, and you all fold, all the way to those at the top,' he bit back.

'That's enough Chief Inspector! Enough,' Ridgway cautioned. 'You're going too far. You're way out of line. I can have you suspended.'

'Fine,' Kalus snapped back. 'Suspend me. I think we both know that's a course of action creating unwelcome questions for you and your bosses from the media. I don't think that you or your masters' would want that, would they?'

There was a pause before Ridgway responded, his voice lowering a notch. 'Peter, if this goes to the press…well, let's say it's not the only thing that's going to get dragged through the mud, is it? You're a good copper, Peter. Even after Handsworth I still put a great deal of faith in you. For God's sake, I went out on a limb. Your record, our past, gives you a little leeway with me, but you've got this all wrong,' he soothed. 'Harper's been after me for years. He'd stoop to anything. He's building himself a career in politics on the back of this whole *West Midlands* thing. You know me, Peter. Trust me on this. I know that you're under tremendous pressure. I'm just anxious for you to conclude it. For you to get the right result.'

'Then keep the fuck out,' Kalus retorted unappeased. 'Let me investigate.'

'Listen to yourself,' Ridgway advised. 'Maybe you do need a break. Take a day or two. Spend time with the family. Your dad. Mallen's more than capable of fronting things for a while. You know he is.'

'I won't be side-lined,' Kalus persisted.

'No-one's side-lining you.' Ridgway exhaled slowly, considering his words. 'But fact is that maybe you need a little time to get things in perspective. I pushed you, was desperate to get you back. Maybe too far, too soon. You're not yourself. Handsworth. Your father's illness. I blame myself for putting you in the firing line. Finish up the day and then stay home.'

'Is that an order?'

Ridgway weighed his response. 'It's the advice of a

concerned friend, Peter. A friend who happens to be your superior officer,' he reminded. 'But yes. Yes that is an order.'

The line went dead.

Kalus slammed the receiver back onto the cradle and slumped back into his chair.

'Jesus!' Mallen commented.

'Did you get all of that?' he asked.

Mallen nodded. 'The gist.'

Kalus shoved the phone away. 'Seems like we're being fucked on all sides.'

'What's he say?'

'It's what he didn't say.' He sat back, staring at the phone. 'I've known the man for five years. Five years', he repeated, 'and he's never once overruled me. Not once.' He steepled his hands in thought. 'He's hiding something.'

'Hiding what?'

He shook his head. 'I don't know,' he admitted.

'You think maybe it's linked to all these noises about the Crime Squad being investigated?' Mallen offered. 'This Harper? Sounds like he's got the bit between his teeth.'

Kalus screwed up his face. 'Some.' He considered the idea. 'None of them are lilywhite. Frank was there longer than most.'

'So why would that make him release Kevin Terry?' Mallen pondered.

'I don't know if it did. But what it does do is make DCS Frank Ridgway vulnerable to pressure from above. Pressure from those who can protect him. Those who can see to it that he's either eased into a safe retirement and that cosy pension or tossed to the mob.'

'Sounds like a *Le Carre* novel,' Mallen observed.

'I know,' Kalus accepted. 'A dark and scary one.'

A deep silence lay between them. Mallen hesitated. 'Peter. You're sure… I mean, it's a hell of a leap. Accusing a man like Ridgway. Suggesting a conspiracy to derail a murder enquiry.'

Kalus fixed him with a glare. 'You mean I'm fantasising?'

'No… I mean. Well, like Frank was saying. Handsworth…

Your dad. Maybe you just need a day or two to get... sorted. I mean, it's not been so long since... everything.'

'You too, eh?' he accused.

'What?'

'Seems like everybody wants me off this damned enquiry.'

'What? That's' so sodding unfair,' Mallen protested. 'You think I'm in this conspiracy of yours?'

'I don't know...I mean...No...No. Of course I don't. It's just....' he stumbled to a halt. He shook his head in exasperation, gathering himself. 'Earlier, you had ideas about Riordan. What his role was. Whether he was what he said he was. What Ridgway said he was.'

Mallen shrugged, flicking his hair. 'Doesn't mean to say it's a conspiracy. Like you said, it's more than likely just Whitehall or whoever covering their backs. Keeping one of their own at the centre of things. Making certain there are no nasty political surprises.'

'Maybe. Maybe,' he conceded.

Mallen rose from his chair. 'Look, I'll go and find out if anyone knows what's happened to Kevin Terry and his dad. Where they are. We might still be able to go round and talk with them. Off the record, so to speak. If it's not him, then maybe after this arrest he'll have every reason to co-operate.'

Kalus nodded. He had no real grasp of what he was thinking at all. Everything was shifting. There were no certainties. Nothing was as it seemed. Everything was hedged by darkness.

Was that true, or was that him?

Was he putting his own issues onto the enquiry?

Maybe he did need that break. Maybe it was time to admit what he believed to be true – what others were now seeing. What they'd been suspecting, what they were clearly discussing. He was no longer up to it.

It was time to finish.

He would take Ridgway's instruction. End of the day. Maybe the end of it all. Maybe it was no bad thing. Finally admitting what he had kept so deep in him for so long.

He couldn't cut it anymore. That it was time to go

* * *

It was White who found the letter, read the contents, realised the significance. He took it immediately to Kalus.

'When did this come in?'

'Must have been yesterday, day before at the earliest. We're way overstretched,' he added defensively. 'It's a wonder it got looked at today. Tucked somewhere in the pile. I'm sorry, guv. I can't see how I overlooked it. I swear I went through it all. It's a wonder I found it now. Low priority pile. We're dealing with hundreds of calls, people who claim to have seen groups of men acting suspiciously. It's hardly surprising given there are gangs of pickets being shipped in from all over the county and beyond. Then there's the wild goose chase calls trying to run us around, tie up resources, people who think by doing that they're helping the miners. Even had one old couple seeing an alien spaceship land by the Co-Op. I'm telling you guv, it's open season out there for nutters and wierdos. But they all have to be logged. Referenced. Letters get low priority.'

'Okay. It slipped through. So what do we know about this bloke…Brody?'

'From what he says, he's a journalist of sorts.'

Roberts looked up from the report he was writing. 'Brody? Matthew Brody?'

'Yeah.'

'You know him?'

Roberts half-nodded, half-shrugged a response. 'Sort of.'

'Sort of?'

Roberts considered what had been the precise nature of his meeting with Brody. 'He's a mate of Eddie Kramer's. I spoke to him the other day. He wanted stuff for a story. Background.'

'And you didn't see fit to tell anyone?'

'I was helping out a mate, guv. Eddie. He said that all this

Brody wanted was a bit of inside stuff. He was asking about Jackson's background. His military service. Seemed harmless. He wanted something as background for a story.'

Kalus wafted the letter. 'Seems from this that he's got himself one. Says he wants to meet me to discuss the fact that our investigation is being sabotaged from the top. That he has knowledge of Jackson, some secret that proves we're being misled into perverting the course of justice.'

'Fuck me!'

'What exactly did you tell him?'

'Nothing.' Roberts answered. 'Eddie said he was a colleague who he wanted to help, a favour he owed. Said it would be good for him. Considering how helpful Eddie's' been to us in the past…well, I felt CID owed him something. It didn't seem much. He just asked about what we knew of Jackson's background. Did we know he was ex-army? Seemed really interested in that. I thought he was going to write something about the death of a man who'd served his country.'

'And?'

'And I said of course we knew he was ex-army. Did he think we were incompetent or something. We knew Jackson wasn't local. He'd been at the pit a few months before the strike.'

'That it?'

'Yeah.'

Kalus looked out of the window.

Roberts looked at him expectantly. 'Guvnor?' he asked.

Guvnor. Boss. Chief. 'He was pumping you Mick. Wanted to find out what we knew. If we knew what he knew. Had what he had. If we were genuine or part of some conspiracy.'

'And?'

'I think we'd better get him in. Have a talk with our Matthew Brody.'

'Matthew Brody?' Mallen asked approaching the table.

Kalus turned. 'Yeah why, you know him, too?'

'No, but there's something you should know. Something's just come in on the wire from Brum.'

Twenty-six

The first blow dropped him forward. Swung from above and to his right, it struck him above the right ear just behind the temple. He wouldn't have heard the sound. Nor would he have at first realised he had been struck. At about the time his cognitive faculty began to warn him as to what was happening, the second blow fell, this time a return swing up from left to right making contact just below the rear of the skull, its impact shattering the parietal cranial bone, and from that point on rendering him helpless.

His head crashed forward, his chin smashing into the desktop. His head flopping, lying to the side, forehead coming to rest just in front of the Olivetti. The letters on the keys the last thing he saw before his optic nerves shut down leaving him trapped in a numbing darkness. Had he, at this point possessed control of his faculties, he would have been in a state of confusion, unable to comprehend the assault. The blows that pounded his head into the desk were something of a coup d' grace. Heavy hands. The impact not only shattered what was left of the right side of the skull but drove splinters from the desk up and into the cheek pressed against it.

Eric Doyle, squinted over the top of the spectacles perched on the end of his nose. He lowered the paper from which he had been reading. 'Does that satisfy you Inspector? Or would you like a second opinion on this?'

'That's more than sufficient, Doctor.'

Doyle tucked his handwritten notes into a manila folder, which he then slid into a larger leather document case. He waved the case over his shoulder for the grasping hand of Donald Osborne to gather and slip into the black Gladstone medical bag that sat at his assistant's feet. 'It's just that I've come to see how little you people seem to think I can divine as to the nature of truth from such humble signs. Isn't that right, Donald? Seem to think that, because we can't find a coal dust covered handprint on a corpse, that we're not up to it anymore. Can't give the bosses the coal miner murderer they want.'

Donny Osborne nodded. He knew better than to try slipping a word in, even one of concurrence.

Kalus offered Doyle the expected words of homage. 'Look, Doctor, we all know the good work you do.'

'Well, maybe you could pass that up the line of command to your superiors. They all seem to think that because I can't tell them that it was a miner who killed that Jackson fellow, that I'm somehow past it. Ridgway for one has been a constant pain in that regard. Ringing my lab every day, twice a day.'

'I'm sure it's just a concern to get to the bottom of it all.'

'I'm a scientist, Inspector, don't talk to me about being sure or certainty. I state what is there. What is present. What is sure. What is fact. I am not divine, I don't deal in delivering whatever it is that your superiors' wish to be. I deal in what is. Tell your DCS Ridgway that for me, will you?'

'Yes, I will. He's aware of your reputation.'

The pathologist paused in removing the Tyvek suit. 'A reputation that's been earned over thirty years. Call out's at all times of the day and night. Expected to slide into sewers and slums. Walk knee deep through bodily fluids. Scenes that would turn most men's stomachs - and to then deliver sage judgments on the spot that point you to the killer.' He finished slipping off the suit. 'It can't be done, you know. Cause of death, time of death - all of these things are possible in good time. Easy when it's the husband, the wife, the lover, the jealous neighbour, the angry drunk. But stuff like Jackson... stuff like this. It's messy. And not just in terms of the gore.'

Doyle pulled on the jacket held out for him by Osborne. He didn't need to look, he knew it would be there. He shrugged his way into it, tugging it into place. Osborne picked up the doctor's bag and the deposited over-suit, a coal truck to Doyle's engine. Jacket on, Doyle surveyed the room.

Kalus stood expectant, Doyle pushing his glasses up to the bridge of his nose. 'Inspector, I have at present no idea as to the certainty of anything beyond the fact that this poor fellow died sometime yesterday afternoon or early evening from blows to the head. There were at least four, maybe half-a-dozen. He used a lump hammer, big and solid. And the perpetrator himself was big. Actually, maybe not big, but certainly strong, muscular. From the probable sequence of blows indicated by the blood splatter marks, they're also someone who knew what they were doing. Not crazed. Motivated.'

Doyle nodded a farewell, and took his leave, Osborne towed in his wake.

Mallen uttered the expected 'Wanker!' serving as the now almost obligatory salute to Doyle's exit from any crime scene.

'Yeah, but he's right.'

'About?'

'About almost everything. The Jackson case, for one. We both know there's real pressure for a result, the *right* result. Ridgway's feeling it too. Part of it, even, whatever *it* is.'

'But what's he expect? Course we want a result. No one wants it to be one of our own. But it doesn't mean to say that we want Doyle to put his precious reputation on the line. Put a tarnish on that brass plaque he calls a conscience.'

'Very poetic Richard.'

'Fuck you!'

Kalus half-smiled. 'That's more like it.'

Mallen ignored the comment. 'And what's he mean, *motivated*? What the fuck's that supposed to mean? Fucking footballer's are supposed to be *motivated*. Fucking Villa are supposed to be *motivated*, not hammer killers.'

'I don't know. I suppose it's his way of saying it needn't be some Charles Atlas type.'

'Little bloke, big hammer?'

'Maybe,' Kalus conceded.

'So what *have* we got?' Mallen pursued, his emphasis on the *have*.

Kalus considered the question. 'We've got two bodies. Two males.'

'Both early thirties,' Roberts offered as he passed by.

'A miner and a journalist,' Mallen put in.

'A journalist covering the miner's story,' Kalus stated.

'A journalist who says he has information that would be of help to us, that the dead miner had a secret,' Roberts developed the point.

'Both bludgeoned to death,' Kalus said, bringing the process full circle.

'So we assume that whatever it was that Brody had, whatever it was that he wanted to tell us, was sufficient for someone kill him. So we're looking for someone who knew what Brody had. Someone who knew what he was about to tell us. Something that threatened them themselves. *Ipso facto*, Jackson's murderer.'

'Take the place apart. There must be something. The man was a reporter. He would have records, notes - details of who he saw, what they told him.' Kalus spread his arms to take in the room. 'Somewhere in here, there's got to be something that we need to know.'

'Guv.'

Roberts stood with a sheet of typewritten paper he'd fished out from a book on the coffee table. 'Take a look at this.'

On the sheet was a phone number, the name *Brian Terry* scribbled beside it. 'Why would our man Brody be interested in contacting Terry senior?'

'He's writing about the strike. Both Terry's are key men in it. A useful source.'

'Maybe. Maybe Brody had something that he wanted to ask him about, either that or to share what he already had. Maybe something about the arrest and the links to Jackson. This secret he was going on about.'

'The same thing he wanted to talk to us about?'

'Possibly.'

'Why would he want to share that with Brian Terry?'

'Maybe he wanted a comment.'

'Or a denial?'

'And instead got a visit?'

'Brody's letter said that whatever he had concerned Jackson's life. Maybe he had evidence that Jackson was fucking the daughter-in-law. Maybe he had proof of a motive.'

'Brian Terry's a violent man,' Mallen stated.

'Brian Terry's a very violent man,' Kalus agreed.

'And he and his son were both on the picket the day Jackson was bludgeoned to death. Kevin was responsible for deployment. Who went where. He could have set a trap.'

'But Kevin was still in hospital at the time Doyle says Brody was killed.'

'Perfect alibi.'

'But his dad wasn't in custody.'

'But then why all this stuff about our investigation being sabotaged from above that Brody talked about in his letter?'

'Maybe he knew that Kevin was going to be released. You said yourself that you thought Ridgway was giving in to pressure from the top brass. This civil rights group. Maybe Ridgway was agreeing to the releasing of Terry to get Harper off his case. Maybe that was what Brody was aware of. He was left wing, yeah? Militant Tendency. Man like Brody must have had contact with people like Harper and the left-wing civil liberties lot. He would have known the father too. Brian Terry is well known on the left.'

'So he tells Brian Terry that he's written a story. That he knows that Kevin's the killer. He wants a comment, maybe even some background on Kevin to fill it out. Contacts us because he picks up that the Civil Rights lot are pressuring Ridgway to get Kevin released. He's worried. Thinks Kevin might come after him. He contacts us because he wants to show us the evidence to stop Kevin's release. But before he can talk to us, the dad, Brian Terry comes round. There's a confrontation. Maybe Brody turns his back on Terry and sits down. Doctor Doyle reckons the perpetrator was standing over Brody whilst he was at his desk.'

'Maybe he's going to show him something that's on his desk. Maybe the evidence.'

'Terry smashes his skull in.'

'Like father, like son.'

* * *

They sat in a car across from Brody's flat. They'd arrived just after picking up the police radio traffic they'd been waiting for. They'd phoned it in themselves. A neighbour who didn't want to leave a name who'd heard raised voices, an argument that had sounded violent '...*this big man running from the block of flats...*'

Since arriving they had watched the comings and goings of the ambulance crew along with that of the pathologist and his assistant. There was no need for Riordan to go in. He was more than familiar with what they would find. Besides, it was better he wasn't present when they found the sheet with Brian Terry's phone number along with the research notes on Brian and Kevin Terry he'd placed there.

On the back seat was the actual file Brody had compiled. It was a mix of photocopies of news articles from the local and national papers along with the journalist's handwritten notes.

Riordan had skimmed through it. 'Not bad,' he'd offered by way of review. By chance or good intelligence, Brody had managed to identify key elements of *Silver Fox* and those involved. The Minister's name was underlined in an article on the policing of the strike - though given the man's profile it was hard to tell if this was just a lucky and obvious guess or genuine investigative skill.

'Looks like the dogs have got the scent,' Riordan stated as he watched Kalus and then Mallen and Roberts exit the house and make for their car.

'Even the local plod can't have missed that one,' the Specialist said. 'Tied up with ribbon. Just enough left for them to do to make them think it's all their own idea.'

'So we're set for the next step.'

The Specialist nodded. They had been over it a number of times. It held up. 'What about the wife?' he asked.

'I read her statement. She was more than likely fucking Jackson. And if she wasn't... well she surely wished she was. She certainly thinks her husband believes she was. That'll be enough.

She won't be a problem.'

'We need this to be tidy. No ragged edges. It's got to be final. This investigation ends today. Ends with the outcome we need. The outcome they've asked for. The one *She* wants.'

Riordan nodded. 'Understood.'

'Kalus and his team need to be convinced that they've solved this by themselves. Kevin Terry and his dad killed Jackson because they believed he was fucking Kevin's wife. Kevin lures Jackson to a lonely spot. They batter him to death, believing suspicion will fall on the police. They're confident that any investigation will get caught up in the politics. They think they're okay. Then this Brody comes along with evidence of what happened to Jackson. He's going to tell the authorities, get their interest by alluding to a secret he's found about Jackson which boils down to evidence that Jackson was fucking the Terry woman. But he's a journalist. He's ambitious. He wants a scoop. So, stupidly he contacts Brian Terry and lets slip his evidence of his son's involvement. Brian kills him, takes the evidence and runs.' He sat back, hands flexing on the steering wheel. It was good. Robust. A narrative that could be sold. He didn't do pride, but if he did, this would be one for the trophy cabinet. He turned to Riordan. 'Now, all we require is for the Terry's to disappear. Our friends at passport control will put them down as having boarded a flight to Spain or Rio, never to be seen again.'

'It's tidy,' Riordan confirmed. 'It's end stopped. There's no connection of Jackson or his murder to any intelligence operation. It's domestic. A crime of passion. His past is irrelevant. His identity holds up to any surface questions. And there's no real trial. Everyone moves on – the local police, the media, the politicians, the miners and the public.'

The Specialist nodded at the certainty of it heard in the mouth of another. 'And, of course, it's imperative that there's no trial. No opportunity for grandstanding or introducing doubt.' The Specialist gripped the wheel, fingers squeezing. 'So, they disappear. Part of the resolution of Bishop's Mitre.'

Riordan knew it had been agreed the previous day. A

plan approved at the highest level. Brody's murder not simply protecting one operation, *Silver Fox*, but offering the opportunity of concluding a second. *Bishop's Mitre*: the eradication of an active IRA cell engaged in the planning of a terrorist outrage.

'The Terry's won't be sticking around,' the Specialist stated, turning over the engine. 'They're on a timescale. They know there's police suspicion over Kevin if not Brian. They have a job to finish, one they're desperate to conclude. They'll want to get those explosives delivered as quickly as they can. Get their money.'

Riordan knew what would follow, every detail had been laid out at their meeting the previous day. Track the Terry's to the meet. Take out the IRA cell. Recover the explosives they knew to have been taken. To finish them. All of them. He'd seen the draft press release The Minister had prepared: *An IRA cell is neutralised and missing explosives recovered. The Terry's bodies are among the dead, labelled as John Doe's. Unidentified IRA men.* As far as Whitehall was concerned they might be Libyan terrorist, Red Brigade, or whatever fitted the current political agenda. Unidentified and unidentifiable corpses.

The government had an anti-terrorist triumph and *Silver Fox* continued unhindered, unknown.

Better. The police had their proof of miners killing miners that could be trumpeted to the media.

As they moved off, he tossed the folder to the back seat. A footnote to the history of the strike. Unknown. Never to be revealed.

Twenty-seven

Mallen stood in the doorway of Kevin Terry's living room and took in the scene of disarray. He blew out his cheeks, exhaling a long stream of air that conveyed to those gathered in the corridor his assessment of the task facing them. 'So, what's the plan now?' he asked.

Kalus, standing slightly ahead of him, surveyed the trashed room. He nodded in the direction of the dark stains on the carpet. 'The usual. All this blood makes it even more pressing.' He turned to Roberts. 'Get the word out. Find out what make of car Terry senior drives – registration, colour, the works. Dangerous occupants. Do not approach. Send for back-up.'

'You think it's the wife's blood? That they've hurt her?' Roberts' response was more observation than question.

Kalus shook his head. 'You tell me. Can't see who else's it could be.'

Roberts blew out his cheeks at the mystery and left for the car radio. He turned in the corridor, calling back in. 'Guv, that WPC you asked for is here.'

'Send her in.'

Kalus and Mallen moved to the centre of the room. The drive to Kevin Terry's house had been filled with radio traffic requesting uniformed back-up, specifically Lawrence, a WPC Kalus assumed capable of looking after the wife and children whilst at the same time probing her for more details.

On arrival there had been no answer to their knocking. A look through a window had revealed the damage in the house, legitimising a forced entry, one establishing that none of the Terry's were anywhere to be found.

Like the rest of them, Lawrence couldn't hide her alarm at

the disarray confronting her.

Kalus looked over to her. 'WPC,' he acknowledged, 'Looks like we may not be needing you after all.'

'What happened, sir? Is she okay?'

'Don't know and don't know,' Mallen answered. 'Lot of blood though. Bit more than a domestic,' he offered moving towards the kitchen.

Kalus lifted a child's toy from the floor. He held it up in front of him for a moment before placing it onto the sofa. 'What were they like when you were here before?' he asked.

'Concerned...Worried,' she responded. 'Like everybody we visited.'

'But you felt that it was more than that. That the letter confirmed what you suspected.'

She took a moment to consider. 'She'd seemed more disconcerted than the husband. Odd in a way now I come to think of it. Distracted, yet at the same time she had a lot of questions.'

'Questions?'

'Who might have killed him.... What we were looking for.'

'How did she seem with him? Her husband, Kevin?' He picked up a few more ornaments, righting them. 'Did she seem worried? Frightened?'

'Not at the time. Not frightened. At least, not so much that I noticed. She just asked a lot of questions about whether we had any idea of the motive of whoever killed Jackson.'

'She didn't offer one of her own?'

Lawrence shook her head. 'Not at the time, no. She was just concerned at the effect the whole thing was having on her family. She said her husband was finding it tough to deal with. *Hadn't been himself* she said.'

'What did you think she meant by that?' Kalus asked, turning to face her, now appearing a little more interested.

She mulled over a suitable response. 'Until her letter, not that much I suppose. Lot of families round here have been having it tough. Hard going. The women especially. Their men struggling. No food on the table. The kids. We don't know the half.'

'Their own fault,' Mallen threw in, reappearing from the kitchen.

'That's as maybe, sir,' the WPC said turning towards him. 'But it falls hard on a community. Especially one as close as this. The women with young kids worst of all.'

'They chose to put themselves on those picket lines. All of them. Jackson too. He knew what he was doing.'

'My uncle's a striking miner. Two of my cousins as well.'

Mallen shrugged his *couldn't give a shit* response. 'Mines' a butcher. So what?'

'The wives suffer. They worry about their kids and their men.'

'Maybe they should get them back to work, then. Solve all our problems.'

'Hey,' Kalus interjected. 'Let's keep the party political out of this. Save it for the canteen or the soap box.'

'Your father was a miner, wasn't he sir?' Lawrence asked.

'Like I said, constable, let's keep all of that to one side while we try to figure out exactly what's happened here. We need to find where Kevin Terry, his dad, and his wife and kids are.'

Mallen, whistling tunelessly, turned back into the kitchen, busying himself with leafing through a pile of letters and bills he'd taken from the mantelpiece.

'Sorry, sir,' Lawrence apologised. 'It's just... Well, I thought that you'd...'

'What?'

'Be... sympathetic.'

Kalus rubbed a hand across his brow. His head throbbed. His eyes blurred. 'Sympathy's not in my job description. Solving stuff is what I'm supposed to do. Leave all that tea and biscuits stuff to...'

'Us women, sir?' she interjected.

Kalus paused. 'Those that do it better than me.'

'Sorry, sir.'

Kalus shrugged it off. 'So, Karen Terry offered you nothing of any real consequence until she sent you that letter?'

'Just that they were finding it hard going.'

'Like the rest.'

'Like the rest,' she echoed. 'Tinned food donation boxes at the corner shops. Garden lawns turned over to vegetables. Collection boxes, welfare funds. You know how it's been, sir. They were like the rest of the mining families around here.'

Kalus nodded. He knew exactly what she meant. Anna donated generously to the collection boxes for tinned food placed on the counters of local shops.

He walked into the kitchen. Mallen was standing at what passed for a breakfast bar going through the pile of papers and folders retrieved from the shed.

Kalus went outside and stood gazing at the small garden. He took in gulps of the cold air, feeling the cooling sweat trickle down the back of his neck and under the collar of his shirt. Concentrate. *Concentrate.* Focus. *Focus on what?* The flagged path, the small scruffy bushes, the shed, the lawn. *The lawn.*

He stepped back inside the kitchen to where Lawrence was standing. 'What did you say about the families round here?'

'Having a hard time?' she tried.

'No, how they were coping.'

Uncertain, she tried again. 'The collections?'

'And the lawns.'

'The lawns?' she repeated, no clearer.

'Turned over to vegetables.'

'Yes. My uncle's been growing potatoes and cabbage on his.'

'Why not theirs?'

'Sorry?' she said more puzzled than ever at what he wanted from her.

'Why is Kevin Terry's lawn still a lawn?'

She shook her head. 'I don't follow.'

Kalus picked up a cabbage from the wire vegetable rack. 'Where's he getting the fresh vegetables?'

'Erm...' Lawrence was lost.

'Allotment. Lots of families round here have an allotment,' he answered.

'You think they're hiding there?' she asked.

'Who knows? Isolated. Quiet.'

She was unsure what was expected, formed a tentative response. 'Isn't it unlikely? They're pretty small. Usually just a potting shed. Lots of coming and goings. Lots of people to see them.'

Kalus shook his head in frustration. She was right. In lieu of a cat to kick, he slid his hands into his trouser pockets, staring at the floor in contemplation. 'There's got to be somewhere they'd go. Somewhere to hold up. Kevin and Brian must know better than anybody there'd be police looking for them. They know that. With the number of roadblocks we've set up to stop flying pickets, they'd realise they'd never get more than a few miles without being stopped once we got onto them.'

'It supposes that they're running.'

'Look around. What do you think?'

'It's a mess.'

'Hardly suggests a quiet family outing or a drive into the country. Someone's been hurt here. Someone - and we're assuming Karen - seems to have been taken against their will. As Kevin got himself released and we know that his dad was with him, we'll assume that it's them doing the hurting and the abducting.'

'Why?'

'In the circumstances breaking and entering seems a little unlikely.'

'No, I mean why hurt her? Why take her?'

'To keep her quiet. Maybe take revenge for Karen dobbing them in.'

'Wouldn't her disappearance be a bit obvious? They'd know that we'd get onto them.'

'Maybe they thought it would take us longer to find Brody. That it'd take us a few days to call round here. Either way, the rule of thumb is that bad people panic. They get caught up in something they can't get out of. They do stupid things because they lose the ability to think straight. Most killings are by people at the ends of tethers.' *Handsworth. Reuben.*

'What about the kids?' she asked.

Before he could answer, Mallen, who had moved deeper into the piles of documents retrieved from the shed, interrupted holding up a piece of paper. 'You mentioned allotments, well what about something bigger? Hurley Farm. This is a copy of a contract signed a couple of weeks ago. According to this, Brian and Kevin Terry as part of their work for the local NUM Welfare Committee negotiated the use of a barn and fields at Hurley Farm for miners' families to harvest vegetables. It's only a couple of miles down the road. They wouldn't pass any roadblocks because it's inside the colliery area.'

Kalus turned to Roberts who was returning from putting out the all-points bulletin for the Terry family. 'Mick, get in contact with McKinnon on the phone. Chances are he'll still be at the NUM offices. Find out what he knows about this Hurley Farm deal. What the NUM have got there. Who's got access.'

'Guv.'

'What about us?' Mallen asked.

Kalus considered the options. He checked his watch. According to Ridgway's orders, he was entering his last hours on the investigation. 'Nothing we can be doing here. Let's get up there ourselves. You never know, we might be about to become heroes.'

***

Kevin stood by the door of the barn. Night was closing in, a gloom deepened by the dark rain clouds covering the sky as far as the eye could see. He let the door swing back into place.

'Nothing.'

'They'll be here soon enough,' his father replied, leaning against a long disused piece of farm machinery.

Kevin slid down and sat on the ground, his back against the

door. 'Fucking mess.'

'Not again, son.'

'Yes again! It's a fucking mess.'

'Time for all that later. When we're rich, son. Rich.'

'When I've got Karen and the kids back you mean.'

'Yeah. Of course. I mean… that's a given. I meant you'll see it all differently a year from now.'

'A few months from now and I'll be a long way from here.'

Brian looked at his son. 'I started this for you. You and your kids. The family.'

Kevin ran a hand over the straw littered earth that he sat on. 'I don't know how you can say that.'

'That's who it's always been for. Your mother. You. Your kids.'

'My family's out there with a fucking Irish terrorist! They're out there because of you.'

'All I ever wanted was to make a better life for us.'

'For you, you mean.'

'Kevin-'

'Don't fucking Kevin me! You know it's true,' Kevin snapped. He glared across the space separating them. The years. The desires. 'Can't you just for once be honest with yourself? This whole thing was your idea. What you wanted. The money.'

'You went along with it.'

'Course I did. What else could I do? You were already up to your neck in it. Was I supposed to leave you to sort it by yourself?'

'Things were supposed to be different.'

'Yeah. That's what you told me. Easy money. Lifting explosives from the colliery. Stashing it away as part of some mad IRA plan to blow stuff up. Bringing down the government in the process. Truth be told, I half-thought it was another bullshit fantasy.'

'You took the money quick enough. You found that real enough.'

'Killing Stephen…'

'Was necessary.'

'Was it?'

'Once you'd run your mouth off. Yes. What would you have done? Asked him to keep quiet? Forget everything he'd heard? He was looking into you, Kevin. He was going to screw us over. Turn us in. Then where would you and the kids have been, eh? Where would your Karen be then? Fucking him, is where. Like the rumours said. No smoke without a fire.'

'No. Not Stephen.'

'Why not? Because he was your friend? Your new best mate?'

'Is that it, dad. Is that really it? Did you really have to kill him? Or was it the fact that his friendship meant something to me? Was that it? That I respected him for what he did? The respect I never had for you. The respect you never showed me.'

'You're talking crazy.'

The sound of an engine labouring close by halted any response. Kevin eased the door open, leaning his head round to peer through the gap.

'They're here.'

The headlights of a transit van glowed dimly through the opening as they bounced along the rutted track.

'You're sure it's them?'

Kevin got to his feet, slipping his jacket into place. 'Who the fuck else would be coming up here? You paid the farmer enough to keep away.'

The van stopped some twenty paces from the barn. For a few moments nothing happened.

'Are they getting out or what?'

Kevin looked through the gap. 'Maybe they're waiting for us to show ourselves.'

'Why would they do that?'

'Maybe they don't think they can trust us anymore. Maybe they think we've got the coppers here with us.'

'When they've got your Karen and the kids?'

'Look, you know them better than me. I don't know what the fuck they might be thinking. I'm going out.'

Kevin pulled the door open and stepped out. The rain beat down. He tugged the collar of his zip jacket closed with one hand whilst waving a large arc as a signal with the other.

The passenger door of the van opened and Loach emerged. He closed the door. Thrusting his hands deep into the pockets of his zipped up blouson jacket, head angled down against the rain, the Irishman began walking towards the barn.

Kevin didn't wait for his arrival, instead quickly closing the distance between them, feet struggling for grip in the mud. 'Where are they, Loach? Where's Karen? Where's my kids?'

Loach looked quizzically at Kevin before breaking into a lop-sided grin.

Kevin brushed past him. 'Are they in the van? Karen! Ricky!' he bellowed as he lurched through the rain towards the Ford transit.

Loach grabbed his arm, swinging him round to face him, a movement slamming Kevin against the passenger door of the van. 'Not so fast!' Loach commanded.

'Fuck off!' Kevin screamed, shaking his arm partially free from Loach's grip. 'Get the fuck off me!'

With his free hand, Kevin reached for the door handle. In the instant the door opened, Loach tightened his hold on Kevin's arm, pushing it round and up behind his back. At the same time, his own free hand yanked the heavy revolver from his jacket pocket, thrusting it under Kevin's chin. 'Stay right where you are, *boyoh.*'

The pressure of the gun under his chin thrust Kevin's head back to a point where he could barely open his mouth. He realised it was useless to struggle. The driver of the van, a huge man with paw-like hands, got out and made his way round the front of the van. He grabbed Kevin's free arm, pulling it behind Kevin's back to join with the other that Loach already held there. A belt, or something like one, was slipped over Kevin's hands and pulled tight. At a nod, Loach removed the gun from Kevin's chin, twisting him round and shoving him violently forward. Unable to hold his balance, Kevin fell face down in the mud.

Loach stood astride and over him and bent down, almost squatting on his back. Kevin once more felt the barrel of the gun on his flesh, this time pushed against the back of his head. 'Now, be a good boy and tell your *da* to show himself.'

Kevin considered what to do. Loach encouraged him by pressing the barrel harder against his skull. 'Now!' he urged.

'Dad!' Kevin shouted. 'Dad!'

Brian Terry emerged from the barn. 'What the fuck's this about, Sean?'

'Brian. Good to see you!' Loach called, wiping the rain from his face. 'Precautions, Brian. Simply Precautions.'

He stood up and moved to the side of Kevin who remained lying in the mud.

The big man moved in, hauling Kevin to his feet and propelling him towards the barn. 'Now, let's all get in out of this dreadful rain,' Loach said. 'You'll be catching your death.'

* * *

Kalus picked up the handset of the police radio. Mick Roberts' voice boomed out of the speaker. 'Guv? It's Mick. You were right. We're up at Brian Terry's allotment. Seems like he doesn't have much in the way of green-fingers. The plot's mostly grass and weeds.'

'Okay.'

'The shed's different matter, though. Brand new locks – three of them.'

'Can you get in?'

'No need guv, it was already open.'

'And?'

Roberts reply was buffeted by wind and rain that was clearly as bad where he was as it was Kalus' end. 'It's weird, guv. There's a bloody big hole in the middle of it. About five or six foot long, two or three foot wide and about three foot deep.'

'A grave?' Kalus asked.

Roberts response was that of a man pondering what he

was looking at. 'Well... Could be. Weird thing is, it looks like something's been dug up rather than they were digging a hole to put something in. There's marks in the soil all around one edge like stuff's been dragged out.'

'Anything else?' Kalus asked.

Roberts tone became more assured. 'Couple of the old blokes on one of the closer plots reckon they saw Brian up here with his lad a couple of hours ago. Didn't see them go, though. Too busy making a brew and keeping dry.'

'Get forensics up there,' Kalus instructed.

'Will do.'

Kalus put the handset control back on its peg. 'What do you think?'

Mallen, driving, half-turned. 'Buggered if I know.'

'Do you think they were digging a grave for Karen?' Lawrence asked from the back of the car.

Kalus half-shrugged. 'Could be. Hard to say.'

'Does that mean they've killed her?' she asked.

'If that was the case, then why leave the hole? Where's the body?' Mallen asked.

Lawrence chewed her bottom lip. 'Maybe they were disturbed.'

'Fucking loonies if you ask me,' Mallen stated.

'I meant interrupted,' Lawrence attempted to explain.

'I know,' Mallen responded. 'Detective joke, WPC.'

'Oh, yes, I see. Sorry.'

'Ignore him,' Kalus said.

'You think they could probably be here at this farm, then?' Mallen asked.

Kalus brushed a hand through his hair. 'God knows where they are, what they're doing. It's open day on stupid. They're running round out there like headless chickens.'

'What about the children?' Lawrence's voice carried her concern.

Kalus thought about the actions of desperate men on the run; uncertain, frightened, panicked. *Rueben*. 'Can't imagine they'd take them with them. Maybe dropped them somewhere.'

'The dad's? Brian Terry's place I mean, with their gran,' she offered.

'Maybe. We've got officers going round there to check.'

Mallen made a right turn down a lane that was little more than a rough single track tunnelled by overhanging trees. About seven hundred yards along it and to their left, a gap in the hedgerow appeared. In it, an open gate led onto a rutted track. The track itself appeared to cut across the field before dipping away over a rise about a hundred yards further on.

'Slow down,' Kalus commanded.

Mallen scoffed, 'This track, you're not joking.' The mud was churning up, the car lurching sideways each time it met a dip or its wheels clumped into a rain filled pothole.

'Someone's' been down here recently,' Kalus stated, pointing at the tyre tracks in the mud ahead of them. 'Lights off if you can.'

They crested the rise and pulled into a gap offering itself between the clumps of bushes. 'Foot now,' Kalus said.

Mallen stared out of the window trying to look up into the night sky. 'In this?' The rain was battering the car's roof with a hollow thunder. 'Reminds me of a caravan holiday I had in Weston.'

'Should we maybe wait for back-up, sir?' Lawrence asked.

'We're not sure whether there's anyone here or not. Those tyre tracks could just as well be a vehicle leaving as one coming in. The farmer out picking his spuds. We'll have a look and make that decision once we know what we've got. You stay here WPC. Richard and I'll go and find this barn.' Kalus opened his door and slid out of the car.

Mallen got out, his right foot immediately sinking into a rut of the clinging red clay that the town and its surrounding villages all seemed to be built on. He stared across the roof of the car at Kalus. 'Great. Second pair of shoes in a couple of days,' he stated gloomily.

'Never mind. Now you can get something a little more

fashionable,' Kalus responded.

Mallen smiled hollowly. 'I hope you're enjoying this.'

Kalus stood and thought. 'You know what? I think I might be.'

Twenty-eight

Kalus cursed out loud as his foot slipped from under him, compelling him to slide down the steep grassy embankment. After six feet or so, he came to a halt when his outstretched right leg slammed into a large sandstone boulder at the bottom. A sharp piercing pain shot up the length of his shin, a pain not for the first time causing him to fear he'd inflicted serious damage to an ankle on the treacherous journey from the car to their current vantage point below the barn.

Slowly he sat upright, massaging the ankle. By now he was unconcerned at the mud and wet soaking through his trousers. His shoes were caked with red clay. Lifting the hem of the trouser leg, he saw his socks had taken on the appearance of dishrags from immersion in the hidden puddles that had littered the pathway they'd followed over the rise. Once they'd crested it, the large barn had appeared at the foot of the slope about a hundred yards ahead of them. In front of it was a dark blue panelled Ford transit.

'Fuck this!' Mallen uttered, sliding to a halt next to Kalus. He sat pulling up his collar in yet another pointless effort to prevent the rain from seeping down his neck. Like Kalus, he was soaked through. He leant across his DCI to peer round the edge of the slope concealing them from the door of the barn and anyone who might be wating in the van. 'What do you think?' he asked, slumping back against the slope of grass they'd slewed their way down.

Kalus stopped massaging his ankle and grimaced. 'Someone's in there. I think I can make out another smaller van round the back. Can't see for sure but it could be Brian Terry's Marina estate.'

'So whose is the van?'

Kalus shook his head. 'God knows.'

'Might be the farmer who's let them the place.'

'And they've let him in there, with them holding Karen and the kids?'

Mallen shrugged, 'So who? Mates? Maybe they've borrowed the van to get through the roadblocks. Easier to stash someone in the back under tarpaulins or stuff.'

Kalus considered the idea. 'Maybe.'

He looked around. The rain poured down, night was settling in. He was facing a situation that was getting away from him. His head ached, and when he blinked it was as much from the pressure behind his eyes as the rain streaming into them. He needed to act.

'Look, whoever is in there, we need to get some support up here.' He inclined his head in the direction of his outstretched leg. 'I think my ankle's pretty well knackered. Get back to the car and get Lawrence to radio this in. Get a team up here. Tell them that we might have a hostage situation.'

'Or what will become a very pissed off farmer going about his lawful business.'

Kalus managed a half-smile. 'I know. Hell, Rich, we both know this is likely my last command in this investigation. So, what the fuck, eh? Might as well go out on a big fuck-up call rather than slip silently away, an embarrassing victim of pressure of the job mediocrity.'

'Your call,' Mallen stated.

'My call.'

Mallen patted Kalus on the arm. 'Don't go away. And don't go being the hero.' He moved off, back the way they had come towards the car.

Kalus sat back rubbing his arms, attempting to massage some life and warmth into them. Although he'd sent Mallen for back-up, he was unconvinced that there might be anything other than the farmer or some NUM welfare committee in the barn getting the site ready for harvesting. A call to McKinnon had confirmed that a sympathetic owner had donated the vegetable crop from some of his fields. All the miners had to do was harvest it, the rota and everything to do with the fields and the barn had all been organised by Kevin and Brian.

He needed to get closer, be certain that he wasn't making a complete fool of himself.

He eased himself into a crouching position and leaned round the slope, evaluating how best to proceed.

The driveway was on a slight incline, which meant he was looking up towards the front of the barn and its large wooden doors. He estimated that he was about thirty paces from the van, which in turn was about twenty paces from the barn.

His ankle hurt like crazy, impeding his movement or a sudden shift of weight. With the rain beating down and the dimming light, it was possible that even with an enforced snail's pace he might creep up behind the van, using it as a shield from whoever was in the barn. From there, he could make his way to what looked like a stack of old tractor tyres which would put him within a few paces of the barn. He assumed that there might be some sort of side window facing out across the field on the far side that was currently hidden from him. If he could get round there he would be able to see in. Even if there wasn't a window, the panelling of the barn looked flimsy enough in places for him to be able to make out what was going on in there.

He moved off towards the van, crouching low. The increased pressure on his lower legs intensifying the ache from a now throbbing ankle. Despite the pain, he couldn't escape the feeling that he was ten years old playing cowboys in the long grass of the park. He was still half-smiling at the ludicrousness of his situation when he became aware of the small access door inset into one of the larger doors of the barn beginning to open.

As rapidly as the pain allowed, he slithered into position at the rear of the van, watching as a figure emerged from the barn carrying a box about the size of a large holdall or cricket bag. The box was oblong, made of metal, and the man gripped it by way of handles protruding from each end. It reminded him of the ammunition boxes his toy soldiers had when he was younger. Whatever was in it, it was clearly heavy, its weight causing problems even for a man as big as this one was.

The man was heading for the van. The van Kalus was hiding behind.

Kalus assumed he would make for the rear doors. But which side? Given his direction, Kalus was sure the man would approach it from the driver's side. As the man closed the distance to his position, Kalus slipped round to the nearside and held his breath.

He heard the squelch of the man placing the box on the ground.

Heard the exhaling of his breath in release from the burden.

There was a fumbling for keys, and then the doors opened, followed by the sound of what he assumed to be the metal box being slid inside the van. The doors closed, Kalus feeling the side of the van vibrate in response against his back. He crouched lower, his head turned to face the rear of the van.

What if he came this way?

Who was he?

How would he react to a man leaping from the darkness, covered in mud and proclaiming himself to be police?

He was still contemplating the point when he heard a squelch of mud from behind him. Before he could react something was pushed violently into his cheek, something that despite the rain and the icy wind felt cold and metallic.

'Well, well, well. What do we have here?' Sean Loach asked before crashing the pistol across the back of Kalus' skull and turning his world black.

* * *

WPC Lawrence couldn't help the sense of resentment welling up. The boys had gone off to play at spies, and she, the woman, was left behind to watch the ranch.

She wound down her rear window, dissipating some of the

condensation building up on the windscreen and back window of the car. Even once that had been done, there was nothing of any real definition outside the car that she could see. The pounding rain and the darkness of night fall had by now taken visibility down to a few yards. Anything beyond ten feet remained blurred shapes, even anything within that distance was hazy and indistinct.

After a few seconds she wound the window back up, the driving rain soaking both the exposed door panel and her side.

She leaned forward to the front control panel and unclipped the radio handset. *Should she call it in anyway?* If there was nothing there, Kalus would be furious at being shown up by stories of a WPC looking out for him. But what if there was something, and Kalus and Mallen were unable to get word back to her? What then? *How long should she wait before taking the decision to call it in off her own bat?*

She released the handset, dropping it back into its cradle and peered out into the rain once more.

There was movement. And it wasn't the trees or bushes.

After a couple of earlier heart-stopping moments in her vigil, she felt she was now accustomed to the pattern the natural vegetation made. This was different. For one thing, this was on the path. More correctly to either side of it. There were figures out there, men moving along the track. Two of them. On their current course they would pass close to the car. Although she thought they were still too far away to have made out her presence inside the vehicle they were bound to get closer. To look in.

Automatically, she hunkered down in the back footwell. She squat there covered by her dark blue greatcoat. Raising a section of the material she was able to see the dashboard. The receiver hanging on its cord was tantalisingly within reach.

Thoughts of what should she do now over-taken by what could she do?

***

It took Kalus some time to accustom his sight to the dark interior of the barn.

He was strapped to a piece of farm machinery, a plough of some sort. A few feet away he recognised the slumped figure of Brian Terry. Another figure, one he assumed to be Kevin Terry, was a further ten paces away than that. Both were tied to what appeared to be the wooden pillars supporting the roof. The older man was held semi-upright by his bonds. Kevin was sitting on the floor, his legs stretched out in front of him. Both had bloodied shirt fronts indicating they had suffered beatings.

Three other men stood a few feet beyond Kevin. The big man from the van, a shorter man with bright eyes, and the man he assumed had been the one who had held the gun to his head.

They had been in close discussion for a few minutes. He had no idea as to who they were or what was going on.

He scoured the barn for any sign of Karen or the children but found none.

As well as the rope holding him tight to the machinery there was another length binding his hands at the wrists. He tugged at the rope holding his wrists together, sliding his hands up and down the machinery to find something sharp he could use to work at his bonds.

'Brian!' he hissed. 'Brian!'

Brian Terry glanced across then turned his head away. The effort to lift his head was immense, but even in that short moment Kalus saw the extent of the beating he'd been given.

'Brian! What the fuck's going on?' Kalus hissed.

Loach turned his attention towards the grouping of bound men. The discussion appeared to be over, some conclusion had been reached.

'Detective!' Loach called out, acknowledging Kalus like he'd just met a neighbour in the street. *Hiya. How are you doing?*

'Well at least that means you know the trouble you're in,' Kalus stated. 'I think you'd better untie me pretty quick so we can sort out exactly what the hell is happening here.'

Loach laughed. It was joyous. A genuine pleasure in the

moment. 'Fantastic! Fantastic! Glad to see you have a sense of humour.'

Kalus wrestled with his bonds. 'Humour be fucked! You'd better release me.'

Loach shook his head. 'Afraid I can't be doing that, at least for the moment. You see you've arrived at a very delicate point in the proceedings.'

'Who are you? Where's Karen Terry and the children?'

Loach held his hands apart in amazement. 'Jesus! It seems everybody's after finding out where Mrs Terry has got herself to.' He turned to Big Man and his smaller partner, 'Hear that lads? The officer wants to know what we've done with Mrs Terry and her toddlers.'

The Big Man grunted. He was busying himself with taking out another of the metal boxes. As far as Kalus could see, however many they'd already removed there were two left in the barn plus the one in Big Man's hands. The smaller man was kneeling by the remaining boxes. He looked up and shook his head in wonder before returning to opening the box directly in front of him.

'It's maybe yourself you should be concerned with rather than the whereabouts and health of Mrs Terry and her kids,' Loach advised.

'Look, I don't know what you people are thinking, or what it is that you're involved in, but there are armed police on their way here.'

Loach stood closer, plucking the police identification wallet from Kalus' inside pocket. He held it open, considering what he saw. 'A moot point, Detective Chief Inspector... Kalus. Hmm. Kalus. Sounds Polish or something. I've read about you. Handsworth, wasn't it?' He tucked the wallet back into Kalus' pocket, patting the jacket closed and moving across to Brian Terry. 'Whatever...The fact of the matter is that you're right. Once your colleagues realise that they've not heard from you for a while they'll no doubt be getting round to sending someone out here. In fact I'm rather counting on it. But that may not be for some time. Bring him in.'

Through the door, two other men appeared dragging between them the slumped figure of Richard Mallen. 'You really think that we wouldn't have posted some men out there on the perimeter? Even if we weren't half-expecting you, you made so much noise coming down that drive a blind man could have found you.'

Mallen was dropped to the floor. There was blood across the back of his head and above his ear, but the fact that his arms were bound behind his back suggested he was still alive.

'Whatever back-up you were expecting will be a while in coming.'

Kalus stared ahead.

'Ah, but don't be disheartened, Inspector. All's not lost. In fact we're expecting our good friends from Special Branch at any minute.' He lifted up Brian Terry's chin from where it had sagged against his chest. 'What's his name, Brian?'

'Riordan,' Terry whispered through broken teeth and swollen lips.

'Riordan. That's the fella.' He let Terry's head flop back to his chest.

'Riordan's Complaints,' Kalus corrected.

'Oh, come now Chief Inspector… Kalus,' Loach savoured the word like some new flavour. 'I'm sure that by now that even you know your Mr Riordan is far more than Complaints, eh?'

Kalus stared ahead. Loach returned the stare, assessing what he found there. Pleased, he turned away. Kalus took the chance to return to rubbing his bonds up and down against the metal of the plough.

'Your man Riordan is Special Branch or MI5 or MI6 or one of them. It matters very little. He's Intelligence.' Loach swung his arm round dramatically taking in himself, Big Man, and the smaller man, 'He's here for us. Or, should I more correctly say, for this.' The sweep of his arm now indicating the metal boxes that the third man was busying himself with.

'What are you? IRA?'

'That's better inspector. Join in with the spirit of the game.'

'Game?'

'The game your superiors have had you playing these past few days.'

Kalus looked at Loach. His face was open. Everything written there.

Loach turned to address his partners. 'Lads, we've either got ourselves a very fine poker player here, or Detective Chief Inspector Kalus genuinely has no idea of what's been going on.'

'What are you talking about?' Kalus demanded.

'I'm talking about why Stephen Jackson was murdered.' Loach closed the gap between them. 'Like yourself, Inspector, I wondered for quite a time just why the death of a man like that - a miner on a picket line - would warrant so much attention. I mean, the political fall-out - the PR of it - looked bad, but nothing warranting so much fancy footwork on the part of your government. But then it became plain as day. Intelligence services. A cover-up.'

'You're mad.'

'Mad?' He stood a few feet away. 'Strikes me that the more I look at this, that there's only one stupid man in this barn - and that'd be yourself, Chief Inspector. It's you. You've been played.'

'How do you get to that?'

'Well, Inspector, perhaps you'd enlighten myself and the Terry's over there as to how come you're here?'

'Fuck you!' Kalus snarled.

'Oh come on now, just when you were doing so well. Surely you've nothing better to be doing for the next few minutes. Indulge me. Enlighten us.'

Kalus stared ahead. He knew it was only a matter of time before someone was despatched to find them. Lawrence was in the car. They'd clearly not found her. Surely she would realise something was wrong. Why not keep this man talking? Keep him involved; keep him from the acts of violence of which he was so obviously capable.

He continued to work his wrists against the machinery. He

needed time. Time was his friend. His back-up. He relented. 'We had Kevin in the frame for the murder of Jackson. After Kevin was released we got a call to another murder. Matthew Brody, a journalist who'd contacted us saying he had information on Jackson's murder found battered to death, just like Jackson. He was in Militant, he knew all about Brian and Kevin. He had Brian's phone number on a pad on his desk, along with a file detailing Mr Terry's violent past.'

Brian Terry gurgled some incoherent sounds. Loach stepped across and pulled his head up. 'Not now, Brian, you had your chance earlier.' He let Terry's head flop back. 'As you can see, inspector, Brian's not himself at the moment. But do go on. I'm sure he and Kevin will be intrigued by your deductions.'

'We went to Kevin's house looking for the two of them. The place had been wrecked. There was no sign of Kevin. No sign of Brian, or Karen and the children.'

'And a bit of the *Olde Detective* work and you find your way here.' Loach concluded. He held up a hand in front of Kalus' face and counted off on his fingers. 'So, your conclusion is this. One; Kevin Terry killed Stephen Jackson because he discovered that he was fucking Karen,' he paused briefly, turning his head towards the recumbent Kevin, 'which, by the way, Kevin, he was - and then Two…' Loach returned his gaze to his fingers and to Kalus. 'Fearing discovery by this journalist, Brian here batters this Brody fella's brains out before, Three; they decide to somehow cover their tracks by doing away with the missus as well. So what do you do then? Obvious. You conclude that they've brought her here to get rid of the body - say in this lovely big shredder over there?' Loach pointed over his shoulder to a piece of heavy machinery on the far side of the barn.

Kalus said nothing.

'Come on Chief Inspector, I'm right, aren't I?' He pushed closer to Kalus, examining his face for clues as to his thinking. He stepped away and began pacing in the space between Kalus, Brian, and Kevin. A lawyer addressing the jury. *Perry Mason*. 'Problem is… Kevin didn't kill Stephen out of jealousy - though no doubt the dirty fucker more than deserved it. In fact, our Kevin here didn't kill Jackson at all.' He paused briefly in his pacing to point at Brian. 'Brian here's your man. Isn't that right, Brian?'

Loach resumed his to-ing and fro-ing, finding a rhythm in both movement and speech. 'A handy man with a club or a hammer or even a brick, is our Brian.' Passing Kalus and turning, he waved a hand dramatically in the air. 'Oh, I know what you're thinking, Chief Inspector. Doesn't really change anything. Your theory still holds up. A crime of passion, a *crime passionale* as the French call it. All that's changed is that Kevin's the accessory rather than the killer you had him pinned for.'

'Maybe. You're the man with the theory.'

'Ah, that's just the point, Chief Inspector. You see, Brian may have murdered Stephen Jackson but he couldn't have killed your journalist informant. Brian's not been out of our sight the past twenty four hours. He's been nowhere near Brum.' He pointed at the remaining metal boxes. 'He's been doing a little job for us, digging up these items here that we'd paid him so very handsomely to obtain for us. I'm his alibi. And, of course, young Kevin was in your custody at the time. It was your man Riordan and his cronies did for the journalist.'

'Riordan? You're crazy. If he's not Complaints, Riordan's still one of us. A copper.'

'And that puts him on the side of the angels, does it?'

Kalus shook his head. 'I don't see it.'

'And that's precisely why your man Ridgway, at his Masters' behest, has put you at the centre of this. You're a policeman. You see things like a policeman. You look for motives that have served you well in the past. Jealousy. Anger. Money. Greed. Maybe even sheer fucking bad luck - wrong place wrong time. You don't see the bigger picture. You don't see it because you don't look for it. You're not expected to. That's why they put you in charge here. *The patsy. The Good Soldier.* The man with a past that he's looking to distance himself from. He knew you'd follow the book. That you'd be taking no more chances. Not after what happened in Handsworth.'

'If I'm to believe you, then where's the motive? Why was Brody killed? Why would a police officer murder a journalist who had evidence that could help us solve a murder.'

'Ah, there we have it. The classic policeman to the end. Motive. How about expediency? You know, something to draw a quick line under everything. All they've wanted from you all along was a quick fix. Ridgway, this Riordan and his Masters. All they ever required was someone to deliver a result pinning it on a miner or a picket. Good PR. That's what your man Ridgway would have done, but you don't need me to tell you that, do you? Failing that, well a copper would do. You know some poor uniform succumbing to pressure of the job, a moment of madness. That would do nicely for them. But you didn't give them what they wanted. So they decided to take a hand, help things along so to speak. Riordan tried to steer you away from whatever it is they wanted to hide. He had what we call a watching brief. But it needed closure quicker than you were looking to give them. Let's face it, Chief Inspector, you were going nowhere. They knew all about Jackson fucking Kevin's wife. Once Karen's misgivings about Kevin had been laid in front of your noses, they saw their opportunity to end it. My guess is that once Kevin was in the frame – and him taking off like he did when they came to arrest him was meat and drink to their cause – they thought they were home. A crime of passion.'

He paused, letting it sink in. 'But then the fly in the ointment: Brody. He starts sniffing around. He's a complication. One getting closer to the truth of things than even he knew. He gets careless. Talks to people. Tells them things. Tries to tell you, Chief Inspector. And that was him sealing his own fate. That's no doubt when they had the idea: two birds with one stone. Get Kevin released and then get his dad in the frame for Brody's murder. Some simple document trail I suspect. Cue panic and a flight.'

'Why get Kevin released? Knowing they'd likely run?'

'So that they can finish them.'

'You mean-'

'I mean that when Riordan and his team get here, he intends to arrive a long time before your back up can. Riordan would undoubtedly report to yourself and Ridgway that they arrived too late to prevent the terrible tragedy of young Kevin here killing his wife, his kids, and his father before ending his own life. Poor Karen. She and the kids will be inevitable casualties in the crossfire. Give it the certain tragic credibility that your media are so fond of. Or maybe they'll tell you they fled the country. Who'd go digging around here looking for bodies if you think they're in Spain or Rio?'

'It doesn't make sense.'

'Come, now, Chief Inspector, of course it does. You know it does. That detective mind of yours. At the very least, it makes as much sense as your own theory. Jackson's death started all this. Jackson was one of their own. Everything since has been a cover-up to keep secret what he was doing here. He was intelligence. Special Operations.'

'Intelligence?'

'Well that's a stretch. A mechanic. A frontline man. A soldier like myself.'

Kalus voiced his disbelief. 'I don't understand.'

'Come on, Inspector, you disappoint me,' Loach tutted. 'An *agent provocateur*. You've heard the stories, the rumours. They're out there. Dozens of them. Their own special unit. The SDS. We know they're there. Lot of them did their time in Ireland, you see.'

He had heard the stories. They all had. Government agents working to stir the miners to violence. Operatives primed to discredit the action, undermine the cause, destroying public sympathy, motivating the police to their own retaliation. A plan to generate support for the quasi-police state operations they'd been carrying out across the country. But one thing gnawed at him, still made no sense. Undermined the theory. He asked the question expected of him. 'Why?'

'Why am I telling you this?'

Kalus nodded.

'Well, you see, I'm part of the complications. It seems that our Mr Jackson whilst going about his own very dirty and shameful business put his nose into the lives of Brian and Kevin at a time when they were in business with us. Brian thought he was onto them, that he knew about our little endeavour. In fact, after discussion with Brian here, we're more than sure that he was. Brian killed Jackson to save himself from arrest, not to mention from what he knew would be our own rather more aggressive if we'd learned of his son's stupidity. A stupidity making himself and his boy a threat to our plans.'

Loach gazed at the slumped Brian Terry. 'I'm certain that a man like yourself, Inspector, must appreciate that such a thing has well and truly put your Masters in Whitehall on the horns of a dilemma. If they reveal the reason for Jackson's death, then the whole lot comes out. The whole can of worms about what they were really doing here. What Jackson's real role was in their nasty little game of undermining the rights of their own citizens. The reason why he came to be here to learn of what was going on between the Terry's and ourselves. And the thought of Brian and Kevin here going to trial and giving evidence as to why they killed him…Well, it doesn't bear thinking about. So you see, it can never get out. The truth of the police state they're quietly building. The undermining of the very democratic process that they maintain they're fighting a war to preserve in my own country.'

'So you're telling me this, for what? A desire to see justice? You want me to tell the world the truth. To arrest Brian and Kevin as murderers. To denounce Riordan and Ridgway as agents in a political conspiracy?'

'No. I'm telling you because it means nothing to me.' He pointed at Brian and Kevin. 'I met these two here to get what I wanted.'

'The boxes.'

'The boxes,' Loach echoed.

'Explosives.'

Loach tipped his head. 'Of a kind. We had a bit of bad luck

with a recent shipment. We needed replacement material rather quickly. We knew Brian here to be a man with sympathy for our cause. More importantly, that he was a man of a very greedy nature. Being responsible for the blast charges at the colliery meant he was handily placed to help us out in our time of need. He got us the keys and the location. We took the stuff and he and Kevin stored it in his allotment. He and Kevin have fulfilled their side of things by also kindly providing us with a van with colliery markings. Our passport through the cordon of police out there shepherding away the pickets. They'll almost escort us out of the area.'

A car horn sounded. It was at a distance, but distinct.

'Time to go,' Loach advised Big Man and the smaller man.

Loach pulled the gun from his jacket, moving behind Kalus. 'Now that I've got what we came for, well I've no longer any use for them.' He waggled the gun at the side of Kalus' head. 'Then again I've no real reason for killing them. Riordan now knows what we've been after, so there's little these two can tell them that'll be of any threat to us. They have no idea as to its purpose. Our plan for using it. Leaving them alive puts the ball back with Riordan and His Masters. Leaves them with a dilemma that we might be able to exploit later on.'

'And you're telling me?'

Loach released the rope that bound Kalus to the machinery, pushing him forward towards the doors. 'Because frankly, you're no threat to us or what we're doing. It amuses me. If Riordan lets you live, I've at least seen to it that you know the truth. Not that there's much you can do about it. No evidence, you see. Or at least, none you'll be able to find in your lifetime. *Official Secrets. Sealed files. Eyes only. Security of the State.*' He stopped, placing a hand on Kalus' shoulder. 'Oh, I would advise you one thing, Chief Inspector. Don't let your superiors know what's been said here. Not if you value your own life or that of any friends or family you might think to tell. Rather, just let them think that you stumbled upon the Terry family whilst pursuing them for Brody's murder. It could go very badly for you if they believe otherwise, if they think that you know what really happened. Of course, they can't let Kevin or Brian here testify. You must know that. So, the question remains: what will you do Detective Chief Inspector Kalus? Who will you save?'

They had stopped close to the barn door. Big Man and the smaller man stood waiting. They had clearly completed their work; a series of wires that ran from the door to the boxes hidden under the straw.

'A little present for your man, Riordan.'

Carefully the door was eased open. Big man was the first to squeeze through, then the small man. They stood outside, holding it ajar for Kalus whose hands remained tied behind him. 'Careful,' the little man warned.

Kalus planted his feet, turning his head back towards Loach. 'What about Mallen?'

Loach looked at the still unconscious officer and shrugged. 'You can't save everyone Inspector. You of all people should know that. A casualty of war.'

Kalus' attempts at resistance were ended with a powerful push shoving him outside. The van had gone, the other two men he surmised. Big man and little man nodded at Loach before they took off over the field towards the main road where he assumed another vehicle would be waiting. Loach led him to the rise above the barn.

'So what now?' Kalus asked.

Loach pulled him to his knees. 'We wait. Shouldn't be too long according to the boys.'

'The car horn.'

Loach nodded.

Within a few minutes, two figures approached the barn from the direction of the drive. They walked in what Kalus could only think to be army style; part crouched at either side of the path offering limited targets to whoever might be inside. They moved closer to the building, the light spilling from the door of the barn illuminating them.

More from his build, Kalus recognised the nearer as

Riordan. The other man was unknown to him. The light showed them to be carrying handguns.

Kalus continued to work at his bonds, finally feeling some give in them. Just a little longer. Just a little more time.

But there wasn't any.

Riordan and his partner were close to the doors. Any moment now and they would enter. No matter how carefully they went in, they would trip the bomb. They would die. So too would Brian and Kevin Terry, along with Karen and her children if they weren't already lying dead in one of the stalls. And Richard. Richard would perish too.

He looked to the side. Loach was on his haunches seeking a better view, his attention on the doors anticipating the moment, savouring it.

No more time.

Despite the agony in his ankle, Kalus pushed himself upright.

The scream was as much the result of the bolt of pain that shot through his leg as it was any warning. He began shouting, 'No! No! It's a trap!' At the same time launching himself upright, lunging to his left, careering into the startled Loach and knocking him sideways.

Kalus toppled forwards and began rolling head over heels down the embankment towards Riordan and his partner. The world span. With his arms still pinned behind him, he had little control as to his fall. He felt the pain course through him as he tumbled closer and closer towards the startled men, at any moment expecting a bullet from the IRA man or even from Riordan or his partner.

He came to a stop part way onto the track, at the turning point where it grew wider. His legs were stretched out behind him, hands still tied. He was face down in mud. He strained to lift his head and shoulders, struggled to catch sight of Riordan or the other man. 'There's a bomb!' he shouted, spitting lumps of mud from his lips. 'The door's been wired!'

At the first shout, Riordan had flung himself to the side of the barn door, taking cover behind the stack of old tyres Kalus himself had noticed earlier. Riordan stared in disbelief at the figure that had splashed into the muddy track some twenty paces from where he crouched. The other man was close by, lying in cover behind a water butt and some upturned wheelbarrows.

'He's up there!' Kalus shouted. 'The embankment!'

Both men scanned the horizon of the embankment but there was no sign of movement or of anyone else being up there.

'Kalus!' Riordan called. 'What the fuck's going on?'

Kalus' face sank towards the mud. The strain of keeping his head and shoulders up was proving too much. He tried spinning over onto his back. The rain beating against his face was almost welcome as it washed the clinging clay away.

'Brian and Kevin Terry are inside,' he shouted across. 'Mallen too. There's no sign of Karen or the kids. They must be tied up at the back of the barn. There was someone on the embankment. He's probably gone by now.'

Riordan and the other man exchanged looks across the roadway. 'Who was it?'

'Didn't catch his name,' Kalus responded.

'How do you know about the bomb?' Riordan called over.

Kalus mind started to kick back in. The flight response was shutting down, the survival instinct hadn't. He strained his arms. The bonds finally gave way. He let them slip into the mud. Despite himself Loach's warning surfaced. *Don't let them know.*

'Heard Richard shout a warning as I approached. We'd better wait until we can get some back-up here. Bomb disposal. Uniforms. Get on the radio.'

The other man scanned the embankment. He nodded at Riordan, who shuffled round to cover him. The man slowly made his way around the side of the barn. Riordan inched his way towards Kalus. 'I think we can handle this one,' Riordan stated.

Kalus managed to haul himself to a sitting position. He held up the remains of his bonds. 'Get these things off me.'

'He's right,' the man confirmed coming back round to where

Riordan hovered over Kalus. 'There's a small window with just enough light. I can make out something wired to the door.' He looked at Kalus. 'Not sure how Kevin or Brian managed to tie themselves up, though.'

Riordan looked in the direction of Kalus. 'Perhaps you can enlighten us, Inspector.'

Kalus shook his head. 'No idea.'

'Who was the man on the embankment?'

Kalus tried to shrug his shoulders but flinched at the pain that shot across them. 'An accomplice. I don't know who he was. Maybe a Flying Picket. Maybe the murderer.' Kalus nodded in the direction of the man standing next to Riordan. 'Who's your friend, by the way? He Complaints, too?'

The man looked at Riordan. 'We haven't got time for this,' he stated.

Riordan nodded. He looked down at Kalus before moving off towards the stack of tractor tyres and the discarded parts of farming equipment scattered around it.

'Seems like you've been rather busy, Chief Inspector,' the man said.

'Who are you?' Kalus asked.

The man smiled.

'Intelligence?'

'Inspector, who I am - what I am - is of little consequence. I'm the man they bring in when something needs fixing.'

'Like this murder enquiry,' Kalus suggested.

The man smiled again.

Riordan returned with a length of plastic rope. 'Just the job,' he observed, before disappearing in the direction of the door of the barn. Kalus could make out Riordan securing one end of the rope to the large bolt before he began belaying out lengths of it as he moved away from the doors and back to where Kalus and the other man waited.

'Him?' The man asked.

'No,' Riordan replied.

Riordan shoved his gun into a holster inside his jacket and

hauled Kalus upright. The pain in Kalus' ankle was growing worse. His right shoulder was bruised and battered. Riordan put an arm under that of Kalus and manoeuvred him along the path back beyond the turning circle.

Kalus was dropped, the man and Riordan hunkering down next to him.

A sudden realisation came over him.

Before he could say anything, Riordan had tugged the rope.

For a moment there was nothing. Then came a roar of sound, a bright eruption of light, and the barn door and the entire front section of the barn disappeared. Flames rapidly took hold of the rest. The wooden construction of the barn meant that even after days of torrential rain it quickly caught light. Within moments the whole structure was ablaze.

The man stood and cautiously made his way towards the burning barn.

'You've killed them!' was all Kalus could think to say.

'No, Riordan said. 'I'll think you'll find that Kevin Terry committed suicide taking his family and a brave officer with him.'

'You won't-'

'What? Get away with this?' Riordan scoffed. 'Look around, Chief Inspector. You're not a stupid man, but here are forces at work here that you really aren't aware of.'

'What about Brody? Was that you too?'

'There's a bigger picture.'

'What would that be?' Kalus demanded.

'The future of the country. The security of the state. The survival of the government. The only leader capable of sorting out the mess this country's in. I doubt it would survive revelations about its own conspiracy, no matter the necessity of the motive behind it. In that matter, it's better that the murder of Jackson and Brody and the Terry's be seen as something else. Something clean with no strings. No messy edges. No repercussions.'

'And what about me?'

Riordan reached down, cradling Kalus' chin with a hand. 'Well Inspector we'd have preferred it for you to deliver the right conclusion to this whole sorry affair. Murder by jealous husband. The rage of a father protecting his son. The driving forces of regret, remorse, and finally suicide. But I doubt we can rely on you to keep your mouth shut. So that leaves two alternatives: your by now well documented emotional breakdown, manifested in the conspiracy theories you see everywhere, or something a little more permanent. We're confident that Frank Ridgway will offer sufficient cause for either conclusion.'

The man returned from the barn. He stood at a little distance from the two and nodded the acceptability of what he'd witnessed inside.

Riordan nodded in return, satisfied at the way things were moving.

He considered the scene, weighing the possible outcomes before turning to the other man. 'It seems that the Chief Inspector feels unable to help us in his official report of the final outcome of his enquiries into the murder of Stephen Jackson and its tragic aftermath.'

The man stepped closer. He held a pick-axe handle in his hand.

Riordan stood back, looking down at Kalus squatting in the red mud. 'No loose ends. There's always the chance of someone listening to you. Some reporter. Some interfering busybody of a politician. One more bludgeoning. One last victim of Brian or Kevin's rage offers a certain symmetry to the case.'

'No messy edges,' Kalus stated flatly.

'No messy edges,' Riordan agreed.

Kalus closed his eyes. Contemplated the darkness.

He saw light. A bright shaft of light burning across his darkness. Was Anna right? Was there light in the dark, a light after darkness?

'Inspector!' a voice hailed the group. Kalus opened his eyes.

Headlights scorched the track. Bright, shining headlights.

Ahead of them a shadow, a silhouette. WPC Lawrence running down the track. Before he could shout anything, he was aware of the sound of engines and yet more headlights dipping up and down as a line of cars came along the track, blue lights flashing illuminating Lawrence, then Kalus and the others.

'I'm sorry,' she shouted, closing the distance. 'I made the call. I saw two men go up the track.' She nodded in the direction of Riordan and the other man, 'I didn't realise it was other officers. I was waiting by the car, and there was the explosion. I came as soon as I heard the squad cars.'

The cars pulled up, doors opening.

Roberts stepped out of the first car trying to take in what he was seeing. The remains of the barn ablaze; Kalus on the floor in the mud; Riordan and an unknown man standing by him. The pick-axe handle in the man's hands.

'Guv! What the fuck's happened?'

Epilogue: 2024

The wind that knifed through the two men walking on the hill was as cold as either could recall. The point where they stood was the highest for miles around, offering little in the way of shelter from the blasts of bitter North Westerly gales that tugged at their coats, swirled up the black dust into their faces.

In every direction, the landscape they looked out over was flat, open. The slag heaps that once dominated the view were gone, along with the winding gear, the shower block, the offices and the canteen: everything levelled. In their place sat row upon row of prefabricated warehousing, light industrial units, grey metal roofs in sympathy with the dull grey of the winter sky.

All that remained was the black dust.

Kalus stood still for a moment, turning his back on the wind, taking in the view to the south. The bulldozers and the developers had made a good job of burying the past. The field where Stephen Jackson had been found lay under a unit making plastic guttering. The barn where it had all ended had been demolished within days of the explosion and had remained open pasture for the forty years since.

But it hadn't ended there.

For days after the fire, he'd been side-lined in a hospital bed with a fractured ankle and exhaustion. There was also the widely circulated view that he had been rendered emotionally fragile at both the death of his fellow Detective Inspector and his wider failure to prevent what quickly became known as the *Horror at Hurley*. A cautionary tale adding to that of Handsworth. Of Reuben.

Beyond his hospital bed, things had moved at a pace. The days after the fire that had destroyed the barn killing all those inside, were a whirlwind of meetings, of comings and goings. Locked doors. Conferences. Damage limitation.

Riordan made his statement and returned to London.

The other man disappeared. Officially he was listed in the record of the enquiry into the operation as an analyst drafted into the area as part of the wider policing of the strike. An officer who, fortuitously, happened to be nearby on assignment at Tamworth Police station where Riordan had co-opted him to accompany him to Hurley Farm. His statement was brief, a mere detail in the whole investigation. With so many officers from different forces coming and going during the strike, it was hard to follow-up everything with any precision. The paperwork was easily lost in the age before computers. Besides, no one had any real desire to follow any of it up. The man's statement was a footnote, a rubber stamp.

The official enquiry was headed by Ridgway in liaison with Complaints and the Chief Constable of a neighbouring force. Much of its work and its findings were based on of Riordan's report. As Complaints and an officer who had been on the ground during the original investigation, he was well placed to inform the enquiry of details and to provide analysis of the police actions taken, particularly those of its SIO, Detective Inspector Peter Kalus.

Riordan's statement of events that night was simplicity itself.

He had heard on the police radio that Kalus was investigating a lead at Hurley farm. He'd needed to speak to Kalus about the way the enquiry was heading. He knew of Ridgway's decision to suspend Kalus. By then, in Riordan's view, the whole investigation was *out of control*. Unofficially, off the record, he had told Ridgway and others that the investigation was '*clueless, headless chickens running around all over the place*'. He had taken a fellow officer with him because he was new to the area and needed someone to drive. On arrival at the farm, they had seen the car that Kalus had been using but admitted that they had failed to see WPC Lawrence inside it. Arriving at the barn at the moment of the explosion, they had hauled the delirious and injured Kalus away from the blaze just as the back-up officers arrived. By then, there was little they or anyone could do for those trapped in the blazing barn. With Kalus incapacitated, Riordan had assumed responsibility as Senior Officer and had alerted the fire and ambulance services.

The wider factual details had been supported by the statements of WPC Lawrence, DS Mick Roberts and the rest of those at the scene.

Simplicity.

Kalus' story, by contrast, had found little in the way of factual support or sympathetic ears. Despite his objections – what Roberts later termed his *ranting like a maniac* - Kalus had been taken to the hospital. His report wasn't asked for until days afterwards, by which time the Riordan version had not only been accepted as gospel but amid much celebration of the sterling work of the enquiry had already been released to the media.

In those early days Ridgway, along with Lawrence, became the faces of the story. In what Whitehall would describe as *a courtesy to the Staffordshire Force who had lost a valiant officer*, Riordan himself was absent from the photographs and media reporting. Instead, it was Lawrence who was presented as the saviour. Lawrence who had initiated the vital breakthrough, pushing the team to take seriously Karen Terry's claim of her husband's guilt. It was Lawrence who had called for the back-up at Hurley Farm. A call sadly too late to prevent Kevin Terry from carrying out a crazed massacre of father, wife, children, and the unfortunate DI Mallen who, it was stated, had bravely gone into the blazing barn in a vain attempt to perform a rescue.

Kalus was sure it was not Lawrence who pressed her cause. She was in part embarrassed by the praise. When met briefly, some weeks later during the enquiries official hearings, she had blushed and avoided him.

In any analysis it was Kalus who came out badly. The man who had '*...pursued too many lines of enquiry for too long.*' The man who '*...pursued fanciful ideas...*' culminating in accusations regarding Riordan and his '*...unfounded speculation...*' as to why Jackson,

Brody, Mallen, and the Terry family had been killed.

A few days after the fire, Ridgway had visited him in the hospital. He had tossed his report back at him, making it clear that any such report would be spiked. He was *clearly under tremendous strain*. Hadn't he, his superior officer, that very day instructed Kalus that he was to remove himself from the investigation?

He was to write up a report that fitted the facts, not the wild speculation of his first draft. There would be an enquiry. Until then he was to be placed on sick leave. Indefinitely.

Angus McKinnon walked across the exposed ground to where Kalus stood lost in it all. 'Penny for them,' he growled.

Kalus smiled, casting adrift his reverie. 'Still old money, then?'

'Ach. I never could get my head around it all. Decimalisation.'

'At least that's one of your troubles you can't blame on Thatcher.'

'Don't mention that woman,' he spat. 'Like the Scottish play as far as I'm concerned. A curse.'

Kalus smile became a grin. 'Old wars, Angus. Old wounds.'

'Raw wounds,' the Scot responded.

A gust of wind whipped up yet another sprinkling of the black dust. Both men turned slightly to face away from it and found themselves sharing the view across to where the winding gear once stood.

For a number of years the long retired McKinnon had made the pilgrimage to the top of this man-made hill. The mine had closed some years later and he'd found that he no longer had the will to move again. Besides, the pits were closing everywhere. It was the end.

The hill they stood on was all that remained. A landscaped mound created to disguise the waste and rubble accruing during the regeneration of the colliery into the trading and industrial state standing in its place. Despite its proximity to several large housing estates, the hill had never been a popular destination for local families, dog walkers or joggers. The wind that rushed across the expanse of open fields proved too inhospitable for all but the occasional, dedicated kite flyer. Kalus liked to think it was more. The sense of darkness.

It had been a few years previous that McKinnon had first seen the figure of Kalus standing almost where he stood now, staring out across the old site of the colliery. They had struck up conversation of times past, of the times that had followed. On many days since then, they had found each other here.

McKinnon had expected to find Kalus here today.

Forty years since the discovery of Stephen Jackson's body.

'Forty years,' McKinnon stated.

Kalus nodded. 'Another world.'

'Aye,' McKinnon said with no real understanding.

'Someone once wrote that... *the past is another world. We can never go there.*'

'And if we could?' McKinnon asked.

'What would I change?'

'I suppose,' McKinnon nodded.

Kalus turned to face his companion. 'Too much. Everything.'

McKinnon shook his head. 'That's wrong. You can't mean that. There was good.'

'Good?'

'Whole communities standing for what was right. Refusing to be bullied.'

'Look how it ended.'

'Yes. Look.' McKinnon gestured at the landscape of industrial units, the distant M42. 'Tell me we weren't right all along. An industry ravaged and destroyed. Communities destroyed, replaced with commuters.' McKinnon sighed, despondent, despairing. 'No one round here works here. They all go to Birmingham to sit in front of their computer screens. No one makes anything, nothing of any real craft. Men aren't proud of what they do. It's just jobs.' He spat the last word. 'They leave nothing behind them. There's nothing for their children to be proud of. Nothing to be inspired by.'

'Thatcher's children,' Kalus muttered almost to himself.

McKinnon nodded. 'Aye. Thatcher's children. Locusts.'

It was a familiar theme of their conversations. The end of the strike the following year had been forced by the slow drift back to work of miners tired of the strike, tired of the violence, tired of the message of their union. They had fought. They had sacrificed. They had bled, but there was little sign of anything changing. The government had been resolute. The strike was broken.

In the years that followed, came the slow strangulation of the pits and the even slower death of their communities. The union became the biggest casualty of the strike. The violence on the picket lines had fuelled public qualms at the power of the unions. It eased the passage of harsh trades dispute legislation that undermined and weakened the position of unions by then too discredited and powerless to stop them. Voices were still raised, but the fight had gone.

'They did their work well,' McKinnon growled. 'The army boys. The secret police. The SDS, those *agents provocateurs*. The Stephen Jacksons.'

Kalus smiled wanly.

'I heard your story.' McKinnon stated.

'Old news,' Kalus responded. 'History.'

'Ah that's as maybe. But they say history is written by the victors. You were stitched up laddie. Like us.'

'Like I said, history.'

When he had finally returned to duty after his period of convalescence, Kalus found his continuing presence in CID difficult both for himself and for others. In the force, exhaustion was the euphemism for breakdown, and he found himself treated with suspicion. The enquiry had required a scapegoat, and he'd been offered up as it.

In the aftermath of it all some parts of his claims had leaked out but they served only to fuel a misguided mass of innuendo and a Sargasso Sea of half-heard truths and inconsistencies as to what had happened. Later came social media and conspiracy theories. Even the stories and enquiries into the SDS had gathered traction. But it came too late.

He was canteen gossip.

A burn-out.

The only consistency in each version of the narrative was that he was responsible.

For many it boiled down to two things: Firstly, he'd screwed up, a nervous breakdown on a case that had become a self-delusional fantasy of wild conspiracy theories; secondly, in his failure he'd got a fellow officer killed.

The Brighton bombing of the Conservative Party Conference had followed within days of the events at Tamworth. The interests of the media and the police moved on. Lying at home recuperating, he'd wondered about Loach and his plan. The operation that was so important. The timetable that couldn't be altered.

The explosive missing from Tamworth was equivalent to that used in the Brighton bombing. In those early days he'd tried to contact the Brighton force conducting the investigation, only to find it was being directed by Special Branch and the intelligence services. They knew all about Tamworth. Knew all about Kalus.

Nothing ever emerged, either then or in the intervening period, about the explosives removed from the colliery other than that used in blowing up the barn. He'd seen with his own eyes the boxes taken out to the van and driven away. The final report of the Ridgway Enquiry ignored this, as it ignored much of what Kalus had said.

The negligence of the colliery manager Gordon Craig in his failure to be aware of the theft of the explosive had led to his suspension before he was finally moved on. The scale of the theft was minimised in the final report written of the Ridgway led Enquiry team. Craig, more than likely wary of his own career and pension, never spoke to anyone about the matter and had never contradicted the amount of explosive said to have been removed.

The year after completing his report, Ridgway retired. Within a few years the long predicted investigation into the practices of the West Midlands Regional Crime Squad had seen that unit discredited and disbanded. It left in its wake hundreds of appeals of wrongful conviction, each one citing the fabrication of evidence and of illegally induced confessions.

The West Midlands forces were reeling from the allegations. The Special Branch, post Brighton, were more than ever focussed on the IRA. No one wanted to investigate the disaster that was Tamworth. The case was closed with no one taking any interest in re-opening it.

McKinnon reached inside his pocket and produced a flask. He unscrewed the top and took a large swig, offering it to Klaus who declined. McKinnon momentarily considering the flask, raised it between them.

'To the miners,' he stated and took a swig.

He proffered it to Kalus, who this time took it and studied it.

'To your daddy?' McKinnon prompted.

'To history.' He drank.

* * *

The hot sun burned her shoulders. Barely eleven o'clock, and already she needed to think about raising the black parasol umbrella above the small bistro table where she sat on the patio. All these years, and she still hadn't got used to the strength of the sun.

She sipped the cappuccino in its elegant white cup, looking again at the article in the English newspaper that Simon had brought back the previous day from town.

Fortieth Anniversary of the Miners' Strike the strapline read, above a small feature on the strike and the consequences for British society.

Consequences.

She stood and wandered across the flagged white stone, the heat of the slabs warm on her bare-feet. She lifted up and inspected the stems of the hibiscus and the subtle pink foliage of the lantanas that filled the terracotta pots on the waist high ledge separating the patio from the short drop of her property down towards the main road. Ahead of her, a pool blue and inviting, jewelled by the morning sun.

Consequences.

A TV programme. *Nationwide*.

She had sat there that evening having returned from the hospital.

Unsure, uncertain. Scared.

What was going on? Who were these people?

Ricky was playing with his toys, Michelle reading her book. She watched her son and her daughter. They were small, vulnerable and fragile. What was she to do? How was she to keep them safe? How could she keep herself safe?

The beating by her father-in-law had terrified her. She hated him. Hated her husband. Hated her life. But she was trapped. There was no escape. If she told all she knew, what would the police do? The WPC that had called had been sympathetic, but who would believe her? Even if they did, what would be the consequences? Kevin or his dad, even if they were arrested would one day be freed and find her. And where could she run to?

Then she had seen it.

On the TV.

Beyond Ricky, playing on the rug.

A clip from a news report. *Nationwide*. A boat in a harbour. A boat used by drug smugglers. She had reached for the remote, turning up the sound.

> *Police and Customs in Essex showed off today the results of a drug seizure thought to be the biggest haul of cannabis ever made in a single raid in Britain.*

> *The drugs were discovered over a week ago on a schooner, moored in the village of North Fambridge on the River Crouch in Essex.*

Eight people are in custody after police had sealed off the village and made arrests under high security.

Armed police and a helicopter were used in the culmination of an eighteen-month investigation called Operation Bishop.

The drugs, over 4.3 tonnes of cannabis, are thought to have a street value of over ten million pounds.

British Customs had been tracking the 85-foot schooner, the Robert Gordon, since receiving information that it had picked up a large consignment east of Cyprus.

Robert Gordon.

The name on the envelope in Kevin's shed. The name that had so terrified her father-in-law and reduced Kevin to ashen-faced shock. The name on the envelope. *Robert Gordon.* A boat. A drug smuggler's boat.

She had rushed to the shed, tore open the desk.

The draw had fallen to the floor. She had ripped open the envelope and counted. Twenty thousand pounds. She had sat there, her mind racing. Possibilities. She remembered looking down at the money, noticing another package taped to the underside of the now up turned draw. A larger package.

She'd ripped that one open. Another ten thousand pounds.

And Passports. Irish passports.

Her own and Kevin's faces; but different names. The children too.

Reynolds. Karen Reynolds.

She'd ran back to the house.

She'd shoved clothes into an overnight bag. She'd thought of taking the suitcase, but that would be noticed. The overnight bag was new. She'd bought it some weeks previous and had stored it in the attic ready for Stephen when he asked her to leave.

Underwear, a few tops and some jeans. The same for the children. Nothing he'd notice.

She'd looked around her. There was little she wanted from here.

She placed the bag in the hall, the children too.

They needed evidence. They needed something concrete. She knew that. The police had told her so. Stephen's body hadn't been enough. Even a motive had not been enough. They needed evidence.

Tentatively at first, she'd picked up a glass vase, dropping it to the floor. It had smashed, shattered into sharp pieces, covering the carpet with water, flowers, and petals.

Tentatively at first. A cup smashed. Coffee stains. Broken china.

Tentatively at first. A picture frame tossed against a wall. The glass splintering across the faces of the bride and groom. The frame distorted. Twisted. Broken.

'Mommy! What are you doing?' Ricky had asked. Michelle began to cry.

'It's okay, darling.' She paused, consoled her sobbing daughter. 'It's okay. It's a game mommy's playing. Ricky take your sister back in the hallway and wait for mommy.'

A game. Mommy's playing a game.

Now, more assured.

Systematically, she'd smashed up her lounge. She'd tipped over furniture, broken ornaments, scattered everything she could find. Finally, she'd picked up the largest fragment of broken glass from the vase, deliberately cut her hand. She'd waited for the blood to flow freely, ensuring that it pooled on the chair where he'd beaten her, the floor where she'd overturned the coffee table. Overturned her life.

She had no remorse. There was no feeling for what her home had been, for those who had been her family.

She'd wrapped a tea-towel around the wound before thrusting the large brown envelope with its cash and passports into the side pocket of her bag and walking out of the door.

She would be listed as missing. Kevin and Brian would have to explain that.

She'd scooped up the children from the hallway and left.

The trip to Ireland had been straightforward. A train. The ferry. A hotel.

Days later, in a hotel close to the railway station, she had read of the explosion at Hurley Farm. The death of Kevin and Brian and a police officer. The death of Karen Terry and her children.

The death of Karen Terry. Official.

She'd spent a few days shopping in Dublin before taking a flight to Spain.

There, she had rented a villa for a few months before buying a property. The estate agents she'd used were Simon's company. In the process of researching where to live, what to buy, she had discovered from Simon that there was a growing boom in building holiday homes for Brits planning to retire to Spain. She was attractive and the money enabled her to dress well. A few months later she had become well versed in the burgeoning property market. She had money to invest. *She was a widow, her husband had died in a car crash. There had been an insurance pay-out.*

She and Simon became partners, later they had married. They rode the boom and her wealth had increased a hundred fold and more. Their property company had expanded.

All the time she shunned publicity. Simon was the face of the business. It was Simon who featured on the web site.

Karen walked back to the table, picking up her iPhone and scanning through the tracks before selecting one to play through the smart speakers dotted through their home. Madonna. She loved the eighties.

Borderline rang out over the patio, the garden.

The sun burnt down.

She stripped to her bikini.

Her figure was still good, so her female friends told her, as did the admiring glances from their husbands.

Her bikini was small and white.

It was going to be a wonderful day.

Printed in Great Britain
by Amazon